JAN 3 1 2012

Washed in the Blood

MERCER
UNIVERSITY PRESS

Endowed by

TOM WATSON BROWN

and

THE WATSON-BROWN FOUNDATION, INC.

Washed in the Blood

A Novel

Lisa Alther

MERCER UNIVERSITY PRESS

MACON, GEORGIA

MUP/H832

Published by Mercer University Press
1400 Coleman Avenue
Macon, Georgia 31207
First Edition

Books published by Mercer University Press are printed on
acid-free paper that meets the requirements of American
National Standard for Information Sciences—Permanence of
Paper for Printed Library Materials.

Mercer University Press is a member of Green Press Initiative
(greenpressinitiative.org), a nonprofit organization working to
help publishers and printers increase their use of recycled
paper and decrease their use of fiber derived from endangered
forests. This book is printed on recycled paper.
ISBN   9780881462579
Cataloging-in-Publication Data is available from the Library of
Congress

For Ina, with thanks for your unflagging
encouragement and great family stories

Also by Lisa Alther

Kinflicks

Original Sins

Other Women

Bedrock

Birdman and the Dancer

Five Minutes In Heaven

Kinfolks

PART I

THE SWINE KING: A.D. 1567

1

The *San Jorge*

The sailors paused in the riggings, like spiders in their webs, to watch the struggles of the drowning dog.

"We can't just leave him," said Diego as he threw off his leather vest and started to climb over the side of the *San Jorge*.

"They wouldn't turn this ship around for you, either," said his uncle Lucas. A foot taller and twice as strong, he pinned Diego against the railing with one hand. "We'll find another dog once we land in Hispaniola."

"But not another Baltasar." Diego pictured the oak grove on the mountainside back home in Galicia where he had trained the gangly young greyhound to herd the hogs and protect them from wolves. "It's my fault. I told him to chase a rat across the deck. It ran out on the bowsprit. When Baltasar followed, he fell off into the sea."

"It's not your fault. Baltasar would chase anything that moves."

Baltasar's front paws flailed in the wake, as though he were trying to rise up and walk on the water. His bark sounded indignant. He sank back down so that only his tapered nose bobbed above the foam.

On the afterdeck, Diego spotted Don Sebastian de Silva, the conquistador who was leading this expedition from Spain to the New World under orders from King Phillip II. His graying auburn hair and stiletto beard were freshly trimmed, and his nose curved like a hawk's talon. His green eyes watched the floundering hound with indifference. Just as he had watched his dead stallion being dumped overboard somewhere off the Canary Islands. Just as he had watched last week as two sailors were swept off the deck by the boom and sank beneath the swells.

Beside him stood Dona Catalina de Alvarado, the natural daughter of the governor of the Canaries. Don Sebastian was escorting her to Santo Domingo, their first port of call on this journey to the unconquered part of the New World called La Florida. She would have a position in the household of a judge. Her chances of finding a respectable husband would be greater in a place where no one knew about her scandalous parentage. Her face was concealed behind a fan that resembled a spread peacock tail. Diego noticed his uncle Lucas sneaking glances at her. He felt a stab of alarm. Such insolence could earn Lucas a flogging.

A week ago a rifleman named Pedro Picado had been discovered hiding in the skiff on deck after the hatch to the first hold, where the soldiers were supposed to sleep, had been barred for the night. He lamely explained that he had wanted some fresh air. Don Sebastian ordered him stripped of his shirt, bound to a mast, and whipped. Diego had averted his eyes, despite Don Sebastian's command that everyone watch. They needed rules, of course. Otherwise the traffic on deck would become so chaotic that the sailors couldn't sail their ship. But why couldn't Don Sebastian have just explained this to Pedro, rather than ripping his bare back into bloody ribbons?

Soon Baltasar was just a faint blotch on the vast indigo ocean, which stretched to the horizon in every direction and faded into the sky. Lucas loosened his grip on Diego. Diego shoved his arm aside and plopped down on a coil of rope from the mainsail. The other soldiers and passengers turned back to Lope Mendez, Don Sebastian's portly surgeon and barber, who resumed his lecture about the poisonous vegetation, insects, and reptiles on Hispaniola, where they would soon land, God and the trade winds willing. Many of the soldiers now spent their sparse time on deck anxiously scanning the horizon for some hint of green.

Down in the hold during the voyage, Diego had often heard the soldiers compare Don Sebastian de Silva to the great conquistadors of the Spanish Empire—Cortes, Pizarro, and DeSoto—who had conquered entire empires of heathens and been rewarded with hordes of gold and silver. As the soldiers tossed dice in the dim light that shined through the cracks in the hull, they discussed Don

Sebastian's ancestors, who had fought in the eight centuries of battles required to drive the Moors out of Spain and back to North Africa. Don Sebastian himself had served as a page to the Captain of the Horse during DeSoto's four-year exploration of La Florida that began some twenty-five years earlier. The soldiers claimed Don Sebastian knew the lay of the land and would lead them to mountains seamed with silver and rivers that flowed gold. They would become rich men.

But all Diego wanted at the moment was to get his dog back. Lounging in his nest of rope, he closed his eyes and silently prayed to the Virgin that Baltasar's end would come quickly. He wished he could warn him not to struggle against the sharks that would soon surround him. Back home, a boy from the neighboring hacienda named Cristobal used to taunt Diego, calling him "Pig Boy" because he tended hogs for the Count of Macedo. Diego had discovered that if he just ignored him, Cristobal and his friends sometimes got bored and left in search of more easily upset prey. Maybe the sharks would do the same if Baltasar stayed still.

On cold winter nights when the hogs that hadn't been slaughtered huddled together in their pen for warmth, Diego had helped his mother pick and comb wool on the wooden bench by the hearth in their little cottage on the Count's hacienda. She had often told him about a contest between the sun and the wind, who were trying to force a wayfarer to remove his cloak. The wind blew and blew, howling around the man like an enraged ghost. But he just clutched his cape more tightly.

Nudging the wind aside, the sun stroked the traveler with its warming rays. Little by little, the man loosened his grip on his cloak. Finally, he shrugged it off and folded it across his arm, and the sun won the wager.

Peering upward through narrowed eyes, Diego studied the sun, which was shielded by a haze, like the film that came over the eyes of a hog once you stuck a knife into the side of its throat to bleed it to death for butchering. That he had tried to live by his mother's story might explain why he had won the affection of his master's daughter, Leonora, over his rival Cristobal. As Diego and Lucas were leaving for Seville to board this ship bound for the New World, Leonora had

whispered from her parents' doorway that she would await his
return with the riches and honors that would force her father to
accept him as her suitor. He had been startled by this notion of
himself as a potential husband. Although Leonora was clearly a
young woman now, he still felt like an awkward child in her
presence. But he would be eighteen by the time he got back home
again, matured by his two years of wilderness adventures. He vowed
to become deserving of her inexplicable confidence in him.

Dr. Mendez concluded his warnings about the natural hazards
of Hispaniola, and Deigo looked up as a barrel-chested corporal
named Arias de Zavallas led the soldiers in a jig to the
accompaniment of a sailor's accordion. This had been their only
exercise during the long weeks in the cramped hold, and their stalled
energy resulted in impressive acrobatics from men who were usually
no more than dour lumps of flesh that lay in the dark longing for dry
land.

As Diego, too, danced furiously in an attempt to dispel his anger
and grief over the loss of Baltasar, he spotted the pudgy face and
wavy chestnut mane of Tomas de Carrion, one of Don Sebastian's
pages. Upon reaching Diego, Tomas proclaimed in his poor imitation
of a court herald, "Don Sebastian will receive you now in his cabin."

"Why?" gasped Diego, bending over to catch his breath. He felt
a deep dislike for that man of ice who could watch unmoved as men,
dogs, and horses sank beneath the sea—and as his soldiers had their
backs lashed to a pulp.

Diego had felt a similar aversion the first time he ever laid eyes
on Don Sebastian. Mounted on a handsome bay stallion with a jet
black mane and tail, he had gazed at Diego with those cold green
eyes while selecting the members of his exploring party from the
clamoring crowd gathered on the Seville quay. Lucas had explained
that many of the applicants were criminals hoping to escape
prosecution, or Jews and Moors being pursued by the Catholic
Inquisition. Hence, their desperation to be picked by Don Sebastian.
Don Sebastian had been decked out in etched bronze dress armor,
thigh-high boots with silver spurs, and a peaked helmet with a scarlet
plume. Diego had never before seen such a vain creature.

Tomas shrugged. "He is the admiral of this fleet and the commander of this expedition, and you are not. That is how it is, Pig Boy."

Diego grimaced to hear his hated nickname, which had somehow followed him onboard the ship. But at least no one had called him "Christ Killer" so far. He still didn't understand why his mother, when she heard Cristobal call him that, had insisted that Diego and Lucas leave Galicia right away. "Christ Killer" was just one among the many insults that Cristobal regularly hurled at him. Diego would have been content to tend his hogs on that Galician hillside for the rest of his life. During the day he had watched the clouds wander around the sky like flocks of wooly sheep. In the distance the silver sea sparkled in the sunlight. And at night he lay on his back in a forest clearing and made up stories about the creatures outlined by the stars flickering overhead. Still, Leonora's father would never have allowed his swineherd to court his daughter.

As Diego trailed along after Tomas, who strutted with his eyes averted from the debased antics of the delirious soldiers, he reflected that this expedition through the lost land of La Florida was his big chance to make something of himself. He vowed to return to Galicia with enough gold to convince the Count that he was worthy of Leonora.

Don Sebastian sat behind an oak table, studying the carved ivory figures arrayed on a chessboard of inlaid wood. The wall of small-paned windows behind him looked out on the wake, which receded like a plowed furrow of foam. Diego imagined striding along that pathway of froth to the horizon and beyond, encountering Baltasar, two bobbing midshipmen, and Don Sebastian's bloated bay. He spotted the tiny white triangles and rectangles of sails from some other ships in their far-flung fleet of twenty vessels. Maybe one of the stragglers would spot Baltasar and take him aboard.

On a high-backed chair in one corner perched Dona Catalina, dressed in a gown of jade velvet with a lace collar. She appeared absorbed in a complicated embroidery pattern.

Beside her sat Brother Marcos Espindola in his brown hooded robe. He was reading a leather-bound Bible. That Brother Marcos had forfeited an estate, wealth, and titles to become a Dominican mystified Diego. That was everything Diego needed in order to win Leonora. Their pursuit was the main reason many in the hold had undertaken this boring eight-week voyage, to be followed by two years of trekking through an unmapped wasteland inhabited by godless savages.

Rumor had it that Brother Marcos had once been a bishop in Burgos. After witnessing the burning of some heretics by the Inquisition, he had resigned his post, donated his wealth to the poor, and requested an assignment in the New World. He rarely spoke or smiled, as though that bonfire of unbelievers had hollowed him out from within. He was probably the only man on this ship whose eyes didn't glitter at the mention of gold.

Diego knew that Lucas had once attended such an auto da fe in Valladolid. He had often described his own horror as a dozen Jews, Moors, and French Protestants, attired in pointed fools' caps and yellow robes painted with the flames of hell, had been bound to posts and burned alive for refusing to pledge allegiance to the Holy Father in Rome. Their screams as their robes ignited haunted his uncle's dreams. And whenever Lucas tried to eat roasted meat now, he would recall the stench of charred human flesh and would sometimes choke and vomit.

Juan Bravo, another page, stood by the wall alongside the hulking Tomas de Carrion. Juan's pointed nose and sly eyes, his bobbed orange hair, and the sideburns that curved along his jaws lent him the air of a hunted fox.

Don Sebastian looked up from his chessboard. "I simply wanted to say that I am sorry about the loss of your dog."

"Thank you, Sire." Diego inclined his head in what he hoped would qualify as a bow. His eyes met Don Sebastian's, which looked sulky. A jagged scar snaked through his auburn beard just beneath his right cheekbone. The soldiers maintained that, as a young man, Don Sebastian had been a favorite at the emperor's court in Valladolid. But he had been banished to La Florida twenty-five years ago as a page to DeSoto's Captain of the Horse, for reasons that no one in the hold could fathom.

Diego was unimpressed by people who possessed the guile necessary to become successful courtiers. He preferred the straightforward country people among whom he had grown up. Although Leonora's father was a count, she was blessedly unaffected compared to her family's fancy visitors from Valladolid, who sniffed nosegays as Diego herded the swine past their gilded coaches. Some women feigned swoons at the mere sight of his herd.

"I know how hard it is to lose a favorite animal," Don Sebastian said. "I noted the care with which you tended my bay. They say he would eat only for you."

Diego shrugged. "He was seasick, Sire. I was, too. I fed us both gruel. But I started too late."

For weeks he had watched the poor horse swaying from the ceiling of the hold on woven bellybands. But each time the handsome bay was lowered to the floor, he snorted and reared like the fierce war stallion he was trained to be. After he nearly kicked a hole in the hull that would have taken them all to the ocean floor, he was confined to his slings. Those strangling slings and the rolling seas destroyed his digestion. He starved to death with barrels of grain stacked right beside him, despite Diego's attempts to coax him into eating the mush that he vomited onto the floor afterwards.

Those on a hardtack diet down in the hold had begged to be allowed to butcher and eat the skeletal horse. But Don Sebastian, dining in his cabin on ham from Seville and fresh swordfish from the sea, had insisted on an ocean interment befitting the stallion's status as his lead battle horse. A dozen soldiers hauled him out of the hold on his slings, his panicked eyes now shut, his black tail no longer lashing in defiance. They hoisted him over the side and lowered him into a watery grave. As the ship pulled away, a swirling vortex indicated that he had been greeted by a pack of sharks as ravenous for fresh meat as the soldiers in the hold.

"What is your name, lad?"

"Diego Martin, Sire."

"Your master is the Count of Macedo, is he not?"

Diego nodded, surprised Don Sebastian should know this. "Yes, Your Worship. My mother was a serving maid at the palace of the Count's father in Pontevedra. Now she works as a spinner and weaver on the Count's hacienda near Ourense. I have been herding his swine since I was a small boy."

Dona Catalina looked up from her embroidery hoop. Her eyes met Diego's. Blushing, she looked back down. Any aristocratic disdain she possessed was pleasantly leavened by the hesitancy of the basely born. She was beautiful, too, with a creamy complexion and hair that flamed like a fire fed by autumn leaves. He understood why Lucas kept risking glances at her, whatever the danger.

"We will need your skills, boy. Swine will be our portable meat supply. And your dog? What was he called?"

"Baltasar, Sire. My uncle trained him for the Count. His ancestors chased down Moors during the Reconquest."

"We will also need good war dogs. But I was unable to turn back. We had an ideal wind from the east."

Diego inclined his head, bewildered that his commander should want to justify his decisions to a boy of no importance. He was also startled by the notion that war dogs would be needed in La Florida. The soldiers in the hold maintained that the natives there would gladly embrace the cross and would show their gratitude by loading down their Christian saviors with baskets of precious metals.

Don Sebastian gestured to Tomas de Carrion, who lumbered over, clutching a tin box painted with colorful arabesques. He removed the lid and extended the box to Diego. Inside were pieces of marzipan shaped like miniature fruits.

"From Naples," announced Tomas, as though displaying the crown jewels to a peasant. "Neapolitans make the finest marzipan in all of Christendom."

"*Sicilians* make the finest marzipan, dolt," snapped Don Sebastian.

"Yes, Sire," said Tomas, "nothing is finer than Sicilian marzipan."

Diego selected a tiny banana.

Waving Tomas away like an annoying fly, Don Sebastian said to Diego, "I must ask you to stay away from our pilot, Francisco. I have noticed that you distract him from his duties, which are crucial to our safe arrival at Hispaniola."

"Yes, Sire." Diego stifled a frown. After tending the hogs and chickens caged on deck, he often visited Francisco at the helm. As the smoke from the older man's pipe of Indian tobacco wreathed his silver hair, he told Diego stories of the sea. But Diego didn't see how this could be distracting. In fact, it probably kept Francisco awake, though it was true that in the heat of an especially exciting tale, Francisco's gnarled hands sometimes left the wheel to gesture dramatically.

"You may go now." Don Sebastian continued to study Diego with his sullen green eyes as Diego backed to the door.

Diego squatted behind a rain barrel on the afterdeck to nibble the marzipan, savoring each fleck. The almond paste flooded his mouth with saliva. It was a relief to enjoy food again after weeks spent vomiting over the railing and into the slop bucket in the hold. He had lost so much weight from his seasickness that his leather shorts now bagged in back, while in the front his hip bones protruded like dulled ax blades.

Don Sebastian had apologized for deserting Baltasar. Maybe he was kinder than Diego realized. But Diego pondered the strange order to stay away from Francisco. Francisco had been crossing the Atlantic for several decades and understood the winds and currents that carried ships in a giant oval from Portugal to the West Indies, up the coast of La Florida, and back toward the Azores. Once, he said, the *San Jorge* had been becalmed in the center of this oval, its sails hanging limp as wet laundry for days. The seaweed had swayed and tangled beneath the hull like the hair of drowning ladies. Francisco told him how the rats took charge, devouring the grain, drowning in the drinking water, attacking the chickens, and gnawing the sailors' ears as they slept. Now, every night before falling asleep, Diego prayed to the Virgin to keep the winds strong until the *San Jorge* reached Hispaniola. But not too strong, because Francisco had also told him about waves the height of cathedral spires, which snapped masts as though they were dry twigs.

Standing up and gazing across the endless waters that glinted and surged in the rays of the noontime sun, Diego wondered whether Baltasar were still struggling to stay afloat, whether sharks were circling him, whether he was distraught that Diego had abandoned him. If he had just jumped overboard, at least he and Baltasar could have been ripped apart together.

Diego had never sailed on the sea until this ship crossed the sandbar guarding the entrance to the Seville harbor that morning two months ago. Fireworks from shore had burst overhead, and trumpets had blared. Francisco claimed to find the sea beautiful. But Diego, son of the soil, found its indifference disconcerting. The ocean would acknowledge Baltasar's death with only a few ripples, as the water opened to receive him and then closed above his head. The earth, on the other hand, enfolded the dead with the tender pity of a bereaved mother.

Diego recalled the day Lucas had first brought Baltasar over from the kennels. The dog wore fir-green armor of quilted cotton that matched Lucas's padded doublet. While Lucas chatted in the kitchen with his sister Manuela, Diego's mother, Diego swept pink mimosa blossoms off the front terrace of the Count's house. Cristobal and his pals rode past. Spotting Baltasar tied to a post, they dismounted, unleashed him, and sicced him on Diego.

Diego had run faster and jumped higher than he ever dreamed possible, grabbing a branch of the gnarled oak next to Leonora's window. The boys laughed as Baltasar snapped and snarled at Diego's dangling feet, like a child leaping up to strike a piñata.

Just when he thought his arms would pop from their sockets, Leonora's shutters had opened. She beckoned Diego inside. He moved hand over hand along the bowing branch. As he swung onto her balcony, Cristobal stopped laughing down below and stared incredulously.

Once inside her shadowy bedroom, Diego gasped, "You probably saved my life, Dona Leonora!" He could see the white of her teeth in the cool darkness. She wore a hood of scarlet velvet, with a net bag at the back of her neck to collect her ebony hair.

"I hate how Cristobal torments you, Diego," she murmured. "It's from jealousy. He can see that you are the one I have chosen."

"Me?" gulped Diego, inhaling the intoxicating jasmine of her perfume.

"Even when you were a little boy, you were my preferred companion. Do you remember those afternoons when I sneaked from the house during the siesta and sat with you in the yard? Do you recall how we used to gaze at our reflections in the still water of the fountain, side by side, with roses nodding all around us?"

"Ever since I was that timid child, Dona Leonora, all my thoughts have been of you. If yours were also of me, I am glad."

"Then be glad, Diego," she said, lowering her long lashes. "But for now, we must get you out of my bedroom. If my father finds you here, he will hurl you back over my railing as dinner for that hideous hound."

2

Landfall

Diego awoke with a full bladder, but the thought of lurching through the dark hold to an overflowing slop bucket repelled him. So he lay there listening to the slap of waves against the hull and to the snorts of his slumbering shipmates. Lucas usually slept beside him in the space claimed by their packs, Baltasar between them. But the indigo blanket Manuela had woven for Lucas, identical to the one now covering Diego, lay heaped on his straw mat. And Baltasar was probably awash in the belly of some shark. Diego wondered whether a whale could have swallowed him whole, like Jonas. The dog might be inside one now, howling in the blackness.

Diego had been dreaming of Leonora. She had loosened her hair from its scarlet hood, letting it cascade over the wrought iron railing of her balcony. He climbed up the hair as if it were a rigging. But when he at last grabbed the railing, she had vanished. To combat feeling so forlorn, he pictured the two of them exchanging gifts alongside the fountain back home—a lump of sugar or a length of velvet ribbon for him, a ripe chestnut or a veined pebble for her.

He felt a great longing to stroke Leonora's cheek with his fingertips and to kiss her soft lips. He had never found the nerve to try this when he was with her. Rolling over on his back, he struggled to think about something else—anything else. The priest who came from Ourense each week to hear confessions and say mass in the Count's chapel on the hacienda had told him that spilling his own seed was a sin. Diego already had a backlog of such sins to do penance for without adding more. And the thought of showing Leonora such disrespect, if only in his imagination, horrified him.

It was finally the lice in his hair that saved him from more sin. He sat up to claw his scalp. Every man in the hold had dragged his clothing and bedding through the saltwater on ropes trying to get rid of the pests. But the fabrics had dried stiff as boards and had rubbed their flesh raw, so now they were resigned to cohabiting with the voracious little vermin—as well as with the fleas Baltasar had probably carried onboard.

The stench in the hold was nauseating—gases from the mouths and bowels of men and horses mixed with the odor of sweat, excrement, and vomit. Even after all these weeks, Diego hadn't gotten used to it. Holding his breath, he tiptoed among the sleeping soldiers, some swaying from the ceiling beams in rope hammocks, to the hatchway. The weather had turned so hot in recent days that the lid was now left open at night so the soldiers below wouldn't suffer heat stroke. But Diego was allowed on deck day or night anyway to tend the dwindling supply of chickens and the one remaining hog.

At the top of the steps he inhaled deeply, studying the glittering pinpricks of light overhead. He hadn't known whether the stars in the New World would be the same as those in Galicia. Nevertheless, he had taught Leonora to locate the Great Bear so that she could look at it from her balcony and think of him, as he, too, gazed at the stars and thought of her. He located the familiar outline and concentrated on Leonora.

Nearby in the night sky he spotted the White Bull. This bull was actually a god in disguise, in love with a princess. He behaved so docilely that she garlanded his horns with flowers and hopped on his back for a ride. Diego's mother had always told him that, like the sun in its contest with the wind, the bull's experience proved that kindness could achieve what force could not.

Upon his return from La Florida as a wealthy man, Diego would ask the Count for Leonora's hand in marriage. He only prayed that she could prevent her father from pledging her to Cristobal first. Cristobal's father was said to own the most sheep in all Galicia. This might be enticing to the Count, but hopefully less enticing than pleasing his daughter. By marrying Leonora, Diego would avenge Cristobal's insulting words to him, which he could not forget: "I have heard how you squat in the mud with your hogs, Christ Killer, watching the doorway for Dona Leonora. From this day forth, shit-eating cur that you are, keep your insolent eyes fixed firmly on the muck in which you crawl, like the lowest of slimy toads."

En route to the latrine holes, Diego noticed the flicker of candlelight behind the window into Don Sebastian's cabin. He leaned against the wall and listened to a lute play a ballad that had been popular on the quays of Seville. The page Juan Bravo began to sing in a pleasant tenor voice:

"Tell me, shepherd,
You who guard the flocks,
If any flocks or mountains
Are as beautiful as the lady you love…."

Diego mused that even the luster of the gold mines of La Florida would be unlikely to equal the radiance of Leonora's smile when she was happy. And when she was sad, it was as though the sun had ducked behind a storm cloud….

Suddenly, what sounded like the death rattle of the lone shoat drowned out Juan Bravo. Abandoning his reveries, Diego walked over to her pen on the foredeck. She lay asleep, breathing noisily.

The odd sound was coming from behind the skiff stored farther down the deck. Slipping through the shadows cast by the sails as they shifted silently in the starlight, Diego spotted a man standing with a woman in his arms. Her skirts luffed like sails around them both. She leaned against the railing, her eyes shut, head thrown back like a conquered dog offering its jugular. It was Dona Catalina. And the man was Lucas. Lucas murmured something, and she moaned in reply.

Diego drew a sharp breath. The handlers of war dogs weren't supposed to embrace governors' daughters, natural or not. Diego's father had been killed in the Netherlands fighting for the emperor when Diego was two, and his uncle Lucas had taken his father's place. Lucas was Diego's protector on this trek into the unknown. Diego wanted to drag this wanton woman away from him. Then he recalled that he himself loved the daughter of a count and was prepared to undergo any hardship to win her. No man in love would heed words of caution.

But how on earth had Lucas engineered this encounter aboard a tiny ship on which each passenger's every move was noted and discussed by everyone else? If Don Sebastian should learn that Lucas was not only on deck at night but was also further blackening the reputation of the woman under Don Sebastian's protection, Lucas would never live to boast to the other soldiers about this conquest.

Diego spotted Francisco in the shadows, also watching the two lovers. He exhaled a stream of smoke from his long-stemmed pipe. On the hand cradling the bowl gleamed a golden ring set with a gem that glittered like a diamond in the moonlight. Motioning to Diego, he led him toward his tiny cabin beneath the bridge, next to the workshop of Gaspar de los Reyes, the ship's carpenter.

Once inside, Francisco sat on his narrow bunk and asked, "Why don't you visit me at the helm any longer, lad?"

"Don Sebastian ordered me to stay away. He says I distract you."

After a moment Francisco nodded curtly. "You do realize that you must tell no one about what we've just witnessed?"

"Yes."

"I fear the future will go badly for your uncle, Diego. A man must learn to tame his desires, or they will lure him into endless hazards."

"She's very beautiful," observed Diego.

"If she truly cared for your uncle, she'd stay away from him. I've seen soldiers hanged for less."

Diego swallowed nervously. Excusing himself, he headed to the latrine holes at the ship's bow, reflecting that his own desire for Leonora was also luring him into unknown hazards. The wooden planks of the ship creaked in the swells, and the brass fittings on the riggings clanked together beneath the dim light thrown by the bow lantern. As Diego released his urine into the sea, a dark shadow swept across him. Looking up, he watched a giant night bird swoop down from the sky to skim the silver wake on outspread wings. Birds meant that land was nearby!

Back in the hold, Diego feigned sleep as Lucas crept down the steps. His uncle stretched out on his mat, rolled up in his blanket, and fell asleep. Sniffing, Diego tried to detect some hint of soil or vegetation carried on breezes from the unseen shore. But the musky scent of Dona Catalina's perfume was too overpowering.

The fingertips of dawn were probing the cracks in the hull when Diego awakened to a shout from the lookout. Jumping up, he scrambled up the stairs to the deck. The sailor roosting in his nest overhead was pointing at the water. Racing to the railing, Diego spotted three dolphins, their arcing backs flashing gold and crimson in the light from the rising sun. Another sign that land was near! As he watched them leap and twist, he fantasized that some compassionate dolphin had already borne Baltasar on its back to the shore.

Gnawing hardtack and dried sardines later that morning, Diego watched an apprentice seaman fish over the railing for Don Sebastian's lunch. The three chickens clucked in their cage, as though encouraging the young sailor, since his lack of success would result in Diego's twisting their heads off before noon. The sails snapped and flapped in the shifting gusts. Diego held his breath and gulped his tankard of chartreuse water. The beer had run out a few days earlier, and apart from the casks of wine he had glimpsed in Don Sebastian's cabin and those of vinegar and olive oil that served as ballast in the bottom hold, this putrid water was the only liquid left on board.

Diego spotted a dark, bumpy shadow that lounged like a sea monster along the western horizon. At almost the same moment the watch overhead called out, "Land! I see land!" This cry was quickly taken up by the watch in nearby ships. Distant cheers erupted from first one vessel and then another.

Soon passengers were crowding every deck. Don Sebastian, Dona Catalina, and Brother Marcos emerged onto the afterdeck of the *San Jorge* to study the distant blotch of gray as it grew larger and began to take on tones of green.

Don Sebastian and Dona Catalina knelt. Diego and everyone else on deck followed their example. Brother Marcos folded his hands and intoned a prayer that Diego couldn't hear. Diego watched Dona Catalina's display of piety skeptically, recalling her behavior in the shadows behind the skiff. Her too-obvious charms might get his uncle killed.

At Don Sebastian's command, a trumpet blared a salute and a cannon fired. Sailors catwalking across the yardarms began to trim the sails. As the scattered fleet struggled to fall into formation behind the *San Jorge*, many passengers started to sing the "Te Deum." Soon this chant echoed back and forth across the vast sea on which twenty tiny ships bobbed and pitched like weary, waterlogged corks.

While the *San Jorge* nosed into the wind and tacked northward, Diego watched the distant shoreline, elated by the notion of at last seeing Santo Domingo, the gateway to Hispaniola, a stepping stone to the New World where brave Spanish conquistadors had saved many a heathen soul for Christ and had been rewarded with chests of gold and silver. If you accumulated enough wealth, people let you be whoever you claimed to be. Many former Jews and Moors in Galicia were now devout Christians who listed as their ancestors those who had fought to drive their actual ancestors out of Spain. Diego was already composing his own tale of origins that would make him a worthy companion to Leonora. It involved a knight named Martin who took a vow of fealty to King Ferdinand at the Santiago cathedral and rode into battle against the Moors at Granada shouting, "Our Lady and Santiago!" Since he knew nothing about his real ancestors, this story could just as well be true as not.

Soon they paralleled a white sand beach flanked by a dense green jungle of palms, vines, and flowering bushes. Sniffing, Diego picked up faint aromas unlike any he had known back home in Spain.

They passed a cleared hillside. Copper-skinned men in ragged clothing hoed seedlings, while a red-faced man on a roan mare supervised. Upon spotting the approaching ships, he herded the laborers toward a square arbor with a thatched roof. A bell began to clang.

The *San Jorge* overtook a pinnace crewed by four fishermen. They glared up at the new arrivals. The soldiers were gathering on deck in their breastplates, quilted doublets, and helmets, weapons in their hands. The fleet would stop at Santo Domingo just long enough to leave Dona Catalina and several others and to clean the barnacles from the keels. All the ships except the *San Jorge* would continue to Cartagena, where they would be loaded with silver from the Incan mines, destined for the treasury of King Phillip back home in Spain. Diego wondered why everyone was dressed as though for an invasion. Why had the farmer and the fishermen seemed alarmed rather than pleased to greet their fellow Spaniards? The bell at the now-distant farmstead was still tolling, joined by others all across the island. It sounded like Easter Sunday in Pontevedra. But were these bells of welcome or of warning?

The *San Jorge* approached a broad bay. A partially constructed stone fortress perched on a promontory to the left. Ringing the cove were many structures of weathered planks, all framed by listing palms. A stone-paved central plaza led to a stuccoed cathedral with a tall bell tower.

Portside from this plaza stood a two-story customs house with a red tile roof and porches upstairs and down. The standard of Castille and Leon, featuring golden castles and purple lions, flew from a pole out front. A pier of wooden pilings extended into the harbor, and many small fishing boats bobbed at their moorings. But Diego couldn't see any people. It was a ghost town—or rather, a ghost village, certainly not the bustling port he had expected after Seville.

As sailors in the riggings overhead furled the remaining sails, Diego watched the fishing boat maneuver between the *San Jorge* and the shore. The fishermen gestured urgently for Francisco to steer the flagship to the left. Spinning the wheel, he did so, no doubt fearing an uncharted reef or sandbar.

The keel ran aground with a splintering thud. The forward movement ceased so abruptly that Diego collided with a mast. The soldiers careened into one another, their armor and weapons clashing. The ballast shifted thunderously in the bottom hold. Several sailors catapulted from the yardarms into the water.

The fishing boat docked, and the crew ran up a street through town and disappeared. As the passengers on the *San Jorge* cursed the fishermen and assessed the damage to their bodies and their gear, the other ships cautiously entered the harbor one by one. They anchored well away from the outcropping on which the *San Jorge* now roosted. The sailors on the other ships launched their pinnaces and began to ferry soldiers and passengers ashore. Those reaching solid ground knelt to kiss the earth as if it were a long-lost lover.

Diego spotted Don Sebastian on the afterdeck with Dona Catalina, his pages, and his bodyguards. For his triumphal entry into the deserted Santo Domingo, he wore a gold brocade doublet, padded trunk hose, and a cape of purple velvet lined with gold silk. His burnished helmet reflected the scorching sun, and his auburn beard was matted with sweat. He watched his battered soldiers limp down the gangplank and wade the spine of coral to the shore, their weapons hoisted above their heads.

Lucas appeared, toting a board donated by Gaspar de los Reyes. He gestured for Diego to follow him. The two of them climbed up to Don Sebastian and knelt before Dona Catalina. Each placed the board on a shoulder and steadied it with both hands. Once Dona Catalina was seated and had arranged the skirt of her emerald green gown, she placed a hand on each man's neck to steady herself. The gentle touch of her fingertips sent a shiver through Diego. He could only imagine what it was doing to Lucas. Diego and Lucas stood up and headed for the gangplank. Upon reaching the reef, they lurched through the shallows. Dona Catalina laughed quietly as she clung to their necks, as though riding sidesaddle on a stumbling mare.

When they arrived at the wharf, Lucas gave Dona Catalina his hand to help her to her feet. Glancing back at Don Sebastian, wading in his finery with his guards and pages sloshing along behind him, he whispered to Diego, "If they tell you I've deserted, don't believe it. I promise we'll meet again."

As the hundreds of sea-weary arrivals lined up to progress across the plaza to the cathedral for a mass of thanksgiving for their deliverance from the sea, Diego watched his uncle and Dona Catalina disappear down a side street. He stifled an urge to run after them and beg them not to leave him.

After Brother Marcos's mass, Diego joined the milling throngs circling the plaza as though they were participating in the paseo back home, their gaits unsteady from all the weeks of shipboard inactivity. Most were uncertain where to go in the absence of townspeople to take them into their homes. As Diego strode back and forth across the paving stones, he felt as though he were missing a limb without Baltasar by his side. And he was terrified for his love-crazed uncle, who would possibly be caught and hanged.

Diego spotted Don Domingo de Santa Cruz de la Sierra, the Captain of the Horse, attired in his dress armor with his plumed helmet under one arm. He was chatting with a voluptuous woman who had been a passenger on another ship. She had jet-black hair and a mole on one cheek. Don Domingo had lost an eye in a fight on the Seville quay just before boarding the *San Jorge*. Gossip in the hold had it that he was injured while defending a serving maid from being raped in an alley by a gang of sailors. Dr. Mendez had salved the wound every day, and Don Domingo now wore a black eye patch. He was the nicest of the senior officers. Upon spotting Diego, he smiled and said, "We finally made it to dry land, lad!"

"Thanks be to the Virgin," replied Diego.

"I've been meaning to tell you I'm sorry about your dog."

"Thanks."

"A dog, you say?" said the lady with the mole. "We saw one swimming in the sea the other day. We decided it was some strange New World fish." She laughed merrily.

Diego lowered his head so they wouldn't see his sudden tears.

As the circling pedestrians swept Diego in their wake, he spotted four Portuguese cavalrymen striding along as though in battle formation. Their Spanish was nearly incomprehensible, so they had kept to themselves in the hold on the trip over. A crossbowman named Nicholas Navarro was the only other soldier who could decipher their strange dialect, and he sometimes sat with them. Lucas told Diego that everyone believed the Portuguese were conversos trying to escape the Inquisitors, who were now pursuing even the Jews and Moors whose ancestors had long since agreed to become Christians. But many in the hold had secrets of their own they were trying to hide, so no one was inclined to expose the Portuguese to Don Sebastian.

As the hot afternoon dragged on toward sunset, some returned to their ships, where they at least had sea rations and a familiar place to sleep. Others moved, uninvited, into the deserted houses. Diego saw Tomas de Carrion emerge from the customs house in which Don Sebastian had ensconced himself and his retinue. Diego wondered when, in the midst of all the confusion of the disembarkation, Don Sebastian would notice that Dona Catalina and Lucas were missing. Tomas scanned the crowds. Eyes settling like sluggish flies on Diego, he lumbered towards him.

"Don Sebastian orders you to find a barge and remove his horses from the *San Jorge*," he announced. "He wishes you to stable them there." He pointed to a quayside shed. "You are to feed and groom them and guard them throughout the night."

Diego nodded, perplexed because this was an honor normally reserved for a page. But he did as he was told, overseeing the hoisting of the two horses from the hold and their transport to shore on a teetering raft poled by a couple of obliging sailors.

Both horses behaved like captives newly released from a dungeon. As he walked them down the quay to their quarters, the ebony gelding staggered from so many days of immobility. The dapple-gray mare whinnied, shaking her head at the bright daylight.

They passed a house with a second-floor balcony lined with a scrolled railing of wrought iron. Huge plants with scarlet blossoms framed the house. A queue of jostling soldiers and sailors snaked into the downstairs doorway. It appeared that at least some of the ladies of the town hadn't fled.

Once inside the dark stable, Diego curried the horses, combed out their manes and tails, and picked clean their hooves. Don Sebastian took almost as much pride in his horses as he did in his wardrobe. These two were beauties. The black gelding had a startlingly blond mane and tail, and the dapple-gray had four pure white legs. As they munched oats, Diego piled straw in the corridor outside their stalls and spread out his and Lucas's indigo blankets.

When the horses had settled down, Diego slipped between the blankets, grateful at last to lie still without the pitch and roll of the sea to keep him awake. What kept him awake instead was music and bursts of laughter from the house next door, the hum from a cloud of circling mosquitoes, and misery over Baltasar's drowning. If he had jumped overboard, would the *San Jorge* have turned back to rescue Baltasar and himself? Or would Don Sebastian have abandoned them both to the waves? Drowning might be preferable to this upcoming journey into the unknown without either Baltasar or Lucas.

The tide was out, and the *San Jorge* listed on the reef, displaying its barnacled hull. Diego joined a line of soldiers and sailors that stretched from the ship across the reef to a quayside warehouse. Everything portable was passed hand to hand and stored in this building. Penitent townspeople were helping. They had sneaked home during the night to find their houses full of sleeping soldiers.

"We thought you were British pirates flying Spanish flags," the man next in line explained as Diego passed him a battered sea chest. His face was sunburned and his hair bleached white by the tropical sun. "We've been plundered by that ruse three times already."

Diego staggered under the weight of the next crate. The lid slipped off. The crate tipped, and several iron chains slithered into the water. As his neighbor retrieved them, Diego noticed that the links ran through rings attached to iron collars. On the road to Seville, he and Lucas had passed a line of Moorish prisoners wearing such collars. When Lucas had asked where they were bound, one said they were headed to La Coruna to row in the galleys of the king. Diego had also seen some African slaves similarly chained on the Seville quay, being bought and sold like cattle. They were the first Africans he had ever seen. Their lot had disturbed him, but Lucas had explained that Africans didn't have souls, so they didn't mind being owned any more than Baltasar did. Still, Diego wouldn't have sworn that Baltasar lacked a soul. The dog had been kinder and more loyal to Diego than several humans he could name.

The crash had shifted some timbers so that the hatch lids to the bottom hold wouldn't budge. This hold was stacked with huge clay jars of wine, honey, olive oil, and vinegar, which Don Sebastian intended to trade with the islanders for supplies for the expedition to La Florida. Gaspar de los Reyes had concluded that chopping the hatches open might collapse the hull. But even after the contents of the deck, the cabins, and the first hold were unloaded, the craft refused to float free on the incoming tide.

Diego stood on the coral reef in saltwater to his knees with the hot sun turning his beardless face pink. Gaspar was inspecting the hull, along with a bare-chested diver from the town and a captain named Melendez, the head of Don Sebastian's bodyguards. Gaspar had eaten a marine diet for so many years that he had begun to resemble a carp, with round, bulging eyes, a blunt nose, and a lipless mouth. His small workshop beneath the bridge contained a treasure trove of tools—awls, mallets, saws, grinding stones. Diego had often helped him during the voyage. In return Gaspar let him handle the tools like so many grails. Which they were. Had those tools been tossed overboard in mid-ocean, the ship might never have made it to shore. They had been used to repair all the cracks and holes that might have allowed seawater to seep into the hollow hull that kept them all afloat.

As Diego reflected that for two months, only a few flimsy boards had lain between himself and the bottom of the ocean, he realized that Captain Melendez was pointing at him. Melendez was tall and muscular with a carefully groomed stiletto beard similar to Don Sebastian's. But his waxed moustache tips twirled up at the corners, giving him a perpetual smile, even though a smile was his least likely expression. He summoned Diego with a crooked index finger. Diego waded along the reef, trying to conceal his lack of enthusiasm for an assignment.

"As the smallest man present," said Melendez, "you will descend on a rope into the bottom hold to inspect the damage from within."

Gulping, Diego nodded. He had no choice other than to run for the swamps. Those who refused orders were flogged, and he knew he would never survive a beating such as Pedro Picado had undergone. But entering that dark hull seemed almost as appealing as jumping overboard in the middle of the ocean. Who knew what bizarre marine creatures might have invaded during the night? Rats might be struggling to stay afloat.

"I can hear the water sloshing," explained the diver with the bare mahogany chest, as they ascended the gangplank onto the deck. "But I can't locate any hole."

Down in the first hold, Diego stood with his arms over his head while the diver knotted a rope around his chest. The stench that usually suffused the stuffy hold had dissipated, replaced by a rather pleasant odor, like a stew simmering. He sniffed several times. Probably this delightful scent was drifting on breezes out from town, where the wives of the town were preparing feasts of apology to the newcomers for the previous day's lack of hospitality.

Diego wiggled through a narrow slot between the floor and the wall. As the rope slowly lowered him into the darkness, he looked around by the light of the torch he clutched in one hand. Tiny red eyes glowed from the tops of casks and from ledges in the curved walls. With water rising to his kneecaps, he found his footing. Then he tiptoed through the murky liquid, praying not to encounter any monsters from the deep.

Stooping, he dipped his fingers in the water. Then he raised them to his nose and sniffed. Eagerly he sucked each finger clean. This seawater was actually a marinade of wine, olive oil, vinegar, and honey. To someone who had spent weeks gnawing moldy sea biscuits, it tasted like nectar from the blossoms of Eden. He laughed out loud, the sound echoing throughout the hollow belly of the beached ship.

Sloshing through the marinade, Diego poked with the toe of his sandal at the shards of jars broken in the crash, searching for a hole in the hull. He found none. He yelled his report up to Gaspar. Then Gaspar yelled down instructions for repairing the feeder pipes to the bilge pumps dislodged by the tumbling casks. Thanks to his onboard apprenticeship, Diego was able to execute these orders. When he finally emerged from the hold, every container anyone could locate was being filled at the pump mouths.

Once relieved of its luscious liquid, like a coconut shell drained of its milk, the hull began to rise up off the reef. Sailors rowed pinnaces attached by cables to the bow, while soldiers stationed on the shoals threw their shoulders against the stern and plied long poles as levers. They finally dislodged the grounded vessel. Back in deep water, the flagship anchored alongside its fleet, unharmed and once more in command.

Tomas de Carrion, with his bulging belly, and the fox-snouted Juan Bravo stood on the quay, eying Diego's heroics darkly. Though it wasn't a task he had chosen, any more than he had chosen to tend Don Sebastian's horses, he could see that they detested him. But, from his years as Cristobal's neighbor, he was accustomed to being disliked. All he knew to do was to ignore those who despised him and pray that they would return the favor.

3

Santo Domingo

Diego sat in a reception room in the customs house at the Santo Domingo port, waiting for an appointment with Don Sebastian. He was mystified as to its purpose. Studying the tiled floor, he tried to calm himself. Several days had passed with no news of Lucas. The retainers of Judge Gonzales, Dona Catalina's new employer, were said to be searching everywhere for the two lovebirds. Rumors were circulating that they had been captured by a band of renegade natives who lived in a swamp at the center of the island.

The door to Don Sebastian's office opened, and three nearly naked men emerged—if one could call them men. Their trunks and limbs were stained blue by swirling tattoos of birds and snakes. Their sleek dark hair was tied up in topknots. They were joined together by a chain that ran through rings on iron collars like those Diego had helped unload from the *San Jorge*. Each neck ring had two prongs that rested on the collarbones to help support its weight. Captain Melendez, with his ever-smiling moustache tips, and two soldiers carrying pikes were escorting them. Alarmed, Diego watched them exit. Could those savages be the ones from the swamp who had seized Lucas?

Tomas gestured to him from the doorway. As Diego entered, Don Sebastian, wearing a jerkin of midnight blue quilted silk, looked up from his desk. He smiled, an expression Diego had never before seen on his somber face. It distorted the horrible scar that snaked through his auburn beard below his cheekbone.

"Do you know anything of your uncle's whereabouts?" he demanded.

Diego was able to answer truthfully, "No, Your Worship." He was flooded with relief. Apparently the crime of the tattooed natives had nothing to do with their having murdered Lucas.

Tomas de Carrion and Juan Bravo stood with their backs to a wall, looking as cross as usual. Don Sebastian gestured for them to leave. They did so, shooting backward glances at Diego.

"Should he contact you," resumed Don Sebastian in a low voice, "you must tell him to remain in hiding until our departure for La Florida. If he is found, I may be forced to hang him. Judge Gonzales is furious, and he is a man with much influence."

Swallowing, Diego nodded. "Thank you, Sire."

"I tell him this from gratitude for your attentions to my horses."

Diego bowed. "I am honored to tend your horses, Sire."

Don Sebastian leaned back in his armchair of carved oak and flashed his strained smile. "I hear that it was you who descended into the belly of the *San Jorge* to repair the pumps."

"I was the smallest man present, Sire. No one else could fit through the opening."

"You are modest, lad. It becomes you. Would you be willing to accompany my steward to farms around the island to select hardy hogs for our excursion?"

"Gladly, Your Worship."

"He will contact you at the stable. Is there anything else?"

Startled to be dealt with almost as an equal, Diego asked, "Sire, who were those natives coming from your office as I entered?"

"They are Orista Indians brought here from La Florida. They will be our guides and translators once we arrive at Santa Elena on the coast north of St. Augustine."

"Yet they wore chains. Will they not help us voluntarily?"

Don Sebastian studied him for a moment, looking almost amused. "It is for their own protection," he finally said. "Should they stray from town, the natives of this island would slaughter them from envy of the favors they enjoy from us. You may go now."

As Diego exited, his knees wobbled with relief. If Lucas hadn't yet been found, it was possible he was still alive. He thought about Don Sebastian's inviting him to select the hogs. He could have merely issued an order. He was surrounded by officers and pages, yet he summoned his swineherd to a private audience. Many other officers also spoke to Diego when they wouldn't even speak to one another. He supposed he was so insignificant that he posed no threat to anyone's authority. He was everyone's favorite lapdog. He shrugged. It beat being Cristobal's jousting dummy. When this journey was over and he was a rich man, he would marry the daughter of a count. Then they would all envy and respect him.

As he strolled along the quay toward the stable, Diego watched the sailors scraping the barnacles off the hull of a ship that lolled in the dry dock beside the main pier. Beyond them he could see the soldiers at work on the Santo Domingo fort. Pascuale Sanchez, a stonemason from Toledo who had slept next to Diego and Lucas in the hold of the *San Jorge*, was overseeing the replacement of the flimsy wooden palisade with slabs of rock. The rock would provide stronger defenses against attacks by French, British, and Dutch privateers eager to plunder the Spanish ports in the Caribbean in hopes of finding some of King Phillip's gold and silver.

He passed a warehouse that had been converted to a mess hall. Alonso Villareal, the head cook, was barking at his cowering kitchen boys, scrawny twins with mops of blond hair. He paused in his rant to nod at Diego. Diego nodded back. Alonso had been a kitchen boy himself on DeSoto's expedition through La Florida twenty-five years earlier. His back was humped, and he walked with a lurch. It was hard to imagine how he had survived that four-year march through dangerous and desolate territory—or how he would survive the upcoming one. Alonso and Don Sebastian had known each other all those years ago. Now he, like Don Sebastian, was graying and wrinkled.

Next to the mess hall sat the bougainvillea-framed house where many soldiers and sailors flocked when night fell. Music and the clamor of drunken men brawling in the street often kept Diego awake until dawn on his bed of straw in the stable.

He glanced at the house. An African girl no older than he sat on the upstairs porch. She wore a red cloth tied around her head like a turban and a long dress with vivid stripes in shades of red, gold, and green. She smiled at him. He looked away quickly. When he glanced back at her, she laughed and tossed her head like a spirited horse.

He hurried to the stable, where he saddled the white-legged dapple-gray. While exercising her, he could explore the path that Lucas and Dona Catalina had followed out of town. If he could find them, he would deliver Don Sebastian's warning and maybe save the life of his besotted uncle.

The dirt road narrowed as the horse trotted inland through the verdant undergrowth. Low-hanging branches swatted Diego's head and caught in his hair. Seedlings seemed almost to sprout underfoot. He saw that, without constant clearing, the jungle would quickly reclaim the little village that perched so precariously on the stormy tropical coast.

Upon reaching a crossroads, Diego had no idea which route to take. He reined in the mare and slid down from the saddle. After tying the reins to a branch, he squatted in the dirt path and tried to imagine which turning he would have taken had he been in Lucas's state of lust and fear.

He heard the barking of a dog. Turning his head, he spotted a silver greyhound streaking down the path from town. He jumped up and ran for the nearest tree. Before he could reach it, the dog caught up with him. His paws tripped Diego, who sprawled to the ground. Closing his eyes, he waited for the sharp fangs to castrate and disembowel him, as war dogs had been trained to do.

Instead, the dog licked his face furiously in between whines and yelps. Looking up, Diego found himself staring into Baltasar's milk chocolate eyes.

"Baltasar! Can it really be you?"

Baltasar whimpered and prodded him with his tapered nose. Diego threw his arms around the dog's neck.

"Come here, Bruto!" shouted a corpulent man who came struggling down the path on stick-like legs.

Diego scrambled to his feet. The panting man carried a coiled leash and a muzzle. Trembling and snarling, Baltasar sidled away from him.

"Where did you find my dog?" asked Diego.

"He's *my* dog," gasped the man. He had gray sidewhiskers and a bulbous red nose.

"His name is Baltasar. He fell off our ship. I thought he had drowned."

"He may have once been yours," said the man. "But I found him swimming in the sea. If I hadn't taken him aboard, there would be no dog to argue about."

"How kind you are to have rescued him, sir. How can I repay you?" Diego grinned at Baltasar, who sat several yards away with a tail that wouldn't stop wagging.

"He's mine now." The fisherman tiptoed toward Baltasar, extending the muzzle.

Baltasar rose and backed away, just out of the man's grasp.

"I would say," said Diego, "that Baltasar belongs to whomever he chooses to belong to."

That night, after a transfer to the disgruntled fisherman of three of Diego's precious jugs of the rich marinade pumped from the belly of the *San Jorge*, Diego lay beneath Lucas's blanket with Baltasar beside him. Both scratched miserably as fleas and mosquitoes feasted on their flesh. From time to time Baltasar licked Diego's cheek. At supper all Baltasar's friends from the ship—the surgeon Lope Mendez, the rifleman Pedro Picado, the crossbowman Nicholas Navarro, the four Portuguese cavalrymen, the stonemason Pascuale Sanchez, the carpenter Gaspar de los Reyes, Alonso Villareal and his twin kitchen boys—had rejoiced over his return. Everyone except the officers, pages, and monks, who were in the customs house with Don Sebastian, dining on their usual delicacies.

As he lay contentedly beside his dog, Diego could hear accordion music lilting from the house next door, along with thumps and thuds as the customers no doubt performed their shipboard jigs, trying to endear themselves to the longsuffering women who worked there. He pictured the girl on the balcony in the red headscarf who had laughed at him that afternoon. He had some wages. If he paid her, she would lie with him just as she did with the soldiers and sailors.

Back home he had been ashamed to awaken from dreams of holding and kissing Leonora. He had rushed to confession in the chapel on the hacienda and recited the Ave Marias and Pater Nosters prescribed by the priest. But those dreams that made him so look forward to sleep always returned. The priest used to sigh whenever he saw Diego coming, always burdened with the same sin. He had finally told Diego that it was better to marry than to burn with desire, because then the possibility of new life existed. Diego couldn't marry until he earned enough gold to go back home and win Leonora. But in the meantime, would it be a lesser sin to lie down with the girl next door than to dream about such acts with Leonora?

Towards dawn, as backyard roosters began to crow, Diego and Baltasar trotted in the coral light to the crossroads at which they had been reunited the previous afternoon. Diego carried Lucas's blanket in a pack basket that also contained a loaf of cassava bread, dried beef, a jug of fresh water, and a vial of marinade. He held out a corner of the blanket for Baltasar to sniff.

"Where's Lucas?"

Baltasar looked up at him and whined.

"Go find Lucas."

Baltasar scurried in tight circles, sniffing the ground. Diego tried to imagine Baltasar's world—all the scents and sounds inaccessible to himself. On the hillside back home, Baltasar used to start growling several minutes before Diego could spot a wolf slinking toward the hogs.

Baltasar's circles became larger and larger. Finally, barking confidently, he headed down a path into a thicket. Diego trotted after him, lugging the basket. From time to time Baltasar sat down and waited for him to catch up.

The path became less detectable as vines writhed like snakes from the overhanging branches. Birds with scarlet and lemon plumage rose into the treetops, shrieking raucously. The odor of rotting greenery gave Diego the sensation of crawling through a pile of manure. As his linen blouse became soaked with sweat, Diego wondered if his uncle and Dona Catalina had managed to survive in this place. But Baltasar seemed convinced he was on their trail.

After what felt like several hours, Baltasar paused before a tree with a trunk the breadth of a hogshead. Its roots hunched up out of the ground, and its branches were draped with filthy rags of gray moss, like the tattered sails of a ghost ship. Baltasar circled the tree, sniffing. Then he backed away and looked up, barking.

"Diego?" called Lucas from the treetop. "In the name of God, is that Baltasar?"

Diego spotted Lucas peering through a curtain of green. "Thanks be to the Virgin! Everyone's been saying you're dead."

"As you can see, they're wrong. Come on up."

Baltasar curled up at the base for a nap while Diego slipped through the moss and clambered up the trunk from knot to knot. Near the crown Lucas had lashed with vines a floor of tree limbs on which Dona Catalina was sitting. Her square-necked green gown was soiled, and her upper chest was swollen from insect bites. Her apricot hair was disheveled. Embracing his uncle, Diego explained about Baltasar's return.

Then he handed Lucas the basket. Removing the stopper, he ran the vial of marinade beneath Lucas's nostrils.

Lucas passed it to Dona Catalina, who drank greedily.

"We've been eating those fruits Lope Mendez taught us about on the ship," explained Lucas. "We're starved. Even those stale sea biscuits would taste good." He ripped apart the bread from the basket, handed a hunk to Dona Catalina, and took another for himself.

Lucas's forearms were swollen with bites. But both he and Dona Catalina appeared intoxicated by life together in their jungle aerie. Diego told him about Don Sebastian's warning.

"Why is he willing to sully his own honor as Dona Catalina's protector in order to spare me?" asked Lucas as he chewed the strange bread.

Diego shrugged.

Lucas's eyes narrowed. "Did he say what he wants in return?"

"He asked me to care for his horses. And to help select hogs for the expedition to La Florida."

"Stay away from him, Diego. If you should displease him, he could have you killed in La Florida, and no one back home would ever know the difference."

"Why would he do that?"

"Do as I say, Diego."

Diego frowned. "But he seems like a nice man."

"Well, he's not. He's a conquistador. Precious metals are priceless to conquistadors, but human life has no value to them whatsoever."

"But he's my commander," said Diego. "Don't I have to obey his orders?"

"Obey them. But lie low otherwise. He's capricious. It's best not to be in his debt."

Diego nodded, his frown baffled.

Abruptly, Lucas asked Diego and Dona Catalina to stand back to back on the platform of limbs.

"Just as I thought. You're the same size," he said. "Diego, I need you to bring us your extra suit of clothing."

"But I have only two sets."

"Take one of mine and ask Miguel Salamanca to cut it down for you."

"Why?"

"If I don't tell you, you won't have to lie if Don Sebastian questions you again. You're one of the worst liars I've ever known." He laughed, putting his arm around Diego and hugging him. "But please make sure you're not followed when you come back. They may be watching you, hoping you'll lead them to us."

Diego nodded.

Climbing down, Diego acknowledged that, although he believed he loved Leonora, he knew nothing about the topic. He understood wanting to win the fame and fortune necessary to qualify as her suitor. She brought out the best in him—his energy, ambition, and determination. But why Lucas and Dona Catalina should seem so enchanted to be starving together in the top of a tree while soldiers searched for them down below remained a mystery to him. What was this elixir called love that drove formerly sane people to risk their lives to attain it?

He thought about the dark-skinned girl in her red headscarf. If he visited her, would what they did together be love? If so, he would be betraying Leonora. But if Africans didn't have souls, as Lucas had assured him, maybe they couldn't love anyway, so there would be no betrayal. And then he himself would be no better than a beast of the fields—like the shepherd on Cristobal's father's hacienda, whom everyone made fun of because he was said to sleep in the woolly embrace of his own sheep on moonless nights.

As Diego and Baltasar headed along the trail back to the village, Baltasar spotted stirrings in the undergrowth and dashed away in pursuit. Diego walked on alone, calling for the vanished dog.

He came to a fork. Having relied on Baltasar's sense of direction, he had no idea which path led out of the forest. Finally picking one, he continued. But the vegetation grew denser, and the daylight filtering through it dimmed. He felt as though hostile eyes were observing him from the undergrowth. He thought he heard labored breathing, as though the forest itself inhaled and exhaled in great hissing sighs.

The path ended, landing Diego on the shore of a lagoon dotted with giant lily pads that bloomed in yellow and purple. He glanced at the log beside him. Embedded in it was a large eye that stared right at him. He jumped backwards. The scaly log stirred and then slithered toward the bank and slid into the water.

Whirling around, Diego tried to retrace his steps, but he merely became more confused. He wandered across a carpet of rotting leaves and stumbled into a clearing. The undergrowth had been thinned as though to encourage the coconut palms that towered all around him. Crossing this jungle orchard, he reached a plot where rows of seedlings were just sprouting.

He discovered that two dark-skinned men in loincloths were approaching him through the trees with drawn bows. They were probably the natives rumored to live in the swamp at the heart of the island. He would tell them about Christ. They would lay aside their weapons and reward him with gold. As they came closer, he realized that both men lacked ears. Around their necks were chokers of scar tissue.

Diego smiled, but they didn't smile back. Nor did they lower their arrows.

"Hello. I'm a Christian. From Spain."

The two conversed in an unfamiliar language. Gesturing with their heads and nocked arrows, they directed him across the clearing.

"I came over the ocean on a ship anchored in the bay," he explained.

One gouged him with his arrow, ripping his linen shirt and searing his side with pain. Diego rubbed the spot and withdrew his hand, which was streaked with blood. As they walked along in silence, Diego's armpits grew slick with nervous sweat. Everyone said these savages ate anyone who annoyed them, and they certainly didn't appear pleased to see him.

Entering a canebrake, they wound along a narrow chute that was hacked through it in a spiral pattern. Now and then they slowed to climb over a tree trunk lashed horizontally across the path. As they emerged into a clearing, Diego spotted round huts roofed with palm fronds. Several naked children played in front of them. They froze in place to stare at him with wide eyes. He wondered if they believed they were inspecting their next meal.

Baltasar came blasting out of the canebrake like a snarling cannonball. The men threw down their weapons and ran, Baltasar snapping at their heels. Diego whistled him back, and boy and dog ran as fast as they could manage out of the maze. With Baltasar in the lead, they trotted toward Santo Domingo.

The streets were empty, but the roar of a crowd came from a field on the edge of town. Diego had forgotten that it was the day for an island-wide fair featuring a market, games, and a feast. As he walked in the direction of the hubbub, Diego tried to figure out why the natives in the swamp lacked ears. Did some insect or disease eat them away? How was he supposed to tell them about the Holy Catholic Faith when they couldn't even speak Castilian? Why did they live in that stinking sinkhole anyway? He felt for the tear in his shirt and poked his fingers through it to the arrow wound in his side. The blood had clotted, but it still hurt.

In the middle of the field, Don Sebastian sat astride the dapple-gray mare Diego had ridden the previous day. He hadn't been there this morning to saddle the horse. No doubt Tomas and Juan had made sure Don Sebastian knew this. He wondered if he were in trouble for his unexcused absence.

Ringing the field were benches of logs where the townspeople, soldiers, sailors, passengers newly arrived from Spain, and farmers from all over the island sat. Everyone was cheering wildly. Diego spotted the red scarf. The girl looked his way and smiled faintly. He was alarmed to feel the dizzy wave of longing that always signaled a trip to the priest for confession.

Don Sebastian wore a quilted doublet of gold brocade, embroidered with black arabesques. His lance was thrust between the shoulder blades of a black bull. Standing in his silver stirrups, Don Sebastian bore down hard on the lance, forcing the bull to its knees. Blood gushed from the bull's wound and flowed down his hide to puddle on the dirt. Don Sebastian's mouth contorted in a strange smile, his eyes glittering like emeralds on ice.

The bull tossed his huge head and rolled his bloodshot eyes. The tips of his horns found a gap in the mare's quilting. Shaking his horns furiously, he ripped her belly open. Her intestines slithered out of the tear and plopped in a steaming pile, sending up a vapor of dust. Nostrils flaring, the dapple-gray threw back her head to emit a shriek almost human.

Diego felt as nauseous as he had during those weeks of vomiting over the railing into the sea. He had butchered hogs all his life and wrung the necks of countless chickens, but that had been for survival, not for entertainment. And he had always apologized to the animal beforehand. Don Sebastian continued to grind the lance into the bull's back as the mare swayed and staggered on the graceful white legs Diego had so carefully curried and massaged. Slowly the bull collapsed. Baltasar whimpered, no doubt smelling the blood.

Don Sebastian dismounted, swept off his black velvet cap, and bowed to the jubilant crowd. The dapple-gray sank to her knees and rolled over against the shuddering bull. As Don Sebastian strode to the gate, some women in the crowd showered him with scarlet flower petals. A lone trumpet blared a fanfare in the hot afternoon sun.

As he retched into a patch of grass, Diego wondered who his new leader really was—a heroic conquistador, a lonely mortal, or a monster who enjoyed inflicting pain.

The audience broke up and groups began to meander along the road back to town. Diego straightened up and wiped his mouth on the sleeve of his dirty, ripped shirt. Snapping his fingers for Baltasar, he joined the ambling throngs headed for the central plaza, where booths for food and games had been erected. The scent of roasted meat drifted on a breeze from the cove. Baltasar began to pant, foamy saliva dripping from the corners of his mouth.

Someone touched Diego's arm. He looked around to see the girl in the red scarf.

"Hello," she said cheerfully.

"Hello."

"Did you enjoy the bullfight?"

"Not really," muttered Diego.

"Me neither. I'm Olivia, by the way."

"Hi. I'm Diego."

"I know. I asked the soldiers."

Diego blushed.

"Why don't you ever come to see us?"

"Don't have time."

"You got all day and all night, just like everyone else."

He could tell that she was laughing at him again. But he didn't want to admit that if he did come to see her, the soldiers and sailors would tease him to the ends of the earth. They regarded him as nothing more than the boy who tended the hogs. It would amuse them greatly to think that he experienced fleshly desires like their own.

"You're a shy one, aren't you?"

He shrugged irritably.

"Where you staying?"

"The stables."

"Well, why don't we go there then?"

His heart in his throat, he walked silently alongside her. What did she want? A private place for a chat or another customer? He wasn't sure either was a good idea. Despite his fevered dreams, he had no idea what to do with a girl. Olivia would just make fun of him.

Leaving the holiday crowds in the plaza, they entered the dark barn. Don Sebastian's sole remaining horse, the ebony gelding with the blond mane and tail, whinnied.

"I see you got a friend," said Olivia.

"The mare that just got killed was also my friend."

"Yeah, you Spanish people sure got some strange ways of having fun."

"It's strange to me, too."

They plopped down on his indigo blanket. Baltasar turned round and round before finally sinking down in the straw nearby. Diego didn't want his dog to witness him being humiliated, but he didn't know how to get rid of him.

"Your shirt's torn." She poked her fingers through the rip and touched his wound. "What have you done to yourself, Diego?"

She lifted his shirt and helped him remove it, revealing his pale chest sprigged here and there with the coarse dark hairs that had just begun to sprout. While she inspected the gash down his side, now caked with dried blood, he told her about his encounter with the natives in the swamp.

"I've always heard about them, but I've never seen them," she said. "The women I work with and I always talk about running away to join them. Why were you out there anyhow?"

"I was hunting for my uncle. He's run off with a woman he's in love with."

"That's sweet. Only problem is that they kill deserters once they find them. And they'll find him. They always do."

They sat silently as Diego tried to digest the reality of his uncle's predicament.

"That's a nasty cut," Olivia finally said. "You better let me clean it out or it could get infected."

Before he could protest, she was on her feet headed out the doorway. She soon returned with a pot of water and rags. He lay on his side and tried not to flinch as she washed the wound, salved it, and bandaged it.

"You probably just want to get some rest?" she asked hopefully.

Diego's body protested, now that her hands had been stroking his chest. But his mind agreed. How could he fumble around with her and then hand her some coins and send her away now that she had been so nice to him? He had started to like her. If he lay with her, and it meant more than the grapplings of two animals at play, he would be betraying Leonora. But one thing was certain: Lucas was wrong. This woman did have a soul.

"Don't worry, Diego," she said, as though reading his thoughts. "You'll have plenty of other chances. I'm going with you all to Santa Elena. A corporal named Arias de Zavallas has just bought me. Turns out I'm worth a lot of coins. I wish they'd pay them to me instead. After all, I'm the one who does all the work. Then I could buy myself back again."

Diego stared at her, startled by this reminder that she was a slave. "Don't you mind leaving Santo Domingo?"

She shrugged. "Unless I could go back home, I don't much care where they drag me to."

"Where's your home?"

"Across those waters." She gestured toward the ocean.

"How did you get here?"

"In the belly of a boat, just like you."

"Who brought you here?"

She got to her feet. "I never saw a man who asked so many questions. Most want to just do their business and then sneak away. I need to go or I'll get in trouble. They're expecting lots of customers next door. All the farmers have come to town."

Diego shuddered on her behalf. "Wait! When will I see you again?"

She smiled at him. "Whenever you get a notion to, Diego. You know where I live."

After the holiday feast in the mess hall, Diego and Baltasar strolled toward the point on which the fort sat. Pascuale Sanchez had told him during dinner that the stone they were using there was unlike any he had ever worked with before. It was crumbly and contained many tiny shells. Although easy to cut and light to stack, Pascuale wasn't sure it would withstand cannonballs.

Upon reaching the construction site, Diego squatted down before some blocks of the stone and ran his hands over one, fingering the petrified debris from the sea. The deep blue evening sky was starting to streak with oranges and reds as the sun sank toward the horizon. Diego was still thrilled to see a discernible horizon and colors other than blue after all those weeks at sea.

At the far end of the point, where it overlooked a beach of white sand, he spotted Olivia in her red turban. She was just standing there looking at the crashing waves, while the breeze off the water stirred her green and gold skirt.

Diego wondered if he should head back to town. Olivia probably had few moments when she wasn't plagued by other people's demands. He was reluctant to intrude on her solitude. Still, he liked her and wanted to talk to her again. In any case, Baltasar had just bounded up to her, and she was now petting him and looking around for his owner.

Diego waved and walked out to the point.

"You spying on me, Diego?"

"I just came to see the fort. That stone with the seashells in it is interesting."

"I come here nearly every evening."

"Why?"

"To think about my family." She looked back toward the sea.

"You must miss them?"

"Yes, I do."

"Why did you leave?"

"It's a long story."

"I'd like to hear it."

"You may wish you hadn't."

She explained that one day her parents took some vegetables to market in a nearby town in the country where they lived, across those wide waters. They left Olivia in charge of her four younger brothers and sisters, instructing them all to climb a tree outside their hut if any strangers came. A couple of strangers did come, men carrying poles with sharp, shiny tips. The five children scrambled up the tree, but the strangers spotted them anyway. They shook the children out of the branches like coconuts. Then they tied them together with ropes around their throats and marched them to a boat anchored in the nearby river. They shoved the five down the steps into the hold, where several dozen of their neighbors were already lying on the floor. The little ones started crying. The boat sailed to an island that had a big stone fort on it. The children were put in a pen with people they didn't know, many of whom were moaning and wailing. The next thing Olivia knew, she was chained in the belly of a ship that wouldn't stop rocking, lying in a pool of vomit, urine, and feces.

"The worst part is," she concluded, "that I have no notion what happened to my brothers and sisters. They were so little and so scared. I was supposed to be taking care of them, but there was nothing I could do."

She turned toward town. "I got to go. All my men friends are waiting for me." Her dark eyes were bleak.

"I'm sorry," said Diego. He reached out and touched her arm.

She pushed his hand away, a wild look in her eye. "Don't touch me, Diego! If you want to be my friend, don't you ever touch me again."

She stalked away.

Diego watched the breakers pound the white sand and tried to picture Leonora with her white teeth and her shiny black hair gathered in the red velvet hood. But all he could see in his mind's eye was Olivia in her red turban with her bleak black eyes.

4

Santa Elena

S quinting up into the bright afternoon sunshine, Diego watched the struggling shoat descend on a leather sling over the side of the *San Jorge*. While treading water, he released her, and then shoved her with his feet toward the shore. She started swimming, squealing frantically. The four Portuguese on their horses on the bank poked at the other hogs with their lances, trying to prevent them from escaping into the nearby thicket of moss-draped cypresses and live oaks.

Diego scrambled back onboard. "She looks like a swimming barrel," he observed to Francisco, who was smoking his pipe by the railing.

"What's this?" Francisco pointed to the crusted scab down the side of Diego's abdomen.

"I got speared by some natives on Hispaniola when I was searching for my uncle."

"Has he turned up yet?"

"No. I'm afraid he may be dead."

"I'm sorry, lad."

"Thanks, Francisco." Forcing himself not to cry, he climbed into his leather shorts and tied the cord, also leather, that he used as a belt.

"Not much of a town, this Santa Elena." Francisco exhaled a stream of smoke that drifted skyward. "Not even a decent port. Yet it's supposed to be the capital of La Florida."

"It does seem pretty crude. Especially compared to Seville." As Diego pulled on his loose linen shirt, he pictured those paved quays, swarming with stevedores, pickpockets, and whores, which had so shocked him upon his arrival from the Galician countryside. He doubted anything could shock him now. He had seen it all.

"Or Lisbon or London or La Rochelle," said Francisco. "But you'll find cities flocked with gold in the interior of this land. As Cortes did in Mexico. As Pizarro did in Peru. I only wish I weren't too old to go along."

"So do I." Diego watched the Portuguese trying to goad the rambunctious hogs along the path toward the town.

"Did you ever hear of Cabeza de Vaca?" Francisco tapped his pipe on the railing. The smoldering ashes fell into the water below, giving off wisps of smoke.

Diego shook his head.

"His expedition shipwrecked on a coast west of here. After being enslaved by some natives for many months, he escaped and hiked to the silver mines in Mexico. It took him seven years. They say King Phillip has ordered Don Sebastian to blaze a trail to link Santa Elena to these mines. Then the silver can be shipped overland rather than across the Gulf of Mexico, which is swarming with pirates."

"How long would such a trail be?"

"No one knows yet. Don Sebastian is supposed to figure that out."

They watched the pinnace loaded with supplies move along the open channel to the wooden dock, which already held mountains of crates and barrels. Stands of marsh grass rustled in the breeze off the bay. A bird with hunched shoulders and a feathered crown rose up to beat a slow retreat on steely blue wings.

"My holds are now empty, lad, and I return to Santo Domingo tomorrow on the morning tide. And from there to Cartegena to pick up some silver for King Phillip. Then back to Seville. And who knows where from there."

"I'll miss your stories, Francisco."

Diego studied the older man who had entertained and instructed him on the ocean voyage. On the hacienda back home, the cast of characters had remained constant. Recently, however, Diego's life had become a series of leave-takings. That was the price you had to pay to make your fortune. Sometimes he wondered if his father, killed on a battlefield in the Netherlands while fighting the Protestant heretics for the Pope, might have been like Francisco. Diego had often struggled to summon some memory of this man who had left when he was two years old, never to return. But he couldn't recall even the slightest detail. All he knew about him was what his mother had told him—his father was strong and kind, honest and loyal. Fancy words with no physical reality.

"You don't know this yet because you're too young," said Francisco. "But you meet only a handful of people in a lifetime with whom you feel at home. As age is no barrier, you are one of those for me."

Laying his pipe on the railing, Francisco removed his gold ring set with crystal and handed it to Diego. "This stone is said to come from a mountain of quartz in the land where you're headed. Wear it on your journey, friend, and sometimes think of me."

Fitting it on his middle finger, Diego turned his head aside so that Francisco wouldn't see his tears.

"Maybe we'll meet again someday, Diego," said Francisco. "On one ship or another. In one port or another. In the meantime, guard yourself well against the evil that surrounds you."

Diego blinked. Was Francisco referring to Don Sebastian? Ever since the ghastly bullfight, Diego had been heeding Lucas's advice to lie low. He had helped Don Sebastian's steward select these hogs at farms around Hispaniola, but the few times he spotted Don Sebastian in the streets of Santo Domingo, he had ducked down an alley to avoid him. He couldn't seem to get the image out of his head: Don Sebastian grinding his lance into the bull's back while his gutted mare staggered beneath him.

Riding the last pinnace into port, Diego surveyed the new capital of La Florida. It consisted of a couple of mud streets lined with huts of wattle and daub. Their roofs were sheaves of marsh grass. Any land that wasn't swamp was a garden or pasture. But the crops at midsummer had reached only half the height they would have in Galicia. The settlers' cattle and hogs looked sickly and stunted, too, as though depleted by the oppressive heat and humidity that had already turned Diego's linen shirt wet with sweat.

Scrambling onto the wharf, Diego retrieved Baltasar from Pedro Picado, who had brought him in from the ship. Pedro's wounds from his onboard flogging had healed without becoming infected, so the rifleman's good humor had returned. He slapped Diego on the shoulder as he handed him Baltasar's leash, almost knocking him over.

Diego and the dog trotted off in search of the hogs. They passed the soldiers' tents, sprouting like puffball mushrooms in a pasture alongside a swamp. They finally located the hogs in a pen of brush that was ringed by the Portuguese cavalrymen and the crossbowman Nicolas Navarro. They looked harried as they prodded at the hogs with their lances like inept fencers.

"Please take these devils, Diego," begged Nicolas. "They keep escaping and racing all over this godforsaken island!"

Diego laughed. "You can fend off attacking soldiers, Nicolas, but a few hungry pigs defeat you?"

Nicolas translated this for the others, and all five roared with laughter.

Diego and Baltasar herded the hogs into a nearby copse of live oaks, where they began to root noisily in the leaf mold. Whenever one wandered off, Baltasar, panting from the heat, struggled to his feet and ushered it back to the drove.

Diego felt lucky to be sitting in the shade while everyone else labored in the sweltering sun. Captain Melendez had put them to work building huts for themselves and pens for the animals. Later they would reinforce the flimsy fort for the colonists before heading inland to terra incognita.

Reclining on a mattress of leaves, his hands behind his head, Diego contemplated love. He concluded that the hardest part about it was leaving it. So far he had left his mother, Leonora, Lucas, Francisco, and Baltasar. Baltasar had miraculously returned. Lucas had promised they would meet again, but Diego had seen no sign of him. If Diego managed to survive the upcoming expedition without Lucas, he intended to go back home to his mother and Leonora and never again stir farther than that oak grove on the hillside.

He glanced around at the mossy live oaks, as shaggy as unshorn sheep, contrasting this setting to his Galician hilltop with its view of the distant silver sea, where puffy clouds had hovered like beckoning sails. Why had he heeded such a vague summons? After all these months of sea and swamp, he was swept with longing for the cool, crisp mountains of his homeland. He understood the homesickness Olivia must have felt as she stood on the beach at Santo Domingo and looked out to sea.

Then he remembered that it was his mother who had insisted he leave Galicia, when she heard Cristobal call him a Christ Killer. But that was just an idle insult, like "whoreson," which Cristobal had also called him since he lacked a father. Diego had hardened himself against these slurs. Why had his mother stirred up such a fuss? And why hadn't he objected to her plan to ship him halfway around the globe under the thumb of a madman? She had always insisted that the boys on the hacienda who tortured animals and insects were the ones who grew up to become murderers. Apparently some became conquistadors, too.

Returning to camp, he and Baltasar enclosed the swine in their pen of brush and tracked down two lancers to guard them overnight. It was a sticky evening, but many fires of green wood smoldered to repel the mosquitoes that swarmed like maggots in rotten meat. The surgeon Lope Mendez had warned that their bites could give a man a fever that would recur for a lifetime. Many coughed from the smoke as they mended clothing or threw dice and exchanged small disks of clay.

Diego walked into the kitchen tent where one of the blond twins served him a bowl of pork stew and a hunk of cornbread. Back outside he sat on a log next to the sturdy corporal Arias de Zavallas, who nodded at him.

As Diego stabbed a piece of pork with the tip of his knife blade, he listened to Nicolas Navarro tell Arias about the escape early that afternoon of the three tattooed translators. "They were unchained," he explained, "because their chief was arriving from the mainland and Don Sebastian feared that the iron collars would incite his ill will. So they promptly slipped into the swamp. We searched until dusk but found no sign of them."

"Why would they want to go back to a swamp after seeing how we live?" asked Diego. He also wondered why the natives were still wearing the iron collars in Santa Elena if the purpose of the collars had been to protect them from the envious natives of Hispaniola.

Before anyone could reply, Tomas de Carrion arrived to announce that Diego was to report to Don Sebastian. As he set his pottery bowl on a stump and stood, Diego felt a stab of dread. What did that strange man want from him now?

Nicolas and Arias watched as Diego departed alongside Tomas, who lurched from foot to foot like a plump duck. Tomas walked with his head held high, not deigning to address a mere hog drover. As they passed the four Portuguese lounging around their private fire, Diego lifted his chin at them in greeting. They nodded back in unison and watched him trail Tomas toward town.

Tomas and Diego approached Don Sebastian's quarters, the largest hut in Santa Elena apart from that reserved for the governor on his trips north from St. Augustine. Its exterior walls were whitewashed. Diego felt apprehensive that Don Sebastian was once again singling him out. The dapple-gray mare with four white legs had been one of Don Sebastian's favorites. She had done her best to serve him well, but he had let the bull rip open her belly. And as she lay there dying, shuddering in the dirt alongside the blood-caked bull, Don Sebastian had walked away without even looking back. If this was how he treated his favorite animals, would his treatment of favored people be any better?

Inside Don Sebastian was sitting on a campstool. Lucas, his hands bound behind his back, stood before him on an Oriental carpet. He had grown a bushy black beard, and his hair was long and unkempt. Diego smiled to see him. Then he stopped smiling as he grasped his uncle's predicament. Normally, deserters were hanged.

"You may be relieved to know that your uncle is still alive," said Don Sebastian.

Diego nodded warily. From the corner of his eye, he spotted the orange hair of Juan Bravo, clearing the dinner dishes from a trestle table. Glancing around to make sure no one was watching, Juan drained the dregs from a pottery wine goblet.

Don Sebastian dismissed the soldiers. Then he ordered Tomas de Carrion to cut the cords around Lucas's wrists.

"Your uncle wishes to marry," he informed Diego.

Diego looked at Lucas. Lucas nodded nervously.

"It seems that my charge, Dona Catalina, is with child."

Lucas hung his head.

Don Sebastian said, "If I execute you for desertion, a lady and an infant are left without a protector. If I execute both you and her, I murder an unborn innocent. Yet if I allow you to marry, my soldiers will believe they can indulge their lusts without consequence. What would you do if were you me, Lucas Martin?"

Lucas stared at the burgundy and peacock blue carpet. "What I feel for Dona Catalina is not lust, Sire. I love her," he murmured. "I beg your mercy for us both."

"I should hope that you love her, soldier. Though is it love to ruin a woman's future and heap shame on her in the present?"

Diego noticed Tomas de Carrion leaning against the far wall, the bottom fastenings on his suede jerkin undone so that his belly could bulge more freely. Beside him stood a young man with European clothing and features, but his lank black hair was topknotted in the native style. His dark eyes inspected Don Sebastian like those of a physician trying to diagnose an illness.

"Brother Marcos will marry you here tomorrow morning. Dona Catalina will return to Santo Domingo on the *San Jorge* to await the birth of your child. You will depart with us for the interior. I need your services as a handler of war dogs. This is why I selected you and your nephew in Seville, and this is the role you will perform."

Lucas fell to one knee and bowed his head. "May God bless you, Sire."

Lucas looked as astonished as Diego felt. He had expected his uncle to be lashed to a pulp, at the very least.

"Get out of my sight!" snapped Don Sebastian.

As Lucas quickly backed out the door, Don Sebastian motioned for Diego to remain. He gestured to the young man by the wall. "Diego Martin, meet Guillermo Albin. Guillermo speaks the native languages. He will accompany you while you graze your hogs so that he can teach you the Indian dialects. In turn, I want you to improve his Castilian. I will need you both as interpreters. Diego, I expect you to attend dinner here each evening so that you can observe Guillermo translating for my guests."

Diego and Guillermo nodded to each other and arranged to meet at the hog pen the next morning. Then Don Sebastian dismissed Guillermo. Gesturing to a campstool, he said to Diego, "You may be seated."

Diego balanced awkwardly in the leather sling, alarmed by his new assignment. Other than the Galician patois and the babblings of the Portuguese cavalrymen, he had never even heard a language other than Castilian.

"How do you find Santa Elena, boy?"

Diego hesitated. "Ruder than I had expected, Sire."

"Our journey has not yet begun. You will see sights in the interior that will astonish you."

"So I have been led to believe, Sire."

"When I was your age, I traveled with DeSoto much of the territory we will soon be covering. Some eight days' march north of here lies a village called Cofitachequi. We arrived there after traversing a barren wilderness for weeks. Men and horses alike were down to bare bones. Just as we were about to succumb to starvation and despair, Cofitachequi appeared as though in a dream. Its huge temple sits atop a high mound. Its roof is crowned by a wooden falcon with a turquoise eye the size of a fist.

"Their beautiful young queen greeted us, dressed in the skin of an albino deer. Bearers carried her on a litter beneath a canopy of white swan wings. Reaching our shore on a ceremonial barge, she draped strands of freshwater pearls around DeSoto's neck in welcome."

As he talked, Don Sebastian's green eyes examined Diego. Diego felt like a canary being appraised by a cat. He glanced toward Tomas de Carrion, who was gazing at a far corner, his hands behind his back and his face twitching with annoyance.

Abruptly Don Sebastian called to Tomas, "Go fetch Miguel Salamanca."

Tomas departed, glancing at Diego with a curled upper lip. Don Sebastian reached for a pile of garments on the floor and held up a doublet of wine brocade. "To attend my dinners you will need the proper attire. Miguel Salamanca will alter these for you. They are items of which I have tired."

"You are more than generous, Sire," replied Diego, silently protesting that he preferred his own leather shorts, linen blouse, and vest of cracked leather. What would happen to him if he proved unable to master the new languages?

Miguel Salamanca entered. He had the darting red eyes and twitching nose of a friendly household mouse. Diego stripped to his coarse linen undergarments and donned Don Sebastian's cast-offs.

"What is this?" asked Don Sebastian, pointing to Diego's hand.

Diego looked at the gold ring set with crystal while Miguel marked the fabrics he wore with a piece of chalk. "Francisco gave it to me, Sire. He said this stone comes from the mountains towards which we are headed."

"Alas, that stone is only quartz. But never mind, we will find gems with true value on our journey."

Diego remained silent. To him, Francisco's worthless chunk of quartz was priceless.

Dismissed by Don Sebastian after the fitting, Diego wandered from fire to fire, trying to locate Lucas. The thought of passing every evening in the company of Don Sebastian and his pages filled Diego with despair. Having been singled out for special treatment, Diego would no doubt be the butt of the pages' incomprehensible machinations, even more than he already was. He would rather eat parched corn with Lucas and Baltasar than dine on delicacies at Don Sebastian's table with those preening young thugs who reminded him so much of Cristobal's gang.

He spotted Lucas on a log. A clean-shaven young man with carrot-colored hair was seated on the ground, leaning against Lucas's legs. Baltasar lay asleep beside them. Lucas looked up and smiled, his white teeth buried in his bushy black beard.

"How did you get to Santa Elena, Uncle?"

Baltasar lifted his head at Diego's voice. Diego sank down beside him and scratched him behind his ears.

"On the *San Jorge*."

"But I searched everywhere for you."

"We hid in the hold with the cattle. I promised the herder part of my share of the gold we'll discover upcountry."

"I can't believe Don Sebastian didn't punish you," said Diego.

"Me either. When they dragged me into his lodge, I thought I was done for."

Studying the boy lounging against his uncle, Diego realized it was Dona Catalina, wearing Diego's extra clothes. Her silky apricot hair had been chopped off, and her milky complexion was sunburned. This expedition was turning into a costume party.

"Congratulations on your upcoming marriage," he said to her, trying not to sound as sour as he felt about the danger she had put his uncle in.

She smiled. "When I left the Canaries, I never imagined I might marry such a wonderful man as your uncle. I'll do everything in my power to make him happy."

Diego forced himself to smile. She was the reason for his uncle's troubles, but she was also the reason for his obvious happiness. "That shouldn't be too hard."

"Don Sebastian is training me as a translator," he said to Lucas.

Lucas snorted. "A translator? You can barely speak Castilian!"

Diego shrugged. "I guess I don't have any choice."

Lucas frowned. "No, I don't suppose you do. I have you to thank that I wasn't beaten or hanged."

"Me?"

"I'm sure Don Sebastian spared me a lashing in order not to upset you."

Diego frowned. "If that's so, then I'm glad. But I wish he'd just leave me out of it."

"Believe me, so do I."

As Diego headed for the tent he shared with the cattle drover from Hispaniola, he spotted Olivia laying a branch on the fire outside Arias de Zavallas's tent. Arias and three foot soldiers sat before it on a fallen log. Diego raised his eyebrows at Olivia, and she nodded curtly. They had scarcely spoken since she had told him at Santo Domingo about her capture by the slave raiders. It appeared the only

way to be alone with her now was as a paying customer. Arias was
charging the soldiers a copper coin apiece to visit her in his tent.

Olivia backed into the shadows behind the tent. Looking around
to make sure no one was watching, Diego circled around to join her.
They stood there watching the orange flames leap and flare. The foot
soldiers chatted quietly, contributing to the low hum that arose from
the camp, while in the swamp frogs and night insects pulsed and
screeched. He wondered if the escaped Orista translators were out
there now, watching and waiting.

"How's your arrow wound?" she asked in a low voice.

"Fine. Almost healed."

"You're lucky. Lots of cuts get infected in this climate. I've seen
people die from smaller ones than that."

"Thank you for cleaning mine."

She shrugged. "Glad I could help."

"What do you think of Santa Elena?"

She snorted. "Not much. But it's all the same to me. I got soldiers
after me half the night, and Zavallas messing with me till dawn. I'm
worn out, and the expedition hasn't even started."

Diego felt a stab of shame for being a man and for having
wanted, and for still wanting, to mess with her himself. "How do you
stand it?"

She glanced at him in the firelight. "Do I look to you like
someone who's got a choice? When you got no choice, you make the
best of it. Or you grieve yourself to death, one. And I'm not ready to
die just yet."

"I wish I could help you, Olivia. But I'm just a swineherd, and I
don't have many choices myself."

"You do help, Diego. You talk to me like I'm a human being.
And you don't grab at me like all the others."

Diego's heart sank. Apparently he could be her friend or her
customer, but not both. And it was too late to be her customer
because she already felt like a friend.

"Olivia!" bellowed Arias. "Where the devil are you, girl? Get in
that tent and earn your keep."

Olivia compressed her lips. Diego reached out to grab her forearm. Then he remembered her injunction against touching her and let his hand fall to his side. She walked around the tent.

As Diego watched her put on a fake smile for the burly soldier scrambling to his feet, he improvised wildly: Tonight the two of them would slip into the swamp as those native translators had done. They would join the Orista. Or he would persuade Francisco to hide them on the *San Jorge* until it reached Spain. Once in Seville he would find a ship to carry her back home....

Then he remembered that he was practically betrothed to Leonora, who could hardly be expected to understand his deserting his chance to earn the riches that would allow them to wed, in order to reunite an African slave with her family. Maybe the only way to stop thinking about Olivia instead of Leonora was to pay Arias to spend time with her. Then she would hate him as much as she did all the others.

Guillermo appeared the next morning as Diego and Baltasar were about to depart for the forest with the hogs. "I know a good spot," he said in his rudimentary Spanish. His chest was bare, and he was wearing Indian leggings and a loincloth. With his topknotted black hair and deeply tanned skin he resembled a native, apart from his lack of tattoos.

Guillermo led the way through the tangled trees to a point that extended into a marsh. It was ringed with a high earthen bank. The two young men and the dog sprawled across the neck, enclosing the hogs as though in a pen. While the animals grunted and rooted in the leaf mold with their moist noses, Diego and Guillermo searched for topics to discuss so they could practice the various languages.

Diego asked about the charred timbers atop the banks. Guillermo explained in his halting Spanish, as Diego prompted and corrected him, that French Protestants had built a fort there before the founding of Santa Elena a few years earlier. Spaniards from St. Augustine had destroyed it, insisting this territory belonged to King Phillip.

"Did you know these heretics?" asked Diego.

"Yes. I'm one of them. My real name is Guillaume, not Guillermo."

Diego glanced at him. The priest back home had warned about French heretics. If captured in Spain, they were hanged by their feet amid fighting war dogs or burned alive in bonfires such as the one Lucas had witnessed. Yet this young man had neither horns nor hooves. Apart from his native topknot, he seemed much like Diego himself.

"I came here from the Cevennes mountains with my older brother."

"To search for gold?"

"No. We hoped to build a settlement where our people could live in peace. The Catholics in France hound us as though we're rabbits with no burrows." He picked up a leaf and began to shred it with his fingertips.

"Where's your brother now?" asked Diego.

"Dead, probably. Many died during the Spanish attack. Some escaped inland to live in native villages. But I've had no word from my brother for several years now."

"How did you survive the attack?" Diego rolled over on his back and put both hands behind his head.

"When we first arrived, we built this fort. We planted crops, but the soil is poor so they didn't grow. Once we'd butchered our livestock, we tried to fish and hunt. But most of us were soldiers with no gift for stealth. We gathered shellfish, nuts, berries, wild greens. We traded our tools to the Orista for corn. Our captain returned in our ship to La Rochelle for more supplies.

"Month after month he failed to reappear. A storm blew down our huts. A fire destroyed our storehouse. Our leader hanged a soldier for disobedience, and then the other soldiers mutinied and hanged our leader. They hatched a plan to sail back home. They built a small boat, caulking it with moss and tar. I had nearly died from seasickness coming over. I believed the Orista would adopt me because I was friendly with the chief's niece. The soldiers stitched their linen shirts and sheets together for sails and embarked for France. And I headed for Oristatown."

"Did they ever reach France?" asked Diego. He realized that beneath his deep tan, Guillermo's chest was covered with puckered scars, as though he had been badly burnt.

"They ran out of food off the Azores. So they ate my cousin, Jean Claude."

After a long silence Diego said, "Some must have survived for you to know this?"

"An English ship rescued them. Our captain returned here with the survivors and some new recruits. That's when the Spaniards attacked. But as I say, I was living in Oristatown by then."

Diego sat up and studied Guillermo, who had just admitted that his compatriots were cannibals. Perhaps heretics were spawn of the devil after all, and the Inquisition was right to destroy them?

Noting his appalled gape, Guillermo replied, "Do not judge these men until you yourself have known a hunger so great that you will roast rats with relish. You will find much here in La Florida to repel you."

Unnerved to have had his thoughts read so easily, Diego asked, "How do you happen to work for the Spaniards, since they despise heretics?"

"As I despise them. I assure you that I'm not a volunteer. They came in search of me at Oristatown and dragged me down to St. Augustine as a translator. Then they sent me here to translate for Don Sebastian. They allow me to live, heretic that I am, because they need my services. They always select young men as interpreters, just as they have you, because we learn new languages faster than older men."

"So what happens if I'm not able to learn them?"

Guillermo glanced at him. "Don't worry. You'll pick them up quickly. You'll amaze yourself."

"Are the mountains to which we're headed really seamed with silver?"

"So the Orista say. I myself have never seen them."

"What are the Orista like?"

"If they need your skills or admire your person, they can be kind and generous. If not, they can be as cruel as we are. But they are our superiors in many respects because they know how to survive in this savage setting and we do not."

Although it was a warm morning, Diego shivered in the shadows of the matted moss, which draped the branches overhead like the lank gray hair of a hag.

5

Orista

Diego squatted beside Guillermo in a canoe stacked high with Don Sebastian's carpets and cushions, watching two burly foot soldiers heave a crate of chains into one of the shallow log boats belonging to the Orista tribe. The boat teetered and nearly flipped, but the loin-clothed native paddlers steadied it in time.

Diego wondered why the heavy chains were being lugged from place to place when they were never put to any use, apart from corralling the tattooed translators who had already escaped. Once they actually reached the wilderness, who would possibly want to flee the safety provided by 130 armed and armored Spanish soldiers? He glanced down at his new outfit—Don Sebastian's renovated wine doublet and trunk hose. He felt silly, but he had been ordered via Tomas to wear them for the upcoming conference with the Orista leaders. Lucas and the other soldiers had guffawed when they saw him. He knew he looked like one of those buffoons from Valladolid who used to arrive at the hacienda in their gilded coaches to visit the Count.

The hogs were being loaded on their backs, their bound feet thrashing. Diego missed tending them, but Don Sebastian wanted him nearby now, with his surprising new language skills at the ready. He and Guillermo exchanged a smile over the antics of the struggling swine. During their days together in the forest learning each other's languages, they had become friends. Diego had told Guillermo about Leonora, and Guillermo had told him about his wife, the niece of the Orista chief, whom Guillermo referred to as Orista Mico. His wife's name was Blue Heron.

Guillermo had also told him more about his flight to Oristatown when his comrades departed for France in their homemade boat. The Orista had welcomed him by tying him to a wooden rack, kindling a fire beneath it, and frying him like a fish. As the flames blistered his limbs, Guillermo screamed for mercy. Blue Heron begged her mother, who was some kind of tribal official, to save him. He was unbound and carried, half-roasted, to the mother's lodge. Blue Heron salved his horrible burns. Once he recovered, she took him as her husband.

They finally set out, the dozens of canoes, paddled by the bare-chested, topknotted Orista warriors, weaving through a maze of canals that crisscrossed the tidal plain. Don Sebastian's raft led this flotilla, with Don Sebastian standing toward the front in his bronze breastplate and peaked silver helmet with its scarlet plume. Captain Melendez in his silver dress armor stood to his left, holding the gold and purple standard of Castile and Leon. The brown-robed Brother Marcos, holding a golden cross aloft, stood to his right with three monks behind him. Each of their horses, splendidly caparisoned, stood in two canoes that were lashed together, front legs in one and rear legs in another, eyes rolling, ears and tails twitching.

"You must be glad to be going home?" asked Diego.

Guillermo nodded.

"How long since you've seen Blue Heron?"

"A couple of months."

Diego had a hard time summoning much sympathy. He likely wouldn't see Leonora again for a couple of years.

Their boat glided past stagnant pools that glowed like old pewter beneath the overcast sky. Flocks of birds—white or slate or rose—erupted into flight with startled cries. Guillermo pointed to a high earthen platform on the far shore, on which sat the Orista council house and Orista Mico's lodge, both rectangular, with mud walls and roofs of reeds, huts not much different from those at Santa Elena.

Upon reaching the Orista wharf, the soldiers disembarked and donned their metal breastplates and helmets. Then they fell into formation. Diego and Guillermo strapped on breastplates and took their places among the bodyguards and pages.

Don Sebastian led the procession on his ebony gelding, flanked by Captain Melendez and Brother Marcos on their best horses, mounts with deep muscled chests, arched necks, and high-stepping hooves. Slowly the army crossed a grassy plaza past hundreds of nearly naked indigo warriors assembled at the foot of the mound. Diego felt a stab of alarm as he recalled Guillermo's tale of roasting on a rack in the middle of this plaza. The Spanish soldiers stationed themselves in orderly ranks alongside the warriors.

After scaling a seemingly endless log stairway up the face of the mound, Diego was short of breath when he reached the summit on which the council house stood. He watched, astonished, as Orista Mico, backed by a dozen headmen, approached Don Sebastian. Hanging from his neck and covering his chest was a shell disk incised with the diamond pattern of a coiled rattlesnake. Indigo tattoos of similar design decorated his limbs. Shell bracelets encircled his biceps and calves. On his head perched the skull of a panther, jaws wide open as though snarling. The panther's pelt draped his shoulders and back. His face was painted indigo and white, with jagged slashes down his temples that emphasized his keen dark eyes. His headmen were outfitted similarly. As strange as they looked to him, Diego realized that the Orista probably thought the Spaniards looked just as strange in their silver armor and peaked helmets, with face guards that revealed only their eyes.

As Guillermo translated, Don Sebastian informed the Orista leaders that they were now subjects of King Phillip II and the Holy Father in Rome. As such, they were required to provide a guesthouse and a full granary for visiting Spaniards. They would also provide boat transport to and from Santa Elena, porters for baggage to their borders, and women servants. If they agreed, King Phillip had sent them gifts.

But if they refused, Don Sebastian continued, with pauses for Guillermo's translation, which was halting, as though delivered with reluctance, "I will seize your wives and children...and I will make them slaves...and I will sell them or dispose of them as His Highness might command."

Diego's jaw dropped open. His eyes shifted to the sea of warriors down below, whose topknots were garnished with garish feathers. At one sign from Orista Mico, they could destroy every Spaniard in sight. Despite the Spaniards' breastplates and weapons of steel, they were outnumbered five to one. But the old man's creased indigo face remained impassive beneath his snarling panther skull.

"And I will seize you and your goods and do you all the hurt and harm which I can…and I declare that the deaths and damage which might grow out of it will be your fault…not that of His Highness, nor mine, nor of these troops who accompany me."

Diego's blood slowed in his veins. Could Don Sebastian be unaware of the cruelties of which the Orista were capable? Diego had often studied the horrible scars across Guillermo's chest. It was a wonder he had survived the Oristas' bonfire of welcome. Who knew how they would celebrate their displeasure?

"Yaa," Orista Mico replied, his face still a study in indifference.

Captain Melendez stepped forward to hand Orista Mico an iron ax, some scraps of taffeta, and a peacock feather. Orista Mico passed the ax and the fabric to his headmen.

But he kept the feather for himself, turning it this way and that to catch the afternoon sun. Finally he replied (according to Guillermo's translation), "Oh Great White Father, who has arrived in a ship with sails like the wings of giant gulls, please know our deep pleasure at your delightful presence and your remarkable gifts. You honor me with this amazing feather. I will eat each meal with it fanning me. I will march into battle against my enemies, bearing this feather as my standard. I will sleep with this feather in my bed and caress my wife with it during the act of love."

Diego glanced at Guillermo as he translated. His eyes were amused, as were those of the headmen. It was clear from the colorful feathers in the warriors' topknots that the Orista had no need for feathers. It was also clear that Orista Mico was making fun of Don Sebastian. Diego felt his terror begin to subside as he realized that these native leaders felt contempt, rather than rage or fear, for the Spaniards and their ceremonies of submission.

That night Diego and Guillermo stayed in a hut on the mound next to Orista Mico's lodge, where Don Sebastian was quartered. The ousted Mico and his tribe were camping outside town, atop the stubble of their harvested corn. Armed soldiers were patrolling the perimeter of the town to keep its rightful inhabitants out. Diego lay on a wooden bench along one wall and wrapped his blanket around himself to fend off circling mosquitoes.

"Orista Mico's speech about the feather was a joke, wasn't it?" he asked Guillermo, who was settling down nearby. "But Don Sebastian seemed to take it seriously."

"Your people are not noted for a highly developed sense of humor," replied Guillermo grimly.

"You seem irritable tonight, Guillermo. Is something bothering you? Apart from Don Sebastian's obnoxious performance on the mound this afternoon?"

"You gauge me well by now, Diego. I've had some bitter news: Blue Heron will be joining us on our march."

"But this is good, isn't it? You won't have to leave her behind."

"The older women go as cooks and servants. The young go for the pleasure of the soldiers."

Diego was too shocked to reply. Finally he asked, "Shouldn't we tell Don Sebastian?"

"He's the one who selected her."

"But if he knew she's your wife...."

"If I complain, he might turn her over to the troops to rescue me from my own sentimentality."

Diego frowned. "Do you really think he would do that?"

"I know he would," said Guillermo. "These soldiers don't take their own marriages seriously. Why should they respect those of people they regard as wild animals?" After a moment he added urgently, "Diego, Don Sebastian shows you his best self and conceals the rest. You must beware. That man is a snake."

Diego didn't reply. He had begun to feel a grudging gratitude toward Don Sebastian. The memory of that awful bullfight remained vivid, but it was a popular sport for many Spaniards. Perhaps he had been judging Don Sebastian too harshly. After all, he had given Diego an interesting new job, the finest food available in this crude country, and a horse to ride on the expedition. Until now, it had seemed worth having to wear foppish clothes.

"If you wake up in the night to find me gone," said Guillermo, "don't be concerned. I'll sneak out to where Blue Heron and her family are camping. But I'll be back before dawn."

The expedition embarked at daybreak. Since he was now a translator, Diego rode alongside Guillermo toward the rear of the vanguard. His mount was a graceful, high-strung chestnut Arabian Don Sebastian had bought in Santo Domingo to replace the gutted dapple-gray mare. The path was wide and well trodden. Wild vines heavy with purple grapes snaked through the wayside underbrush.

After an hour, as they skirted cornfields ready to harvest, Tomas de Carrion appeared alongside Diego and Guillermo, looking like a sack of flour astride his piebald gelding.

"Don Sebastian requires your counsel," he informed Guillermo.

Guillermo cantered behind Tomas to the front of the vanguard.

When he returned, Diego asked, "What was that all about?"

Guillermo shrugged. "Don Sebastian asked me for information about the village up ahead."

As they rode through the village, Diego realized that the huts and earthen streets were completely empty. The cornfields that stretched in every direction had been burnt to the ground and were still smoldering. Diego looked at Guillermo questioningly.

"The people who live here hope that if we find no food, we'll turn back."

"But I thought they'd be pleased to greet us and hear about the Holy Virgin."

Guillermo rolled his eyes. "They have their own gods. Why would they want yours?"

Diego frowned. He had thought saving souls for Christ was the main reason for this trek. That is, in addition to the gold and silver they would gain from spreading the gospel to grateful converts.

As the sun reached its apex, Tomas arrived to fetch Diego. Diego's horse cantered to the front and fell in between Don Sebastian and Captain Melendez. Melendez rode straight and tall in his Moorish saddle, bearing the gold and purple standard. His silver breastplate and helmet glinted in the coastal sun, and his smiling moustache tips drooped with sweat. Brother Marcos, clad in his suffocating robe of coarse brown wool, balanced the golden cross in a holster on his saddle to the left of Don Sebastian.

To Brother Marcos's left was Don Domingo de Santa Cruz de la Sierra, the Captain of the Horse. His black eye patch made him resemble a friendly pirate. He smiled at Diego and winked with his good eye.

"Sire?" Diego ducked his head to Don Sebastian, embarrassed to be singled out like this with the entire army watching. Also, he felt uneasy after Guillermo's warning from the previous evening. Why did Don Sebastian insist on favoring him with unwanted attention?

"How are you enjoying our march, boy?"

"Greatly, Sire. I am honored to be riding your Arabian."

"How does she ride?" With his auburn beard covering his lower face and the visored helmet hiding his forehead, all that remained visible were Don Sebastian's piercing green eyes and aquiline nose, crimson from the sun.

"She is spirited but obedient, Sire."

"Just like yourself," murmured Don Sebastian. "An appealing combination indeed."

Diego felt his face blush. He was glad his sunburn concealed this from Don Sebastian.

"Guillermo tells me you have a rare gift for languages."

"A gift I never knew I possessed, Sire. In Galicia I heard only Castilian and the peasant patois."

"You have a quick intelligence, lad. Why did you leave Galicia?"

"My mother wished it, Sire."

Don Sebastian turned his head to study him. "Normally mothers want their sons beside them and mourn their departure, do they not?"

"A gang of older boys used to beat me up. I guess she worried for my safety."

Don Sebastian smiled whimsically. "She worried for your safety, so she sent you to a wilderness full of savages? What do you hope to gain here, lad?"

"Riches, Sire. To take back home to Galicia."

"You plan to return to Spain?"

"Yes, Sire. A young lady there awaits my return."

Don Sebastian raised an eyebrow. "There will be no lack of native girls on our journey."

Diego blushed again. "I have pledged my heart to her, Sire."

"Your heart, perhaps. Yet you may find that the excitement of chance encounters pleases you more than the prospect of an entire lifetime with just one lady, whatever her charms."

Not daring to dispute this assertion that had also occurred to him, Diego studied the scar that snaked like a length of rope through Don Sebastian's beard. It must have been an appalling wound. He wondered during what battle or joust it had happened.

"Would you not rather rule the world, lad, than the heart of one silly Castilian country lass?" prompted Don Sebastian.

Diego remained silent, unpracticed in the obsequiousness of successful courtiers.

Don Sebastian shrugged hopelessly, seeming amused.

"Sire, may I ask a question?"

Although appearing somewhat startled by such presumption, Don Sebastian nodded hesitantly.

"Why did we threaten the Orista with slavery yesterday? They seem content to aid us in every way."

"Our king requires that formula. It is merely an outmoded formality." He frowned irritably. "You may return to your rank now."

Diego pulled his horse aside and waited for his line to catch up to him. Troubled by the exchange, he sat motionless as Guillermo rode by with a quizzical glance. Next came the riflemen and crossbowmen on foot in quilted cotton armor. They carried their weapons, the guns with fuses smoldering, the crossbows with nocked arrows, as though anticipating an attack. Nicolas Navarro and Pedro Picado nodded to him. Then the infantry marched past, swords at their hips and pikes in their hands, with Arias de Zavallas at their heels to make sure they didn't lag. Behind them ambled Alonso Villareal and his twin kitchen boys, Pascuale Sanchez with his stonecutting tools in a basket on his back, the surgeon Lope Mendez, the tailor Miguel Salamanca, Gaspar de los Reyes with his bulging eyes and lipless mouth, the cobbler, the saddlemaker, and the blacksmith.

Behind the craftsmen came the African slaves, including Olivia. She was balancing on her head a woven basket that no doubt contained Arias's belongings. She smiled faintly as she passed. Diego reflected that this expedition was like a mobile village. It included those who could perform any service anyone might ever need, from cradle to grave.

The bare-chested Orista bearers in their loincloths followed, loaded down with pack baskets. Several carried Don Sebastian's trestle table, campstools, cushions, carpets, and wineskins.

The Orista women carried baskets on their shoulders. Their heads were hanging and their feet shuffling. With a start, Diego noticed that several, although they wore the moss skirts and trailing hair of women, had the muscled chests of men. On their backs were barrels of lead shot or gunpowder.

Bewildered, Diego watched the giant boar, his eyelids stitched shut, meander up the trail, attended by his own private lancer. The other hogs trotted along behind him, hemmed in by the four Portuguese cavalrymen with their lances. Lucas and two other handlers walked Baltasar and two mastiffs on leashes. The sniffing dogs trembled with eagerness to chase the rabbits that only they could smell lurking in the undergrowth. Lucas frowned at him questioningly. Bringing up the rear were the cavalry not assigned to the vanguard.

Turning back toward the vanguard, Diego studied their flashing silver armor as they crested a rise up ahead. Above them on a shimmering cloud of dust floated the gold and purple flag of Castile, flanked by Brother Marcos's golden cross. These symbols of the Spanish Empire as it brought civilization and salvation to heathens in a barren land helped alleviate Diego's sense of shame over yesterday's ceremony on the Orista mound.

When Diego resumed his spot in the vanguard, Guillermo asked, "What did Don Sebastian want?"

"To know if I were enjoying the journey."

Guillermo contorted his face disbelievingly.

"He also asked about my plans for the future," added Diego with a comical smile.

Guillermo shook his head.

The horses in front of them stopped abruptly, so they did too. Diego could see what looked like an expanse of dirty brown water up ahead. While they waited, the sun burned down. Gradually Diego's linen shirt grew wet from his own sweat. He wondered if he could get away with removing his annoying breastplate, now that he was apparently Don Sebastian's favorite underling. But he decided not to press his luck. Gnats began to circle and bite. His Arabian snorted and tossed her head, flicking her tail at the flies that tried to settle on her twitching flanks.

Finally, an order came down the line to dismount. Diego and Guillermo took cheese and biscuits from their packs and ate them in the shade of a gnarled cedar. Their horses, hobbled alongside them, picked at the coarse grass. After eating, both young men stretched out in the sparse shade and fell asleep.

Awakening to shouts and the clanking of harnesses and weapons from up ahead, they discovered that the vanguard were remounting. They followed suit. When they arrived at the water, Diego saw that it was a muddy river. The vanguard were stationing their horses in a line, head to tail, all the way across it, so as to break the force of the current, which swirled and sucked as it fought its way to the sea.

Diego and Guillermo dismounted and maneuvered their horses into position. Diego planted himself alongside his Arabian, braced against her foreleg with the surging water rising to his chest. The coolness of the water felt delicious after baking all morning in his breastplate. He squatted to drench himself all over. He didn't care if his breastplate rusted to pieces. Then he watched as the main body of marchers began to ford on foot, their supplies and weapons hoisted overhead. Some had hung their sandals or boots around their necks.

While the bearers were crossing, one stumbled and fell. The barrel of gunpowder he had been carrying floated off down the river. Several soldiers fought their way through the swift current to grab the floundering young man. They dragged him across to the far shore, where he sprawled on the ground, gasping and coughing up water.

After the rest of the line had crossed, Diego led his mare through the strong current and up the far bank. The sodden bearer had been bound to a tree to receive a flogging. His tattooed blue back was striped with wounds that welled with oozing blood.

"But he couldn't help it!" Diego exclaimed to Guillermo as they remounted.

Guillermo smiled sourly. "Are you sure?"

"He fell on purpose?"

"He was carrying a barrel of gunpowder, which he managed to ruin. He's probably hoping they'll leave him there for dead after the beating. If he survives, he can go home a hero. If he doesn't survive, at least he'll know that he refused to help the Spaniards and has inspired others to copy him."

They rode on in silence. As the sun steamed the moisture from his clothing, Diego discovered dark slugs embedded in his forearms. One by one he plucked them off, leaving punctures that bled like the lash marks on the back of the Orista bearer.

This routine continued all afternoon. They crossed streams, rivers, and swamps, getting soaked, and then emerged to remove engorged leeches from their flesh. There were no more "accidents" among the bearers. Glancing now and then at Francisco's ring, Diego kept watching for a mountain sparkling like crystal up ahead. But all he could see was an endless wetland, studded with hummocks of sawgrass and thickets of gnarled red cedars and slash pines.

They halted for the night on an island surrounded by a swamp over which hovered clouds of mosquitoes as thick as smoke above a bonfire. As the foot soldiers used axes to clear the straggly trees for tents and fires, Diego joined the pages to gather grass for the horses.

"Don't get used to riding, Pig Boy," murmured Juan Bravo, his bobbed orange hair swaying like a silky curtain as he scythed.

"Excuse me?" Diego paused to stare at Juan, his arms full of the coarse grass.

"Don't forget how to use your feet, Swine King. You may think you're pretty special now, but Don Sebastian will soon dismiss you on a whim. He always chooses a young man to amuse him. And he kicks him out when he tires of him. We've watched this a dozen times. Corpses of Don Sebastian's cast-offs are strewn all across the Spanish Empire."

Diego sat at the trestle table in Don Sebastian's campaign tent of pale Peruvian wool, eating salt-cured ham from Santo Domingo with the officers and bodyguards. He had left Lucas outside squatting on the damp ground, chewing a stew of parched corn. As Diego sipped wine from a clay cup, he felt guilty knowing that the soldiers would be getting down on their hands and knees to suck up the swamp water that had collected in their boot prints.

"You may go now," Don Sebastian told his guests once the meal was over.

As Diego stood up, Don Sebastian gestured for him to sit back down. Once the others had departed, he pointed to a leather cushion on the Oriental carpet and said, "Make yourself comfortable."

Diego perched on the plump cushion, feeling like a hen hatching a giant egg. Juan Bravo had warned him that Don Sebastian would dismiss him once he was no longer amusing. He resolved to be as boring as possible.

As though aware of Diego's discomfort, Don Sebastian asked, "Do you understand why I must maintain myself as I do—with my fine clothing and horses and lodgings and delicacies?"

Diego said, "You are our commander, Sire. You may do as you wish."

"It is not a question of what I wish. I am at heart a simple man."

Tomas de Carrion, who stood along one wall, raised an eyebrow and suppressed a simper. Juan Bravo was too busy guzzling the dregs of wine in the cups from dinner to have heard this.

"Because I am your commander, I must behave like one in order to earn the respect of my troops."

Diego nodded, thinking it might impress the troops even more if their leader shared their hardships.

"I will teach you by example how to be a leader of men."

"Thank you, Sire." Diego wondered why Don Sebastian assumed that he even wanted to be a leader of men. He had been perfectly happy as a leader of hogs.

"The role of the page is to serve, so as to observe and to learn." He nodded toward Tomas, who was pretending not to listen. "These dolts watch, but they learn nothing. This is why I have selected you."

"Thank you, Sire." Don Sebastian had just thrown him to the wolves. He could feel Tomas's fury wafting his way. It seemed that Don Sebastian insulted those like Tomas and Juan who served him well, rewarded those like Diego who tried to avoid him, and excused those like Lucas who deserved punishment. Was generating confusion his secret to effective leadership?

"Sire, how many days will it take us to cross this swamp?" asked Diego, hoping to change the subject to something less offensive to the surly pages.

"Perhaps another week. DeSoto's expedition landed on a different coast. We passed through territory as sodden as this, but with hostile archers behind every tree. The Orista, however, are content to aid us. Orista Mico told me that other white men came in ships before the French heretics. They invited Orista warriors on board. The ships sailed away, and the warriors never returned.

"Later more ships arrived, bringing pale-skinned colonists. Most died the first winter with what the Orista call the Spotted Disease. The survivors wandered from village to village, begging the Orista for food. Wherever they passed, Orista sprouted weeping pustules and died. Those who now remain believe that unless they do as we command, we will destroy them with the Spotted Disease, or carry them away forever on our ships."

Don Sebastian moved from his stool to a cushion on the carpet opposite Diego. "But soon we will arrive at Cofitachequi," he said. "The women there are beautiful and willing. The soil is rich, and the crops bountiful. Their river flows with pearls. Several of DeSoto's soldiers escaped into the wilderness there. I'm certain they will have put the natives to work mining silver. We will claim these mines for King Phillip and return to Spain as heroes."

Diego studied Don Sebastian's glinting eyes. He had thought Don Sebastian wanted to find the native queen in the white doeskin who had welcomed DeSoto with strands of river pearls. But apparently his real goal was the same as that of his soldiers: precious metals. However, Diego hadn't realized these metals would have to be seized rather than accepted as gifts for introducing grateful natives to Christ.

As Diego stood up to leave, Captain Melendez arrived, holding by the upper arm a young Orista woman in a sleeveless doeskin shift. Her dark eyes appeared sullen and wary.

Don Sebastian gestured to the cushion Diego had just vacated. Captain Melendez seated the woman on it and backed to the doorway.

Diego found Lucas sitting by a fire, poking at a huge blister on his heel. Baltasar lay with his chin on Lucas's thigh. When the dog caught Diego's scent, he whimpered. Baltasar and Diego saw little of each other these days. Diego squatted beside him and stroked his head apologetically.

"So, nephew," murmured Lucas, "you're keeping fancy company lately."

Diego nodded. "But I prefer you and Baltasar."

"And I would prefer that for you. I can't figure out what that man wants from you."

"He told me about the town where we're headed. He says it's full of beautiful women."

"The only woman I want is in Santo Domingo," muttered Lucas.

Diego studied his uncle. He missed Leonora, too, but his yearning for her seemed less urgent than Lucas's desperate ache. The balladeers on the docks at Seville had proclaimed love the highest virtue. It was apparently what Lucas felt for Dona Catalina and what Guillermo felt for Blue Heron. It turned formerly vigorous men into languid ghosts. The more Diego saw of it, the more it seemed almost as appealing as the Spotted Disease. At Santa Elena, a wish to protect Olivia, which might have been the first symptom of love, had spurred in him some dangerous fantasies of escape into the swamp that would have gotten them both killed. Since then he had managed to bottle up his affection for Olivia and seal it tightly. The best he could do was to spare her his deadly heroics and abandon her to her unpleasant fate.

En route back to the tent he shared with Guillermo, Diego passed that of Arias de Zavallas. A cluster of soldiers sat by the fire with Arias. Someone emerged from his tent. Another man stood up.

"Make it fast!" called a soldier by the fire.

"Not a chance," replied the man as he ducked beneath the flaps. "Tonight I get my money's worth from this black bitch."

Diego suppressed a scowl and walked on, soon passing the clearing where the native bearers were lying in the damp marsh grass. A few guards sat by a fire, where a soldier was pointing out a woman to them. A guard got up and walked over to her. He bent down and unlocked the iron collar around her neck with a long key. Grabbing her by the upper arm and raising her to her feet, he led her back to the soldier, who handed him a coin. Studying the sleeping bearers sprawled across the grass, Diego realized that they all wore those collars, connected to one another by long chains that clanked whenever anyone stirred. At last he understood their grisly purpose.

Diego entered his own tent. Guillermo was already asleep on his bedroll. Diego reclined on a mattress of bark he had gathered, intended to repel the moisture seeping up from the soggy soil. It was a trick he had learned during his nights in the open, tending the hogs back home. He lay in the moonlight that streamed through the tent flap and tried to erase the image of those chained bearers by picturing Leonora on her balcony, gazing at the Great Bear. But he could no longer remember the exact location of the mole on her cheek. Her image was all he possessed of her, and even that was beginning to fade.

"Are you awake?" he murmured to Guillermo.

"Yes."

"I just walked past the Orista camp. They're all chained together by neck rings."

"Does this surprise you?"

"I just hadn't realized that the Orista would need to be chained."

"You thought they'd walk a hundred miles carrying baskets that weigh sixty pounds apiece just for fun?"

"I thought that once they heard about Christ, they'd be glad to help us."

Guillermo snorted derisively. "Diego, sometimes I forget what a rustic you are. One day you'll understand that, although Spaniards regard the Orista as savages, the Orista also regard Spaniards as savages."

Diego lay in silence, inspecting this new idea.

"Did you see the Orista woman Melendez brought in to Don Sebastian this evening?" asked Guillermo.

"Yes."

"That's Blue Heron."

Diego turned his head to look at Guillermo in the moonlight. "And she has to spend her nights with Don Sebastian, in his tent next to ours? But that's unbearable."

"During several visits to Orista from Santa Elena, Don Sebastian ordered Melendez to bring her to his quarters. She says he just sat with her in silence and then called Melendez to take her away. He hasn't touched her. But maybe he's courting her? Maybe he feels that to take her without her consent would shame him? Maybe he believes that it honors Orista Mico to show such favor to his niece?"

"Maybe," said Diego, understanding nothing about Don Sebastian, who rarely did what others expected of him. He had never seen Guillermo less than calm and amused, but tonight he seemed upset.

"She'll come to me here tonight, Diego. It's torture to watch each other all day long and not be able to touch or to talk."

"Won't they chain her up after she leaves Don Sebastian?"

"He's ordered Melendez to leave her unchained as a sign of respect, since she's Orista Mico's niece. She could head for home, but she stays because of me, and to lend courage to her people who are chained. Of course, Don Sebastian is conceited enough to believe that she stays for him."

"I could move to my uncle's tent so you two could be alone."

"No, you must stay here. No one must suspect us. We could be killed."

"Surely not," said Diego. "To love is no crime."

"To love as we do is. At least in the eyes of your people."

"But soldiers all across this encampment are passing the night with Orista or African women."

"But that's not love," muttered Guillermo.

Diego turned over, every muscle in his legs and hips aching. If he were this sore from riding, he could only imagine what agonies the foot soldiers must be enduring.

Diego awoke to urgent whispers from Guillermo's bedroll. The birds in the swamp had begun their halting hymn to the new day. Someone slid out from under Guillermo's blanket and stood up. In the dim light through half-closed eyelids, Diego watched Blue Heron. She had the chest of a man—but a beardless face framed by a woman's dark trailing hair. She, or he, donned a doeskin shift and slipped out the doorway into the dawn.

Diego lay completely still, trying to digest the fact that his new friend Guillermo was not only a heretic and a cousin to cannibals, he was also a sodomite.

6

Cofitachequi

As Diego sat at the trestle table in Don Sebastian's campaign tent, he could see the harvest moon hanging huge and low outside the flaps. Its beams bathed the parched plain on which they were camped in hues of peach. The soldiers' cooking fires danced and flared as though greeting the rising moon. Many of the troops hadn't even bothered to pitch their tents because the stakes wouldn't hold in the sandy soil. So they sat or lay around their fading fires, some already asleep in their bedrolls.

A couple of days earlier they had abruptly left behind the wetlands for a never-ending desert. Rolling sand dunes had replaced the marshes and swamps. Ticks and gnats had elbowed aside the mosquitoes and leeches. But at least there were no more broad brown rivers to ford.

"So what do you think, Guillermo?" asked Don Sebastian. "Have our fugitives headed back to Oristatown, or are they somewhere out there preparing to attack us? Should we go in pursuit of them?"

All the officers at the table strained forward to hear Guillermo's response. Before moonrise that evening, six Orista bearers who had somehow managed to file off their collars had slipped away into the darkness.

Diego watched Guillermo's eyes shift as he replied, "They must be halfway to Oristatown by now, Sire."

Diego could tell he was lying. Besides, he knew from Guillermo's descriptions of the Orista that they would be unlikely to flee when members of their tribe were still captives.

But the officers relaxed their tense postures and returned their attentions to their wine goblets, which Juan Bravo was repeatedly filling from a leather wineskin.

Soon Don Sebastian dismissed everyone but Diego. As he placed his inlaid chessboard on the table between them and shoved the black pieces in Diego's direction, he said, "DeSoto used to call sleeping under the stars 'The Moon's Inn.'"

"What was DeSoto like, Sire?" Diego started setting up his army. The more time they spent together, the more Don Sebastian allowed him to ask questions, although Don Sebastian still did most of the talking.

"DeSoto fed on danger like a horse on grain. If his officers counseled retreat, he attacked." He advanced a white pawn, which Diego confronted with one of his own.

"Sire, why have we seen no natives since Oristatown? Why are their villages always deserted and their cornfields torched?"

"No doubt they think that if we find nothing to tempt us to stay, we will leave." With a flourish he captured Diego's black knight with his white bishop.

Sliding his rook sideways to challenge the white bishop, Diego reflected that the natives' scorched earth tactics were working. The soldiers, half-starved on their rations of biscuits and cheese, were grumbling. The Orista bearers were growing listless under their heavy loads. The only factor the vanished villagers hadn't reckoned on was Don Sebastian's indifference to this hardship.

As the game progressed, Diego studied his dwindling ranks. It was all he could do to remember how the different pieces moved, much less to plan those moves in advance. He reflected that this expedition wasn't turning out as he had imagined aboard the *San Jorge*. There were no friendly natives eager to learn about the Christ child. To the contrary, any able to cast off their chains vanished into the night. Not only did they not want to hear about Christ, they wanted to kill anyone who might try to tell them.

As though sensing Diego's unease, Don Sebastian launched into his standard eulogy about Cofitachequi, its temple as overflowing with pearls as a gristmill with grain, its storehouses bursting with dried venison, its women as skilled as the courtesans of Naples. Diego realized that one of his jobs was to pass this information on to the others. Don Sebastian probably counted on its flowing throughout the camp to douse any smoldering coals of mutiny.

"Checkmate," announced Don Sebastian with a sly smile as he moved his queen along one side of the board to Diego's back row. "You notice how I distracted you with my bishop into leaving your king unprotected?"

Diego studied his trapped king and sighed.

"We will play often," promised Don Sebastian. "It will help you develop a sense of strategy."

"Yes, Sire," said Diego unenthusiastically. Surely there were others who could offer him a more challenging match. But it was clear that Don Sebastian loved to win. And the larger the margin, the happier it made him.

Upon returning to the tent he shared in secret with Guillermo and Blue Heron, Diego lay down, rolled up in his blanket to fend off the sand fleas, and fell asleep.

He awoke to whispering from the next bed. Although he tried not to listen, their murmurings made him miss Leonora more than ever. He wished there were someone to whom he could murmur sweet promises in the night. It needn't even be Leonora. In fact, his love for her had begun to seem pretty barren. He wanted a real woman whose burdens he could share, not some remote phantom he could approach only in his dreams.

He slipped out from under his blanket and pulled on his clothes and sandals. Reaching into his pack, he grabbed a sandal. Every soldier had an extra pair for the day when his current ones fell apart. In the meantime, they were used as currency, since most had squandered their wages brought from Santo Domingo and Santa Elena. Who knew in whose baggage all those coins were now stashed? Diego slipped out of the tent and walked through the clusters of snoring men sprawled by the smoldering embers of their fires.

Outside Arias de Zavallas's tent sat half a dozen soldiers waiting for Olivia. He was never able to talk to her. They marched all day and then set up camp. She cooked for Arias and entertained soldiers half the night. Sometimes he spotted her on the march, lugging a heavy basket, looking exhausted and disgusted.

Diego arrived at the fire where those guarding the remaining Orista were seated, their pikes and swords lying on the ground beside them. The Orista, still chained together by the rings on their iron collars, lay huddled in awkward heaps, no one able to shift position without waking up the entire line. Diego held out his sandal to Pedro Picado.

"Decided to give it a try, boy?" asked Pedro, struggling to his feet.

Diego shrugged, hoping to appear experienced in these matters.

"Look them over," suggested Pedro. "Take your time. Pick one you like the looks of."

Diego walked among the slumbering women. Most were bare-breasted with tiny moss skirts that concealed their loins. They looked dirty and sweaty. But if the escaped Orista attacked, he hated to think he would die without ever having known a woman. Besides, the priest on the hacienda had said that lying with a woman was a lesser sin than dreaming about it, because it might produce new life.

A young woman with trailing black hair lifted her head to look back at him. He saw misery in her dark eyes—and anger, and hatred, and fear. She twisted her head, clearly in pain from the chafing of the iron ring around her neck with the prongs that lay across her collarbones. His desire fizzled like embers doused by water. He tiptoed through the sleeping forms back to Pedro.

"I guess I'm not in the mood," he muttered to Pedro, trying to sound bored instead of appalled.

"Here, lad, take your sandal." Pedro handed it back to him with a sympathetic smile.

Clutching his sandal, Diego wandered back to his tent. He wanted to stay true to Leonora, but she was in Galicia and he was stuck in this forlorn desert. Olivia didn't want him. The Orista women didn't want him. And he didn't want *them* if he had to take them by force. Unlike Don Sebastian with his bullfighting, Diego found no pleasure in causing other creatures to suffer. But if he lay

down to sleep in his current state, he would have dreams about
embracing Leonora or Olivia or some faceless female. Then he would
have to confess to Brother Marcos and spend his sparse spare time
reciting Ava Marias on his knees. The only solution appeared to be
not to sleep, so that he couldn't dream.

When he reentered his tent, Diego found Blue Heron and
Guillermo asleep, breathing slowly and steadily beneath Guillermo's
blanket. Lying on his bedroll, Diego tried to keep himself awake and
fantasy-free by thinking about Blue Heron. He could now identify
him on the march, male-chested and moss-skirted amid the women.
But when Melendez escorted him to Don Sebastian, Blue Heron
always wore a demure doeskin shift. Was Don Sebastian aware that
this muscular porter was the same person who came to his quarters
each night, with his long hair hanging loose across his shoulders like
a silky black mantilla? If so, why did he summon him? If not, would
Don Sebastian punish him for this deceit once he discovered it?

Diego wondered if he had an obligation as an obedient Catholic
to report Guillermo's secret sin to Brother Marcos. That would be one
way to become head translator, since the Inquisition condemned
sodomites to death by fire, along with anyone else who was different
in appearance, beliefs, or behavior from ordinary Christians. But he
realized that he had no wish to be head translator. He wished,
instead, to understand this odd young man who had become his
friend. If not reporting him was a sin, it seemed a lesser one than
betraying a friend. In any case, Guillermo was a heretic, and maybe
lying with another man wasn't a sin for heretics. Life in La Florida
had taken on complications Diego had never imagined possible back
in Galicia, where the line between good and evil, and between men
and women, had seemed self-evident.

Diego was jolted from his meditations on the nature of sin by the
sound of distant yipping and howling, like a pack of wolves
welcoming a rising moon. He sat up. So did Guillermo and Blue
Heron. All three jumped up and started pulling on their clothing.

When Diego emerged from the tent, the camp was wide awake.
The moon was down and the sky was black except for a faint golden
glow at the western horizon. Weapons and armor clashed and

clanged as soldiers rushed around readying themselves for combat. The officers shouted orders as the howling chant moved ever closer. Baltasar and the two mastiffs began barking and snarling.

"What are they saying?" Diego asked Guillermo.

"It's a war chant," said Guillermo. "But they won't attack. They're just letting their friends know that they're still out there."

"Are you sure?" asked Diego.

"That's what Blue Heron says."

The soldiers massed along the western perimeter of the campsite, their weapons clutched in unsteady hands. Don Sebastian sat on his ebony gelding in the front line, staring into the darkness. Diego wondered if he would insist on charging out into the night, chasing a weaponless enemy who would evaporate at his approach. Apparently that's what his idol DeSoto would have done.

The howling ceased as abruptly as it had begun. No one stirred for a long time. The snorting of Don Sebastian's gelding finally broke the silence.

Don Sebastian leaned over and said something to Captain Melendez. Melendez barked an order for the troops to fall out and resume sleep.

On the tenth day out from Oristatown, as the sun rode low over the endless swells of packed sand, Diego realized that the path along which his Arabian plodded was rising ever so slightly. Before long, her hooves began to slip and stumble as the sand shifted to fine pebbles. The scraggly pines and dune grasses gradually gave way to stands of hardwoods with leaves tinged scarlet and gold.

The mood of the soldiers was also shifting. He heard banter and laughter behind him from men who had passed the morning tromping in grim silence. The escaped Orista had been chanting all night long for the past five nights. When the Spaniards slept at all, it had been a shallow, anxious slumber in which hands clutched weapons as though they were paramours and muscles stayed tense and tight.

The vanguard arrived at a shallow creek. They turned their horses north to follow a worn path along one bank. The waters leaped among boulders in the streambed, rather than just swirling and sucking like the muddy coastal rivers. The calls of forest birds replaced the strange screeches of the desert fowl.

They soon reached a settlement of deserted huts. The cooking fires were still smoking, but not a living creature was anywhere to be seen.

Captain Melendez assigned Diego and Guillermo a hut two doors down from the Mico's lodge in which Don Sebastian was installing himself. The hut's interior was strewn with tools, clay pots, and hides, testifying to the inhabitants' hasty departure. Clearing off a bench along one wall, Diego spread out his blanket. Then he took his line and hook from his pack and went outside. The enforced camaraderie of this march was starting to get on his nerves. He was accustomed to being alone with his hogs and his dog, an occasional wolf, and now and then a neighboring shepherd.

Wandering among the clusters of huts, he finally found the one in which Lucas was settled, along with Baltasar, the two other handlers, and their mastiffs. Lucas was napping on a bench within, with Baltasar curled up beside him on the floor of packed earth.

Shaking Lucas awake, Diego explained that he wanted to borrow Baltasar for company while he fished upstream.

"Is that wise, Diego?" demanded Lucas, propped up on one elbow. "These woods are probably crawling with those enraged Orista, longing for a chance to kill a lone Spaniard. And what about the inhabitants of this town? Surely you don't think they've just happily donated their village to us? They're out there right now, plotting their revenge."

"That's why I'm borrowing Baltasar," said Diego. "If they're nearby, he'll know it. We'll rush right back and warn the rest of you."

Lucas shrugged. "I'm too tired to argue with you, Diego." He lay back down and was instantly asleep.

Diego and Baltasar walked beside the stream past some naked soldiers who were splashing their swollen bites, blisters, and sunburns with the cool, clear, leech-free water. Nicolas Navarro and two of the Portuguese tried to grab the darting trout with their bare hands. Their faces, red from the sun, contrasted startlingly with their pale torsos, which were pelted with dark, curly hair.

Well upstream, Diego cut a pole from a tree and tied his line to it. Baiting his hook with a grasshopper, he tossed it into the water. Baltasar's nostrils and ears twitched as he dashed around sniffing. Finally satisfied that they were safe, he wound round and round himself and sank into a bed of weeds. This was proof enough for Diego that anyone who wanted him dead wasn't nearby at present. He drew a deep breath and sat beside Baltasar while the flailing grasshopper made his line tremble.

In the valley below, Diego could see scores of soldiers swarming the unburnt village fields, ripping the unharvested corn from the stalks and devouring it raw, cobs and all. Unless Cofitachequi turned out to be the paradise Don Sebastian had portrayed, with storehouses bursting with venison, it might be hard to keep the hungry, sleep-deprived soldiers moving forward. Diego could imagine a mutiny such as Guillermo had described among the French heretics at their fort near Santa Elena. He could think of several desperados in the ranks who wouldn't hesitate to loop a noose around Don Sebastian's neck and hoist him high on a tree limb.

Yanking in his straining line, Diego discovered a large trout on his hook. As it flopped on the bank, it flashed rainbow colors in the light from the sinking sun. Diego unhooked it, ran his rawhide belt through one of its gill holes, and submerged it by the bank. Then he rebaited his hook and tossed it back into the stream. For the next hour, fish continued to strike his bait as enthusiastically as hogs rooting in an oak grove.

By the time Diego headed back to camp, he was lugging fifteen trout on his belt. He delivered them to a delighted Alonso Villareal beneath the kitchen awning. While Diego cleaned, gutted, and boned the fish, the blond twins ground corn between two stones and sifted the meal through squares of chain mail.

As he watched Alonso bread the fillets and lay them in the frying pans, Diego asked, "What was Don Sebastian like when you two were on DeSoto's march?"

Alonso looked up from the flames. "I have no idea. I was a kitchen boy, and he was a page to the Captain of the Horse. He never spoke to me. He seemed unhappy. He had a fresh wound on his cheek that appeared infected. You can still see the scar through his beard."

"How did he get it?"

"No one knew. He already had it when he joined the expedition in Spain."

Spotting Olivia cooking for Arias de Zavallas in a fire pit outside a nearby hut, Diego excused himself and walked over to her. She straightened up in her long skirt with the gold, red, and green stripes.

"How's it going, Olivia?"

"I'm bone tired, if you really want to know."

"I can imagine. I'm tired, and I get to ride a horse."

"Lucky you. I bet you get to sleep at night, too?"

Her posture had somehow shifted. She was standing with her hands on her hips as though supporting her lower back. Her belly was slightly rounded, like a new grave. All at once he realized why. "You're not...?" He nodded toward her belly.

She looked around to see if anyone had overheard. "You mustn't tell anyone, Diego. If I can't keep up on this march and can't earn Arias lots of sandals, he'll leave me by the side of the path for the Indians or the wolves to finish off."

"But he's going to see it for himself before long."

"I've been trying to get those Indian women to tell me how to get rid of it. But they can't understand me, and I can't understand them. Back in Hispaniola there were plants the women used to make tea. But I don't recognize the plants around here."

"I'll ask Guillermo."

"Would you do that, Diego? It might save my life."

Diego knew he sounded more certain than he felt. The priest back home had always said that killing an unborn baby was a sin— maybe an even worse sin than for a man to spill his seed on barren ground. If he helped Olivia kill her child, he would be as guilty as she. But if he didn't, she would be dead, and not preventing murder was also a sin. He needed to talk to Brother Marcos before getting involved. The next day was a Sunday. Brother Marcos would insist they remain in this dreary little village for a day of confession, penance, and atonement. He had already set up shop in the council house, where he would conduct mass for the confessed the next morning.

Diego returned to his empty hut. He knelt on the earthen floor, his elbows resting on the bench where he had laid his bedroll. Burying his face in his hands, he asked the Holy Spirit to help him examine his conscience and make a good confession. Then he ran through the catalog of sins one by one—anger, hatred, blasphemy, envy, greed, malice. As usual, the one that tripped him up was lust. He reviewed the torrid thoughts and dreams he had had that week. Jesus had suffered horribly on the cross to redeem Diego from his pursuit of such impure fantasies. Try as he might to outwit Satan, Diego always failed. He apologized to God the Father and His Son, the Lord Jesus Christ. And he swore to try harder in the future to avoid his usual lurid reveries.

Several soldiers stood in a silent line outside the council house. Diego recognized Pedro Picado and several whom he had seen lounging around the fire outside Arias de Zavallas's tent, awaiting their turn with Olivia. Many on the march confessed their carnal failures every week, just as Diego did his. Then they rushed out and sinned some more, just as Diego did. It felt vaguely comforting to have so much company.

Finally entering the council house, Diego spotted Brother Marcos's trunk-hosed legs protruding from a bench. His face and torso were concealed by his brown robe, which hung from a ceiling beam like a curtain. Motes drifted in the shaft of daylight through the roof hole overhead. Opposite Brother Marcos was a bench for the sinners.

Crossing himself, Diego sat down with clasped hands. "Bless me, Father, for I have sinned." Resolutely he held in his mind the image of a merciful God who would forgive him for his frailties, rather than an avenging tyrant who would punish him.

"Gratia vobis et pax a Deo Patre nostro et Domino Iesu Christo," replied Brother Marcos.

"Amen. Father, it has been one week since my last confession." He went on to itemize his unclean thoughts, including his thwarted attempt to purchase an Orista woman for the night. "I burn with shame, Father, when I reflect on the goodness of Jesus compared to my own sinfulness. I am weak in the face of the wicked longings of my own flesh. But I pray that with His help I will sin no more."

There was a long silence behind the brown curtain. Finally Brother Marcos cleared his throat. "To lie is also a sin, my son."

"Why do you say that, Father? I'm not lying."

"I hear this same sin from you week after week. If you were truly penitent, you would reform yourself, would you not?"

Diego sat in startled silence. The priest on the hacienda had never questioned his sincerity—nor his inability to reform himself.

"My son, God gives us our earthly bodies. A gift from God can only be holy. You must use this precious gift to create pleasure and goodness for yourself and for others. God has made you in His own image. Surely you would not call God a sinner? That which pleases you will also please Him. I don't think you're a sinner. I think you're just a normal, healthy young man who ought to be back home in Spain courting some comely young woman."

Diego was stunned. The priest on the hacienda had always insisted that the body was evil and its pleasures sinful. Both these men were priests, but how could both be right at once? And after all, Brother Marcos was more than a priest. He had once been a bishop.

"Is that all?" asked Brother Marcos in a tired voice.

"No, Father. I wish to speak of a sin I have not yet committed."

Brother Marcos sighed but said, "All right, go ahead."

Diego explained Olivia's situation and his own dilemma over helping her. She had helped him when he was wounded in Santo Domingo, and he wished to repay her. Besides, she was his friend and she was in trouble. But helping her meant murdering an unborn infant. Yet sparing that infant might condemn both mother and child to a horrifying death alone in the wilderness. He asked the priest which path one should follow, when every path led to sin.

"Since you are made in God's image, it is natural that you wish to assist God's creatures," said Brother Marcos. "If you do nothing, a mother and a baby will die. But if you help to abort an unborn, you may save the mother. The baby is not yet born, but the mother is alive and in danger here and now. Your own conscience is perfectly well equipped to calculate the lesser of the two apparent evils. Misereatur nostri omnipotens Deus...."

As the priest promised him God's forgiveness in Latin, Diego reflected that it was no wonder Brother Marcos had signed on to this exploring party. If he hadn't fled Spain, the Inquisition would have burned him alive for his unorthodox interpretation of God's will.

The officers sat at the trestle table in Don Sebastian's borrowed lodge, gobbling the fried trout and guzzling wine. Don Sebastian turned to Diego, who sat beside him. "Is there no end to your talents, lad?" He pointed to the fish.

"Any country boy could do the same, Sire."

Tomas scowled at him from across the table. Diego wondered if there were some way to earn the approval of the belligerent pages other than by killing himself or vanishing into the forest.

"Cofitachequi is just upriver on the opposite bank," Don Sebastian announced to the group, as he extracted a stray bone from his fillet with the tip of his knife. "Their scouts will have noted our arrival by now. In the morning they will doubtless send a delegation to greet us."

Turning to Guillermo, he announced, "Tomorrow we will release the Orista. The following day we will depart for Cofitachequi, carrying our own baggage. It isn't far, and it will make a better impression on those at Cofitachequi if we have no chained bearers. Also, the Orista territory ends here, and it is onerous having to force homesick bearers onward, or to slow our pace for women growing sluggish with child. Let them go home to the coast and bear their bastards at their leisure. Those natives who have survived smallpox will soon be swamped by the sons of Spain, who are even now waxing strong in Orista wombs."

At the far end of the table Captain Melendez, eyes bleary, curled moustache tips unfurling, raised his cup. "To the bastard sons of Spain!"

Some of the other officers and bodyguards raised their cups and echoed the toast. Don Domingo in his black eye patch and Brother Marcos in his brown robe studied the toasters with distaste.

Diego glanced at Guillermo. His eyes had gone black with fury. Diego himself felt dizzy from the strain of trying not to show his disgust. He knew what it was like to be taunted with the title of whoreson. It wasn't something for drunken brutes to boast about. And now Olivia faced death because of their depravity. But he couldn't deny that it was a depravity in which he too would have participated had shame not overwhelmed him.

Dismissing his drunken officers and pages, Don Sebastian invited Diego to recline on a leather cushion on his burgundy and peacock carpet, with its geometric emblems that resembled the Orista pyramid.

"You are upset by the crudeness of my officers," observed Don Sebastian. He picked up a pitcher and filled his silver goblet with wine. Then he sat on the carpet with his elbow propped on a cushion.

"I know what it is like to lack a father, Sire."

"Your father abandoned you?"

"He died in battle in the Netherlands."

"Do you remember him?"

"No, Sire. I was only two when he left."

"My remarks at dinner were insensitive."

Diego glanced at him, baffled that Don Sebastian should notice the distress of an underling. After all, he had refused even to talk to a kitchen boy for four years on DeSoto's march.

"I, too, know what it means to lack the support of a father. Mine lived at court in Valladolid. When he came home, he beat me. I once said, 'Father, if you treat me like this, I will grow up to treat those weaker than myself similarly.'

"He replied, 'This is why I do it. To break you of your compassion.'"

Don Sebastian paused for a long moment. Then he seemed to shake himself from his reverie to announce briskly, "But it is time for sleep, boy. You may go now."

As Diego stood up, Melendez and Blue Heron appeared in the doorway. Guillermo claimed Don Sebastian had never yet laid a hand on Blue Heron. But was Blue Heron lying to spare Guillermo's feelings? Diego and Blue Heron exchanged a glance of recognition, both at the mercy of a man they couldn't figure out.

Diego awakened on the bench in his borrowed hut to hear Guillermo say to Blue Heron, "I'll return to Oristatown as soon as I can."

"You must try to escape, Guillermo. They may know about us. They will arrange to have you killed." Blue Heron's voice was as deep as a man's, but his inflections lacked the gruffness of most men's voices.

"If I desert, they'll hunt me down and kill me for sure. And you and your people as well for protecting me. No, I must complete this expedition and train Diego to take my place, so that they will release me voluntarily. Then you and I can live in peace."

Remembering his promise to Olivia, Diego sat up and said in Orista, "Forgive me for interrupting your farewell, Blue Heron. But do your people have potions to expel the unborn?"

There was a long silence. Finally he replied, "We do, but why do you ask?"

"I may as well tell you. But I count on you both to tell no one else: Arias de Zavallas's slave woman is with child. If she can't get rid of it, she'll probably be left alongside the trail."

"How far along is she?" asked Blue Heron.

"Who knows? You can just barely see it."

"I'll give you some herbs for her to chew. If they don't work and she's cast aside, tell her to ask any natives who approach her to bring her to Oristatown for a reward. Teach her the words to ask for me."

"I will. Thank you." Diego exhaled, feeling hopeful about Olivia's future for the first time since he had learned about her situation.

As the Orista raced back downhill toward the sandy plain that would lead them home, the Spaniards marched upstream on a rutted path alongside the streambed, constantly ascending. The higher they got, the crisper the air and the sweeter the water that danced in the sunlight from rock to rock. Through a grove of pyramidal poplars up ahead, Diego caught a glimpse of a distant cliff of cream-colored rock. Word spread down the ranks that the fabled Cofitachequi lay at its base. The troops at Diego's back buzzed like a beehive invaded by a bear. Soon they would be eating fresh venison while exotic native women danced for them. Maybe Diego could at last find a woman who would be pleased to lie with him. After all, Brother Marcos had practically given him permission.

Guillermo hadn't said a word all morning. He rode listlessly, his shoulders slumped, one hand loosely holding the reins. If a rabbit had crossed his path, his horse would have bolted.

Diego finally said, "I'm sorry Blue Heron had to leave."

Glancing at him, Guillermo said, "At least she's free now from Don Sebastian's incomprehensible machinations."

"Guillermo, I do realize that Blue Heron is a man."

Guillermo stared at him, suddenly alert.

"Don't worry, I'd never tell anyone."

"You're mistaken, Diego. She's not a man."

"But I saw him, Guillermo. I looked up one morning at the wrong time."

"The Orista believe that if a Frenchman feels himself to be Orista, then he is Orista," he said urgently. "And if a person with a male body feels herself to be a woman, then she is a woman."

Diego rode in silence, considering this odd point of view.

"Blue Heron is a shaman and a healer," continued Guillermo, sitting up straighter in his saddle. "She is highly valued by the Orista because they believe that the Sacred Spirit fashioned her specially, with the strengths of both a man and a woman."

Diego glanced anxiously at the neighboring horsemen to make sure no one had overheard this rant that could get Guillermo executed by the Inquisition. And this time there would be no Blue Heron to rescue him from the flames.

As the cliff loomed before them, a palisaded wall appeared at its base. Behind it rose an earthen pyramid nearly twice the height of the Orista mound. A large structure stood atop it. It was sided with painted mats, some torn and others hanging askew. The roof beam was capped with a row of pinkish conch shells. At its peak was a giant wooden falcon with a turquoise eye. The temple was just as Don Sebastian had described it, so maybe the rest of his claims were true as well.

The vanguard assembled on the high bank opposite the town. Diego could detect no noise coming from within the walls. The sentry boxes appeared vacant. The Spanish trumpeters' fanfare drew no response.

"I expected to be welcomed by the Cofitachequi headmen," said Don Sebastian to his officers as he sat on his gelding studying the spiked palisade. "But it appears we must camp here tonight. The town will probably send barges tomorrow to transport us across the river, as they did DeSoto and his troops."

No barges arrived the next morning. In fact, not a sound came from the village. Don Sebastian ordered Gabriel de la Zarza, the engineer, to build a bridge across the ravine. Several dozen soldiers chopped down a grove of tall poplars, trimmed their branches, and lashed them together. This structure was braced and then lowered on ropes to the opposite bank.

Don Sebastian, clad in full armor, crossed first on the swaying bridge toward the eerily silent town. Melendez, also armored, strode along behind him, leading his own horse and Don Sebastian's balking ebony gelding. On the far shore Don Sebastian mounted the gelding and trotted through a gateway in the wall of sharpened log posts.

Diego and Guillermo followed on foot behind the bodyguards, in case interpreters should be needed. Diego was so fearful of the ambush they might encounter that his knees shook as he walked. He remembered Don Sebastian's saying that DeSoto fed on danger like a horse on grain. Apparently Don Sebastian did, too. But Diego didn't. Terror terrified him.

The earthen streets within the palisade were overgrown with a tangle of thistles and wild blackberry canes. The huts appeared empty. The roofs of several had fallen in.

"Search the huts," Don Sebastian ordered the Portuguese cavalrymen.

Don Sebastian rode across the brambled plaza and began to ascend the stairway of rotting logs up the face of the mound. His retinue trailed after him on foot, clutching their swords and shields. With their helmet visors lowered, they looked around in every direction, braced for an attack.

As Diego climbed the crumbling steps, he could see the plain below, across which the released Orista were crawling toward Oristatown like a line of drunken ants, no doubt delighted to be rid of those cruel collars and clanking chains. He glanced at Guillermo, who was studying them intently, probably trying to identify Blue Heron.

Outside the temple with its walls of tattered matting loomed six pairs of fully armed and armored wooden warriors in menacing poses. Diego followed the bodyguards inside, his heart pounding like native drums.

He gasped. In the dim light he could see hundreds of human skeletons stacked on benches along the walls. Scraps of dried skin rustled in the breeze through the doorway. Spiders had woven webs among the bones. These webs were studded with the corpses of insects that had swarmed inside to feast upon the flesh. Wild animals had apparently dismembered some of the bodies and strewn their limbs across the floor of decaying mats. Scattered skulls stared back at the intruders through vacant sockets.

Don Sebastian raised his helmet visor. "It doesn't make sense," he muttered. "An enemy would have burned the village."

They ate a somber dinner that night in the campaign tent on the riverbank opposite the ghost town. No doubt the dejected officers were as haunted as Diego by that charnel house full of skeletons, in place of the alluring women and bursting storehouses they had been promised throughout their weeks of deprivation. Don Sebastian quickly dismissed them, signaling for Diego to remain seated at the trestle table.

"There was a magnificent queen here," he insisted, absently fingering his grotesque scar. "She wore a dress laced from the hide of an albino deer. It was as supple as silk. She draped strands of river pearls around DeSoto's neck. Shapely young women danced for us in the plaza afterwards. Then they entered the huts of the men who pleased them most." He seemed dazed, as though talking to himself.

"It sounds like a paradise, Sire." Diego was surprised to find himself feeling sorry for Don Sebastian. He had been as eager to reach Cofitachequi as a priest to reach heaven. Instead, he had found himself faced with a boneyard.

"Many wanted to stay here and pan for gold in the river," Don Sebastian continued. "Or mine silver in the mountains. But DeSoto wished only to seize the treasures of others, so he insisted that the march continue." He studied his own hands, as though surprised they were still there. "What am I to do now?" he asked Diego abruptly, staring at him with haunted eyes.

"About what, Sire?" asked Diego. Looking into those forlorn green eyes, he realized that he had begun to care for this confusing and complicated man as he might have cared for the father he had never known. He wanted somehow to comfort him in the face of this disaster.

"I had planned to ask the queen here where DeSoto's deserters have gone. It appears she is dead, so I am without a plan."

"The bodies were neatly stacked by survivors, Sire. Perhaps they moved elsewhere, and we can locate them."

Don Sebastian nodded thoughtfully. "Did I ever tell you about DeSoto's death?"

Diego shook his head, bewildered to have been giving advice to his own commander.

"Once we left Cofitachequi, we wandered for three years among savage tribes that tried repeatedly to slaughter us. Finally we arrived at a river far west of here called the Mississippi. DeSoto told the natives there that we were Sons of the Sun. He came down with a fever and soon died. We stuffed his body into a hollow log and sank it in that river. If the natives had realized we were mere mortals, they would have murdered us on the spot.

"During our march we had collected several hundred native slaves. After a couple of years together in the wilderness, some of the soldiers and their native women had become like husband and wife. Some women had given birth. As we boarded our boats to retreat downriver to the Gulf of Mexico, the natives begged us to take them with us. They said they were far from their homes and surrounded by hostile tribes. They claimed that even if they managed to reach their own villages again, their people would never accept their half-Spanish spawn. But we left them there on the riverbank."

"You deserted a woman you loved," Diego realized.

Don Sebastian poured a cup of wine from the clay pitcher on the table and drank it straight down. "We hadn't enough food even for ourselves. We needed silence to drift past the hostile tribes who lived along the riverbanks. We couldn't have risked the crying of babies."

"Who was she, Sire?"

Don Sebastian's eyes darted around his tent like a trapped bird. "She was the only woman I have ever loved," he finally replied. "But I abandoned her and our son, whom everyone said looked just like me."

Halfway up the narrow path that switchbacked across the face of the cream-colored cliff, Diego looked down at the line below him. Since there had been no bearers to draft at Cofitachequi and the Orista were long gone, the African slaves and the packhorses were heavy-laden. The cavalry had donated their extra mounts for the humiliating task of carrying supplies.

Diego spotted Olivia's red scarf among the slaves. He had slipped her the bundle of herbs from Blue Heron. She immediately stuffed some in her mouth and started chewing. He hadn't yet heard if they had worked.

Overhead Diego could see Don Sebastian on his ebony gelding. Brother Marcos rode behind him, bearing the golden cross, followed by Captain Melendez with the gold and purple standard.

Don Sebastian had averted his eyes from Diego's as the vanguard fell into formation at dawn. Diego realized that he needed to sidestep any future confessions from his commander. He now knew things that both he and Don Sebastian wished he didn't. Don Sebastian seemed to want to unburden himself of his past sins and gain absolution, but he needed Brother Marcos for that, not his swineherd.

When Diego and Guillermo at last crested the lip of the limestone cliff, they discovered a wooded plateau spread out before them. Its stands of hardwoods sported the muted mustards and mauves of a fast-fading fall. Far to the west rose a range of mountains that were partially veiled by a haze the hue of a heron's wing.

"That's where Don Sebastian will find his infernal gold and silver," muttered Guillermo, pointing to the mountains. "It was in the mountains of Peru that Pizarro seized his loot. I hope you will all soon be rich and will go back home to Spain and leave us alone."

"You could wish that no more earnestly than I do myself," muttered Diego.

Once the army had reassembled atop the plateau, the march resumed. They followed a path that wound through trees taller than any Diego had ever seen. The forests of Galicia seemed dwarfed by comparison. So dense was the canopy of leaves overhead that only occasional shafts of sunlight penetrated it. The forest floor was carpeted with giant ferns that rose nearly as high as the horses' backs as they wove along the trail packed down by generations of passing natives.

Entering a chestnut grove, Diego glanced over his shoulder. He wondered how the Portuguese lancers would prevent the hogs from running wild over the fallen nuts. When he turned back around, he saw that Melendez and two bodyguards were plunging on their horses through the ferns alongside the path. They appeared to be in pursuit of something—perhaps a deer for Don Sebastian's lunch?

Baltasar streaked up from behind, his broken leash lashing. He shot through the woods after the horsemen. Lucas was nowhere in sight.

Diego spurred his Arabian. Then he pulled in on the reins so hard that the horse reared and nearly toppled sideways, snorting and neighing. He looked toward Don Sebastian. Mouth set, Don Sebastian nodded permission. Diego loosened the reins, and the Arabian charged off after Baltasar through the giant ferns, while Diego ducked and dodged low-hanging limbs.

Diego reined in the Arabian for a rest. She was white with lather, and he was breathing heavily. In the sudden silence he heard Baltasar snarling up ahead. He whistled a command for him to freeze.

Dismounting, he walked in the direction of the snarls. As he parted a curtain of tangled vines, he spotted the crouched greyhound. Clutched in his jaws was the thigh of a native perhaps a few years older than Diego himself. The young man lay motionless, his eyes numb. He wore only a loincloth. A quiver of arrows was strapped to one shoulder. There was no sign of his bow. His head was shaven on both sides, with a crest of bristling hair on the top of his head that resembled a rooster's coxcomb. The crest grew long enough in back to form a braid.

"Drop it!" ordered Diego.

Baltasar reluctantly opened his jaws to free the leg, which was pocked with small rips that welled with blood. Lucas ran into the clearing, gasping for air, chagrined by Baltasar's escape. He and Diego each seized an arm and lifted the dazed warrior to his feet.

As the Arabian trailed along behind them with dangling reins, they dragged the struggling boy back through the woods to Don Sebastian. He was sitting on his gelding, holding an arrow that had evidently missed its mark—himself. Melendez and the guards reappeared from the woods, dismounted, and seized the trembling boy.

"Ask him his tribe," Don Sebastian instructed Diego.

After he had done so, the boy merely stared at the ground. Diego couldn't tell if he had understood the question or not.

"Put your knife to his throat," Don Sebastian instructed Melendez, who obliged.

"Ask him who his king is."

The warrior muttered something.

"No king," translated Diego. "A queen."

Don Sebastian's sullen green eyes flared.

"Ask him her name."

No reply.

"Tell him he must take us to her. Tell him I am her old friend."

No reply.

"Tell him we will kill him if he refuses."

Nothing.

"Remove the right ear," he ordered Melendez, who gestured to the bodyguards to drag the young man to a fallen tree trunk.

"Sire," murmured Don Domingo de Santa Cruz de la Sierra, the Captain of the Horse, "I urge you to be cautious. We are strangers in this foreign land. We should court this lad's aid, not his rancor."

Don Sebastian glared at Don Domingo in his black eye patch.

"Continue," he ordered Melendez.

Diego watched Melendez draw his sword and chop off the boy's ear as though slicing bread. The boy didn't so much as flinch.

The guards dragged the boy, blood dribbling down his neck and shoulder, back to Don Sebastian. All at once the boy wrenched loose his arms and ran for the undergrowth. Stopping and turning around, he seized an arrow from the quiver on his shoulder and held it tip-first toward his chest. He stared at Don Sebastian as he plunged it into his heart with both hands, a quarter of the way up its shaft. Still gazing at Don Sebastian, he worked the arrow in a circle with both hands so that his blood spurted from the wound and splattered the ferns. He sank to his knees, still twisting the arrow to maximize his blood loss. As red flooded the floor of golden leaves, he collapsed on his side. His eyes fluttered slowly shut.

The vanguard sat silently on their mounts. What Diego could see of Don Sebastian's face beneath his silver helmet had turned pale. He spurred his horse, and the march resumed. Rank after rank passed the copper body that lay twitching on leaves soaked mahogany.

As Olivia approached, she caught Diego's eye. He raised his eyebrows questioningly, and she shook her head. Diego took this to mean that the herbs had not worked, and his heart sank for her.

Diego walked over to the boy. He looked down at the bloody gash where his ear had been. Was this what had happened to those natives on Hispaniola?

"How could Don Sebastian have ordered such a thing, or Melendez have committed it?" he demanded of Lucas, who was tying Baltasar's knotted leash to a tree.

"Have I or have I not been trying to warn you?" replied Lucas.

"You have," mumbled Diego. "I just didn't believe you."

"This isn't something you would ever do, so you don't expect it from someone else. But you must learn to protect yourself from the cruelty of others, Diego."

Diego nodded as he and Lucas gathered armloads of leaves to spread across the boy's body. Baltasar whimpered and strained against his leash at the scent of the fresh blood.

Diego remounted and cantered up to his spot in the vanguard. With his eyes fixed on the hazy mountains that scalloped the horizon, he asked Guillermo, "Why didn't that boy just take Don Sebastian to his queen? Wouldn't she have been pleased to see a friend?"

"You don't actually believe that story, do you?"

"I guess I do. Or did."

"Diego, there is no native alive who regards a Spaniard as his friend. That's like asking a sheep to love a wolf."

They pitched camp on a grassy savannah where jackrabbits were as plentiful as lice in the holds of the *San Jorge*. Diego watched Nicolas Navarro, the four Portuguese, Arias de Zavallas, Pedro Picado, and several others form a large circle and close in, driving a dozen rabbits to the center. Once they were shoulder to shoulder, the men tried to beat the animals to death with sticks. But most escaped and bounded away.

Still in shock from the native boy's death, Diego retrieved Baltasar from Lucas and hiked far away from the hubbub of the camp. Baltasar chased down and retrieved a dozen rabbits, and Diego slit their throats. Then he collected a satchel of chestnuts from the forest floor, all the while trying to fathom the implications of the tragedy that had just occurred. Would the boy's tribe find his body? What might they do for revenge?

After skinning the rabbits for Alonso outside the kitchen tent, Diego went in search of Olivia. She was bent over by the fire pit in front of Arias's tent, stirring something in a cast iron pot.

"The herbs didn't work?" he asked quietly.

She looked up. "Not yet. If they don't soon, I'm done for."

"Maybe not," said Diego. "Let's wait to see what Arias does once he learns about it before we panic."

"You're sweet to care, Diego."

"You're my friend. You'd do the same for me."

"The next time you're with child, Diego, you can count on me." She smiled wryly.

As the officers sat at the trestle table devouring Alonso's rabbit and chestnut stew that night, Don Sebastian raised his cup. When everyone had fallen silent, he said, "Let us drink to the young native who died today. As warriors ourselves, we can all admire such bravery and loyalty to one's commander."

Everyone drank, and Diego wondered if these men actually felt loyalty like that toward their own commander, or if Don Sebastian were merely indulging in wishful thinking.

Don Sebastian continued, "These natives have much to teach us about courage. During DeSoto's campaign, we were once attacked by several hundred of them. We fought them off. Their survivors sought refuge in a lake. We surrounded the banks, waiting for them to crawl ashore. Half a dozen swimmers would lift an archer up out of the water to shoot at us. One such arrow pierced my own breastplate, barely missing my heart. After two days, when they could no longer stay afloat, they sank down silently into watery graves."

Don Sebastian dismissed the others, motioning for Diego to remain, as usual.

As his commander set out his chessboard, Diego asked, "Sire, why did that boy refuse to lead you to his queen? Didn't you say that you were her friend?"

Don Sebastian replied, "She and I were friends while DeSoto was romancing her. But he quickly lost interest. She was too willing. He preferred to take women who objected. He had found no gold or silver at Cofitachequi, so he announced our departure. Some soldiers who hadn't yet found women to lie with broke into their temple and assaulted their sacred virgins. The queen protested. DeSoto put her in chains. When we resumed our march, she was with us, still chained."

Don Sebastian held out both fists. Diego picked the left one, which held a black pawn. He was struggling to digest the notion that DeSoto, the hero of most on this march, had enjoyed rape. Of course, many on this march apparently did as well. On the one hand, they revered their mothers back home in Spain and the Holy Virgin in heaven. On the other, they had no qualms about forcing themselves on any female unlucky enough to cross their paths. He didn't understand. If this was what it meant to be a man, he guessed he would rather remain a boy.

"Several days into the mountains, the queen and her attendants, guarded by DeSoto's African slave, went into the forest to relieve themselves. DeSoto didn't know that the queen and this slave had fallen in love. They fled, along with some other slaves and soldiers."

As Diego set up his ebony army on the checkered squares, Don Sebastian assembled his ivory pieces.

"Did your wife come from Cofitachequi?" asked Diego, forgetting his pledge to invite no more such confidences.

After a strained silence, Don Sebastian replied, "Yes. She traveled with me from Cofitachequi to the banks of the Mississippi, where she gave birth to our son. After DeSoto's death I tried to escape with her and our baby. My comrades tracked us down and threw me into a boat, leaving them on the shore. If my son has survived, he is only a few years older than you. The young man who impaled himself on his arrow today could have been he, for all I know."

Diego thought it best to stifle his next question of why, if the native boy could have been his own son, he had ordered his ear amputated. Don Sebastian had curious ways of expressing affection.

After a moment Diego asked, "Did you come back here to find your son?"

"No doubt he and his mother died. They had no food. They were surrounded by natives who hated Spaniards. Cofitachequi was many weeks distant by foot. The forests were full of panthers, wolves, and poisonous snakes."

For the first time Don Sebastian looked old and haggard.

"I deserted them to save myself. My comrades dragged me away. But if I had insisted, I could have stayed. A few did stay. We could have banded together and figured out how to survive. But I was a coward." He wrapped his arms around himself, lowered his chin to his chest, and closed his eyes.

"We floated downriver to the Gulf of Mexico," he continued in a choked voice. "Then we paddled along the coast for many days, until a Spanish fishing fleet from New Galicia rescued us. I sailed home to Spain and put my woman and my son out of my mind. I amputated my own heart."

Diego's impulse of compassion for Don Sebastian clashed with the picture seared into his brain of the young warrior sprawled earless beneath his shroud of gory leaves.

7

Joara

"Sire, the men are exhausted," Don Domingo said at dinner in Don Sebastian's tent in a poplar forest somewhere in the middle of nowhere. "We left Cofitachequi nearly a fortnight ago, and we haven't even reached the mountains yet."

As he chewed his pork, Diego studied Don Domingo with his jaunty black eye patch. His remaining eye was blue.

"Since we found no bearers at Cofitachequi," continued Don Domingo, "the men must carry all the supplies. And since there was no food there, they are now eating nuts and roots. They are too weak to march all day with heavy packs and then scavenge in the forest for their dinners when we halt. We must consider turning back. At the very least we must butcher more hogs for them."

Several other officers murmured fainthearted agreement. Don Domingo, whose father was a large landowner near Leon, was the only officer with enough prestige to challenge Don Sebastian. Some of his and Don Sebastian's cousins had intermarried, so they were remote kinsmen.

Don Sebastian glared at the malcontents until they fell silent. He clenched and unclenched his jaws so that the scar across his cheek writhed like an agitated snake. Then he dismissed them all before they had even finished their meals.

Diego stood up, pocketing a hunk of pork for Lucas. He glanced at Don Sebastian to see if he would gesture for him to stay. But the commander just gazed glumly into his silver goblet and began to massage his temples with his fingertips.

As Diego and Guillermo headed back to their tent, they passed a throng of soldiers jostling outside Arias's tent. Arias was now charging Olivia's customers a portion of their evening biscuits. Since Cofitachequi had not yielded the skilled concubines Don Sebastian had promised and since the Orista women had returned to the coast, many were half-mad with lust, on top of their hunger and exhaustion.

"Didn't you tell me that Arias's slave woman was with child?" whispered Guillermo.

Diego nodded.

"Did the herbs Blue Heron gave you work?"

"No."

Guillermo looked at him with consternation. "Don't those soldiers know about her condition?"

"I guess they either don't notice or don't care," said Diego.

Guillermo shook his head. "Is there no degradation to which these men would not stoop?"

"None," Diego assured him. He hesitated and then asked, "Guillermo, if I helped Olivia escape, would the Orista take us in?"

Guillermo said nothing for a long time. Finally he replied, "They would certainly take you in. What Don Sebastian would do to them in retaliation is the real question."

Diego nodded. Then he remembered that he himself was Guillermo's ticket back to Oristatown. Guillermo was counting on his assuming the post of head translator so that Don Sebastian would release him to return to Blue Heron.

Despite Don Domingo's courageous plea, the march resumed at dawn. As Diego's longsuffering Arabian plunked one hoof in front of another, Diego studied the mountains ahead, their peaks piercing the skyline like the scales on a dragon's neck. They were already tipped with snow that glowed pink in the rising sun.

By mid-morning foothills began to break up the monotony of the dense woodlands and rolling savannas. These hills appeared to have been burnt over. Large herds of deer grazed their coarse grasses, which were tinged by frost with a mustard tint. The irony was that, although those distant deer were venison steaks on the hoof, none of the soldiers knew how to hunt them.

During the lunch break in a wide meadow at the foot of a hillside forested with giant oaks, the advance scouts returned to report a palisaded town snuggled into the base of a rocky escarpment two hours' march ahead. Energized by the prospect of women and food for the taking, the flagging troops doubled their pace and raced along as though pursued by the Furies. By mid-afternoon the trail began to widen and the undergrowth thinned.

Diego heard what sounded like the piping of flutes, accompanied by a rhythmic rattling. Winding down the path from the town came a line of bare-chested young men, clad in fringed deerskin skirts to their knees. As some blew into reed tubes or shook painted gourds, others hopped and skipped, extending and contorting their arms and hands in gestures of apparent welcome.

Behind the dancers strode two dozen older men in hide togas that covered the chest and fastened at one shoulder. Draped over these were capes, some of painted deerskin, others of luxuriant fur. Around their necks hung strands of gray river pearls or yellow metal beads. Similar pearls and beads dangled from their earlobes. Their heads were shaven on both sides, leaving coxcombs that were braided in back, like that of the young warrior now dead among the fallen leaves. Hide boots rose to their ankles or calves, and their thighs were bound in soft leather. Most were tall, muscular, and well proportioned.

With a start, Diego realized that three of these dignitaries were women who wore doeskin shifts and mantles of overlapping feathers. Their dark hair hung long and straight with bangs across the forehead.

Their leader stepped forward. A wizened old man with skin like the cracked leather of Diego's old vest, he wore a cape fashioned from the feathers of what seemed an entire flock of blue heron. Where his nose should have been were two holes and a mass of scar tissue, like a wormy dried apple. He gazed up at Don Sebastian on his ebony gelding and addressed him.

Don Sebastian turned to summon Guillermo and Diego for a translation. Dismounting, they approached the old man. But when he spoke, they couldn't understand him.

Another headman stepped forward. Swathed in an auburn fur, he towered over the others. The white tail feather of an eagle was secured in his black braid. He announced in the Orista language that he could translate Joara Mico's speech into Orista, which Guillermo and Diego could then render into Spanish.

In this halting fashion they learned that the town ahead was called Joara. The Joara, forewarned by their scouts that the Spaniards were approaching, had summoned the chiefs of the mountain villages to the north and west. All had gathered in Joara to pledge their fealty and their aid.

Following these remarks, Joara Mico summoned a dozen young men who carried covered pack baskets, from which came a cacophony of yapping and whimpering. They opened their baskets to display wriggling mounds of plump puppies.

"Well do we recall how DeSoto's troops savored the roasted dogs of Joara," mused Joara Mico with a smile of fond remembrance.

Diego exchanged a glance with Guillermo as he translated Don Sebastian's solemn praise for such generous hospitality. Don Sebastian went on to announce to Joara Mico that, as an expression of gratitude, his troops would camp in the field outside the town rather than evicting the Joara from their homes.

Then Don Sebastian launched into his speech about the Joara now being subjects of Philip II and the pope in Rome and, as such, having certain obligations. If they accepted them, gifts would flow. If they refused, the Joara would be enslaved and their civilization destroyed.

The assembled Micos wisely chorused, "Yaa."

Diego and Guillermo headed back to their tent from a dinner of fresh venison sent to Don Sebastian by Joara Mico. Pleased by this lavish welcome, Don Sebastian had announced at dinner that the army would rest at Joara for a few days before tackling the pass into the mountains, which notched the ridge beyond the village. They would also build a fort in the meadow for future use as an outpost along the route to the Mexican silver mines.

Diego and Guillermo passed a campfire around which Nicolas Navarro and the four Portuguese were still feasting on roasted puppy.

"It's delicious. Try it," insisted Nicolas, holding out what looked like a drumstick for Diego to sample.

"Baltasar would never forgive me," replied Diego.

As Nicolas translated, the others chuckled and sucked their greasy fingers clean.

Since the soldiers were under strict orders not to enter the village of Joara, several were now standing below the palisaded wall, serenading some native women peering down from the ramparts. Their lusty Catalonian drinking song appeared to mystify the women, who whispered among themselves.

As they lay in their tent trying to sleep amid this ineffectual courtship, Diego said to Guillermo, "At last some people who seem pleased to see us!"

"They can run for the hills, leaving their village to be plundered. They can fight and die. Or they can feign hospitality and try to save their homes and supplies."

"You are a hopeless cynic, Guillermo. Maybe they're just hospitable people."

"They *are* hospitable people. But they learned from DeSoto the price of hospitality to jackals. Mark my word, Diego: soon they will inform Don Sebastian of piles of gold lying unclaimed in the land of their enemies."

The next morning Diego and Guillermo stopped en route to Don Sebastian's tent to watch several soldiers lever a tree trunk twice the height of a man into a deep ditch so as to form the palisade for the new fort. When they entered the campaign tent, Don Sebastian was already seated on a stool opposite Joara Mico and an adolescent boy clad in a loincloth, leggings, and a fringed leather shirt.

"At last," muttered Don Sebastian with a glare at the tardy translators. "This is Terrapin," he said, gesturing to the boy. "He will translate Joara Mico's speech into Orista for you. Then you can translate it into Castilian for me."

Diego listened closely to the ensuing discussion, trying to identify the basics of the Joara dialect. He soon realized that Guillermo and Terrapin were carrying on a private conversation as they translated for their respective chiefs.

"We seek metals of gold and silver," Guillermo said to Terrapin in Orista. *"What is your Orista clan?"* he added.

Terrapin spoke to Joara Mico and then replied in Orista, "We have many such deposits. *My mother is clan mother of the Turtles.*"

Guillermo translated only the first sentence for Don Sebastian, who replied with a question.

"In what direction do these deposits lie?" Guillermo asked Terrapin. *"How long have you been here?"*

"In the mountains to the southwest," translated Terrapin. *"I was captured on a hunt five years ago."*

"Will your scouts take my captain there? *I have heard of your disappearance. Do the Joara treat you well?"*

"Yes, whenever you wish. *The Mico treats me as his son, but I long for Oristatown."*

"Then let them depart tomorrow. *I will tell the Turtle Clan of your whereabouts. Your kinsmen will find a way to rescue you."*

Once Joara Mico had left, Don Sebastian ordered Guillermo to prepare to leave for the mountains the next morning with Captain Melendez, Terrapin, the Joara scouts, and a smith from Toledo named Julio Gomez, a purported expert on precious gems and metals.

As they left Don Sebastian's tent, Diego said to Guillermo, "That was a dangerous game you and that boy were playing."

"Why? No one could understand us but you, and I know you would never expose us."

"That's true enough. But, look, Guillermo, I want to apologize. That trek through the mountains will be exhausting and dangerous. I want you to know that I didn't ask to stay here."

"It's clear that Don Sebastian wants you by his side," replied Guillermo. "I know it's not your doing, unless you're to be blamed for being so pleasant and entertaining. But you should know, in case I don't return, that this is what I wanted—Don Sebastian relying on you, in the hope that he will soon free me to return to Oristatown."

"However much I would hate to see you leave, Guillermo, you know that I'll help you however I can."

"As I will you, Diego. And you may need help more than I before this trip is finished."

"Why?" asked Diego, puzzled. "Don Sebastian has his episodes of cruelty, but they're never directed at me. To the contrary, he's showered me with privileges." He was sick of everyone's veiled warnings about Don Sebastian. He couldn't help wondering if they stemmed from envy.

Guillermo shrugged.

Diego sat on a stool in the corner of Don Sebastian's tent, only half listening to his conversation about the new fort with the engineer Gabriel de la Zarza and the stonemason Pascuale Sanchez. The soldiers had woven lathes between the posts of the palisade, which they were now plastering with orange clay from a nearby pit. Gabriel was recommending square log sentry boxes at the corners. Pascuale was urging that the walls be skirted with stone, which would be fireproof.

"You may be right, Pascuale," said Don Sebastian, "but we don't have time. As soon as Captain Melendez returns from the mountains, we must resume the march."

"But why not rest here awhile, Sire?" asked Pascuale. "The Joara are hospitable, and the men and horses are worn out from their weeks in that wilderness with no food."

Don Sebastian glared at him until he lowered his gaze. "We must blaze a trail to the Mexican silver mines and locate DeSoto's deserters," he finally replied. "We can rest once we get back to Santa Elena."

Don Sebastian had been plagued all week with requests from his officers and from the native headmen, each with his own formula for currying favor. Diego had had to sit through it all for times when translations were required. At first he had needed the assistance of the huge Orista-speaking chief in the cape of auburn fur. But he had picked up the Joara dialect quickly, allowing this man to depart for his village in the mountains.

"Turn away any supplicants who arrive this afternoon," Don Sebastian called to Tomas de Carrion as Gabriel and Pascuale exited. Tomas and Juan Bravo stood outside the entrance, armed with halberds.

"Yes, Sire," replied Tomas.

"My head is pounding," he murmured to Diego. He closed his eyes and pinched the bridge of his nose with thumb and index finger.

"Shall I summon Dr. Mendez, Sire?"

"No. I'll lie down and rest awhile."

"Shall I leave, Sire?"

"No. Stay." He shrugged off his jerkin and reclined on his cot in his linen shirt.

Diego stretched out on the Oriental carpet alongside him, feeling like a favorite hound. To his surprise, Don Sebastian began to talk in a muted voice about his family's hacienda near Valladolid, where he had spent his childhood studying under a Jesuit. He had also received military training from a veteran of Cortes's conquest of Mexico. This soldier often described the capture by several hundred Spaniards of a town on an island in the middle of a lake, defended by 8,000 Aztec troops. Don Sebastian said that he had been fascinated by the veteran's descriptions of the Aztec soldiers. The Eagle warriors wore plumed helmets with gaping beaks and carried feather-fringed shields, while the Jaguar warriors peered out through the snarling jaws of the jaguar skulls that formed their headdresses.

Don Sebastian's beautiful mother had rarely emerged from her bedchamber, and when she did, she ignored him. He identified her with the Virgin Mary, to whom he was passionately devoted.

When his father came home from court, he, too, was ignored by his wife. So he filled his time by beating Sebastian. These beatings pleased Sebastian because they proved that his father was aware of his existence, however irritating he might find him. Sebastian vowed that one day he would be a conquistador like Cortes, bringing heathens in garish headdresses to heel. At last he would win his mother's notice and his father's approval.

Abruptly, he sat up and stared at Diego, seeming startled to find him still there. "But why do I bore you with these trivial memories, boy?" His expression turned haggard.

Diego felt a flicker of fear. With knowledge of someone came power over him, and Don Sebastian ceded power to no one. "I am honored, Sire." He ducked his head to indicate that he posed no threat, the way he had seen curs submit to Baltasar.

"I suppose you remind me of myself at your age —so innocent and so idealistic."

"Innocent of what, Your Worship?"

Don Sebastian studied Diego. "Innocent of your own capacity for wrongdoing."

Diego frowned. He was only too aware of his own capacity for sin. It had already required him to spend hours on his knees reciting Ava Marias. But he had never admitted this to Don Sebastian—and never would.

Standing up and stretching, Don Sebastian said, "I know Joara Mico from DeSoto's mission. We passed through this village. It had a different name then."

Diego scrambled to his feet. "Do you think he remembers you, Sire?"

"I don't believe so. I was just a boy. Our troops were angry to have to leave Cofitachequi. Two infantrymen who tried to escape were hanged on a gallows in this meadow. Several raped and looted here. Others stewed every dog they could capture. Joara Mico was a young war chief then. He threatened retaliation, so DeSoto ordered his bodyguards to cut off his nose and feed it to a mastiff."

Diego shuddered.

Don Sebastian shrugged. "DeSoto didn't respond well to threats."

"But you were with your woman from Cofitachequi then, weren't you, Sire?"

His face darkened. "She...." He fell silent.

Diego figured out too late that he was supposed to have pretended not to remember this.

"You may go now," murmured Don Sebastian.

Joara Mico and two of his headmen, attired in their hide togas and fur capes, stood across the trestle table from Don Sebastian as Diego translated their bitter complaint that two young women had been lured from Joaratown the previous night by soldiers who offered them swatches of taffeta. Each woman was dragged into a tent. The Joara explained that men were lining up outside the tents when a Spaniard arrived with a snarling dog. (Diego inserted Lucas's and Baltasar's names here, since it was they who deserved the credit.) Lucas had warned the soldiers to let the women return to Joara, or they would find themselves lacking the equipment with which to rape.

Outside Don Sebastian's tent, Diego heard Captain Melendez's voice demand of Tomas de Carrion and Juan Bravo an immediate audience with Don Sebastian. Diego felt relieved to know that the mountain mineral hunt was over and that the men on the mission had apparently returned alive and intact.

"Let Captain Melendez enter," Don Sebastian called to Tomas.

Melendez burst into the tent, the smith Julio Gomez at his heels. The headmen stepped aside to make room for them. Proudly the two men placed four chunks of stone on the trestle table before Don Sebastian. Don Sebastian studied the rocks for a long time, turning them this way and that.

Glancing down at Francisco's ring on his middle finger, Diego felt a surge of excitement. One of the rocks looked as though it could have been hacked from the same mountain as the chunk of crystal in his ring. Perhaps this was the quartz peak that Francisco had promised him they would find here in the interior.

Pointing to the rocks one by one, Don Sebastian said, "Mica. Iron ore. Quartz. Copper. Worthless!" With both hands he shoved them off the table onto the Oriental carpet. Waving his hand irritably, he dismissed Melendez and Gomez.

As the discomfited men skulked from the tent, Joara Mico stepped forward. "A tribe called the Chisca, who live in a valley beyond these mountains, mine a yellow metal that they use for trade and for adornment," he announced.

Diego studied the Mico's face as he translated this. The Mico looked alarming with those two gaping holes where his nose should have been.

"Their streams run so plentifully with this metal that it lights up the night sky as the sun does the day," continued Joara Mico.

Don Sebastian's eyes glinted. "I am told that DeSoto was given this same information by the Coosa to the south. He sent two men to explore the rumor. But the mountains were so high and the trails so steep that they turned back."

Diego noted Don Sebastian's pretense that he himself had not been with DeSoto.

"They were mistaken not to continue," said Joara Mico, his black eyes scanning Don Sebastian's face like a soldier searching a palisade for a gap.

"Do you know a town toward the sea from here called Cofitachequi?"

The Mico appeared to search his memory. "Alas, no."

"DeSoto reported a young queen there who dressed in the hide of an albino deer. Later in life she may have had as her consort a man with a dark face and curly hair. Did you ever encounter such a couple?"

Again the Mico replied no. But Diego thought he detected a nervous shift to his eyes. Joara Mico would have had to know this woman, Diego realized, since she was the queen of his nation when he himself was a young war chief. He also realized that Don Sebastian knew this. His questions were a test of the Mico's truthfulness, a test the Mico had just failed, and probably knew that he had failed—had failed purposely. This entire conversation was as complex as a chess game, and, as usual, Diego was several moves behind Don Sebastian.

After the Mico's departure, Don Sebastian took to his cot and asked Tomas de Carrion to summon Lope Mendez. The portly Dr. Mendez arrived and gave Don Sebastian a potion to drink for his aching head. Then he bound Don Sebastian's temples with a vinegar-soaked rag. Prescribing an afternoon of complete quiet, he gestured for Diego to leave.

On his way back to his own tent, Diego passed that of Arias. Olivia was sitting in the sun on the ground outside it, knees drawn to her chest and eyes closed. There were bruised half-moons under her eyes, and her cheekbones stood out like burls on a mulberry branch. Down her dark cheeks ran several salty tracks of dried tears.

"Olivia?" he said softly.

She opened her eyes. Once she saw him, she tried to smile.

"Are you okay?"

She looked down and didn't reply.

"What's wrong—apart from the obvious?"

Slowly she extended her fists. When she opened her hands, he saw that her pale palms were covered with red welts.

Diego sank down beside her, took one of her hands in his, and studied the sores. "What is it?"

"The pox."

He stared at her. "The pox?"

She nodded.

"Are you sure?"

"Yes. A couple of women at my house in Santo Domingo had it."

Diego shook his head. He had never doubted the goodness of God before. But why was Olivia being punished like this? She was not the one who had impregnated herself or given herself pox.

"Have you told Arias yet?" he asked.

"No. I'm trying to work up the courage. He may kill me when he hears."

That night Diego, Guillermo, and Baltasar watched from the shadows behind Arias's tent while a mob of Olivia's former customers clamored for her death. Diego intended to sic Baltasar on anyone who tried to touch her. Dr. Mendez had examined her and confirmed her self-diagnosis. He had added that she had had the pox for a long time and had probably brought it with her from Santo Domingo.

One soldier yelled at Arias, "You knew she was sick! You sold us the services of a diseased slave! We ought to hang you up by your thumbs!"

"Why would I have lain with her myself if I had known she had the pox?" Arias yelled back.

Eventually the soldiers began to drift away, some to Dr. Mendez's tent to learn if they too were infected.

"What do you think will happen to Olivia?" Diego asked Guillermo.

Guillermo shrugged. "Those men want to kill her. Arias probably does, too. But he paid a lot of silver for her. He may try to sell her to the Joara. They seem fascinated by her dark skin. Have you noticed how they stare at her all the time?"

"What will the Joara do with her?"

"It's hard to say. Either make her their queen—or torture her to death."

The next morning Arias came up to Diego outside the kitchen tent during breakfast and asked, "Do you have a free moment, lad? I need you to translate for me in Joaratown."

As Arias and Diego strode across the meadow toward the Joara palisade, Diego said, "I was sorry to hear about Olivia's illness."

Arias spat a wad of saliva into the undergrowth. "I can't believe that bastard in Santo Domingo sold me damaged goods. If I could get my hands on him, I'd wring his neck!"

"Are you sick, too?" Diego asked hesitantly.

Arias glanced at him and said nothing. After a while he muttered, "Yes."

When they reached the main entrance to the town, a guard stepped forward to block their passage with a spear. He wore the usual Joara outfit—a loincloth, boots, leggings, and a fringed leather hunting shirt. His head was shaved except for a coxcomb on top and a long braid in back.

Arias said to Diego, "Ask him if he knows of any Joara who would want to buy my African slave woman."

"Shouldn't you warn him about her disease?" asked Diego.

"Why should I? No one warned me."

Remembering Guillermo's private conversation with Terrapin when he was supposed to be translating for Don Sebastian, Diego asked the guard if he had seen a dog with a silver coat pass by recently, in order not to ask the guard about selling Olivia.

The guard shook his head no.

"I don't think he's interested in buying a slave," Diego told Arias.

"Tell him to ask around the village. I'll come back tomorrow."

Diego said to the guard, "If you see my dog, could you please send word to Diego in the soldiers' camp?"

The guard nodded yes.

As they headed back across the meadow, Diego asked, "Arias, will you sell Olivia to me?"

Arias stopped walking to look at him. "Why would you want a diseased African whore who's going to die soon?"

"Because she's my friend."

Arias's mouth fell open. "Well, what's your offer?"

"I don't have much, Arias. I'm just a swineherd. But I can give you this ring." He slipped off Francisco's ring and passed it to Arias. He hated to part with it, but it was the only item of any value that he owned. He suspected Francisco wouldn't object if he knew the reason.

Arias studied the ring. "It's handsome, Diego, but it's just quartz." Arias handed it back to him. "It has very little value."

Diego had a sudden inspiration: "I could guarantee you a fish or a bird or a game animal for supper every single day for the rest of this march."

Arias's eyes flickered with interest. "All right. But I want you to take her right now before I strangle her. I can't stand the sight of that pox-ridden bitch for another minute."

When they reached his tent, Arias called for Olivia. She crept out, looking all around her, expecting the worst.

"Diego's just bought you," he told her. "Gather your stuff and get the hell out of my life."

After digging for worms, Diego baited his hook, tossed the line into the water, and sat on a shelf of limestone. Since Don Sebastian was laid low with another headache, Diego was using the idle hours to catch a fish for Arias's supper. The warm ledge heated his buttocks through his leather shorts. He heard axes chopping and mauls pounding at the new fort in the meadow behind him. From upstream drifted the banter of Joara women fetching water. Several Joara men were repairing a reed trout weir on the far side of the river. Downstream, soldiers on a lunch break were squatting on the shore, sifting sand in flat-bottomed baskets, searching for the flecks of gold that washed down from the mountains. A couple of soldiers were said to have panned nuggets, which they hid in their rectums when they slept.

Diego closed his eyes and tried to picture Leonora. But her image was becoming fainter with each passing week. If it could fade so quickly, was what he had felt for her really love? Or was it just self-absorption? Seeing himself through her eyes had allowed him to regard himself as finer than he actually was. Olivia also saw him as finer than he was, but he had at least done something to merit her good opinion. She was so grateful to him for buying her from Arias that she was doing everything she could think of to make his life easier—washing his clothes and straightening his bedroll. It was driving him crazy.

A blood-curdling scream upstream interrupted his musings. Laying aside his pole, he jumped to his feet and ran along the path by the river. He spotted soldiers racing from the fort site, clutching their pikes.

Arriving at a clearing by the water, Diego saw Pedro Picado standing there with his leather shorts down around his ankles. Before him stood a bare-breasted Joara woman, her deerhide skirt askew. In one hand she held a shard of stone. In the other she held Pedro's genitals. She made sawing gestures with her stone knife. Pedro was begging for mercy, sweat rolling down his forehead and soaking his beard.

The soldiers halted at the edge of the clearing, pikes poised. Beside them appeared more bare-breasted Joara women, gourds on their shoulders. Diego spoke to the outraged girl in her own language. Eventually he persuaded her to let Pedro go. As she headed back to the village with her indignant friends, Pedro collapsed on the leaves, hiccupping with relief.

The soldiers doubled over with hilarity. But Diego wasn't sure it was funny. He had heard the rage in Joara Mico's voice a couple of days earlier as he complained about the attempted rape of the two women lured from Joaratown with promises of taffeta.

Certain that Don Sebastian needed to know about this, Diego ran across the meadow and through the maze of alleyways among the tents. When he reached Don Sebastian's Peruvian wool tent, Tomas de Carrion and Juan Bravo crossed their halberds in his path.

"I have something important to tell Don Sebastian," Diego gasped, trying to catch his breath.

"Don Sebastian is ill," announced Tomas. "Nothing can be more important than his recovery."

"Let him enter," Don Sebastian called weakly from within.

Don Sebastian was lying on his cot with a vinegar-soaked cloth wrapped around his forehead. He looked seasick. Diego stood over him and reported the incident by the river.

Don Sebastian replied wearily, "Men without women will do whatever they must to acquire them. Now that that African slave woman has come down with the pox, we must make other arrangements. The women of Cofitachequi were pleased to entertain visiting Spaniards. They regarded us as gods. We have perhaps been too lenient toward these Joara women. They are, after all, our subjects. They owe us whatever form of tribute we require. Can you rub my temples?"

Diego sat down at the head of the cot and removed the damp cloth from Don Sebastian's forehead. Placing his fingertips on his commander's temples, he began to stroke them in the small circular movements he used on his Arabian's legs when she was weary from the march. Don Sebastian heaved a sigh. Diego felt sorry for him. His glorious mission to locate the queen of Cofitachequi and to blaze a trail to the Mexican silver mines was degenerating into a quest for enough food and sex to keep his rowdy troops from murdering him. His carrot was the promise of gold. His stick was the threat of his own unpredictable cruelty. But he seemed too exhausted today to manufacture enough cruelty to intimidate anyone at all.

It was hot there in the wool tent under the afternoon sun. Don Sebastian threw off his blanket with one arm, revealing his linen undergarments, the finest Diego had ever seen, as supple as silk. A pulse throbbed at the base of his throat. Outside, the mauls pounding at the new fort punctuated the sawing whine of a plaintive cicada.

"Rub the base of my skull."

As Diego did so, he inspected the ugly scar that meandered across Don Sebastian's cheek through his beard. Although the beard was flecked with grey, Diego could see the wounded boy beneath the grizzle—spurned by his mother, beaten by his father, forced to abandon his woman and child, feared and loathed by his own men, despised by the natives.

Diego's life, despite his father's death and Cristobal's taunts, seemed charmed by comparison. He had worked hard since he was a small boy, but he had always had plenty to eat and a warm hearth to come home to. And he had known he was loved—by his mother, by Lucas, by Leonora, by the Count, by Francisco, and perhaps now by Don Sebastian, Olivia, and Guillermo as well. Silently he pledged never to abandon Don Sebastian, as had everyone else in his life.

Don Sebastian groaned as Diego's fingers kneaded the knots of inflamed muscles in his neck. Once his breathing had slowed and he appeared asleep, Diego stood up.

"Ask Juan Bravo to summon Joara Mico right away," Don Sebastian murmured, not opening his eyes. "Return here to translate when he arrives."

Don Sebastian had donned his midnight blue jerkin to receive Joara Mico, who stood before him in his mantle of heron feathers. Don Sebastian's hair and beard were combed and trimmed, and no one except Diego would ever have known that his head probably felt as though an axe had cleaved it. Diego reluctantly conveyed to Joara Mico Don Sebastian's demand for young women for his men.

Joara Mico, noseless face impassive, dark eyes averted, said nothing for a long time. Finally he replied, "Our shaman tells us an early winter is on the way. Once the snows begin, crossing the pass beyond our village becomes impossible. If you wish to find the gold of the Chisca, you must go now. If you delay, you will be trapped in the mountains until spring."

Don Sebastian appeared to think this over. "My men and horses are well fed and rested now. The fort is almost finished. We will depart for the Chisca in two days' time. I will, however, still require porters to carry our supplies and women to keep company with my soldiers."

Joara Mico's eyebrows met in a frown above the scar tissue where his nose used to be. "How many?"

"Thirty bearers and ten concubines."

The Mico turned aside for a moment, as though struggling to master himself. Unsuccessful, he glared at Don Sebastian, his black eyes flashing and his upper lip curled beneath the gaping nostrils. "We have welcomed you to our village. You were hungry, and we shared with you our food stored for winter. We summoned the heads of the mountains towns to pledge you their aid. We led you to our sacred peaks in your search for the yellow metal you prize above all else.

"But always you demand more. You Christians are vagabonds— rude, crude, and greedy. You wander through the homelands of others, seizing their huts, their corn, and their hides. You chain our proud warriors and force them to carry your goods. Now you demand our women to quench your lust.

"You speak of your king and your shaman across the great waters, to whom you say we owe tribute. Yet we have our own kings and queens, our own shamans. We are neither your subjects nor your slaves. We are your hosts. Those who are guests cannot demand or require. They can only receive what they are offered with gratitude...."

Diego was nearly tongue-tied trying to translate this torrent into a Spanish of equivalent fury.

Don Sebastian said nothing, his jaw clenching and unclenching. Finally he waved his hand at Joara Mico in dismissal. Then he waved Diego away as well.

As Diego wove along among the tents, he felt sneaking admiration for Joara Mico—mixed with dread. Once inside his own tent, he found Guillermo awake on his bedroll with his hands behind his head. He had been chatting to Olivia, who sat on her own bedroll in her striped skirt and red headscarf. Diego summarized the Mico's tirade.

"He's a brave man," confirmed Guillermo. "But what choice does he have? To live like a cowering cur on scraps tossed his way by the Spaniards, or to die like a panther in full attack."

"He's trying to send us to the Chisca," said Diego. "He says their streams are overflowing with gold."

Guillermo laughed grimly. "What did I predict, Diego? If your fields were being devoured by crows, wouldn't you inform them of the lush corn patches of your enemy?"

Diego frowned.

"Must you be so insistently naive, Diego? You are gripped in the talons of a dragon."

"Don Sebastian is my friend."

"Don Sebastian is not your friend. Please awaken to this truth and protect yourself."

"You don't know him as I do. He's been hurt."

"And nothing is more dangerous than a wild beast that has been wounded," Olivia said quietly.

Diego and Guillermo sat in Don Sebastian's tent the next morning, idly observing his meeting with the brown-robed Brother Marcos concerning the upcoming dedication of the new fort. All of a sudden Captain Melendez pushed past the pages and burst through the flaps into the tent to announce that the village of Joara was completely deserted.

Don Sebastian looked up. His face flushed. "Send squadrons in every direction," he barked. "Do what you must to bring them back. Capture them or kill them if necessary."

He stalked round and round the tent for a long time before sitting back down and resuming his discussion with Brother Marcos.

By mid-afternoon Captain Melendez returned to announce that the patrols had come back empty-handed. There were no signs of the vanished Joara. But Pedro Picado was now missing.

"Send the cavalry out to retrace the route his patrol followed," ordered Don Sebastian. "Fan out through the forest on all sides. Don't return without him."

The pages had just lit the oil lamps in Don Sebastian's tent when Captain Melendez returned to report finding no traces of either Pedro or the fleeing Joara.

Standing at attention on the parade ground inside the new fort the next morning, Diego watched Brother Marcos offer Fort San Juan to the greater glory of God. Diego glanced up at the ramparts, where a double watch was patrolling. He envied the thirty infantry assigned to remain at this fort. They had these walls to cower behind. The rest of them were headed into a wilderness swarming with enraged natives.

The thirty men passed one by one before Don Sebastian, pledging to hold the fort unless and until ordered to depart. Six of Olivia's customers who had contracted the pox, including Arias, were among them. Dr. Mendez had given each a tube of mercury salve and wished him luck. Diego had apologized to Arias for not being able to pay for Olivia with the daily fish and game he had promised, and Arias had canceled the agreement, in a fine mood since he had been released from the march.

"Do you so swear?" Don Sebastian demanded of each. "Under pain of perjury and of infamy?"

"I so swear," each vowed.

Afterwards, Diego and Guillermo mounted their horses and assumed their places in the vanguard. The foot soldiers, wearing all the armor they owned, shouldered their packs and grabbed their pikes. The riflemen lit the fuses on their guns, and the crossbowmen fitted arrows into their bows. As the cavalcade moved out, the cavalry flanked the line and brought up the rear, scouring the woods for concealed warriors.

Olivia walked among the other slaves, but Diego had refused to let her carry his belongings. He had rolled the little that he and she owned into his bedroll and tied it behind his saddle. Then he had filled her pack basket with a few light things so that no one else would ask her to carry something. Diego had wanted to give her his horse and walk himself, but she had pointed out that it wasn't his to give. And Don Sebastian would be unlikely to feel enthusiasm for contributing his fine-boned Arabian to a diseased African slave.

The path in the valley could support six riders abreast. But it gradually narrowed to single file as it wound steeply to the pass. Dense stands of mountain laurel and rhododendron loomed on either hand.

"Do you think they'll attack us?" Diego asked Guillermo as his guts churned with fear.

Guillermo shrugged. "Why would they want to delay us now that we're finally leaving them to harass their worst enemies, the Chisca?"

As the vanguard approached the pass, Diego's Arabian began to snort. Horses up and down the line whinnied and pranced in place, tossing their heads against their reins. The line stalled. Diego could hear Baltasar barking urgently behind him.

Up ahead Diego could see Brother Marcos's golden cross. Captain Melendez's gold and purple standard hung limp beside it in the still morning air. Beyond them something was swaying from a branch that overhung the trail. It flashed silver in the feeble shafts of sunlight that pierced the purple clouds.

Juan Bravo and Tomas de Carrion came running along the narrow pathway from up front. They motioned the vanguard forward, but they halted those on foot halfway down the incline. Diego could just barely see a speck of red from Olivia's scarf. He was glad she was among those ordered to stop. The steep climb with her heavy belly and her fever from the pox would exhaust her soon enough.

Upon reaching the pass, Diego joined the rest of the vanguard crowded into the narrow opening. He inspected the dangling silver bundle that hung from a branch overhead, surrounded by a cloud of buzzing flies. It was a breast-plated torso—headless, limbless, and studded with arrows.

Then he saw the helmeted head. It was perched on a boulder above the path. Pedro's bearded jaws were wide open, as though screaming.

8

Cauchi

By late afternoon Diego looked down on the village the Joara had called Tocae. It sat in a bowl on the far side of the mountaintop on which Pedro Picado had met his grisly death. Five streams roiled down from the surrounding peaks and converged there to form a shallow river, which exited the bowl through a ravine that cleaved a ridge to the west. Wisps of smoke still drifted from the roof holes of the huts, but the streets were deserted. Several storehouses on tall stilts were ablaze, sending wavering plumes of smoke into a sky already dark with angry black clouds.

As his Arabian picked her way down the steep path from the pass, Diego wondered if the Tocae had learned about Pedro's murder. Had they fled, fearing Spanish fury? Diego was distressed to recognize the limits to that fury: his comrades in their shining armor were clearly not so invincible as they had all believed.

Diego and Guillermo hobbled their horses in a field outside Tocae and carried their packs to a hut that appeared hastily vacated, with bowls, tools, and furs strewn around the benches along the wall. Diego cleared off one bench and rolled out his bed. Then he exited into the street of packed earth and looked around for Olivia.

The soldiers were pitching their tents in the grassy central plaza. They seemed subdued, as though somehow sensing the atrocity at the pass, despite the secret burial of Pedro's remains. The vanguard had pledged themselves to conceal the brutal murder so as not to unnerve the other soldiers.

Yet Diego reflected that there were many other reasons for them all to feel unnerved. They were now trapped in a mountain valley with little food. The only exits were through the narrow pass overhead or the ravine to the west. At their backs were hundreds of enraged Joara. Who knew what lay ahead? Diego imagined how furious *he* would feel if a pack of filthy rogues in bizarre outfits descended on the hacienda in Galicia, stole the food stored for winter, assaulted his mother and Leonora, and then chained him by the neck and forced him to carry their baggage to Pontevedra.

A woman's scream pierced the uneasy stillness. The soldiers in the plaza froze, as though acting in one of the tableaux the Count's guests sometimes performed for after-dinner entertainment in his drawing room on the hacienda. Diego wondered if the scream was a signal for a native attack. If the warriors from all the mountain towns joined together, they could easily decimate the one hundred Spaniards now cowering amid the huts of Tocae.

The eerie shriek recurred, echoing along the darkening ridges.

"A panther," called Guillermo from inside their hut.

Diego laughed nervously. "A panther!" he called to the paralyzed soldiers. Abruptly, their activities resumed, everyone pretending his heart had not been lodged in his throat.

Diego spotted Olivia with his basket propped on her shoulder, stumbling up the path from the plaza. "We're in here!" he called, pointing to the hut.

He walked down the path to meet her and took the basket. She lumbered alongside him. When they reached the hut, she entered and collapsed on a bench along the wall.

"Diego, promise me that if you have to abandon me, you'll kill me first," she requested in an exhausted voice. "I don't want to be ripped apart by a panther in the night."

Diego and Guillermo exchanged a glance.

"I mean it," she said urgently. "Promise me."

"I promise. But I'm not going to abandon you, Olivia." Killing her was a promise Diego doubted he could keep, in any case. He tried to imagine, if the day came when she was too weak to travel, choking her with his leather belt or stabbing her with his knife. But he doubted he could do either, however grisly her fate might be if he failed.

One of the blond kitchen boys appeared in the doorway, shifting nervously from foot to foot.

"What is it, lad?" asked Guillermo.

"My master says Don Diego must come right away. He needs him to kill some hogs for dinner."

Grinning at being addressed as Don Diego, Diego followed the boy through the village to an open-air shelter that Alonso had turned into his kitchen. Don Domingo de Santa Cruz de la Sierra was standing with Alonso, talking to him in a low voice.

"How many hogs do you need?" asked Diego.

"Three large ones or five smaller ones," replied Alonso.

Diego raised his eyebrows. "Has Don Sebastian agreed to this?"

Don Domingo shrugged. "There's nothing else to eat here. The fields have been harvested and the storehouses are burning. We'll smoke whatever meat is left over and carry it with us. We simply cannot go on like this."

Diego stood there, unable to decide whether to obey an order, however sensible, that he knew Don Sebastian would condemn.

"As your superior, I order you to butcher those hogs," said Don Domingo pleasantly. "Don't worry, Diego. I'll take full responsibility for this with Don Sebastian."

Diego found many eager helpers among the soldiers as he organized the hog slaughter in a meadow outside the town. They erected three gallows from which to hang the carcasses and dug fire pits beneath them for scorching off the bristles.

Once the hogs had been bled and butchered, the roasts were buried in the ember-filled pits. Some of the starving soldiers cleaned the intestines, while others chopped up the entrails with which to fill them for sausage. The rank terror of their current situation faded from their minds as they occupied themselves with these everyday chores familiar to many from their rural boyhoods.

At dinner Don Sebastian tried to pretend that the pig project had been his idea. His only alternative was to confront Don Domingo with his insubordination. But he was no doubt aware that the soldiers, happy to be so well fed on the roasted pork, would likely protect their new benefactor. Still, it was an insult and a challenge that Diego realized Don Sebastian was not likely to forgive or forget. The only real question was what form his revenge would take and when it would strike.

As Diego, Guillermo, and Olivia lay in their bedrolls late that night, listening to the troops bravely sing drinking songs by a bonfire in the plaza, Diego told Olivia about Pedro's death at the pass. He had promised not to tell the other soldiers, but he had not promised not to tell his own slave. In any case, he needed to discuss the death with Guillermo in order to find the courage to continue on this insane trek.

"Why did the Joara have to be so cruel?" he asked Guillermo, picturing anew the headless, limbless torso hanging from the branch and the helmeted head balanced on the boulder with its terrified expression.

"Are they any crueler than we are?" asked Guillermo.

Diego pictured the iron collars and chains, the amputated ears and noses, the gutted dapple-gray. "I suppose not."

"Don't forget, we *are* invading their homeland."

After a long silence Diego murmured, "I don't want to invade their homeland. All I want is to go back to my own homeland."

"I guess we all do," said Olivia.

"Except Don Sebastian. I gather he has no home to go back to," said Diego.

"He has a home," said Guillermo. "It's called hell."

"Guillermo, you know that I like him."

"That's what worries me most."

At sunup Diego and Guillermo rode among the vanguard along the banks of the frothy river as it swirled westward out of Tocae toward the valley of the Chisca. The cliff alongside them suddenly veered into the trail, plunging right down to the water. They rode out into the shallows and crossed to the other side, where they picked up a new trail. But it ran for only a short distance before it, too, was terminated by a wall of rock. Again, they forded the river to a path on the other side. This continued all day long. Sometimes they had to wade downstream in the racing waters between two cliffs of jagged rocks for long stretches. But the gradual descent was a relief after the steep climb to the pass the previous day.

On the second afternoon out from Tocae, Diego was riding the Arabian along a narrow footpath by the river, through a deep canyon with walls so high on both sides that he could barely see the blue of the sky up above. He realized that this was the perfect spot for an ambush. The vanguard had to pick their way carefully along the rutted path in single file. The march was stretched out over half a mile. The Joara archers had only to stand on the opposite cliff and pick them off one by one. It would be as easy as spearing fish in a fountain.

Diego heard a shrill voice call, "Don Diego?"

Looking down, he saw one of the blond kitchen boys splashing through the shallows below the path. Diego reined in his horse and asked, "What is it, lad?"

"My master told me to come get you, Sire." He was panting, evidently having run from the back of the march. "Your slave woman has fallen down and can't get up."

Diego dismounted and led the Arabian into the water so that those behind him could get by. Don Sebastian was so far ahead that he would never realize that Diego was breaking rank. Unless some passing soldier or craftsman told him, which was unlikely. Ever since the pig roast in the Tocae meadow, it seemed as though Don Sebastian had been demoted to an honorary role, like an elderly uncle, and that the real authority now rested with Don Domingo, a far more compassionate man than Don Sebastian.

Sending the kitchen boy racing back to Alonso, Diego led his horse across shelves of slippery rock along the water's edge until the last of the rear guard had passed him by and the trail was empty. Leading the Arabian back up to the path, he remounted. The horse picked her way among the piles of manure deposited by the hogs and horses. Diego kept scanning the cliff tops anxiously for Joara archers.

Finally, he spotted Alonso, seated in the dirt with the twins standing beside him, their eyes wide with fear. Olivia was lying in the path, her head on Alonso's thigh.

"What's happened?" asked Diego, sliding off the horse.

"She's burning with fever," said Alonso. "She can't even stand up. Everyone said just to leave her. But I thought you should be the one to decide that."

"Thanks for sending for me, Alonso, and for staying with her. I won't forget your kindness. Now go catch up with the others. I'll deal with her."

Alonso seemed relieved. As he turned to go, he looked back with concern.

"Go!" said Diego.

Alonso lurched along the path as fast as his humped back and stunted leg would allow. The twins stumbled along behind him. Diego only hoped they could reach the rear guard before the Joara spotted them, an old man and two young boys, alone and defenseless—pitted against bowmen who rarely missed their targets.

Diego sat in the dirt, lifted Olivia's head, and laid it on his own thigh. He studied her handsome face with its high cheekbones and arched eyebrows. Now what? This was probably as good a place to die as any. Should he resist the encircling Joara with the knife on his hip? Or should he take his own advice to Baltasar after he fell off the *San Jorge*: Don't struggle. That way attackers sometimes got bored and went away. He could speak the Joara dialect, so maybe he could talk his way out of this. Beg for mercy. Perhaps Olivia's dark skin would fascinate them into sparing at least her.

Olivia opened her eyes. They shone unnaturally, glazed with fever. "Kill me, Diego," she murmured. "You promised. Do it now and then go catch up with the others."

He studied her. If he left her and the Joara didn't find her, she would starve or be ripped apart by wolves or panthers. She couldn't walk. He wasn't strong enough to carry her. Don Sebastian's fine-boned Arabian could carry only one of them. He stood up. For a moment he did contemplate climbing up on the horse and leaving Olivia for the Joara. No one would blame him. No one would know. Except for himself and her.

"Give me your hands," he ordered Olivia.

She did so, perhaps believing that he was going to drag her to the river and hold her under. Instead, he hauled her to her feet and half carried her to the horse. Leaning her face first against the horse's side, he said, "Help me, Olivia."

"Help you what?" She opened her eyes and inspected the horse, alarmed.

"Help me get you up on this horse."

"I can't ride a horse, Diego. Just kill me and get it over with."

"I'm not going to kill you, Olivia, and that's final!" Squatting and positioning one shoulder beneath her buttocks, he shoved her upwards with all his might. To his amazement she ended up lying across the saddle on her swollen belly like a sack of feed.

"Swing that leg around so you're straddling the horse's back."

Soon she was sitting in the saddle, hunched over, barely conscious. Diego arranged her striped skirt to cover as much of her long legs as possible.

He took her hands and placed them around the pommel. "Try to hold on there while I lead the horse."

"Maybe you won't kill me, Diego, but Don Sebastian is going to kill *you* once he sees that you're letting me ride his precious horse."

"Now is hardly the time to be worrying about that."

He grabbed the reins and dragged the startled mare down the shadowy pathway beneath the towering cliffs. At each step he expected to be showered with arrows and spears from overhead. But as he pictured Pedro's severed head with its screaming mouth on the ledge overlooking the pass from Joara, he realized that an arrow would be preferable to being captured alive. Diego hated pain. He would be a failure at being tortured. He would betray everyone he knew to avoid it.

He began repeating to himself, in rhythm with his hurrying footsteps, a line from his mother's favorite psalm: "Yea, though I walk through the valley of the shadow of death, I will fear no evil for Thou art with me."

After several hundred repetitions of this brave sentiment, Diego spotted an armed and armored soldier on a horse. Ahead of that soldier were more soldiers. It was the rear guard! Sighing with relief, he trailed the guard out of the canyon and down into the valley in which the rest of the expedition was already setting up camp for the night. The soldiers and slaves paused in their domestic activities to watch Diego lead Don Sebastian's Arabian past them, with Olivia sitting on it, slouched over with her black hair in damp tangles, to the tent that Guillermo had already pitched.

Guillermo looked at Diego disbelievingly when he saw them coming. "Get her off that horse right now!" he muttered. He helped Diego lift Olivia out of the saddle and carry her into the tent, where they lay her on her blanket.

Diego went back outside, mounted the horse, and rode her to the field where the others were hobbled. Juan Bravo, unsaddling Don Sebastian's gelding, looked at him and said, "Don Sebastian will love hearing that an African whore rode his cherished Arabian all afternoon."

Diego shrugged. "Tell Don Sebastian whatever you need to, Juan." His hours of terror, leading the half-dead Olivia beneath cliffs that might have been teeming with Joara warriors who wanted to hack off all his limbs, made anything Don Sebastian might do to him seem insignificant.

After hobbling the horse, he went in search of Dr. Mendez and found him in his tent, looking into a hand mirror and clipping his beard. Dr. Mendez was so heavy that there was room for little else inside his tent. Diego wedged himself into a corner and described what had happened to Olivia.

"I'll give you something for her to drink that may bring down her fever," said Dr. Mendez. "But I'm afraid it's just part of the syndrome."

"What about her baby?"

"She may miscarry. Frankly, it would be a blessing. Babies born to mothers with the pox usually have an awful struggle themselves. Some are stillborn. Others are sick and cry all the time. Some go blind. Usually their mothers are too ill to care for them. It's heartbreaking to watch."

He poured some powder from a bottle into a clay cup and told Diego to add water. He also gave him a tube of the mercury ointment.

"She should apply this to her sores. It could help the baby, if the baby lives. But it may be too late."

Back at the tent Diego helped Olivia drink Dr. Mendez's potion. He also gave her the ointment and told her how to use it. Then he changed into a doublet and went to dine at Don Sebastian's tent, prepared to be berated or punished. Don Sebastian could decapitate him in front of the entire army, for all he cared.

Instead, Don Sebastian was in a good mood. He chatted and joked with the officers and happily defeated Diego in five games of chess afterwards. Diego played even more poorly than usual because he was distracted by trying to figure out what to do about Olivia if she couldn't walk the next day. In his desperation he even considered confiding in Don Sebastian, but he came to his senses in time to remain silent.

During the night Olivia's fever broke, soaking her shift and bedding in sour sweat. The next morning she took her place among the slaves, with Diego's nearly empty basket balanced on her shoulder. Before mounting the Arabian, Diego told her that if she could walk until the lunch break, he would find her so that she could ride the horse for several hours.

"Don't, Diego," she whispered. "It's too dangerous. Who knows what that man would do to us both if he caught me riding his horse. I'll send for you again if I can't manage to walk."

At the end of the afternoon, Diego spotted a rounded mountaintop up ahead. It was so high that its crown rose above the tree line and was carpeted with coarse grass. Although it was nearly twilight down below, the setting sun bathed this bald in gold so that it glowed like a gilded cathedral dome.

When they reached the base of the bald, they discovered a village with no palisade around it. Some fifty huts encircled a grassy central square, which featured a seven-sided council house at one end and a large longhouse at the other.

A giant in a mantle of auburn fur emerged from the council house to greet Don Sebastian, backed by six of his headmen. Studying the white eagle feather in his braid, Diego realized that he was the same man who had helped him translate at Joara. He didn't seem surprised to see them. No doubt he had been forewarned and had decided not to flee, for whatever reasons. He told Don Sebastian that his village was called Cauchi and that he was Cauchi Mico.

A welcoming dinner had already been prepared in the council house. Diego sat on a tiered bench with the officers and pages. Facing them on another bench were the Cauchi headmen. Cauchi Mico, his priest, his war chief, Don Sebastian, Brother Marcos, Don Domingo, and Guillermo sat on benches up front behind a fire that smoldered in a pit in the floor. The smoke rose in a steady column, exiting through a roof hole overhead. After the meal of venison, stewed corn, beans, and squash, Don Sebastian stood up and gave his speech about Cauchi subjugation to Philip II and the Pope.

The Mico nodded his consent a second time, having already given it at Joara. "Since you are now our patrons," said the Mico as Guillermo translated, "will you aid us against our enemies? Warriors from three of our clans will soon attack a Chisca town in the valley to retaliate for the murder of some clan members on a hunting trip."

Don Sebastian hesitated before replying, "Certainly, Cauchi Mico. Captain Melendez, my most valiant officer, will lead twenty of my best soldiers on your mission. My remaining troops will build a fort outside your village."

Strolling alongside Don Sebastian back to their huts afterwards, Diego asked, "Sire, why are we building a fort in this forlorn spot?"

"As another outpost on the route between La Florida and Mexico," he replied. "And to anchor our campaign for Chisca gold. It was near here that the queen of Cofitachequi disappeared with DeSoto's slave. It is possible they never even returned to Cofitachequi. Cauchi Mico may know of their whereabouts. I must figure out what would induce him to tell me where they have gone."

Don Sebastian invited Diego into his borrowed lodge, a spacious hut with walls of wattle and daub and a bark roof. He set his inlaid chessboard on his trestle table and proceeded to demolish Diego in three straight games.

As he stood up to leave, Diego said, "I'm sorry, Sire, that I can't give you more competition."

"You'll soon learn this game, lad. In the meantime, I'll enjoy the slaughter!" He smiled whimsically, contorting the scar that snaked through his graying auburn beard.

As he exited, Diego reflected that since Don Sebastian seemed so cheerful, he must not have been told about Olivia's riding his horse. Either that or he didn't care. Which was it?

Diego and Guillermo were seated in Don Sebastian's lodge listening to Captain Melendez describe to the assembled officers the upcoming march upon the Chisca: "The Cauchi war chief says that we will descend a narrow valley and cross a forested plain to a river they call the Nolichucky. This river flows through a canyon that opens onto the field in which the palisaded Chisca town sits. They estimate that we will return in eight days' time."

"Take any side trips necessary to view the Chisca gold mines," ordered Don Sebastian from his campstool, with one hand propped on his hip, as though posing for a portrait.

"Yes, Sire."

"We look forward to your return, Captain Melendez," Don Sebastian said. "We will await news of your victory over the Chisca and information concerning the exact location of their gold mines."

Diego and Guillermo exited from the lodge with the other officers. The Cauchi warriors were secluded in their seven-sided council house, performing purification rites for the upcoming battle. Their drums had been echoing throughout the valley for three days running.

"That drumming is getting on my nerves," murmured Guillermo. "They must have committed a lot of sins if they have to dance for so long to expiate them."

Diego smiled. "I guess I should apologize for a second time, Guillermo, that I get to stay here while you wander in the wilderness."

Guillermo shrugged. "I've already told you that I want Don Sebastian to regard me as dispensable, so that I can go back home to Blue Heron."

May Guillermo live so long, Diego prayed silently.

Diego watched the loin-clothed warriors trot down the path out of the village. They were painted red all over, with black circles around their eyes. Squares of dried venison jelly and parched cornmeal bulged in pouches at their waists. Each wore a quiver of arrows on one shoulder and clutched a bow and a war club in his hands. Diego waved farewell to Guillermo, who rode alongside Melendez. Melendez sat rigid in his Moorish saddle, his eyes grim above his grinning moustache. Behind them marched fifteen armored infantrymen, a handler and his mastiff, and two riflemen with the fuses on their rifles smoldering. Diego felt envious that they would get to see the Chisca mines. But what if they met an end similar to Pedro Picado's instead?

Diego joined the remaining Spaniards at the altar Brother Marcos had set up at one end of the Cauchi council house. The golden cross gleamed behind him as he petitioned God for protection for their comrades.

Then he delivered a long sermon on lust, which concluded, "We saw the wages of our lust at Joara. We lost several of our bravest soldiers to disease, and we alienated our allies, the Joara. We must now look to a new Paymaster. Savages or not, these Cauchi women are not to be forced. They are under the protection of Our Holy Virgin. To insult them is to insult the very Mother of Christ."

As the soldiers filed forward for communion, Diego calculated that with thirty men left in the fort at Joara and twenty en route to the Chisca, they were down to some eighty at Cauchi. But the woods were full of hundreds of angry Joara and any allies they had managed to assemble.

Don Sebastian was riding his ebony gelding in the plaza, illustrating for Cauchi Mico and his remaining warriors the feints and charges of mounted warfare. Diego sat beside the Mico, whose huge frame teetered precariously on a campstool. He was wrapped in his cape of auburn fur, his expression indifferent. His eyes were so close set that they appeared to be trying to stare at each other across the bridge of his prominent nose. Horses were said to intimidate natives, but Cauchi Mico appeared unimpressed.

Don Sebastian dismounted, tossing his reins to Juan Bravo. Sitting beside the Mico, he awaited his reaction. Receiving only silence, he said, "I could arrange for you to own one of my horses, Cauchi Mico."

Diego translated this, wondering if Don Sebastian intended to give him the Arabian. Maybe he knew the Arabian had been defiled by Olivia, and this was his way of ridding himself of the mare while gaining the Mico's good will. But wasn't the Mico too large to ride the graceful Arabian?

"The price would be too high," replied Cauchi Mico.

"It would be a gift."

"We learned from DeSoto that a gift from a Spaniard is the honey that heralds the sting of the bee."

"But I am not DeSoto," said Don Sebastian.

"Yet you are a Spaniard."

"And should I judge you by the Joara who, as you no doubt know, murdered one of my soldiers at their pass?"

"Perhaps," replied Cauchi Mico. "If you are a man of wisdom."

The two men locked gazes for a long moment.

"Tell me this," said Don Sebastian. "Do you know the whereabouts of the woman who was queen at Cofitachequi when DeSoto passed through? She wore the skin of an albino deer."

Cauchi Mico shook his head.

"Her consort after DeSoto might have had black skin and curly hair."

"No such woman exists in these mountains," Cauchi Mico assured him.

Don Sebastian fought to conceal his disappointment. Diego wasn't sure whether this disappointment, evident to Diego if not to the Mico, was due to his believing Cauchi Mico, or to his realizing that his ploys to win the Mico's confidence had failed.

Back at his lodge Don Sebastian invited Diego inside. Still wearing his breastplate, he lay on his cot and asked Diego to rub his temples.

"Would you like me to unstrap your breastplate first, Sire?"

"No. I prefer to wear it."

Perplexed, Diego sat at the head of the cot and proceeded to massage the commander's aching head. Don Sebastian had taken to wearing his breastplate at all times, indoors and out, as though fearing an attack not just from the Joara, but also from the Cauchi— and maybe even from his own men.

Satisfied with the massage, Don Sebastian gestured for him to recline on the carpet alongside the cot.

As Diego lay there in the dim light, Don Sebastian began to talk in the low, tortured voice he seemed to reserve for the times when his headaches were at their worst.

"No doubt you've wondered about this ugly scar across my face?"

"No, Sire," murmured Diego politely, half asleep.

"No need to dissemble, boy. Everyone stares at it, but none dares to ask its cause. I will now tell you the tale that few have heard."

Despite his curiosity, Diego didn't really want to hear it. Every time Don Sebastian confided secrets to him, he was cold and withdrawn afterwards, as though he hated Diego for having witnessed him being human. But there seemed to be no stopping him.

"When I was fourteen," he began, looking up at the tent roof, "my father took me to a grandee at court in Valladolid. He was a bent old man with a pointed gray beard and cloudy irises. He accepted me as his page. For the first time in my life I experienced kindness from an older person, and I flourished like a plant brought into the sunshine from a cave. All I had ever known was indifference from my mother and violence from my father. But the grandee played chess with me by the hour and showed great interest in my plans to become a conquistador.

"Sadly for an old man, he was in love with a serving girl at his palace. Her name was Elvira. At that age I was growing so fast that I was hungry all the time, and Elvira was constantly slipping me choice bits of food from the pantries. She was my friend, nothing more. But he became convinced that she resisted him because she loved me. In reality, she regarded him as nothing but an old fool.

"One night I awakened to find him looming over my bed with a stiletto in one hand. He slashed my cheek with his knife, saying, 'Now we'll see how pretty Elvira finds you!' The next morning he sent me back to my father.

"My father was outraged—with me, not with the deranged old man. He insisted I had purposefully alienated the grandee, who could have showered us with the wealth and honors my father had always dreamed of. He bought me a post on DeSoto's expedition and said he hoped I would rot in a swamp in La Florida. I never laid eyes on that old grandee again, though I will bear his brand to the grave. Nor did I ever see my father again. He died while I was in La Florida."

As he fingered the gnarled scar across his cheek, Diego said, "I'm sorry, Sire. That's a very sad story."

"Far worse things happen to people," he snapped. "I survived it. Save your sympathy for someone who wants it. You may go now."

As Diego walked back to his hut, he tried to analyze what had happened as though it were a chess problem. Don Sebastian had appealed for sympathy. When Diego offered it, he rejected it and acted offended. Like much of Don Sebastian's behavior, it made no sense.

Diego and Baltasar stood on the riverbank watching the Portuguese, who had just worked all day on the fort, frolic in the chilly shallows with several young Cauchi women. The afternoon sun beat down from a hazy blue sky as they drifted downstream in derelict canoes, laughing and splashing, teasing and taunting, babbling to each other in their mutually incomprehensible tongues. After Brother Marcos's stern lecture, the soldiers were trying their best to charm their way into the good graces of the native women rather than simply taking them by force.

Diego smiled at their antics, watching water bead on the breasts of the women as the men maneuvered like caballeros cutting out steers to be branded. He wanted to join them. But he also wanted to stay true to Leonora, half a world away. More to the point, he had no idea how to persuade a girl to sneak into a corncrib with him or what to do once he got her there. Olivia could probably offer him some pointers. But she now regarded men and their lust with such disgust that he avoided the topic. She spent most of her time lying inside the hut. Sometimes she made weak attempts to perform chores, so that Diego wouldn't appear quite so ridiculous to the others for having bought her. He supposed what he felt for her was the higher form of love, which the priests recommended as leading to salvation: he wanted to help her, without expecting anything in return. It felt nice. Still, he would like one day to know what the lower forms of love felt like.

Leaving behind the Portuguese lechers, Diego decided to follow to its source a creek that flowed alongside the village and emptied into the river. Its water seemed warmer than that of the other nearby streams. It might yield some unusual fish for Don Sebastian's and Olivia's dinners. He fetched his hook and line from his hut and summoned Baltasar, who lay asleep beside Olivia, toward whom he had developed a great devotion.

As Diego and Baltasar waded upstream, the water became increasingly warm. Passing through a cleft carved by the current through sheer rock, they arrived at a stretch of eddies that had been floored and sided with flat stones. From them bristled colonies of black mussels. Stooping, Diego filled his leather satchel with the dark shells while Baltasar lapped playfully at the briskly flowing water.

Farther upstream, Diego reached a dam of stones. Scaling it, he discovered a deep pool behind it, which was steaming like a soup kettle. Opposite the dam a spring bubbled out from a limestone cliff. He circled the pool, squatted, and held his hand before its mouth. The water spurting from the depths of the earth was hot.

Noticing that the sun was about to plunge behind the bald, he headed back to camp with Baltasar trotting beside him.

At dinner that night in Don Sebastian's lodge, Alonso served the mussels Diego had gathered, steamed in a broth with crisp wild tubers contributed by a Cauchi woman. Diego noticed that Don Sebastian waited until the others had sampled the stew before he himself did so, as though to make sure Alonso wasn't trying to poison him. As they all critiqued the strange new vegetable, Don Sebastian removed an oblong gray pearl from his mouth.

Passing it around the table, he said, "It's similar to those the queen at Cofitachequi hung around DeSoto's neck."

Surrounded by his armed bodyguards, Don Sebastian inspected the mussel beds the following afternoon. He seemed annoyed to find so few shells. Nevertheless, he ordered Tomas de Carrion and Juan Bravo to collect them in their baskets.

"Take them back to camp and pry them apart with your knives," he ordered. "The natives will tell you to throw them into the fire to open them. But fire scorches the pearls and ruins their value."

Don Sebastian, Diego, and four bodyguards continued up the creek to the dam and pool that Diego had discovered the previous day. As they stood on the bank inspecting the steaming water, Don Sebastian ordered Diego and the guards to scale the surrounding cliffs and keep watch while he bathed.

Reaching the ridge, Diego sat on a cushion of fallen leaves. Baltasar scurried around poking his long nose here and there. All Diego could see from his vantage point was wave after wave of trees with bare branches, interspersed with pointed evergreens. He wondered how Guillermo and the others were faring with the Chisca. The eight days designated for their foray had just expired. The delay in their return might mean they had found the gold mines. If so, everyone on the march would soon be rich. This whole grueling journey would seem worth it, assuming they could make it back to Santa Elena alive with their stashes of gold intact.

He heard Don Sebastian calling for the guards, so he got to his feet, whistled for Baltasar, and descended the cliff. He found Don Sebastian shirtless, fastening his trousers. Although his torso was lean and taut, the wrinkles and discolorations of his skin betrayed his age. The scar across his cheek was minor compared to a puckered one in the center of his chest, probably from the arrow shot by the archer in the lake during DeSoto's march. Faint scars also striped his back, perhaps from his father's strap.

Don Sebastian pulled on his linen shirt and buckled his breastplate over it. Then he slipped his metal helmet over his graying auburn hair, damp from his swim. They walked back to camp, the only sound the tromping of their boots on the forest floor and the plaintive call of a mourning dove from a branch overhead.

In the cooking area near Don Sebastian's lodge, the pages, along with Alonso and the blond twins, were wrenching open the mussels with their knives. They paused to watch Don Sebastian stride toward his lodge in his silver breastplate. Diego trailed him to the doorway, uncertain whether to follow him inside.

Don Sebastian turned back to glance at him irritably. "What is it you want?"

"I await your command, Sire."

"Help them with the mussels." He gestured distastefully toward the scene of the carnage. "Juan, come with me."

Juan Bravo laid aside his knife, glancing at Diego with a sly smile. He stood up and followed Don Sebastian inside his lodge.

Drawing his knife from its scabbard on his hip, Diego squatted by the pile of black shells and picked one up. Why had Don Sebastian rejected him in favor of Juan? It was true that the cache of mussels was small, but surely that wasn't his fault. Nor was it his fault that Captain Melendez hadn't yet returned with reports of caverns full of gold. Had someone finally told the commander about Olivia's having ridden his horse? Or was he still sulking over Diego's role in the slaughter of the hogs at Tocae? Who knew what this strange man might be thinking or feeling? His unpredictability was probably the source of his power over others, though that power seemed to be dwindling of late.

Watching Alonso, Diego copied his technique for prying his shell open. Poking and prodding through the still-throbbing gelatinous mess inside, he found a small grey pearl. He plucked it out with his fingertips and dropped it into the pottery bowl beside Alonso. Then he tossed the shell onto the mounting pile.

Some Cauchi stood watching. One warrior named Bear Claw, who had scars down his cheeks, arms, and chest, wore an expression of outrage at the wastage of the sprung mussels, which lay dying by the hundreds in the dirt.

When Diego arrived at Don Sebastian's lodge for dinner that night, Juan Bravo and Tomas de Carrion crossed their halberds in his path.

"There will be no dinner tonight," announced Tomas. "Don Sebastian is unwell."

"Would you ask him if he needs me for anything?" requested Diego.

"His instructions are to admit no one—not even you, Swine King."

Diego waited, knowing that Don Sebastian lay within, able to hear this confrontation and intervene if he wished. But he remained silent.

Diego went in search of Lucas's fire and its pot of stew. He would eat some himself and then carry a bowl to Olivia in his hut. He greeted Lucas and Nicolas Navarro, who scooted down the log by their fire to make room for him.

On the fifth morning past the day designated for the war party's return, Diego reported to Don Sebastian's lodge to find him lying on his cot in his breastplate and helmet, just as he had been every morning since the deadline had passed. Diego shifted uneasily from foot to foot on the Oriental carpet, awaiting instructions. The previous mornings Don Sebastian had curtly dismissed him for the rest of the day.

Probably no one except the pages and himself realized it, but their commander was in a state of collapse. It was alarming. Eighty men were essentially leaderless here in this wilderness, surrounded by natives who wanted them dead. Diego was beginning to wonder whether he should mention Don Sebastian's bizarre behavior to Dr. Mendez or to Don Domingo. Or were they already aware of it?

Tomas entered the lodge to announce the arrival of a messenger from the Spanish governor in St. Augustine.

Blinking, Don Sebastian rolled off his cot. He removed his helmet and combed his scrambled hair with his fingers. Then he stroked his shaggy beard. Sitting behind the trestle table, he said to Tomas, "Show him in."

The man was splattered with mud. He look exhausted, having ridden alone all the way from Santa Elena through dangerous territory in only two weeks. He stared at the disheveled Don Sebastian with wide eyes, as though seeing a ghost.

"You may speak," said Don Sebastian.

"Sire, a fleet of French warships is headed for Santa Elena. The governor orders that you return there immediately with your troops to assist in its defense."

"Give him some food and a place to sleep," he told Tomas.

When Tomas and the messenger had left, Don Sebastian slumped at the table and buried his face in his hands. "I must obey the governor," he murmured, as though to himself. "But if I return now, my expedition is a failure. I have found no gold, and I have not yet completed the trail to Mexico."

Jumping up, he stalked around the lodge like a caged war dog. Leaning out the doorway, he called to Juan Bravo, "Summon my officers."

To Diego he said, "You are dismissed."

Don Sebastian's meeting lasted for hours, erupting now and then in shouts that Diego couldn't make out as he lay on his bedroll in the hut with Olivia and Baltasar napping nearby. He was surprised not to have been included in this meeting. True, no translations were required since no Cauchi were present. But Don Sebastian had been treating him almost like an advisor ever since Oristatown, requesting his presence at all the meetings, whatever language they were conducted in, and asking his opinions afterwards.

Diego was worried about Guillermo. Would Don Sebastian return to Santa Elena before learning the fate of the missing men? Surely he wouldn't abandon Captain Melendez, his favorite officer. And then he remembered what had happened to Don Sebastian's favorite mare in the bullring at Santo Domingo.

The next morning Don Sebastian summoned the entire army to the plaza. Attired in quilted armor of burgundy cotton, in addition to his helmet and breastplate, he announced their immediate return to Santa Elena. Diego felt a surge of excitement. If he could make it back to Santa Elena and survive the French attack, maybe he could find work on a ship bound for Spain. Although he had accumulated no riches, all he wanted now was to get back home to the hacienda and to Leonora. He might be able to figure out how to get Olivia back home to her family as well.

"Ten soldiers will be left here at Cauchi to complete Fort San Pablo and to staff the fort," he continued, "along with Captain Melendez and his patrol upon their return from the Chisca."

Diego was shocked to hear that Don Sebastian was evidently abandoning his old friend, Captain Melendez.

Don Sebastian gestured to Tomas de Carrion, who stepped forward to read the list of the ten men who would stay. As Tomas announced the names of these unfortunate ones, Diego realized that several had somehow displeased Don Sebastian. Julio Gomez had mistaken copper for gold at Joara. Don Domingo had repeatedly challenged Don Sebastian's decisions and currently enjoyed much more popularity with the troops than did Don Sebastian. The four Portuguese cavalrymen had probably asked to stay, lending credence to the rumor that they were fleeing the Inquisition. Brother Marcos had no doubt volunteered to remain, intent on martyrdom. But Diego couldn't imagine what the crossbowman Nicolas Navarro or the stonecutter Pascuale Sanchez had done to merit inclusion on this roll of rejects.

The last name Tomas read was Diego's. Diego felt his face go pale. Lucas caught his eye, looking horrified.

When Diego arrived at Don Sebastian's lodge after the muster, Tomas de Carrion and Juan Bravo were guarding the doorway with crossed halberds. They greeted him with smiles like those on the mouths of the possums Baltasar liked to harass in the woods.

Don Sebastian called for them to let him enter. He was sitting on a stool in his breastplate while Lope Mendez trimmed his beard. At a sign from Don Sebastian, Lope packed up his leather satchel and exited, glancing back at Diego with a sympathetic frown.

"What is it you want?" asked Don Sebastian, not meeting his gaze.

"Sire, I'm curious to know why I've been assigned to remain at Cauchi."

"Because you know the native dialects. This is why I trained you thus."

"Yet Guillermo is among those returning from the Chisca."

"We do not know that he will return."

"You believe our men to have been slaughtered, Sire?"

"Perhaps."

"Yet you leave in this fort only ten soldiers, Sire?" Diego was astonished by his own insolence. But he had nothing to lose. Don Sebastian had already relegated him to the wilderness.

"The Cauchi are our allies, and they are formidable warriors."

"Yet many of their best warriors marched on the Chisca. They may be dead as well."

"I have no choice. The governor requires my troops as defense against the French."

"I had thought, Sire," said Diego, " that you were training me as your page."

"Alas, the moment has come for us to part."

"But why?" Diego dropped the "Sire." His patron had become his executioner.

"You have prospered from my favor, have you not, Diego? From a pig sty to a cushion on the carpet of your commander is an impressive achievement, especially for one so young."

"I thought we were friends, Don Sebastian."

"*Friends*?" He laughed incredulously. "Because of your youth, I found you decorative. But you mean no more to me than this carpet beneath my feet. I take pleasure in looking at it and walking on it. But like Cortes, Pizarro, and DeSoto, I am one of the great conquistadors of the Spanish Empire. Why should I interest myself in a boy of no importance?"

Diego studied Don Sebastian. "That's what I've been asking myself this whole time."

"You may go now," said Don Sebastian.

Back in his hut Diego plopped down on his bedroll, his heart numb. The man he had cared for like a second father now wanted him dead. Why had he not heeded everyone's warnings—or even his own perception that Don Sebastian needed to defy anyone's expectations of him? Diego knew he would never emerge from this wasteland alive. Never lay eyes on Galicia again. Never court Leonora nor hold her in his arms.

Olivia stirred, sat up, and looked at him. "What's wrong, Diego?"

He sighed. "Olivia, although I meant well, I'm afraid I've condemned us both to a horrible death in this godforsaken place."

"What's happened?"

He told her. "Maybe I can persuade some soldier to take you back to Santa Elena with him."

"It's my fault Don Sebastian has turned on you like this. I never should have agreed to ride his wretched horse. I'm sorry, Diego."

"I doubt if that had anything to do with it, Olivia. One way or another, he wanted to get rid of me. I have no idea why. But there's no reason why you have to share my fate."

"I'd never make it back to Santa Elena alive. Since I'm dying anyway, I might as well die here with you."

"Whatever you want."

"Are you saying that I'm a free woman?"

Diego smiled. "Yes, I guess you're free to choose where to die, Olivia."

He got up and left the hut. Finding Lucas plastering the palisade of the new fort, he followed him to a log by the rushing river. They both sat down.

"It's a death sentence," agreed Lucas. "I went to Don Sebastian and asked to trade places with you. But he refused."

Diego looked at him, amazed. "Thank you, Uncle. But I would have refused, too. You have a wife, soon to give birth, who's waiting for you in Santo Domingo. But I don't understand. Why would Don Sebastian grant me all those privileges, only to condemn me to death?"

"You yourself have been known to gorge a hog on all his favorite foods prior to slitting his throat."

"Thanks," said Diego. "That's a nice comparison. What makes me saddest of all is to know that I'll never again sit by the hearth with my mother. Never return to Galicia with the wealth that would have won me the hand of Leonora."

Lucas studied his clay-caked hands. Finally he said, "Perhaps you'll die here, Diego. We may never meet again. Therefore, I must tell you something."

Diego looked at him questioningly.

"You're upset because you can't return to Galicia. I need to tell you that you could never have gone back in any case."

"What?"

"You've never understood why your mother wanted you to come with me on this expedition, so I must explain: My sister Manuela is not your mother. Nor am I your uncle. And your father didn't die in battle in the Netherlands."

Diego stared at him.

"Manuela was a serving maid in Pontevedra, just as she has always told you. But we served your parents, not the Count. Your father was a physician to the old Count, Leonora's grandfather. Your grandfather was a Jew, and your father converted to escape the Inquisition. Yet he had many enemies who envied his success. They convinced the Inquisitors that your parents were judaizing in secret. Your parents' townhouse was sold to their foes at a bargain price to finance their trials."

"My mother was also Jewish?"

"Her parents were also conversos. Your parents' cook testified under torture that your mother never served pork at her table. This was true. Neither of your parents had grown up eating it, and it didn't appeal to them. The Inquisitors seized on this as proof of their Hebraic practices. The Count made you his swineherd to protect you from such charges."

"How old was I when they were seized?"

"Two. We've often wondered how much you remember."

"I remember nothing."

"The soldiers pounded on the door while you and your parents were at dinner. Your mother shoved you beneath Manuela's skirt. 'You must remain as still as a stone statue,' she told you. 'No matter what you hear, son, don't make a sound.' Then she opened the door. She and your father exited calmly. Manuela and I rushed you to the young Count. He sent the three of us to his hacienda outside Ourense."

"What happened to my parents?"

Lucas frowned. "They appeared before the Tribunal in Valladolid. They were tortured. They could have saved themselves by accusing others, but they refused to. The Count sent me to their auto da fe, hoping my presence might comfort them. They marched to their pyres in pointed hats and yellow robes painted with flames. I was as close to their path as I could manage. I caught your father's eye. By my nod I hope he knew you were safe. They were bound to stakes within sight of one another. As the flames licked their calves and ignited their robes, they were gazing into one another's eyes."

A wave of nausea swept over Diego.

Lucas laid an arm across his shoulders. "They were wonderful people, Diego."

He reached under his shirt to extract a leather pouch on a cord around his neck. Opening it, he dumped out a pendant of red stone on a gold chain. "This was your mother's ruby. Manuela told me to give it to you when I told you this story. I should have told you sooner, but I was waiting for a right moment that never came."

Diego handed it back. "Lucas, if you get back to Galicia, please give this to Leonora."

Lucas smiled. "Manuela predicted you would do that. She told me to insist that you sell it and make a life for yourself here in the New World. But I'll tell Dona Leonora your story, if I'm ever able to."

"Tell her I'll come back someday if I can." His eyes filled with tears.

"Diego, you must never go back. Somehow Cristobal knows about your parents. That's why he called you a Christ Killer that day. He'll see to it that you're seized by the Inquisition. In any case, the Count would never allow his daughter to marry the son of executed conversos. You must make your life here. And you must release Leonora to her own fate."

"Cristobal is not her fate. She loves me. She told me so as we were leaving for Seville."

"Is it love to want her to waste her life waiting for a man who may never return? Waiting for a man who would condemn her and your future children to a lifetime of danger? People can love more than once, and so will she. And so will you."

"*You* can tell me this, who are wasting away to a ghost over Dona Catalina?"

Lucas shrugged. "I tell you what would be best for you, Diego. But I know you'll do as your heart, not your brain, commands."

Diego smiled, tears dripping from his chin. "Just as you have."

"Just as I have," agreed Lucas. "I do believe that we both might just be dumb enough to perish for love."

"What about Baltasar? Could I keep him with me?"

"I'd like you to. But I guess you have to ask Don Sebastian."

"He'll refuse. He wants me dead. I know too much about him. I've seen him sick and sad and weak."

"You're probably right. But ask him anyway. Maybe he'll recall that he had great affection for you until recently. If a man like that is capable of affection."

Tomas de Carrion and Juan Bravo crossed their halberds in Diego's path at the entrance to Don Sebastian's lodge, but Don Sebastian called from within for them to let him enter.

Don Sebastian was lying on his cot, a damp cloth that reeked of vinegar knotted around his forehead. Diego looked down at the pinched mouth and squinting eyes, the grizzled beard and the breast-plate he never removed, which looked as uncomfortable as a hermit's hair shirt. Was his betrayal of Diego causing him to suffer as well?

"What is it you want?" he asked weakly.

"I want to ask you to leave me my dog, Don Sebastian. I have lost my homeland, my mother, the lady I love, my plans for the future, and the regard of my commander. At least leave me Baltasar." He kept picturing Pedro Picado's torso swaying above the trail through the Joara pass. Baltasar couldn't save him from a similar fate. But surely he deserved a fighting chance.

"Done." Don Sebastian's eyes were tightly shut, as though he were wincing. "I am also leaving you a dozen hogs. And you may keep the Arabian. She is too fine-boned for anyone heavier than you or your slave girl."

Diego studied him. So he knew about Olivia. Is that why he had turned on Diego? But it didn't sound as though he cared about Olivia's riding his horse.

"Allow me one last question," said Diego. Not waiting for permission, he posed it: "What crime have I committed, other than doing all I could to make your life more pleasant?"

"The more you demand an explanation, the angrier I become," he murmured.

"I have demanded nothing. I have merely requested clarification, as one friend does to another. And know, Don Sebastian, that you will never again have as loyal a friend as I."

"I have heard otherwise."

"Because you have heard lies from those who envied me, you are condemning me to the wilderness? Just as your father did you? Just as you did your son? And will you go through the rest of your life committing on others the crimes that were committed on yourself?"

"Get out!" snarled Don Sebastian.

As he turned to go, Diego took a last look at this man he had served, admired, and loved. He lay as pale and rigid as a marble statue on a catafalque, eyes closed and lips compressed.

"Imagine," marveled Juan as Diego brushed past the two pages. "From Pig Boy to page and back again, all in less than a year. What a miraculous feat for one so basely born!" He swept his bobbed orange hair off his forehead with the back of one hand.

"Yes, how the mighty have fallen," lisped Tomas.

Diego studied Tomas's wavy chestnut hair and bulging belly, his simpering smile and hate-filled eyes. "Vipers coil together," Diego observed, "and will someday sink their fangs of venom into one another."

9

Land of the Lost

D iego stood next to last in the line of men in the Cauchi plaza who were passing one by one before Don Sebastian to deliver their pledges to defend Fort San Pablo to the death. Don Sebastian wore the same etched bronze breastplate and scarlet-plumed helmet as he had on the Seville quay when Diego had first locked eyes with him a lifetime ago. The other soldiers stood at attention in formation behind him, ready to depart for Santa Elena. The bald loomed overhead, bathed in sunlight.

"Do you so swear?" Don Sebastian demanded of Diego, his eyes averted. He looked almost sane today compared to last night and the previous week. Maybe he was as relieved to be returning to civilization as Diego was distressed not to be. "Under pain of perjury and of infamy and of falling into less value?"

"I so swear," Diego murmured, trying to catch Don Sebastian's eye for a final farewell.

Don Sebastian looked past him to Gaspar de los Reyes, the carpenter who resembled a friendly carp. He had recently lost his leg to gangrene from an infected blister. Dr. Mendez had performed the amputation while Gaspar was in a drunken stupor. Aided by a crutch, he lurched forward on the new wooden stump he had carved for himself. It was doubtful he could provide much help against attacking Chisca, but it was certain he could never hobble all the way back to Santa Elena.

As Diego moved aside, he glanced at Juan Bravo and Tomas de Carrion. They stood in the front row of troops in their dress armor looking pleased with themselves. They had won this largely silent struggle, just as they had predicted they would.

As the rear guard rode up the riverside trail that led through Tocae to Cofitachequi and back to Santa Elena, Diego surveyed his new home—and probable gravesite. Cauchi sat along a swift river with high cliffs on either shore and the bald overhead. The new log fort stood at the western end of the narrow valley, surrounded by harvested fields.

Among the remaining Cauchi were the women and children, the old and ill, and the men who did women's work, plus some seventy warriors from clans not involved in the Chisca dispute. En route to the village from the west were either twenty Spanish soldiers and thirty Cauchi warriors—or an untold number of Chisca warriors intent on destruction. Several hundred Joara warriors might also be closing in from the east. To defend Fort San Pablo were two arquebuses, seventy-five pounds of powder and sixty pounds of lead, two crossbows with 120 bolts, a few halberds and swords, the Cauchi's sticks and stones, five horses, Baltasar, and ten Spanish and Portuguese rejects. Who knew what role the Cauchi might play? Were they now friend or foe? Had he been they, Diego doubted he would feel much enthusiasm for helping to defend a bunch of abandoned Spanish invaders.

Diego and Baltasar hiked up the steep trail to the crown of the bald. Standing in the coarse grass that lay wind-flattened like scythed wheat, Diego looked out over the mountains that rippled row upon row to the western horizon, where they abruptly fell off into a golden valley through which snaked several tawny rivers. Smoke from a couple of distant fires curled skywards. Somewhere out there were Melendez, Guillermo, and the others. But were they alive or dead?

In the opposite direction, Don Sebastian and Lucas were marching double-time to Santa Elena. If Diego could have seen far enough, he would have glimpsed the sea, upon which Francisco was piloting his treasure-laden caravel back to Spain. Across those endless waters lay Galicia, where Leonora was either still watching the Great Bear and waiting for him, or was already trying to make the best of it with Cristobal.

Bending to stroke Baltasar's head, Diego reflected that he had left Galicia a swineherd and had become an interpreter and confessor to a mad conquistador. He had left speaking Castilian and the Galician patois and was now fluent in French and three native dialects as well. He had left a Spanish Catholic, the son of a soldier and a serving maid. But he now knew himself to be the son of Jewish conversos. He had left loving Leonora. He had come also to love a man who now wished him dead, as well as an enslaved African woman and a French Protestant sodomite.

Raising his hand, he studied Francisco's ring as it glinted in the sunlight. He had never found that peak of crystal. He had found instead cruelty, horror, and betrayal. He no longer knew what to make of this species to which he belonged. It was not so much that he feared his upcoming death. But he did fear the torture that might precede it. And he would lament having to exit this earth in a state of such bewilderment.

Diego was awakened in the barracks within the palisade of Fort San Pablo by the growling and whining of Baltasar. Sitting up, he heard pounding at the barred gate, running feet, and hushed voices. His scalp prickling with fear, he pulled on his clothes and dashed into the yard, where he nearly collided with a panting Guillermo. They threw their arms around each other.

"Praise be to God!" exclaimed Diego. "I was afraid I'd never see you again."

"You nearly didn't. But I have to sleep. Then I'll tell you the whole horrible story. I've been running for three days."

"At least tell me this: Where are the others?"

Guillermo shook his head. "All dead. It was a slaughter."

Diego struggled to take this in—both the loss of his comrades and also what that meant for his own fate.

Guillermo fell to his knees. "I must sleep," he muttered, collapsing in the dirt.

Diego dragged him into the barracks and stretched him out on a bench along the wall, covering him with a fur.

The next morning Cauchi Mico, his headmen, the remaining Cauchi warriors, and the abandoned Spanish soldiers assembled on the tiered benches in the seven-sided council house to hear Guillermo's account of the attack. Diego stood beside him and interpreted his Cauchi into Spanish for the other soldiers: "To reach their village we passed one at a time through a narrow chute between two cliffs. They dropped boulders on us. Several were crushed. Others were impaled by arrows as we emerged from this ravine.

"The Chisca village was surrounded by a high stockade with a tiny entry door. We laid siege, setting their rush roofs afire with arrows bound with dried moss. We could hear their screams and smell their flesh burning. We tried, without success, to drag down their palisade with our horses.

"The Cauchi had never before encountered soldiers whose goal was total obliteration. Their war chief and I tried to persuade Melendez to retreat, but he refused.

"Once the Chisca realized that they would eventually be destroyed, their village fell silent. We wondered if they had departed during the night. After breaking down the gate, we found only a few famished curs prowling the streets. When we entered their council house, we discovered the Chisca sprawled on benches and lying on the floor. The women, children, and elders had been strangled. Some warriors were impaled on arrows. Others were dangling by their necks on their bowstrings from the ceiling beams.

"As we set this charnel house on fire, the Cauchi scouts informed us that a war party from other Chisca towns was headed down the valley toward us. Before we could retreat, the fields outside the palisade filled with archers, and we were trapped inside this village of death. By day the Chisca shot arrows as plentiful as flocks of migrating birds. By night they danced, keeping us awake with their chants and drums. One by one our warriors and soldiers fell. Finally, the Chisca managed to climb the village walls. They fell upon us with their scalping knives.

"They shoved pine splinters under Captain Melendez's skin. They set these on fire and forced him to dance. Then they stretched him over a bonfire in his armor, which heated up like an oven. They amputated each digit and limb while he was still alive. Finally, they ripped off the top of his head. He was a brave man even in death. He never uttered a sound throughout all this agony.

"They didn't harm me," concluded Guillermo, "because I figured out a few words of their language and pleaded for mercy. A Chisca headman who had lost a son during the battle decided to adopt me. As we marched toward his village, I escaped. But having destroyed thirty Cauchi warriors, they will now come here to claim their women, children, and goods."

As the Cauchi discussed the situation among themselves, the soldiers looked at one another.

"What are our chances of defending Fort San Pablo against several hundred warriors?" asked Nicholas Navarro.

"We could always go back to Santa Elena," suggested Pascuale Sanchez, the stonemason.

"If we show up there, we'll be hanged as deserters," cautioned Domingo de Santa Cruz de la Sierra, whom Don Sebastian had appointed as commander of the San Pablo garrison, all ten of them. "Remember our vow?"

"We could join forces with the soldiers at Fort San Juan in Joara," proposed Julio Gomez. "Would that be considered desertion?"

"We must honor our pledge," said Brother Marcos, "and beseech God for succor as we face our deaths."

"You may like the idea of having your limbs hacked off, Brother Marcos," snapped Gaspar de los Reyes, "but I sure as hell don't. Losing one leg is enough for me."

As the soldiers argued, Cauchi Mico stood up, as enormous as a bear in his fur cape. He signaled for silence. With Guillermo translating, he said, "Your fort is useless. You are ten warriors and we are seventy, facing Chisca as thick on the ground as crows in new corn. Ever since DeSoto's time, we have been known as a tribe who aided the Spaniards. The Chisca have long wished to destroy us. So you must flee quickly and save yourselves."

"We cannot leave here," explained Don Domingo. "We have pledged to our king, our God, and our commander to remain in this fort until ordered to depart."

"To stay is to die," said Cauchi Mico. "We Cauchi will not stay. We will cross the mountains to our winter hunting camp. We have need of warriors to replace those who have fallen. Our clan mothers will adopt any of you who wish to make our path your own."

The Spaniards talked urgently among themselves, reviewing all the options and arguing loudly with one another.

Don Domingo finally stood up and replied, "Cauchi Mico, your people shame us with their generosity. Guillermo Albin, who has made no pledge to remain at this fort, will return to Oristatown. Those under my command who wish to risk the gallows may accompany him. Those who wish to undergo the trials of the forest or to seek refuge at Fort San Juan are free to depart. But I myself will accept Cauchi Mico's offer to join with his people as one of them."

Every other soldier came to the same conclusion.

After the meeting, Brother Marcos gathered the nine soldiers together before the golden cross at the back of the council house and delivered an impromptu sermon. He told them that just as Aaron had loaded a goat with the sins of the Jews and sent him into the wilderness, so had God chosen them to carry away the evils of the Spanish Empire, its armies and its conquistadors. He quoted from Leviticus: "And the goat shall bear upon him all their iniquities unto a Land not inhabited." He assured them that God would protect and sustain them in the ordeals that lay ahead.

Diego listened intently, trying to believe the priest's earnest reassurance—but feeling only dread. He couldn't get the image out of his head of the somber Captain Melendez with his smiling moustache tips, dancing for the amusement of the victorious Chisca with pine splinters flaring beneath his skin. If the fierce Melendez were helpless in this wasteland, how did Diego stand a chance?

Guillermo lay on a bench in the barracks, watching Diego pack his gear. They could hear the Cauchi doing the same throughout their village, interrupted now and then by mournful chanting for their lost warriors.

"I'm curious," said Guillermo. "Are you comforted in your current plight by the notion of yourself as a goat of God?"

Diego laughed. "I'll miss your smart mouth, Guillermo."

"I'll miss you, too, Goat King."

Olivia stirred on her pallet in the corner.

"Are you finally awake?" Diego asked her.

"Yes. What are you doing?"

"Packing." He explained to her the decisions from the meeting in the council house. "You can go with me to the Cauchi winter camp. Or Guillermo has said he'll take you with him back to Oristatown. It's up to you."

She lay there in silence. After a while she said, "I can't travel anywhere very far or very fast. The time may have come for you to honor your promise to kill me."

"I'm not going to kill you, Olivia, and that's that."

"But you promised me."

"I lied."

All three started laughing.

"Don Sebastian left me the Arabian. You can ride her to the Cauchi camp or to Oristatown, whichever you want."

"I know I'm a burden," she said, "so I guess I'd better burden the man who owns me."

"I'd be happy to take you with me if you want to go back to the coast," insisted Guillermo. "I'm sure the Orista would adopt you."

"I guess I'd rather live out however many days are left to me as far as possible from all those awful men who slobbered all over me."

"Good!" said Diego. "Then get busy sorting your belongings. We're leaving right away. Do you want these?" Diego offered Guillermo two fistfuls of the fancy doublets and trunk hose Don Sebastian had given him. "I guess I won't be needing them."

Guillermo smiled wryly. "They never suited you, Diego. I didn't know how to tell you."

Diego tossed them into the corner. "Why don't you come with us, Guillermo? Oh yes, I forgot that Blue Heron is waiting for you at Orista."

"Love does simplify one's decisions, doesn't it?"

"If you see Lucas, will you tell him that I intend to survive and that maybe one day we'll meet again?"

"I'll tell him. But I'll tell everyone else that I am the sole survivor from Fort San Pablo. Otherwise, knowing Spaniards as I do, I suspect they would send out a search party to bring you home in chains for breaking your vow. Why did Don Sebastian assign you to remain here anyway? I thought you were his golden lad?"

Diego shrugged. "Who knows? I can't make any sense of it."

"That's a good sign. The only ones who can make sense of the insane are those who are themselves insane. I did try to warn you that you were being fanned in the face by the wings of a demon."

"Yes, you did. I wish I had listened to you."

"There probably wasn't much you could have done. He singled you out to play his little tricks on. If you hadn't gone along with him, you'd probably be lying in a forest grave right now."

"Yes, I guess he's crazy," said Diego sadly. "He would have to be to want to be a conquistador in the first place."

The Cauchi and the Spanish soldiers headed up the trail toward the bald. Guillermo set out on a little-traveled shortcut to Santa Elena, jubilant to be returning to Blue Heron. As he and Diego waved farewell from adjoining ridges, Guillermo danced a sailor's jig.

With Baltasar by his side, Diego paused atop the grassy bald to look down at the village and the fort, guilty about deserting his post. But the choice to stay was a choice to die, and suicide was at least as serious a sin as breaking a vow. Guillermo had assured him that with reasoning like that, he could join the Jesuits.

Bear Claw and another warrior named Ten Killer were torching the village and the newly built fort. Cauchi Mico had explained that this way the Chisca might believe the Cauchi were already decimated by other enemies and not attempt to track them to their winter camp.

If you had to be chased through the mountains by murderers, reflected Diego, you couldn't wish for stauncher companions. Bear Claw and Ten Killer looked far more lethal than Cristobal's thugs or Don Sebastian's pages. Bear Claw had earned his name and the scars down his face and body in hand-to-hand combat with a mother bear after shooting her cub. He had strangled her with his bare hands and now wore her claws on a thong around his neck. And Ten Killer's nickname was the result of his having scalped ten simultaneous Iroquois attackers when he was out hunting by himself.

Cauchi Mico, swathed in his cloak of auburn fur, led the way. Brother Marcos followed, stubbornly toting his golden cross as the wind tugged at his brown robe. Gaspar de los Reyes limped along on his wooden leg, assisted by Julio Gomez. Pascuale Sanchez's slender frame was bowed beneath his pack of stonecutting tools, which he had insisted on bringing in case they should be needed at the winter camp.

Babies were strapped on boards to their mothers' backs. Several native men dressed in women's shifts carried three elders on litters. Children and mangy dogs walked silently, curbing their capers.

The four Portuguese and Nicolas Navarro led the horses, which seemed to sulk at having to drag poles to which supplies were lashed. One bore the wrapped bones of Cauchi ancestors. Olivia sat slumped over on the Arabian, wrapped in Diego's indigo blanket. The horses' hooves and the ends of the baggage poles were bound in skins to minimize their tracks. Diego and Baltasar brought up the rear, herding the dozen hogs. Bear Claw and Ten Killer would follow shortly behind, erasing any footprints and droppings that might betray their route.

As the crimson sun set beyond the valley of the Chisca, they stopped for the night. Since fires might signal their whereabouts to Chisca scouts, none were lit. Diego and Olivia sat in a circle with the other soldiers, all silently gnawing dried venison. A couple of young warriors stood atop the ridge, scouring the valley floor and the coves that cleft the cliffs for any sparks from the fires of pursuers. Glancing at their silhouettes, Diego felt a flash of panic. What if this gesture of hospitality on the part of the Cauchi were all a ruse to lure the Spaniards to their winter camp? Once there, maybe the Cauchi would torture and kill them, or turn them into slaves. He remembered Orista Mico's tale of the Orista warriors who were invited on board Spanish ships and then carried away forever, no doubt into slavery in the Caribbean. Maybe the Cauchi would take revenge on Diego's motley companions on behalf of the Orista.

As he rolled up in his blanket and tried to calm his anxiety enough to sleep, Diego reminded himself that he had just experienced the ultimate in treachery from Don Sebastian. But this didn't mean everyone else was intent on deceit and betrayal. He lay on his back with his hands pillowing his head and watched the glimmering stars etch their eternal patterns, while down below prowling panthers screamed in the gloom.

The refugees departed at dawn, gnawing hunks of cornbread as they marched along above the tree line. Lakes of milky mist engulfed the valleys and turned the peaks into jagged islands of indigo and mauve. During the night Diego had concluded that he had no choice but to accept the apparent kindness of the Cauchi at face value. It was the only option that held out the promise of survival, under whatever terms.

When the sun was nearly overhead, they descended from the crest to cross a sparse forest of stunted saplings with trunks scaled gray from lichen. After wading a roiling creek on shelves of slippery stone, they ascended again to the balds, which stretched into the distance like a necklace of tawny pearls.

They traveled for five days and nights at a pace that kept Diego and the hogs panting. But the advance scouts traveled even faster, racing ahead to inform those at the winter camp of the slaughter of their kinsmen.

On the sixth day Diego realized that they were now descending without corresponding ascents. Snowflakes began to sift from a glowering sky. Soon snow was driving hard against him, stinging his cheeks. He smiled, knowing that the new snow would further conceal their trail from any pursuing Chisca.

In mid-afternoon two young men in belted hide shirts and laced leggings appeared from nowhere. The march stopped as they talked intently with Cauchi Mico. Up ahead Diego could see a valley carved out of limestone by a narrow river. High hills strewn with boulders encircled this bowl, which was drifted with the new snow. Looming over the hills was a bald similar to the one at Cauchi.

Along the river stretched several dozen round huts, like over-turned baskets. Their floors were sunk well below ground level, and dirt was banked up around their sides. Smoke spiraled from their roof holes. Noticing Baltasar's nostrils twitching, Diego concentrated and was able to pick up the scent of wood smoke and roasting meat. His mouth began to water.

As they tromped down the hillside, the dogs and children broke ranks to romp and roll through the snow. Distant figures emerged from the huts.

Approaching this group, Diego realized that they were mostly women, children, and older men. The young men were probably hunting or standing watch on the cliffs. Some women carried babies on their backs and held toddlers by the hand. Many adults already wore the ashen paste of mourning on their faces.

One stocky older woman, whose silver hair hung long and straight, held the arm of a man with dusty ebony skin. His head was shaven on both sides, but his graying coxcomb curled crisply, as did his beard and moustache, which Cauchi men never wore. This woman clasped forearms and exchanged words with Cauchi Mico in his auburn fur. He bent over to talk right in her ear, as though she were hard of hearing. She shook her head and leaned heavily on the arm of her companion. Cauchi Mico gestured to the soldiers. She studied them, nodding.

Diego watched her approach, limping through the snow. The ragged Spaniards stood to attention, sensing themselves in the presence of someone formidable.

"Welcome, wanderers. May our path be yours from this day forward," she said in broken Spanish.

"Thank you, kind lady, for your generous hospitality to wayfarers in distress," Diego replied in Cauchi.

She fixed her dark eyes on him. "You know our tongue, lad?"

"Poorly."

She smiled. "We are honored that you try. Please tell your comrades that all we own, although very little, is theirs to share."

He repeated this in Spanish, and the soldiers bowed.

"Any skills or goods that we possess are at your service, madam," replied Diego, the self-appointed diplomat.

"We need strong young men. Many of ours have fallen in the valley of the Chisca. Wives are without husbands and children without fathers. Fields lie fallow, and game mocks us unhunted from the forest."

Diego smiled. "Alas, soldiers are not known for their success at the hunt."

She smiled back. "This we already know." She gestured to the older men. "Soldiers are known for living off the efforts of those weaker than themselves. But once stranded in a strange land with no other recourse, they learn overnight how to contribute!"

The men she had singled out laughed uproariously.

The dark-skinned one walked over to the soldiers. "Welcome, cousins," he said in Castilian.

"You're Spanish?" several soldiers inquired at once.

"As you can see, I'm African. But I once lived and served in Seville. My Spanish name was Vicente Sevilla. My Cauchi name means Buffalo. I'm called that because of my curly hair."

"What are you doing here?" asked Diego, already knowing.

"Years ago I deserted from an expedition led by a conquistador named DeSoto."

"Are there other deserters here?" asked Diego, astonished that Don Sebastian's quest had been fulfilled in his absence.

"Three more still living. Three others have died. But they live on through their children." He gestured toward the young people, who exhibited every color combination of skin, hair, and eyes. "A handsome hodgepodge, are they not?"

"She must be the queen from Cofitachequi," marveled Diego, nodding toward the woman with the silver hair.

"So I am," she replied. "But how did you know this?"

Diego blushed, not having meant to say this out loud. "My commander told me of you. But how did you end up so far from Cofitachequi?"

"We returned to Cofitachequi after our escape from DeSoto," replied Buffalo. "But many there were starving because we Spaniards had seized their winter stores. Scores more were dying from the smallpox we left behind. We stacked the dead in the temple and brought the survivors with us to join the Cauchi, who had hidden us after our escape. They were willing to adopt us Spanish deserters because we had helped their queen escape from DeSoto."

"This lady, you mean?" Diego gestured to the woman on Buffalo's arm.

"Nowadays I am what Spaniards would call the queen," she replied. "But at that time my aunt was the queen. I was merely impersonating her while she hid from DeSoto."

"Do you live up here in this winter camp all the time?"

"No, like all the Cauchi we spent warm months in the village from which you've just come," said Buffalo. "But those of us with Spanish connections moved up here earlier than usual to avoid your expedition, lest we be captured and executed for having deserted. Or forced to join you and return to Spain."

"You prefer it here in the wilderness?" asked Diego with faint hope.

"My son, if you wish to experience a true wilderness, return to your horde of ravaging soldiers," suggested Buffalo. "If you are here now, I gather it's because you have thrown your lot in with ours. So welcome to the Land of the Lost."

10

The Cave

Diego and the other soldiers helped the Cauchi disassemble the huts by the stream. They carried the poles and sheets of bark up a hillside and stashed them in a cave in one of the cliffs that encircled the bowl. Although the cave mouth was small and partially blocked by rock ledges, it opened into a vaulted hall with walls lined with columns of milky quartz. Many alcoves opened off this hall, and the Cauchi began to move their sparse belongings into them.

Diego had translated as Cauchi Mico explained the plan to Don Domingo. It was hoped that the Chisca would go to Cauchitown, find it in ashes, and return home. But if they came in search of this winter camp, they might not be able to identify the bowl if the huts were missing.

"Should they discover the entrance to the cave," the Mico continued, "there are many winding passages where pursuers can be ambushed. Also, as in a rabbit warren, there are other exits, some used by our sentries to reach their cliff-top outposts. One path extends through the heart of the mountain to open onto the valley of the Chisca. The map of these routes is secure, as it exists only in the heads of our warriors."

That night at a feast in the torch-lit hall, the Cauchi shaman was the first to address the tribe. He wore a skirt of what looked like squirrel pelts, their tails forming a fringed hemline. On his head perched a stuffed owl. Its talons dangled over his ears. Diego stifled a startled laugh when he spotted him. He glanced at Nicolas Navarro, who was struggling similarly not to laugh.

But what the shaman said wasn't funny. Diego interpreted to the soldiers his prayer for the Cauchi warriors and the Spanish soldiers who had been slain by the Chisca: "The sunset burns upon the mountain for your spirits. What will become of us, bereft of your laughter? What will become of us, wandering in the canyons of our lives without the echo of you?"

They all sat motionless in the vast cavern of stone. Even Brother Marcos appeared moved by the words of this strangely attired pagan. He crossed himself, clasped his hands, bowed his head, and closed his eyes.

After a long silence the queen stood. Diego had learned that her name was Silver Vixen. She addressed her tribe, all of whose faces were now caked with ashes. "My people, we must not grieve for long over our lost warriors. We must go on, as they would wish us to. The Sacred Spirit has sent these strong young men to take their places. Misfortunes happen, even to the wisest and best of people. One day we will each of us go out to greet the morning sun, the sweet dark earth, and the long Great Silence—always out of season, always alone."

The Cauchi nodded.

Then she turned to the Spanish soldiers and said, "We wish you to find work to suit your skills and mates to ease your loneliness."

She announced which clan had adopted each soldier. Diego's was the Dragonfly clan. He had no idea what that meant except that Dragonfly women were now like sisters to him, off limits as potential mates.

Next Cauchi Mico stood. Towering head and shoulders above everyone else, he began to circulate among the soldiers with Diego translating. He discussed with each man what jobs he could perform. The soldiers were pleasantly surprised to be consulted rather than commanded.

Sitting on a bench beside the blazing fire pit, Cauchi Mico asked Diego if he would tend the animals. "If you can get the hogs to multiply," he explained, "our dependence on the hunt could be relieved. Likewise, a herd of horses could extend the range of our hunts, and could also give us an advantage in battle. This might help make up for the loss of so many of our best hunters and warriors."

Afterwards Diego and Olivia followed the other soldiers along a path of packed earth, past eerie rose and ochre cones and hourglass pillars, to a rock chamber that Cauchi Mico had assigned them for their living quarters until they should find wives. As they spread out their bedrolls, Brother Marcos piled up flat stones in one corner to form an altar. Then he propped his gold cross behind it.

Diego knelt on the earthen floor with the others and received one of the dwindling supply of wafers, feeling embarrassed for Brother Marcos. In another life he had performed communion in cathedrals for grandees dressed in silks and satins. Now he was offering his silver chalice to a gang of ragged fugitives in a damp and chilly cave in a forlorn mountain cove. Apparently, his longing for mortification knew no bounds.

After communion Nicolas Navarro exited from their rock barracks with a sheepish grin. Diego had watched him after supper as he flirted with a widow who appeared to be emerging from mourning in record time.

Diego lay down and wrapped himself in his indigo blanket. Having accompanied him from Galicia to Santa Elena and throughout the wilderness, the blanket was in tatters. The others were now sleeping under hides or furs. But like a child with a cherished toy, Diego couldn't bring himself to relinquish this last link to Manuela. She may not have been his real mother, but she was the only mother he had ever known. He was unlikely ever to see her again. So he clung to his blanket as he had clung to her hand when he was a little boy faced with something that frightened him.

With his arm draped across the sleeping Baltasar, Diego tried to calm his fears about his future as a Cauchi by planning the pens and stalls he would construct inside the cave entrance to replace the current ones of brush and branches.

At dawn the next morning, Diego and Baltasar left the cave. Baltasar herded the hogs while Diego led the five horses, gaunt from the flight along the ridge tops dragging heavy baggage. Hobbling them in a stand of withered river cane at the mouth of a spring, he conducted the hogs through the crusty snow to an oak grove partway up the side of the bald.

Perched on a rock ledge while the hogs nosed aside the snow and grunted over the acorns beneath it, Diego looked down to the river in the valley, a radiant silver ribbon that wound through the landscape of white. Several women were submerging themselves in the chilly water. As the sun, veiled in swirling mist, rose over the rim of the bowl, they turned to face it. Chins lifted, they raised their arms, palms up. The sun's rays sliced through the mist, pointing like golden daggers at the worshipping women.

Diego forced himself to avert his gaze as they emerged from the water to dress. But when he looked again, his eyes settled on a young woman in a doeskin shirt and leggings. She wore strapped to one shoulder a quiver made from what looked like the pelt of a silver fox. She joined the hunters, among them Domingo de Santa Cruz de la Sierra and Nicolas Navarro, as they headed down the river and through a cleft in the cliffs.

While the hogs fanned out across the hillside, Diego opened the leather pouch he wore on a cord around his neck and removed his mother's ruby pendant. He turned it to catch the light from the rising sun. He recalled Manuela's instructions to sell it and use the proceeds to make a fresh start for himself in the New World. There was no one here to buy it and nothing to buy it with. Nevertheless, he *was* making a fresh start, and he vowed that if he ever fathered a daughter here, he would name her Galicia and would hang this ruby around her neck in honor of his brave birth mother whom he couldn't even remember, who had managed to save him from the Inquisitors' pyre that had consumed her and his father.

As the sun melted the snow and warmed the air, the Cauchi emerged from their cave. Some women began to scrape fat from hides alongside the river. Some older men, Buffalo among them, gathered around a spine of rock, which they used like an anvil as they chipped and flaked shards of stone into arrowheads and spearheads. The shaman and his two young assistants, a boy and a girl, dug roots and collected dried seed pods on the hillsides. Some girls gathered nuts in a walnut grove, while a pack of boys shot at winter birds with their blowguns.

At sunset the hunters returned, carrying on poles across their shoulders an array of deer, birds, possums, and coons. After a meal of fresh kill in the cave, the hunters butchered the remaining carcasses and laid their flesh in strips over racks by the fire to dry. The restless children raced and wrestled in the smoky cavern, which was lit by several flaming pine knot torches.

Diego sat beside Nicolas Navarro, warming himself at the fire pit, while Pascuale Sanchez argued in Spanish with Buffalo about his proposal to construct a fortress of stone by the river.

"It would intimidate our enemies," Pascuale insisted. " We could go about our lives without having to move into this cave each time danger threatened."

"A fortress would invite assault," said Buffalo. "Our enemies would then know our exact location."

"At the very least we need to build a stone palisade around the mouth of this cave," insisted Pascuale. "We could shelter behind it to fight off attackers."

"Spanish soldiers are trained like falcons," explained Buffalo. "We plunge at our prey. But native warriors imitate the hummingbird. In a Cauchi myth, the Sacred Spirit fashions the first hummingbird from the fluff of a dandelion, so that he can dance nimbly on the breezes. This is how they fight. No rigid ranks. No last stands. No stone fortresses. Their warriors are carried along by the gusts of a battle—surging forward and falling back. They feel no shame in retreat, only in fighting without joy."

Diego and Nicolas Navarro glanced at one another. Fighting and joy were two categories Diego was unable to combine. But he could easily imagine himself darting away from danger like a wary hummingbird.

Diego stood up, leaving Baltasar asleep on his blanket, surrounded by Olivia and the slumbering soldiers in their cavern of stone. Lighting a torch from the embers of their fire, he walked to the cave mouth to check on the animals. The horses stood asleep in their stall of branches, forelegs poised as though about to step out. The hogs lay piled atop one another, heaving grunts as they no doubt dreamed of a land where acorns showered like hail from the sky.

Diego returned to the empty hall. The smoky air was ripe with the odor of stale food and animal waste, a stench almost as revolting as that in the hold of the *San Jorge*. But at least the floor didn't roll. He had been assigned to keep watch that night on a cliff top, accompanied by the young woman he had seen bathing in the stream that morning. He had learned that her name was Doe Stalker. While hunting, she apparently donned the skull and hide of a doe. She could mimic a doe's movements so exactly that she moved through a herd undetected, until she threw off her cape to shoot the lead buck point-blank.

Strolling past alcoves in which the Cauchi were settling down for the night, he spotted Doe Stalker through an arched stone doorway. She was sitting on a fur-padded bench beside a smoldering fire in her hunting shirt and leggings. A small boy sat on the ground in front of her. Silver Vixen, Buffalo, and a young girl sat across from her. Bear Claw was also there, the scars down his cheeks highlighted by the flames.

Another young woman was chewing something. She took it from her mouth and placed it between the lips of a withered old woman who smacked her lips and ground the masticated food between her gums.

Buffalo called, "Come in out of the shadows, Pig Boy. Join us by the fire."

Blushing both to have been caught eavesdropping and also to hear his old nickname newly minted, Diego entered. He sat on a bench. Bear Claw gave him an unfriendly look that made him realize that Bear Claw was a suitor and thought him one, too. He didn't even know what clan Doe Stalker belonged to. She must not have been a Dragonfly or else Bear Claw would have had nothing to worry about.

"This is Silver Vixen's mother, Corn Silk," said Buffalo. "And my younger daughter, Doe Stalker, and her sister Vine. And Vine's children, Wake Robin and Bowlegs. I believe you already know Bear Claw."

Diego nodded to each in turn. Bowlegs was the boy seated on the ground. Doe Stalker was braiding his miniature crest of black hair. With a start Diego realized that both her hands had a second thumb sprouting from the joint between her thumbs and her index fingers. Diego had seen extra toes on some cats that lived in the barn at the hacienda. At a fair he once saw a calf with an extra leg. But a person with twelve fingers was a first for him. He tried not to stare.

"Tell Diego the story about DeSoto, Grandmother," requested Wake Robin. She shivered, as thrilled at the prospect of a DeSoto tale as Don Sebastian's officers had been.

Silver Vixen looked at Diego apologetically.

"Yes, please do," he said politely. He had already heard about DeSoto and the Queen of Cofitachequi two dozen times from Don Sebastian, but Silver Vixen's version might be different from his.

"I was no older than Doe Stalker when I first met Hernando DeSoto," said Silver Vixen. "I was wearing my aunt's best robe, made from the hides of albino does. Around my neck hung her three strands of river pearls.

"On the far side of the river that ran alongside Cofitachequi I spotted the men whose approach had stirred such fear in our village. We knew all about them and their murderous ways. Our scouts had informed us of these hairy barbarians, hacking their way through the pine barrens. They coveted corn, women, and yellow metals. They couldn't hunt. They bargained for food until they ran out of trade goods. Then they just grabbed it. By the time they reached us, they were so starved that they were prepared to kill for it.

"I studied their chief's silver clothing and peaked war bonnet, which arrows were said to bounce off of. He and his headmen sat on horses, the first we had ever seen. We thought they were giant deer. We lacked enough warriors to fight them because over half our people had died that winter from the Spotted Disease. The council agreed our only hope was to give them what they wanted and then send them to the Chisca with promises of yellow stones, just as other tribes had so kindly sent them to us.

"The litter bearers helped me into our ceremonial canoe. I sank down on the cushions beneath an awning made from the wings of white swans. If my mission failed, my people would be butchered and enslaved—as other tribes had already been. Our war leader, who was also my brother, had opposed my putting myself in such danger. But I knew if I did nothing, I was doomed for certain, and my aunt and our people along with me.

"The paddlers lifted me onto the shore. I stood looking up at that haughty creature on his white stallion. Hair encircled his mouth and nose like the fur around a bear's muzzle. His tiny eyes were cruel. In words that a trader's boy beside him translated, he told me my people were now subjects of his king and his shaman across the great waters. He got down from his horse.

"Ignoring his arrogance, I replied, 'We welcome you, Sire, to our homeland. All that my people and I possess is yours to share. We have set aside half our village to quarter your warriors, and we urge you to accept the corn stored in the cribs on that side of town. Our supplies are low, and we need the storehouses on our side to sustain us until our new crops come in. I offer you a token of the respect with which we regard you.'

"I draped my aunt's pearls around his neck.

"He fingered them. 'These are lovely,' he said. 'Where did you get them?'

"'Our fishermen collect them from mussels in the river.'

"'Do your fishermen find nuggets of yellow stone in your river as well?'

"'We have no yellow stones,' I assured him. 'But beyond the mountains lies the land of the Chisca. There, pebbles of yellow line the creek bottoms and spill from the mountain caves.'

"Our paddlers conveyed his army across the river. Our men carried him in a litter alongside my own into the nearly empty village. Many had fled to clan members in mountain towns. The only ones left were the young women who had volunteered to remain, hoping to prevent our huts from being torched and our temple and storehouses from being sacked. The sacred virgins had also volunteered to remain, sequestered in the temple, to lend us courage. When we reached the council house atop the temple mound, the men lifted DeSoto and me off the litters.

"'We have prepared our best lodge for you, illustrious brother,' I said. 'I regret that it must seem so modest, compared to your dwellings in the sky.'

"Appearing not to notice my sarcasm, he said, 'This lodge is a palace to one who has been bivouacking in pine barrens for many a night.'

"'Tonight you and your most honored warriors are invited to my quarters.' I pointed to my aunt's longhouse. 'We will feast together and smoke the pipe of peace and friendship.'

"When he arrived, he had shed his shell, like a silver locust. He wore a crimson doublet over leather shorts, tights, and high leather boots. In place of his helmet was a soft black cap. Behind him came four soldiers, similarly attired. Two dozen more, wearing their silver shells and carrying long spears with jagged points, surrounded the building.

"I motioned for DeSoto to sit on a platform along the wall, which was cushioned with bear pelts. I introduced my brother as my husband, hoping this might discourage any amorous designs. I had also slathered my limbs with rancid bear grease."

As everyone smiled, Buffalo got up to throw a log on the fire, which had already filled the rock room with smoke that stung Diego's eyes.

"We ate acorn bread and a stew of beans, squash, and venison. We drank from a flask DeSoto offered, which contained the famous firewater our traders had sampled at the coast.

"At the meal's end, as we passed the smoldering pipe, DeSoto said, 'And now may we speak in private as one ruler to another?'

"This was the moment I had been dreading. I knew Spaniards traveled without women, apart from abducted natives. They included no women in their councils and appeared to regard us as useful for only household chores and erotic play.

"As my brother stood up, DeSoto asked, 'I am sure you will not object, noble sir, to sharing the favors of your wife with a guest from the gods?'

"My brother looked to me, anger in his eyes. With a movement of my own eyes I signaled for him to go.

"Alone except for the translator, DeSoto announced, 'And now you and I will speak together the language of the human heart.'

"He dismissed the trader's boy. I knew if I refused him, he would take me anyway, and would enjoy doing so. The only hope for our village was to gain his good will by whatever means were necessary. But I was determined to deny him the pleasure of forcing me. So I stood up and unbelted my white robe. Seizing my shoulders, he pressed his mouth, stinking of firewater, against mine. The fur around his lips scratched and tickled. It was like rubbing noses with a cur that has been rooting in garbage. I struggled to conceal my disgust.

"He pushed me down on the bearskin. I could smell sweat and swamp mud, tobacco smoke, and the excrement of horses. My stomach convulsed. Our people bathed daily in the river, but Spaniards smelled as though they never bathed at all. I turned my head aside. But I assured myself that this man was a creature like myself, with a spark of the Sacred Spirit glowing somewhere deep within himself. For a few moments we would be as one. He would understand that to harm others was to harm this most precious part of himself. He would go away without beating, killing, looting, and enslaving my people.

"After his departure I went outside and stood alone on the temple mound. Down in the village I could see the soldiers lounging around fires with women who were my friends and cousins. They were singing and laughing. A few were dancing. I looked up at the Great Bear. Its familiar stars twinkled just as they always had.

"A woman screamed. I could only hope it was from pleasure or amusement. Horses snorted and neighed. An owl hooted from the forest, my brother's sign that he and the warriors were there, prepared to forfeit their lives in our defense.

"I kept watch all night. When the sky paled and mourning doves began to coo, I followed the path to the river. Several women were already submerged. I removed my robe and joined them. As a sliver of sun peeped over the cliff, we turned to face it. When the fiery globe burst into full view, we murmured, 'Thank you, Mother Sun, for creating the world afresh each day. Renew our purity, blackened in the night.'"

Diego tried to reconcile Don Sebastian's version of this story with that of Silver Vixen. As with a wound that goes numb until you are strong enough to bear the pain, Diego felt his first stab of anguish at the knowledge that he would never again recline on Don Sebastian's cushions and listen to his troubled confessions.

"I knew a friend of yours from DeSoto's company," said Diego.

Silver Vixen turned to look at him. "I had no friends among DeSoto's men, except for his slave." She nodded at Buffalo.

"His name was Don Sebastian de Silva. He was a page to the Captain of the Horse."

She looked blank.

"You remember him," Buffalo assured her. "He was the boy with the horrible scar across his cheek."

She closed her eyes. "I do remember him," she said. "When DeSoto announced their departure, Silva and some others broke into our temple and defiled our sacred virgins. When I protested, DeSoto put me in chains and announced that I would accompany them.

"One of these virgins was the daughter of my aunt. She would have been our next queen. Silva put an iron collar around her neck and chained her to his saddle. She walked while he rode. If she tripped, he dragged her until she could regain her footing. Her eyes were red from weeping. On her arms and at her throat were bruises. When I escaped, I had no choice but to leave her behind. I have never seen her since. Why do you say that such a fiend is my friend?"

"He was our commander," muttered Diego. "He was trying to find you. He claimed to be your friend."

"Don Sebastian de Silva is a friend to no one. He is infested by demons he mistakes for himself. He marches through this world spreading his contagion to others, like a Spotted Disease of the spirit."

The roar of a subterranean river grew louder as the light from Doe Stalker's torch danced in a clammy draft. She and Diego passed a rock wall that soared overhead beyond reach of the torchlight. On it entire herds of animals were painted in tones of ocher, scarlet, and charcoal—bucks and buffalo, bears and elks and panthers, eagles and hawks—some as large as life, others doll-sized, as though approaching from afar in an endless stampede.

"Why is your mother called Silver Vixen?" Diego asked the young woman striding ahead of him. In Galicia there had been servants like Manuela and ladies like Leonora. On the march there had been slave women like Olivia. But Doe Stalker's attitude toward him, of comradely self-assurance, was baffling. He had no idea how to behave with her.

"Silver because her hair turned white after she encountered DeSoto," replied Doe Stalker over her shoulder. "Vixen because she was canny like a fox in her dealings with him."

Leading the way up steps that were chopped into the wall, she propped the torch against a boulder and vanished through an aperture. Climbing the remaining steps, Diego reached the opening and joined Doe Stalker on a cliff top. He followed her into a shelter of evergreen boughs where Ten Killer sat wrapped in a buffalo robe. He stood up and handed Diego the robe. The moonglow illuminated his crooked nose and long earlobes.

Diego watched him slip back into the cave. Then he and Doe Stalker sat in the shelter side by side and encased themselves in the heavy robe.

The mountains below, rolling to the horizon like swells on the sea, were swathed in the bright moonlight. Their beards of firs cast bristly black shadows. Diego's task was to watch these shadows until dawn, making sure none moved. He could see that the temptation to doze would be strong. But a single ill-timed nap might spell destruction for the entire tribe.

He heard the howl of a wolf paying court to the mottled ivory moon. Scanning the snow-patched ridges, he wondered if he would even notice a Chisca creeping toward this cliff.

As he looked up at the stars, he spotted the Seven Sisters. He had often studied them while tending his hogs on the Galician hillside. Resembling a bunch of luminous grapes, they hung just to one side of the White Bull, who was so in love with a princess that he let her ride on his back and garland his horns with flowers. He remembered how Manuela had maintained that, like the sun in its contest with the wind, the bull knew that kindness could accomplish what force could not. He smiled sadly, having learned in La Florida to have his doubts.

PART II

THE SQUABBLE STATE

1

The Five-Chicken Baby: 1818

Doc Moore's horse staggered up Silver Valley, Doc's belly propped on the pommel like an overripe pumpkin. Struggling down from the saddle, he crossed the porch and opened the Martins' oak door. The main room was crammed to its ceiling beams with the five Martin sons, their father Reuben, and their grandfather Zachariah, all awaiting the arrival of the new baby currently dawdling in Barbary's womb.

Waving to the men, Doc lumbered into the bedroom, greeted Barbary, and parted her knees to inspect her progress. After washing up in a basin on the washstand, he returned to the other room, where a dozen plucked chickens sizzled on a spit in the stone walk-in fireplace. Reuben removed a roaster with his remaining arm (the left one having been abandoned in the fallen leaves on King's Mountain during the battle against the British nearly forty years earlier). He laid the fowl in a pottery bowl and extended the bowl to Doc. Doc carried it out to the front porch, sat in a rocker, and started dismembering it. Now and then he called through the open window into the bedroom, "You all right in there, Barbary, honey?"

Once he had sucked the grease off the bones and tossed them to the hounds lurking in the yard, he lay back in the chair and began to snooze.

As the sun sank behind a cliff and a cool blue shadow stole across the pasture, a contraction hit Barbary so hard that she howled like a trapped wolf. Doc snapped awake and heaved himself to his feet.

Examining her again, he murmured, "It's gonna be a while yet, Barbary."

"Doc, I don't think I can stand it no more," she gasped.

"Appears to me you got no choice," he replied cheerfully. "I watch them come and I watch them go, and life just plods along at its own pace, whether we like it or not."

As Doc lingered by the fire, Reuben offered him another chicken. Returning to the porch, Doc devoured the second of what he hoped would be the entire flock. Then he licked his fingers clean, picked his teeth with his thumbnail, clasped his hands atop his belly, and fell into a deep slumber that even a mosquito feasting on his billowing chins didn't disturb.

Toward midnight, as the moon bathed the pasture in a pale golden glow, Reuben prodded Doc awake. He came to with a jerk and a snort, rose slowly to his feet, and stumbled into the house, tiptoeing with sudden cat-like grace around the sons sprawled fast asleep on the floor. Zachariah sat smoking a pipe by the fading fireplace embers. Doc eyed the three remaining chickens now nesting in a crock on the trestle table.

Barbary lay writhing in the four-poster bed, her teeth clenched and her hair slick with sweat. But Doc soon placed in her arms a tiny girl with an olive face, curly charcoal hair, and bewildered black eyes. On each miniature hand was a second thumb.

"Have mercy, Barbary!" he exclaimed, "Have you been locked in forbidden embraces with those Indians across the mountain?"

"Lord no," she said, smiling down at the baby. "I don't even like it with Reuben, much less with rank strangers. In fact, I aim to give it up now. I can't go through all this again. I'm way too old. It like to killed me this time around."

"I've heard that before," said Doc. "After almost every delivery I've ever done. But a year or two later they all come looking for me again."

"Well, not me. This is it for me."

Back in the other room Reuben said, "Doc, we sure do appreciate you, but I ain't got no more than a few coins to pay you with."

"I'll take the roasters for the balance, Reuben."

As Doc departed, grease soaking through a sack across one shoulder, Reuben went in to inspect his first daughter, the fruit of aged loins. He cradled her in his arm, examining her delightedly.

"Well, darling," he said, leaning down to kiss Barbary's damp forehead, "looks like Doc give us a bargain this time—a five-chicken baby. My uncle Henry had an extra finger on each hand and an extra toe on each foot. He used to chase us kids around the house, waving his hands and scaring us all to death."

"I want to call her Galicia after your grandmaw," said Barbary. "She was always so sweet to me."

"That would tickle Daddy to death. She left me that red stone she used to wear on a leather cord around her neck, to pass along to the next Galicia in the family. Said she got it from her grandmaw, also named Galicia. Claimed it came over from across the waters with the ancients in times gone by. So I guess it belongs now to this little bitty gal."

By the time Galicia was six months old, she had enchanted the entire citizenry of Couchtown, Virginia—all 250 of them. Reuben would clasp her tiny feet in his palm. She would stiffen her trunk and clamp her arms to her sides. Flexing his arm, he would press her above his head and hold her there as though on a pedestal. She would look down placidly on her adoring audiences like a pagan goddess.

Galicia's brothers fought to carry her on their shoulders into Couchtown. The townspeople, too polite to ask, tried to position themselves as they chatted so as to catch a glimpse of the tiny extra finger that sprouted between her thumb and pointer on each hand. They speculated about Galicia's foreign-sounding name, inherited from her father's grandmother, when every other girl in town was called Sarah or Sally, Mary or Polly. But nobody ever claimed the Martins weren't a motley bunch. They had every sort in their family, and they appeared to love them all alike.

Reuben and four of his sons spent their days trapping, hunting, farming, fishing, or herding, depending on the season. Abner, the next to youngest, worked as a clerk at West's Trading Post in town. The three-story log blockhouse had been built long ago as a stockade and warehouse for the Tidewater fur traders, who used to cross the Sturgeon River at the ford just above its junction with Otter Creek. They had rested themselves and their horses at the blockhouse before tackling the steep paths through the Smokies to the Cherokee villages snuggled into the river valleys that snaked their way among the towering mountain peaks.

But the vast herds of deer the Cherokees had hunted no longer grazed the hillsides. The Cherokees were mostly farmers now, and no more fur traders forded the Sturgeon. The outlanders who arrived these days were hungry for homesteads, not hides, and they settled down rather than just passing through.

While everyone else was working, Galicia remained at home with her grandfather Zachariah. Whatever the weather, the skinny old man was chilly, so they huddled by the fire while he carved small animals for her from chunks of wood. Galicia played with her animal collection on the braided rug by the hearth.

One brisk autumn afternoon Zachariah decided he needed to tell Galicia about her ancestors so she wouldn't forget them when he was dead and gone. He wanted her to know that she came from a long line of fine pioneering people, that her name Galicia and the dark red stone she would wear on a thong around her neck had been passed down from ancient days to a woman in most every generation, sometimes to a Galicia with a different married name than Martin, but always returning to a Galicia Martin whenever one was available.

"Everyone used to call our valley Silva Valley," he began. "Nobody knew why. And then some hunters found an old mine shaft they claimed some Spaniards had dug in days of yore, so they started calling it Silver Valley, which they still do, right down to this very day."

Galicia gazed up at him from the rug, her twelve fingers toying with a wooden horse he had carved for her.

"I recollect the day them traders first come down the path into this valley. Like you, I wasn't hardly more than a lap baby myself. But I remember them all dripping wet in their buckskins, driving their train of pack horses, more horses than I had ever seen before, and them horses plumb loaded down with rifles and hoes and hatchets, casks of rum, what have you. The river was surging real high from the spring runoff, and when they tried to wade it, a tree trunk come along and knocked them crossways, soaking their gunpowder and cornmeal and bolts of calico. I'd never seen nobody so mad as they was that day—just a'stomping and a'swearing.

"When they reached this house, they looked as shocked as treed coons. In them days of old, folks around here spoke a little bit of everything and not much of anything. But my papaw managed to converse with them, and they asked him how come us to be living in a stone house like they had them back on the coast, instead of in bark huts like the Indians. Papaw said they was no lack of stones in these mountains, and the ancients had known how to stack them so they stayed put. They asked was the ancients Spaniards. Papaw said he'd heard tell they was some of them Spanish, some Porterghee, some Indian, some other things he disremembered.

"The traders stared at him like they'd seen a haint and asked could they pitch camp in our meadow—that same meadow you can see right out that window there today. When they left, Papaw went along with them as a guide. Them mountain paths was all scrambled up by the Cherokees to keep enemies out. You had to know where you was going, or you'd end up at the bottom of a gorge.

"My daddy went along, too, as a horse handler. When he come home, he'd changed his name from Navarre to Joseph. Them traders told him Navarre was Spanish, and they didn't want nothing to do with no Papists. They told Daddy a bunch of Bible names, so he could pick him a new one that God would like better.

"When I turned sixteen, the traders hired me, too. Sometimes they was a hundred pack horses or more, loaded down with trade goods on the way over, and with skins and furs on the trip back— deer, bear, coon, squirrel, possum, beaver, panther, elk. Just like Noah's ark. If the loads wasn't balanced just so, they could topple a horse off a cliff. Sometimes we brought slaves with us for the traders to sell back at the coast—black Africans who'd escaped from the Tidewater and hid out in the mountains, or enemy Indians the Cherokees had captured in battles. One time a bunch of them that was chained together jumped off a cliff so they wouldn't have to go back to being slaves."

He fell silent, remembering arriving at the Indian villages after weeks in the wilderness. The trading girls would come out with their hair cut short, so the traders could tell them apart from the warriors' wives. Traders who messed with warriors' wives never made it back to the blockhouse alive. But for a hand mirror or some beads, a trading girl would take you off to a hut and pleasure you in ways that his wife Nancy could never have even imagined. But Nancy must have suspicioned why he was always so eager to trod them harrowing mountain paths, rain or snow, heat or sleet, because when he'd get back home, she'd act all evil-like. He'd soon have her smiling at his nonsense. But she'd usually lay a baby in the bed between them, so he couldn't get at her till she was good and ready to forgive him for his sins of the flesh indulged in far afield.

2

Couchtown: August 1837

As the raft across the Sturgeon River bucked the current, Daniel Hunter's mare stamped and snorted. Daniel gathered her reins more tightly and patted the white blaze down her forehead. Across her haunches hung leather saddlebags containing his most cherished possessions—the journals of George Fox and John Woolman, and William Penn's *Some Fruits of Solitude*. If this ferry capsized, he could manage without everything except those books. They might prove his sole consolation here in this wild backcountry.

As a muscular young slave hauled on the rope cable that stretched from shore to shore, Daniel studied two men waiting with their horses on the Couchtown landing. One had sideburns and whiskers as tangled as the nest of a messy bird. On his head drooped a floppy black hat. His companion sported a rust-colored stubble on his jaws and skull. His eyes squinted in the sunlight that flickered like flames through the tossing trees. The slave kept glancing at them uneasily.

As Daniel disembarked, he handed the slave a coin, saying, "This is for you, not for your master."

"Thank you, sir." The young slave stuffed the coin into his pocket.

Daniel reflected that he was reenacting a story his father often told about Daniel's grandfather: A Quaker preacher from London visited Daniel's grandparents in their townhouse on Chestnut Street in Philadelphia. As he was leaving, he pressed gold coins into Daniel's grandfather's palm, saying, "Please use these to compensate thy slaves for their many kind services to me."

Daniel's grandfather had stood there staring at the coins while
his carriage driver guarded a blank expression by the front door.
Daniel's father, six years old at the time, had asked himself in bed
that night how a kind man like his own father—who said he believed
each person possessed an inner flame that was the indwelling
Christ—could own his carriage driver and tell him what to do all the
time.

Evidently, Daniel's grandfather questioned himself similarly
because a week later he announced at dinner that their cook and her
husband, the carriage driver, were free from that moment forth. They
kept their jobs and their rooms in the basement, but Daniel's
grandfather gave them emancipation papers and began to pay them a
salary.

Daniel noticed that the men waiting on the Couchtown landing
were staring at him. He knew he looked bizarre in his garments of
raw linsey-woolsey. But he had renounced colored clothing, even the
black that many other Friends favored. He had a special horror of
blue, knowing that its use fuelled the indigo plantations of South
Carolina. Most of the slaves who worked in the dye vats there died of
horrible diseases within five years. It was said that even buzzards in
the sky refused to fly over the reeking vats in which slaves labored
from dawn to dusk.

Daniel led his mare up to the main street of Couchtown, a
packed clay roadway lined with puncheon sidewalks. The street was
dominated by an old three-story log blockhouse chinked with orange
clay. Along the sidewalks stood workshops—a forge, a harness
maker, a tannery, a boot maker, a wheelwright, a cooper.

A gaggle of men dressed in hide shirts and leggings were
gathered in a vacant lot next to an inn with a wide front porch. They
cheered on two black and red cocks that slashed at each other in
midair with flashing silver spurs. Some of the spectators had the high,
beardless, copper cheekbones of Indians, others the anthracite
coloring of Africans. Some seemed too light complexioned to be
either, but too dark to be Englishmen. Apart from their rustic dress,
they reminded Daniel of the exotic sailors and stevedores who had
populated the dock district of Philadelphia. His father had taken him

as a small boy to witness these men stumbling from taverns and brawling in the streets, as an example of how not to behave. But Daniel had always been secretly intrigued by men who did exactly as they wished without worrying about anyone else's disapproval. He himself had always been a model child—quiet, polite, obedient, a good student. Boring, in short.

James and Vera Perkins, friends of his parents whom he had just visited on their sheep farm in the Shenandoah Valley, called this border area the Squabble State because for many years it had been claimed by North Carolina, Virginia, and Tennessee alike. It was unclear whose laws, if any, were applicable. Amid the contention, many free people of color, fleeing the coast and the Deep South, had purchased land or squatted on it unchallenged. Some refused to pay taxes to any state or to serve in their militias. Missionaries from the north had established schools among the Cherokees, but these mixed people in the mountains had been on their own—until now. James and Vera had identified Couchtown as a place in need of a school. Their Mulberry Monthly Meeting and Daniel's parents' meeting in Philadelphia had donated money to get Daniel started as a teacher. If only he could figure out how to begin.

A sign over the doorway of the blockhouse read West's Trading Post. Some trappers milled around outside, their strapped bales of hides and furs resting on the ground like slumbering bears.

Within the blockhouse, Daniel was assaulted by a rank, gamey odor. He spotted a carrot-haired young man in a hide apron counting the deerskins in a bale. Glancing Daniel's way, he called, "Can I help you, sir?"

Hefting his saddlebags across one shoulder, Daniel strode over to him. The man had the freckles and green eyes of an Irishman. Many indentured servants in Philadelphia had been Irish. They were rumored to have started the recent riots there to protest the employment of free Negroes. Several Negroes had been murdered.

"Daniel Hunter." He extended his hand.

With an apologetic grimace, the clerk wiped his hand on his apron. "This is a nasty business," he observed as he shook Daniel's hand. "Abner Martin. Glad to know you, sir. New in town?"

Martin, noted Daniel. Rogue or not, he was English, not Irish. "Yes, I'm from Philadelphia."

"Just touring our southern mountains, sir?"

"No, I'm here to open a school."

Abner blinked.

"Do you think anyone would come?" Daniel asked. His words came out haltingly, like those of a foreign tongue. He had decided to drop "thee" and "thy" so as not to alarm the parents of his prospective students, who might fear that he intended to proselytize. But he often stumbled, and rarely remembered to use contractions. It was especially hard for him to say "sir" or "ma'am," "Mr." or "Mrs." Quakers didn't believe in these distinctions of rank and called other people "Friend" or addressed them by their first names. Daniel understood that this seemed disrespectful to those who weren't Quakers and was trying to correct it.

Abner hesitated. "To tell you the truth, Mr. Hunter, the way most live around here don't leave much time for studies—hunting and trapping in the winter, fishing and planting in the spring, hoeing and suckering all summer, harvesting in the fall. Your students wouldn't likely do no more than drop in between seasons."

Daniel smiled ruefully. "Well, at least you are honest, Mr. Martin."

"But some might send their younger children. And I would sign on myself. We need someone around here to read all these land grants and deeds that newcomers are always waving in our faces."

Abner excused himself to speak to a man in a vest and frockcoat at the rear of the store. He returned to offer Daniel an empty store-room upstairs for his classroom. He also directed him to the house of the widow of the previous store manager, who had extra beds and needed someone to do chores.

Widow Reeves's cheekbones cradled her keen mahogany eyes as she stood in her doorway considering Daniel's request. Her copper cheeks were filigreed with fine wrinkles, as though she had just walked face first through a spider's web. She agreed to provide him a room and meals in return for chores and a small rent.

"This is where my children slept," she explained as she led him up to a loft lined with rope bedsteads topped with cornhusk mattresses.

"How many do you have?"

"Fourteen. All grown now and farming down in Silver Valley."

Once she had gone downstairs, Daniel spread his undyed wool blanket on a mattress, stacked his leather-bound books on the windowsill beneath the gable, and laid his extra set of clothing in a cupboard built into the wall. Then he placed his slates, chalk, and George Fox primers on the floor by the stairway, to carry to his new classroom the next day. He would hire someone to make puncheon benches and desks. Then the only thing lacking would be students.

Lying on his blanket with his head propped against the chinked wall, he watched daylight fade through the tiny gable window. Exhaustion from his journey began to creep along his limbs like a fever. He now owned only a horse, tack, and saddlebags and their contents, but he felt more at peace than he ever had during those years of working for his father's textile import firm on the Philadelphia docks. His life had a true purpose now. Before, he had worked for money and for his parents' approval. Now he would work for the welfare of those less advantaged than himself.

Daniel knew that his parents, as well as James and Vera, hoped that he and their daughter Abigail would marry. They had known each other as children, before the Perkinses moved south, and they had just spent many pleasurable hours together at her parents' sheep farm in the Shenandoah. He was twenty now, and it was time for him to consider this step. Once their engagement was over, he would be twenty-two and she twenty-one. But he wondered if Abigail could find fulfillment in this rude village. She wore dresses of a modest cut, yet he could tell, since it had been his trade, that their dark fabrics were the finest silks and taffetas money could buy—and he himself would earn little as a schoolteacher.

As twilight descended, Daniel pondered his favorite Bible verse: "Be still and know that I am God." Lying there in the dark, he closed his eyes and waited for guidance from his own inner light in this strange new land. Although he had listened all his life to descriptions of this inner light, which apparently guided the decisions of all true Quakers, he was not certain he had ever experienced it. Not that he had admitted this to anyone else.

The following evening, Daniel inspected the Martins' farmhouse. Mossy stones had popped out of the walls and lay on the ground, but the structure had evidently been standing for a long time. The Virginia creeper climbing one wall was as burled as Mrs. Reeves's fingers and as thick around as his own forearm. Some cows and horses inhabited sheds ringing the yard. A few raggedy sheep grazed a pasture beyond.

Abner greeted him at the doorway, his red hair slicked back. He ushered Daniel down a stone-paved corridor. His family was already seated on benches around a plank table at one end of a large room that featured a walk-in fireplace. The rear windows overlooked a creek bank lined with poplars that towered overhead like green pyramids and swayed in a breeze off the water.

As Abner introduced him, Daniel struggled to remember the various names, all of which seemed to be taken from the Old Testament. But the best he could manage was to note a cacophony of colors—eyes of blue, green, chocolate, and black; hair of butternut, auburn, and charcoal; skin several hues of brown, copper, olive, and cream. The Martins were the oddest-looking Englishmen he had ever seen.

"So you're starting a school in town, Mr. Hunter?" asked Abner's mother, Barbary, as she served him a bowl of venison stew. Her graying hair hung lankly to frame a chubby, cheerful face.

Daniel nodded. "Yes, ma'am."

"Do you think my son, Nathan, could attend?" asked a young woman, whose face was the color of a ripe chestnut. Around her neck on a rawhide thong hung a stone the color of clotted blood.

The little boy looked up from a small wooden horse he was swaddling in a napkin.

"By all means," said Daniel. "And anyone else in the family so inclined."

"I'm afraid Nathan here is our only little fellow of leisure," said Abner's father, Reuben, who was missing his left arm. His right one was grotesquely muscular and as broad around as a thigh. "Abner tells us you hail from Philadelphia, Mr. Hunter?"

"Yes, sir. I traveled down the Shenandoah on horseback. That valley has become quite a thoroughfare."

"So I hear. But they say Couchtown ain't an easy place to find. You got to scale some right smart hills at the foot of that valley."

"Yes sir, that is true. I rested on a sheep farm before starting the climb to Couchtown."

"We hope you like our little town, Mr. Hunter," said Barbary. "We need a school here, and we need some educated people."

"Daniel said he would learn me to read and write," said Abner.

"Good idea," said his father, gnawing a hunk of venison speared on the tip of his hunting knife. "This fellow turns up here a while back with his tripod and chains and starts blazing trees with his ax all around my farm. When I asked him his business, he showed me a piece of paper. Since I couldn't read it, he told me the government had laid out plots for soldiers who fought them Red Stick Creek Indians at Horseshoe Bend during the second war against the British. I told him my family had farmed this land since ancient days, and I lost my arm fighting in the first war against the British, and if he didn't get offen my land right quick, somebody would have to carry him off."

"What happened?" asked Daniel.

"He went away, and he ain't been back since."

"Daddy, tell Mr. Hunter the story about how that general cut your arm off with his sword," requested Nathan. He had his mother's dark, shining eyes and curly black hair.

Reuben smiled at him. "I wouldn't want to take away Mr. Hunter's appetite, Nathan."

"Did you fight in the Revolution, sir?" asked Daniel. His parents had always assured him that nothing gained through fighting was worth having. Quakers believed in turning the other cheek, no matter what the provocation. Nevertheless, men willing to kill for their beliefs had always intrigued him, and at school he had studied the Revolution and the War of 1812 with fascination.

"No sir, not really. Not the whole war. Just a little skirmish at King's Mountain when I was about your age."

"But King's Mountain was a very important battle, sir. It stopped the British from invading Virginia and heading north." Daniel was astonished to be talking to a man who had actually fought in the Revolution—at King's Mountain, no less. The older Quaker men he knew had all found ways to avoid fighting, believing that the way to combat evil was to focus on doing good instead.

Reuben shrugged. "I just didn't want them burning down my corn patch."

"Go ahead, Reuben," said Barbary with a longsuffering sigh.

"My family has heard this story a million times," he explained to Daniel.

"But it's interesting every time, Papa," insisted a son named Joshua, whose eyes shone like sapphires in the light from the setting sun that poured through the windows overlooking the creek bank.

"Well, Captain Barnes, the head of the Couchtown militia at that time, sent out a call for us to muster in town. I didn't go because I hadn't finished harvesting my corn. But the next thing I knowed, Barnes was on my doorstep telling me to grab my rifle and come on.

"I says, 'Where at?'

"He says, 'The Tories is fixing to come up here and kill our wives and children.'

"I says, 'What's the Tories?'

"He says, 'Ain't you never heard of them Loyalists?'

"I says, 'Yeah, but I ain't give them no thought.'

"He says, 'Well, you better cause they're headed this way.'

"'What have they got agin us?'

"'That we won't take the loyalty oath.'

"'Nobody never told me about no loyalty oath. If I'd ever heard of it, I might of took it. Loyalty to who?'

"'To the King of England.'

"'Well, I don't care nothing about no kings,' I told him, 'but I do like them English. They give my daddy and my papaw jobs on their trading trips.'

"'Them traders was Virginians,' Barnes says. 'And it's the Virginians heading up this fight to get us free from the English.'

"I pondered this. The traders had always told my daddy they was English. They talked about the Virginia planters on the coast who hated the English king because he taxed their tobacco. But the traders hated the planters because many of the traders had worked as servants chopping the planters' tobacco. So was this war meant to save these planters from paying taxes, or what? The whole thing didn't make no sense to me, so I pointed to my corn still on the stalk.

"Captain Barnes says, 'Let me put this another way, Reuben: If the Tories win, we will every one of us get run offen our land.'

"I says, 'This here is my land.'

"'The king done give the Indians all the land west of the Blue Ridge, and that's just exactly where we're standing right now.'

"I says, 'But the ancients used to say some of our people was Indians. So I guess we ain't got no quarrel here.'

"'Martin, them ancients of yours is dead and gone," said Barnes. 'Prove that you own this land. Show me your deed.'

"'The ancients didn't read nor write. But that don't mean I don't own this land.'

"'All right, Reuben,' says Barnes. 'Here's your last chance. If you don't come with me right now, Colonel Cleveland will have you hanged in town for treason.'

"'Why didn't you say so right off?' I asked, and headed into the house for my rifle."

As night descended out the windows along the creek, Barbary lit beeswax candles while Reuben described how his militia rode all night through driving rain without so much as a swallow of rum to warm them in their sodden buckskins. The next day the scouts reported Tory troops camped atop a low mountain just ahead. The militia crept up the steep slopes, slipping from tree to tree, concealed by the morning mist.

All of a sudden everyone around Reuben began to yell, "The sword of the Lord and Gideon!" So Reuben joined in, even though he had no idea who this Gideon fellow was.

The Tory drummers formed a ragged line on the mountaintop and beat a frenzied tattoo. As the rebels neared the summit, the Tories charged with their bayonets. The rebels retreated downhill and the Tories followed. Then the rebels circled around and cut off the Tory route back up to the top. As the Tories scurried among the trees like panicked mice, the militiamen patiently shot them down one by one.

When Reuben's unit reached the summit, the Tory commander, Colonel Ferguson, led a charge right at them. Ferguson's horse stumbled and collapsed from bullet wounds. Ferguson, a corpulent fellow in a fringed hunting shirt, staggered around slashing wildly with a saber. Someone in a red uniform jacket brought him another horse, which he mounted as eagerly as a bear climbing a honey tree. Then he charged Reuben's rank again, this time lopping off Reuben's arm in passing. As Reuben fell, so did Ferguson, with his boot caught in his stirrup. While Ferguson's horse dragged him around the campsite, Reuben's comrades riddled his body with bullets.

The candlelight flickered across the remains of the dinner, and the air around the table filled with the sweet scent of melting honeycomb. Reuben described how someone cauterized the stub of his arm. How he lay there all night on the mountaintop, surrounded by the dead, listening to the screams and groans of the wounded, wondering how on earth he could harvest his corn with just one arm. The next morning two of his cousins loaded him on a stretcher and headed for home. They stole sweet potatoes from a roadside patch and built a fire from fence ties to roast them.

"I've never tasted anything more delicious before or since," concluded Reuben. "I'd drunk so much apple brandy that I didn't hardly feel the pain, and I was just as tickled as a puppy in a weed patch, gobbling my yams and knowing we'd stopped them British in their fancy red coats from coming up our way. It seemed worth losing my arm for at the time—though I've often doubted that since. I named my firstborn twin after that Gideon fellow, just to honor my lost arm, lying there rotting on that forlorn summit, gone all goose-bumped in the winter winds."

On the ride home Daniel stopped his horse to vomit alongside the trail over the image of Mr. Martin's goose-bumped arm abandoned on the mountaintop. His parents were right. No victory was worth robbing a man of his limbs for the rest of his life. It was clear that his romantic notions about war were just the heroic delusions of a silly child.

Back at Mrs. Reeves's he climbed into bed and tried to calm his agitation by reading James Naylor: "There is a spirit which I feel that delights to do no evil, nor to revenge any wrong, but delights to endure all things…. Its hope is to outlive all wrath and contention, and to weary out all exaltation and cruelty…."

He fell asleep, determined to be a living example of the spirit of conciliation, whatever challenges this savage land might serve to him.

Daniel led his horse down the street to the forge. The farrier, a tall, bald man with a deformed left ear and a missing eyetooth, introduced himself as Ben Jones. As he pounded the molten horseshoe intended for Daniel's mare, Daniel told him about his school and asked if he knew of any likely students.

Ben straightened, holding the glowing shoe in tongs, and studied him. "You're not from around here, are you?"

"I am from Philadelphia."

"A city boy. Can you fight?"

"Well, no. I mean, I never have. I do not believe in fighting." Daniel figured this was truer than ever now that he carried that image of Reuben Martin's severed arm in his head.

Ben laughed grimly. "You don't have to believe in lightning to get yourself fried to a crisp during a thunderstorm. Tell you what, I'll do your fighting for you, if you'll teach my son and daughter how to read and write."

"Agreed." Daniel extended his hand, then realized that Ben's were fully occupied.

Daniel dropped wood into the box by Mrs. Reeves's charred stone fireplace. She had had to hobble outside and show him how to use the axe and wedges. It had taken him an hour to assemble this meager armload. It was going to be a long winter. He squatted to toss one of his precious logs onto the smoldering coals. Then he sat at the long walnut dining table.

Ladling corn, squash, and beans into pottery bowls, Mrs. Reeves asked, "Aren't your parents sad to have you so far from home, young fellow?"

"I imagine so," replied Daniel, as he scooped up a chunk of pumpkin on a hunk of cornbread. "But as I was leaving, my father told me they named me Daniel, after Daniel in the Bible, because they wanted me to face challenges without fear. He said I was fulfilling all their dearest hopes for me."

"So Couchtown is your lion's den?" Her sly smile narrowed her mahogany eyes to slits.

Daniel blushed, realizing he had offended her. "No, ma'am. But I do think it will benefit the town if some of its citizens can read."

"Those who can't read may have more to offer than educated folks might imagine, Mr. Hunter."

"I am certain they do, Mrs. Reeves. But Mr. Martin, for instance, says it would help him if he could read the papers of newcomers who want his land."

"You've already met Reuben Martin?"

"I had dinner at their house yesterday evening."

"The Martins are my oldest friends. Their children are almost as precious to me as my own children. Reuben's father Zachariah and I used to ride on trading trips together. My husband was the chief trader. Zachariah was a guide, and I was an interpreter."

Daniel studied the hunched old woman in her calico skirt and blouse and tried to imagine her navigating on horseback those narrow mountain tracks on which he had barely escaped plunging to his death in the valleys below. "The Martins seem like an interesting family. Are they English?"

She snorted. "Abner over at the store likes to swan around like he's English. But the only true Englishman around here was my husband Roger."

"Are you English, too?" He knew she wasn't, but he didn't know how to ask if she were as Indian as she looked.

"No. I grew up in a town three mountains over called Tocaru."

"You're Cherokee?"

"Some call us that. Others call us Tsalagi. The cave dwellers. Our ancestors called themselves the Principal People. But most whites these days just call us a nuisance." She chuckled.

"How did you happen to marry an Englishman?"

"The unmarried girls in our village used to entertain the visiting traders. We didn't much care for the men themselves because they rarely bathed and had scratchy beards. But they brought us hair-brushes, mirrors, satin ribbons, calico cloth, bead bracelets. Our town encouraged us because we made the traders eager to return. Sad to say, our village had by then mostly forgotten how to make our own weapons and tools and clothing. So we actually needed the traders as much as they needed us."

"Yet you married one of these unappetizing traders?" Daniel was trying to digest the fact that his landlady had just confessed to being a prostitute, and that she didn't seem remotely ashamed of it.

She smiled. "Oh, I didn't say they was all unappetizing. In fact, Roger Reeves was as delicious a man as I've ever seen, before or since. A vagabond and a thief, but a charming one. They put him in prison in England for stealing a horse. Then they loaded him on a ship bound for Virginia. He hoed tobacco for four years before he got fed up and headed for the hills, where some traders hired him as a horse handler. One afternoon at Tocaru he came swaggering toward me with a gleam in his eyes, which were the tint of sunlight through pond water. I knew right then that I wanted him near me for the rest of my days."

"Did he own the trading post?"

"No, the export company at the coast hired him to run it for a while."

"When did he die?"

"It's been a good twenty-five years now. I hadn't ever imagined a life here in Couchtown without him. I'd never been alone before. I grew up in a lodge at Tocaru surrounded by my entire family. And this house here had been so crammed with our children that it never occurred to me that they would grow up to live like the English— each couple in a separate house with children of their own. My grandchildren marrying British settlers and then claiming to be pure British themselves, like their grandfather.

"I decided to move back home to Tocaru. I knew it would go easier for my children and grandchildren if I left. The settlers think it's romantic to have an Indian ancestor from times gone by. But if you have an Indian mother or father, they see you as nothing but a trashy half blood. I hadn't visited Tocaru for years. At first I was too busy raising children. Later, the journey was too dangerous. The Cherokee raiding parties and the settler militias were trying to destroy each other. They both wanted the same land—the land the Cherokees had lived on since time began."

As the fire crackled and popped, she described riding on horseback along the no longer familiar paths, hiding in the bushes each time a traveler approached. At night she slept beneath rock ledges, with a fire to keep the wolves and panthers away.

Reaching Tocaru, she passed a huge old oak tree under which she had often rested while hoeing corn. Sliding off her horse, she hugged the trunk like a long-lost friend. The cornfields were overgrown with brambles. The fruit and nut trees lay rotting alongside their jagged stumps.

As she walked toward the town, she discovered that its log palisade had collapsed and that many huts were no more than charred ruins. The seven-sided council house lacked its roof.

Wandering the familiar streets, she came upon half a dozen lodges with smoke spiraling from their roof holes. She called out a greeting and approached one. A young man in a wide calico headband emerged, cradling a rifle. In rusty Cherokee she explained who she was.

"We know of you," he replied. "You are Sali. You married the trader Reeves?"

"Yes."

"You have been away for many winters."

"Yes, too many."

"You belong to the Deer Clan?"

She nodded.

"Many of your people now lie buried in that mound on the hillside." He pointed to a hillock covered with saplings and brambles.

"So I have heard."

"Your sister Wren lives a half day's walk downstream. Only the Bird Clan remains here in Tocaru. But you may stay with us tonight and seek your sister in the morning light."

"I accept your generous offer," she replied. "But what has happened to Tocaru? Why do so few live here now?"

"When the militias attack, they burn down the town. We have wearied of rebuilding our lodges. Besides, since the wild animals have now vanished from the forests, we rely on cows and pigs, orchards and gardens. We need to live near them in order to protect them from the settlers."

The next day, plodding on her horse along a path that paralleled a broad, shallow river, Sali had passed several deserted cabins. Toward noon she arrived at a cornfield in which four women in calico skirts, blouses, and sunbonnets were hoeing weeds. Beyond them children tussled in the dirt yard of a small log cabin.

She recognized Wren immediately, even though her black hair had gone silver and her cheeks had shriveled up like dried apples. But Wren's greeting was so cool that Sali felt she needed to introduce herself.

"Of course I know who you are," Wren assured her. "But I have only reproaches for you, so it is best that I say nothing at all."

"I have stayed away too long."

"These grown women are your nieces whom you have never met."

Sali smiled at the three young women, and they nodded back shyly.

"Come sit in the shade and give me your news," said Wren.

They sat on a fallen tree trunk. Sipping water from a bottle gourd, they talked about the years that had passed. Sali learned that her uncles, brothers, and male cousins had either been killed in skirmishes with the settlers or were in hiding farther south.

"It is good to see you, Sali," Wren finally admitted. "How long can you stay?"

"I had thought of staying permanently." Sali lowered her head and awaited Wren's response, which didn't come for a long time.

"You long ago chose the traders over us."

"But I am still a member of the Deer Clan, as are my children."

"Have you raised them to speak our tongue? Have you offered hospitality to other members of our clan? Have you sought vengeance against those who have harmed us?"

Sali shook her head. "Yet I remember how you all encouraged my alliance with the traders."

"The traders once seemed to bring us all we could wish for. But in the end they took everything away, including my baby sister Sali. Of course you may stay here if you wish, Sali. But it seems to me that your place is now among your children and their children."

Mrs. Reeves smiled ruefully at Daniel in the firelight. "After Wren said that, I realized I couldn't go back to Tocaru anyhow. I'd become too used to the comforts of my life in Couchtown. So I guess I'll end my days just as old Zachariah Martin did: babysitting my grandbabies down in Silver Valley. My children love me and will take me in when that time comes, whatever hardships it may cause them to have newcomers know that they're half bloods."

As Daniel arranged the new desks and benches, Ben, the farrier, appeared in the doorway with a boy and a girl, both with complexions the rich golden brown of cured tobacco leaves. Daniel looked back and forth among the three, realizing that Ben was perhaps a mulatto. Or his wife was. Or these weren't his children.

"Is there a problem?" asked Ben, with a defiant tilt to his chin and a belligerent tone to his voice, as though he had often known trouble and had learned to anticipate it, even where there wasn't any.

"Not at all. I am happy to see you again, Mr. Jones. Are these your children?"

Ben nodded, relaxing his scowl. "Mr. Hunter, let me present Sampson and Rebecca."

Daniel shook hands with the solemn children and led each to a bench.

"When school's over, come to the forge," their father told them as he left.

"We will—we'll wait a little longer to see if anyone else is coming." Daniel sat at his desk and studied his new students in their neat homespun clothing. "Does either of you know your alphabet?"

Both children shook their heads.

Daniel looked up to discover Nathan in the doorway, dressed in a calico shirt, leather leggings, and moccasins, clutching his wooden horse. Behind him stood Abner, his orange hair ablaze in a shaft of morning sunlight. Sampson and Rebecca stared at Nathan, and he stared back at them.

"Nathan wants to learn to read and write and do sums," said Abner.

Nathan nodded eagerly.

"So do I," he continued. "And Mr. West likes the idea, too, so he's giving me time off to take your classes."

Daniel stood up. "I'm pleased to have you both. Nathan, would you share that desk with Rebecca?"

Nathan did as he was told, and Abner sat beside Sampson, his lanky legs folding up like chicken wings until his chin could almost have rested on his knees.

Daniel laid a slate and a stick of chalk before each student. "First we need to learn our letters."

Gently he freed the wooden horse from Nathan's grasp, saying, "I—I'll take good care of your pony until after class." After placing the horse on his desk, Daniel printed an "A" on his own slate and watched his students copy it.

As they practiced the letter, he sat behind his desk. Picking up the horse, he studied it. It looked to be carved with a hunting knife, every muscle perfectly molded by someone who knew horses.

3

The Shenandoah: October 1837

Daniel sat astride his mare, lulled by the steady clop of her hooves on the packed clay road. To his right roiled the Sturgeon River, its waters white and turbulent from the autumn rains. To his left tobacco curing in a weathered barn laced the breeze down the hillside with an acrid tang. Beside the barn stood a two-story plank house, some outbuildings, and three small log cabins. He spotted two slaves chopping wood and three more butchering a hog that hung head-down from the limb of a huge oak with leaves gone mauve.

This valley appeared quite prosperous compared to Silver Valley. The buildings and fence posts stood straight. The fields were cleared of trees and brush. The sheep and horses looked sleek and healthy. The hogs were penned and the cattle fenced, rather than wandering throughout the neighborhood. And there were the slave cabins, which, of course, explained all the rest. On the docks in Philadelphia some of his father's competitors used slaves to load and unload their ships. Their profit margins were greater than his father's. But his father always insisted that there were higher rewards than money for those who refused to exploit their fellow human beings.

Since most of his students were currently harvesting corn and tobacco, Daniel had decided to visit Abigail. He had either to propose marriage or to set her free to find someone else. He had no idea which he would do. He was sometimes lonely for someone who shared his background and beliefs. But he simply couldn't imagine performing the carnal duties of a husband with her. He had grown up listening to inspired testimonies from traveling women preachers, including Abigail's own mother Vera. Another woman preacher, Mary Dyer, had been hanged by Puritans on the Boston Common for her faith. Mating with such pious creatures as women seemed a sacrilege to Daniel. He wondered how their husbands managed it.

He had attended a revival the previous night, held in the vacant lot next to the Couchtown Inn, a site that normally hosted cock fights. Farmers had brought their families in wagons to hear a Methodist circuit rider named Reverend Foster, who had a reputation for conversion.

As Daniel listened to his panting descriptions of "the gates of heaven and the grates of hell," some in the audience swayed, trembled, and shouted. Others swooned to the ground and lay there jerking and babbling gibberish, while the stench of sweat and manure wafted into the night sky like yeoman's incense.

Daniel had spotted Nathan riding on Abner's shoulders near the front, clutching his wooden horse as he observed this bacchanal. The two men Daniel had seen at the ferry dock when he had first arrived had stood near the street scanning the crowd. One wore a floppy black hat, and the other had rusty stubble on his jaws and head. Daniel watched Ben Jones, the bald farrier, glance their way and assume an expression that seemed to mix contempt with alarm. Beside him stood Sampson, Rebecca, and an attractive African woman wearing a blue headscarf. The next time Daniel looked for the Jones family, they had vanished.

As his horse plodded along, Daniel reflected that he had grown up in a world in which spiritual experience had been private and reserved. He had been startled by this public frenzy. Yet his new neighbors had seemed so sincere in their faith and so passionate in its expression that he now wondered if they were experiencing some truth that had eluded him all these years because of his preoccupation with his own dignity. After all, the early Quakers had preached at open-air markets and street fairs, earning their sobriquet from their converts' convulsions as they opened themselves up to illumination. But the Friends at his parents' meeting in Philadelphia had frowned whenever anyone betrayed an emotion that threatened to disrupt the decorum of their silent sittings.

The descent from the mountains took two days, the road surging and plunging like the swells on an angry ocean. At night Daniel ate

Mrs. Reeves's cornbread and venison jerky from his saddlebag and then rolled up in a blanket beneath a rock ledge. Although accustomed to such rude accommodations from his trip down the Shenandoah, he was not accustomed to the utter silence of the mountain nights or to the occasional screams of panthers and howls of wolves. Should one attack, he would have no notion of how to fight it off. Like a cowardly gladiator, he would have to let it eat him alive. Could pacifism thrive, or even survive, in such a savage setting as this?

On the third day Daniel reached a landscape that merely rolled. The leaves drifting into his path were still only faintly tinged with orange and gold. Up ahead he spotted a man in a broad-brimmed straw hat riding a dapple-gray gelding. A coiled blacksnake whip hung around one shoulder. A rifle butt protruded from a leather holster strapped to his pommel. Before him trudged some Negroes dressed in frayed homespun—two adolescent girls, two younger boys in shirts with long tails and sleeves that exposed their wrists, and an older man with a tightly curled gray beard. A woman in a yellow calico turban carried a squirming toddler.

Riding up alongside the mounted man, Daniel asked, "Where are you headed, sir?"

"To Mulberry Courthouse," the man replied, revealing a mouthful of crooked yellow teeth, like dried corn kernels. "How about you?"

"I am visiting some friends on their farm near Mulberry Courthouse."

They rode on in silence until the slaves began to sing a sorrowful hymn in a minor key.

"What's happening to these people?" asked Daniel.

"Their master has died, leaving his widow in debt. They have to be sold."

"Are they a family?"

The man nodded.

"You will of course see that they are sold together?"

The man shrugged. "Once I deliver them to the auctioneer, it's out of my hands."

After a moment, Daniel spurred his horse to a canter, pounding down the road until his mare's neck turned slick with sweat and he himself was gasping for breath. As he slowed her to a trot, he was relieved to discover that the slaves' lament had been replaced by the mournful wail of dying cicadas. He had seen slaves before on the docks of Philadelphia, but never an entire family in bondage, about to be dispersed.

He pictured himself hiding in the bushes and then leaping out to disarm the man with the yellow teeth. He would tell the slave family that they were now free. And then what? Where would they go? How would they earn a living? What would he do with the man? Would he have to kill him to keep him from recapturing the slaves? How could he kill him? He didn't even know how to shoot the rifle in the man's holster. Besides, Quakers didn't kill people. They believed in peace. They turned the other cheek. But how could you turn your head aside when you saw people being mistreated? If he were a true Quaker, like his parents, like Vera and James Perkins, his inner light would give him the answers to these questions. But no matter how long he waited, answers never came. He was nothing but a fake Quaker.

Daniel realized that several dozen sheep were grazing in the pasture to his left. He recognized them as the Saxons James Perkins had herded down the Shenandoah from Pennsylvania. James was trying to persuade his neighbors to improve their flocks so they could sell their wool to northern mills. He always had several schemes percolating, designed to relieve the local planters' dependence on tobacco and hence on slave labor. He had recently persuaded the entire Philadelphia Quarterly Meeting to smash their pipes in a gesture of protest.

Knowing Abigail was now just a few minutes away, Daniel was invaded by alluring memories—of the lavender scent of the hand-kerchief she pushed up her sleeve, of the rustle of her taffeta skirt as she walked past him. Thoughts of what to do about her erased his anguish over the plight of the slave family and his own spiritual inadequacies.

Arriving at the Perkins house, a two-story log cabin planked with whitewashed boards, Daniel slid down from his horse, walked up to their door, and knocked. Abigail and her parents greeted him, clad in their best black garments. He almost laughed out loud at the contrast of their grim attire to the gay calicos and vegetable-dyed stripes of mountain clothing. The Perkinses resembled a coven of alabaster-faced witches.

"Why do we amuse thee so?" asked Abigail in her quiet alto as she escorted him upstairs to the guest room. He had almost forgotten how her voice had stirred him during his last visit. Its restrained intensity had suggested that beneath that dour black bodice glowed a molten heart that could boil the ice water that trickled through his own chilly veins.

"I was smiling simply because I am happy to see thee." Reverting to "thee," he felt as though this were now a foreign language, too, and that he had become a man without a native tongue.

"I am happy to see thee, too," she murmured, looking away. "I had hoped thou might write to me."

He studied the fitted black jacket that overlapped the waistband of her long black skirt. Each wrist-length sleeve featured a row of tiny buttons up the forearms that matched those securing the front placket running from her waist to her throat. It must have taken several hours to hook them all closed. "I wanted to," he replied. "But there is no postal service in Couchtown. I had great difficulty even finding a traveler passing this way to bring thee my note about this visit."

"So my parents assured me."

Daniel glanced at her lowered head and the neat knot into which she had twisted her shiny auburn hair. If he removed a protruding ivory pin, the hair would cascade down her shoulders and over her bosom, like water coursing from a breached dam. She had evidently been discussing him with her parents. If he did not intend to propose marriage, he should probably go right back to Couchtown. But now that he saw her again, he felt his doubts about his own desire for her melt like spring snow. However, his doubts about her happiness in Couchtown remained.

As she looked up, her gray eyes met his, and his heart leapt into his throat. He almost spoke to her of these feelings. But instead, he forced a smile. After a moment she smiled back. Impulsively, he reached out an index finger and stroked a vein that throbbed up the back of her hand. Her lips trembled as though she were about to speak, but she said nothing.

Vera Perkins appeared in the doorway. Her silver hair was parted in the middle and gathered into a bun, which she had encased in a translucent white cap that tied with sashes beneath her chin. Prior to her marriage she had traveled for religious service, preaching all over New England, the West Indies, and the British Isles. Once during Tecumseh's War she had reportedly ridden alone and unarmed along the treaty line between the white settlers and the Shawnees, to demonstrate her confidence in God's protection.

As a boy, Daniel had heard her preach in Philadelphia. People throughout his meeting had closed their eyes and covered their faces with one hand, in rapt inward concentration. Yet as a hostess, Vera rarely spoke, and then she said only the most commonplace pleasantries. He found her thoroughly intimidating, even though she and her husband insisted Daniel call them by their first names. Could she tell that he had never really experienced his own inward light? Did this make him unworthy of Abigail? Might Vera oppose their union on such grounds?

"Let Daniel clean up, my dear," she said to Abigail. "Then come have some dinner, Daniel. Thou must be famished from the road."

After changing his clothes, trimming his closely cropped beard, and brushing his hair, Daniel went downstairs to join his hosts. As he described his new students, Daniel watched Abigail rise to assist the serving woman. Like all Quakers, she didn't stand on rank or ceremony. Perhaps she could fit in at Couchtown better than he had been imagining?

"I attended my first tent meeting earlier this week," said Daniel, somewhat sheepishly.

"Who was the preacher?" asked James. His head was as bald as a toadstool. A tuft of gray whiskers at his chin made him resemble an amiable goat.

"A Methodist circuit rider named Reverend Foster."

James laughed indulgently. "Oh my goodness, yes. Our meeting calls him the 'circus rider.'"

They all smiled, but Daniel felt like a traitor. He could still picture the ecstatic faces of his impoverished neighbors. Was their form of worship any less worthy of respect than his own?

"But he did affect a lot of people," added Daniel.

"Yes, but affected them in what way?" asked James. "Their lives are tedious, and he stirred their passions—their desire for heaven and their fear of hell. This is entertainment, not spirituality."

"Perhaps not," conceded Daniel. But to *them* it had been spirituality, and who could swear that it was not as profound as the elusive inward light of the Quakers?

"But I keep thinking," said Daniel, "about George Fox and all those early Friends who got thrown into jail for disrupting Anglican services. Many were beaten and stoned for blasphemy. What if Reverend Foster is the current George Fox?"

James chuckled, thinking he intended a joke. Rather than risk a confrontation with his potential father-in-law, Daniel switched topics. "I passed a family of slaves on the road today. They were walking to Mulberry Courthouse to be sold for their master's debts. The overseer said it was not certain they would be sold together."

"Alas, that happens all too often," replied James.

"Is there nothing to be done?"

James shook his head. "It is like trying to stem the ocean tide with a pile of seashells. Thy parents' meeting sends us as much money as they can spare for our emancipation fund. We bought and freed more than two dozen slaves last year. But over half have since been seized and resold. So this year we have bought five more in the name of our meeting. They work for us for wages, but if anyone should kidnap them, we can prove ownership. But we now face expulsion as Friends for slave owning, which as you know has been forbidden to Quakers for the last half century. Sometimes the path to righteousness is thorny indeed."

"Can we not do something for this family that is headed to the auction block?" asked Abigail, frown lines etching her pale forehead.

She looked almost ill to Daniel after his months surrounded by people with skin every shade of golden brown, cream, olive, and sable.

"How many of them are there?" asked James.

"Seven," replied Daniel. "One is just a toddler."

"We could perhaps afford three or four."

"But they are a family. They belong together," protested Daniel.

James nodded. "I know how shocking thou must find this, Friend. But to guard thy sanity, and thus be able to help, thou must learn to observe this madness clearly, without allowing it to infect thine own being."

Alone in his room after dinner, Daniel read the letters his mother had been sending him in care of James and Vera. The familiar routines of her busy life in Philadelphia filled him with homesickness. But she also spoke of the pride she and his father felt in him for undertaking such a demanding mission, and he knew that being a responsible adult required one to endure loneliness and hardship with equanimity. But not forever, if one could find a partner to assuage him....

Daniel watched rainwater drip from the brim of James's wide black hat and bead on the shoulders of his broadcloth coat as they rode toward Mulberry Courthouse the next morning. Reaching the streets of shops and hostelries, they left their horses at a livery stable. A neighboring farmer in muddy leather boots greeted James, and they followed him up the steps and into the red brick courthouse.

The slaves to be auctioned lined the hallway. Their eyes were wide with apprehension, numb with resignation, or smoldering with rage as potential buyers lifted their eyelids and upper lips and searched their bodies for evidence of handicaps and diseases, for the scars or amputations that would identify troublemakers.

Daniel indicated to James the family he had passed on the road. The mother in the yellow turban kept repeating, "My baby must stay with me. Please, sir. Please leave my baby with his mother. Please, kind master."

Listening to her litany of pain, Daniel felt nauseated being a member of the race that was performing this horrific deed. As they walked past the auctioneer, Daniel heard him explain to a dealer in a black eye patch that he would prefer to sell her entire family as a unit. The dealer shook his head. He looked up and glared at James, probably having bid against him in the past.

They stationed themselves against one wall. James said in a low voice, "We must make some hard decisions, Daniel, and then wait to see how the bidding goes. The sons must be sacrificed. They are young and strong and can survive on their own. Keeping the child with his mother is our priority. Then the sisters, who are of an age to be debauched. Then the father, who is nearly too old to work."

They watched as the slaves near the entrance were bought one by one. Then the brothers, dressed in their long-tailed shirts, were purchased by the dealer with the eye patch. Daniel watched them look toward their parents and siblings for what all present knew was most likely the last time.

The mother was bought as a cook by the farmer who had greeted James outside. As the auctioneer tried to lift the child from her arms, she clutched him more tightly, and he began to scream. James stepped forward and spoke to the auctioneer. Then he went over to the woman's new owner and talked to him in a low voice. The farmer nodded. The mother was allowed to continue holding her baby.

James bid on the two sisters himself, outlasting a dandified dealer from the coast, with a gold watch chain draping his checked waistcoat. James also bought the father at a bargain price because of his cloudy eyes.

As the new owners crowded around the clerk's desk to complete their bills of sale, James approached his neighbor and asked him to lease the sisters and father for a nominal fee. In return, James offered him a slice of woodlot along their common boundary. The farmer agreed, delighted to have gained five slaves and a woodlot for the price of one slave.

As Daniel and James mounted their horses outside the stable, a coffle of slaves with bound wrists trudged past, heading for the main road. Daniel spotted the two sons in their long-tailed shirts. The face of one was wet with tears.

"I have looked Satan in the face," Daniel murmured to James, "and I have seen that he is stronger than we are."

"Stronger than we are perhaps, but not stronger than our God."

Daniel gathered up his reins, wishing his own faith were as stalwart as that of James.

An icy rain was pelting down the next morning, and the Perkinses' only means of conveyance to the Mulberry Creek meeting house was an open cart. So they sat at home in silent communion until dinnertime.

After the meal they lounged by the fire. Daniel leafed through some newspapers, not having had access to any during his weeks in Couchtown. In the back pages of a *Richmond Register* he came across several ads offering rewards for fugitive slaves. One was headed by the silhouette of a fleeing slave with a walking stick over his shoulder, from which hung a bundle. Then followed a description so detailed that Daniel felt he almost knew the runaway.

"This is appalling." Daniel spread out the page for the others. Abigail and her mother nodded, as though already familiar with such ads.

James handed him the pamphlet he had been scrutinizing. "Read this report from the Virginia Yearly Meeting and tell me what thou thinkest."

Daniel discovered that it concerned a schism over the involvement of certain members in the Underground Railroad. The tract maintained that abolitionists stirred up such antagonism that even the moderate slaveholders turned against abolition, thereby harming the very cause for which the abolitionists were fighting.

"What dost thou think, James?" Daniel asked, wondering if he were being tested as a potential son-in-law.

"Well, although I oppose slavery, I also oppose theft."

"Even when the property being stolen is another human being?"

"We must operate within the framework of existing laws until we can change them, Daniel. That is why I purchase slaves to free them, even though I abhor such negotiations."

"Yet Quakers have always refused military service, which surely breaches the law?"

James looked at him with new interest. "I fear thou art turning into a rabble rouser, Daniel."

"What is the punishment for aiding fugitives?" asked Daniel.

"Fines, exile, public whippings. A few have been hanged."

Daniel grimaced. "Yet some would say that laws that are wrong must be disobeyed."

James waved a warning finger at him. "That path leads to conflict, Daniel, and it is peace we seek to cultivate—peace both within and without."

"Yet I have not felt a moment's peace since our trip to that auction. Perhaps peace is not always desirable. If the sun shone ceaselessly, the soil would bake and the crops would wither."

James smiled. "Beware, Daniel! Isolated mountain living is transforming thee into a philosopher."

"No, Father," interjected Abigail. "Into a poet—and an eloquent one at that."

Daniel glanced at her gratefully, and knew all of a sudden that he wanted to look at her lovely face in the firelight every evening for the rest of his life.

The next morning James led Daniel out to a workshop in his barn to show him samples of copper, mica, and iron ore he had extracted in the foothills to the south. He explained that he hoped to persuade his meeting to buy those tracts and open mines and then operate them with free labor.

"Another abuse of slavery," James explained, "is that it undermines the landless whites and free people of color, who are unable to earn living wages."

"On the way down here I was struck by the contrast between the farms that use slave labor and those that do not," said Daniel as he picked at the chunk of rusty iron ore with his fingernail.

"Well, a farmer must purchase slaves and pay for their upkeep. But this expense is negligible compared to hourly wages."

Daniel's armpits and palms were slick with sweat. He needed to get this marriage question over with, whatever the outcome. Clearing his throat, he croaked, "James?"

James turned to look at him, the tuft of his beard sticking out stiffly, like the tail of a wagging dog.

Daniel struggled to rally his courage. "I wish to request thy permission to ask Abigail to be my wife."

James tortured him by saying nothing for what felt like half an hour. "Canst thou support a wife?" he finally asked.

"I believe so, or I would never have presumed to ask. I have twelve students now who pay me in kind. I do chores for my room and board. I receive a stipend from my parents' meeting. Thy meeting has also been very generous. My school will be closed each year for planting and harvesting, and I hope to find farm work during those months. In any case, there is very little on which to spend money in those mountains. Eventually, I would like to buy some land and build a cabin. It would not be a life of luxury, but I do not believe that Abigail requires luxury. She would, nonetheless, enjoy the luxury of my undivided devotion."

"Well spoken, Friend," replied James. "I believe thou hast good reason to hope that Abigail will look with favor on thy request. Thou must ask her thyself, but with the blessing of Vera and me. We admire thy parents. We find thee to possess both a good heart and a sound head. We admire thy work on behalf of the free coloreds in the mountains. We know that thou will work hard to provide for Abigail and thy children."

Daniel blushed at being reminded by the word "children" of the act that produced them, an act that he might soon be expected to perform, should he ever succeed in undoing those hundreds of tiny buttons.

"I thank thee, Friend," he murmured. "Having been granted thy kind permission, I will now take my leave to ask Abigail herself."

Stumbling into the house, he located Abigail sitting alone in the living room, staring tensely into the fire. Sitting beside her, he fought to calm his sudden anxiety that she might refuse him.

"I have just spoken with thy father," he began, not looking at her, "who has given me permission to approach thee about a subject of importance to us both."

She looked up at him.

"Or rather, it regards us both should thou consent to join thy future to mine..."

She waited, a smile twitching at the corners of her lips.

"That is to say, I love thee, Abigail, and I wish thee to consider becoming my wife."

"Yes."

"On the other hand, perhaps in time..."

"Yes," she insisted, placing her hand over his stammering mouth. "Yes," she repeated, gazing into his eyes so intently that he lost the wish to explain his reasons for asking and his doubts about her acceptance.

Daniel rode back to Couchtown in a stupor of happiness. Vera and James had, of course, insisted that they wait two years before marrying. Nevertheless, they had invited him to visit as often as possible. During his next stay, he and Abigail would present their marriage plans to the Mulberry Creek Monthly Meeting for their approval and advice. Daniel, as well as James and Vera, had written his parents asking for their blessing. Two years seemed an eternity, but Daniel knew he needed to solidify his school and ready living quarters for his future wife.

Meanwhile, he had the memory of their last moment together to sustain him. Downstairs, James had been stuffing one of Daniel's saddlebags with newspapers and pamphlets, while Vera filled the other bag with food for the journey. Upstairs, supposedly assisting his descent, Abigail took his hand and placed it on her multi-buttoned bodice, atop her left breast. His palm could feel the steady pumping of her heart. As her eyelids fluttered shut, he knew with certainty that to perform the duties of a husband with her would prove not only possible, but perhaps the most wonderful experience of his entire life so far. Though his inner light was perversely refusing to ignite, he had no doubt that the flame now flaring in the pit of his stomach would eventually provide delicious consolation.

4

Mulatto Bald: October 1837

Daniel's mare tiptoed through the sea of grunting hogs that overflowed the main street of Couchtown. These drifts of swine, fattened like water bladders on the rich mast of the autumnal uplands, were headed to the Carolina cotton plantations. The drovers stopped off at Couchtown to rest their hogs and horses, while they themselves stayed at the inn, loaded up on supplies, and cavorted with any local women bold enough to venture to the Friday night dances in the barn behind the trading post.

The wagons of local farmers, bound for the hog pens with piles of feed corn for sale, further clogged the congested street. Daniel spotted two Martin brothers, Elijah and Gideon, standing in their wagon, laughing helplessly at the chaos. They appeared to be identical twins, with the same chestnut hair and eyes to match. Joshua, haggardly handsome with his sapphire blue eyes and sleek black hair, slouched on the driver's seat. Daniel waved, but only the twins waved back. Joshua looked about as unhappy as Daniel was happy.

Finally reaching Mrs. Reeves's house, Daniel stabled and fed his exhausted mare. Saddlebags slung across one shoulder, he entered to find his landlady sitting by the fire, over which a pot of aromatic stew hung from a wrought iron crane. Even though it was only late afternoon, she insisted he sit down and eat, while he told her happily of his engagement.

"When will this marriage take place?" she asked.

"In two years' time."

Her eyes widened. "When I was a girl in Tocaru, if a couple wanted to marry, the boy gave the girl a haunch of venison and she gave him a shock of corn. Then the holy man knotted their blankets together, and the boy moved into her mother's lodge that very night. Don't you worry that your hearts will go astray during all this delay?"

"If they do, then it's best that we not wed, in any case."

She shook her head disbelievingly. "What religion are you, anyhow?"

"Quaker."

"I don't know nothing about Quakers. What else do you all believe in?"

As he began to tell her, there was a knock at the door. Mrs. Reeves greeted Joshua Martin and invited him in. Daniel greeted him, too. But from the misery evident in his bright blue eyes, it was clear he had not arrived for a social call. So Daniel said, "I'm just back from the Shenandoah, Joshua. Please excuse me if I unpack and get some rest."

Although he tried his best to do just that, he couldn't sleep with daylight out the window. It felt like being a small child again, put to bed on a summer evening while other children still played outside in the park across the street. In addition, he could hear the conversation in the kitchen below through a knothole in the floorboard. He fought not to eavesdrop, but he lost the battle when he heard Mrs. Reeves say, "But if she's carrying your child, Joshua, then you've got to marry her."

"Well, that's what we both want, Aunt Sali. I'm hoping you can tell me how to do it, since you and her is both from down Tocaru way."

"Did you ask her parents?"

"Yes, and they said no. They call me the Soolekohste."

Mrs. Reeves burst out laughing. "Pest," she explained.

"They also call me a half breed. They say I look like a corpse."

Daniel heard Mrs. Reeves sigh. "There's a legend in Tocaru about the tribe buried in the mound on your daddy's farm at the head of Silver Valley. It's said that they adopted too many pale-skinned strangers from across the sea and were destroyed by it."

"Could you talk to her parents for me, Auntie?" begged Joshua.

"Joshua honey, remember that I gave birth to fourteen 'half breeds' myself. The people in Tocaru ain't likely to pay much mind to anything I have to say. How did you meet this girl, anyhow?"

"I spotted her picking blackberries one afternoon when I was out checking my traps. Her family farms down near Tocaru. She said, 'I am called Choo-qua-le-qua-loo.' I said, 'My people say Whippoor-will.' Bit by bit we learned each other's tongues."

Mrs. Reeves chuckled. "In more ways than one, I gather."

"I want to be her husband," moaned Joshua. "I want to be a father to our baby."

"What about eloping?"

"She says her brothers and uncles would track us down and kill me. But in our own minds we're already married. We meet in the big cave. I go in at the top of Silver Valley. She enters through a shaft near Tocaru."

"I remember it well," murmured Mrs. Reeves. "Many before you have trysted down there, my boy."

"We've made a home for ourselves in an alcove of rock. Its floor is padded with the fur of a bear I shot. If her brothers should follow her, I know a route through the cave that leads to the Great Warriors' Path. We might could escape to the north."

"I'm sorry, Joshua honey, to know that you've found such anguish in something that ought to be wonderful. In my day the Tocaru loved the traders and their goods. But now they blame them for the disappearance of the deer and the plague of rum. Your grandfather worked for the traders. I married one. I reckon you and your brothers and sister and my own children remind the Tocaru of all they've lost. It's like a love gone cold, when a mother sees in the faces of her offspring nothing but the features of the man she's grown to despise."

After a long silence Joshua said in a defeated voice, "So you see no hope for us?"

"I didn't say that. Never let anyone harm what's yours—your love and the child it has created. But be canny, Joshua. Unforeseen events can alter situations. Stay alert and grab them when they occur."

"What does that mean, Aunt Sali?"

She gave a throaty laugh. "I don't know what it means, Joshua. I just know that it's so. Let the yarn unwind at its own pace. Don't yank on it, or it might snap."

As his students departed, Daniel stacked the slates and gathered up the chalk. He had a crowded classroom nowadays. Some came from the ridge where Ben Jones lived, some from Silver Valley, and some from the town itself. Several were grandchildren of Mrs. Reeves. Upon his arrival, he had copied what he recalled from his own early education, feeding his students the shapes and sounds of the letters and numbers. He had been elated when they started to catch on. It thrilled him to watch a child finally grasp how letters formed words and words formed sentences. Working for the welfare of these little children felt much more satisfying than conducting commercial transactions on the docks of Philadelphia, which had been strictly for his own material gain.

Daniel descended the steps, waving to Abner, who was weighing ginseng roots in a scale on a dirt-covered back counter. He exited into the street. The days had grown so short that he had to race back to Mrs. Reeves's to finish his chores while there was still enough light to see the logs he tried to split. As the sun sank behind the mountains to the west, a sharp wind set in. He shivered, despite the buckskin jacket Barbary Martin had laced him as payment for Nathan's fall tuition.

Reaching the house, he grabbed a wooden bucket and carried water from the stream to the depleted rain barrel outside the kitchen door. Then he shelled corn for the chickens clucking in the barnyard. He dumped buckets of ear corn into the trough inside the barn before the two horses and the cow. As they ate, he mucked out their stalls, piling the manure behind the barn. Sitting on a stool alongside the cow, he struggled to milk her. She flicked him irritably with her tail. After storing the milk in the springhouse, he split several logs into kindling. Piling the kindling in one arm, he headed for the house.

Once inside, he built up the fire and warmed himself while Mrs. Reeves served supper. As they sat down to eat, the sound of fiddle music drifted over from the barn behind the trading post, where the youth in from the farms were no doubt inspecting that week's crop of exotic trappers and drovers who were passing through.

"You never go to the dances, Daniel," Mrs. Reeves said. "Don't you never get bored listening to the ramblings of an old woman?"

He smiled. "But I'm practically a married man, Mrs. Reeves."

"You don't trust yourself around pretty young women?"

"Quakers don't dance, so there is no point in my going."

She stared at him incredulously. "In Tocaru we danced at the drop of a hat. What do Quakers have against dancing?"

"It stimulates the passions."

"But passion is what being young is all about. Before you know it, you grow too tired and too stiff for passion."

"I'd rather read." Daniel gave a rueful shrug.

"Well, I reckon those who can't read have to dance for entertainment. But I'm worried about you, Daniel. Are you waiting so long to marry because you don't have no house? Because you and your bride can live upstairs and share my kitchen. I won't last much longer here in town, and when I move down to Silver Valley with my children, I'll sell you this place at a bargain price."

He laughed. "I appreciate your offer, Mrs. Reeves. But I'm afraid it won't shorten the wait."

"I will never understand the English. Why bank the fire before the stew starts to boil?"

"It's a test. To see if our love is real or just lust."

"What's wrong with lust?"

"Nothing, I guess," he said, concealing his shock at such a question. "But can you base a lifelong marriage on it?"

"I don't see why not. Roger and I did."

"So you took one look at Roger Reeves and that was it?"

"That was it for me. For him I was just another Tocaru trading girl."

"How did you turn yourself into his wife?"

"It wasn't easy. We spent one wonderful night together. When he left, I put on my brother's extra buckskins and persuaded my brother to run away with me."

She described how they tracked the traders across three mountains and down Silver Valley to their blockhouse. Then they just hung around, doing whatever chores they could find. In return, the traders gave them leftovers and a warm spot to sleep—in a corner by a fireplace among their favorite dogs.

Sali studied Roger from afar, afraid he would send her away. Watching him flirt with the kitchen girls, she grew increasingly miserable, realizing that the night that had been so memorable for her was just his everyday behavior.

As Daniel sopped up gravy with his cornbread, Mrs. Reeves told about how Roger finally looked her way one morning as he saddled his horse. Then he looked a second time. He sauntered over to her. Smiling, he addressed her in his strange language. She met his gaze and smiled back. At that moment he seemed suddenly to recognize her. He said something to the other men. They looked at her, disguised in her brother's buckskins, and burst out laughing. Mounting his horse, Roger reached down and pulled her up into the saddle in front of him.

He taught her English, and she accompanied him as his interpreter. When the hunters discovered that he had a native wife, they traded on more favorable terms.

Once their babies began to arrive, she had to stay behind, so she sewed moccasins and laced snowshoes for him and his men. She also made rockahominy and venison jelly for upcoming trips, so that Roger wouldn't waste away.

"I used to call him Kora-Hah," she said with a wistful smile. "Skin-and-Bones. He was so puny that he'd have blown away in a stiff breeze."

"It seems as though there are only farmers and trappers around Couchtown now. What happened to all those traders?" Daniel pushed back his chair and stretched out his long legs.

"Most married Cherokee women and had passels of children. They lived around the blockhouse where the workshops now sit, and all down Silver Valley. When their children grew up, they courted each other and had children of their own. As the deer herds dwindled, the traders and guides and horse handlers took up farming, and the trading post turned into a store."

Mrs. Reeves sat silent for a long time. Realizing that she was either tired or sad, Daniel lit one of Barbary Martin's beeswax candles in the fire and said good night.

Up in the loft he hung the wrought-iron candleholder from a peg in the wall. The flame wavered in the cold air seeping past the chinking. Removing his leather clothing, he stretched out in his linen underclothes beneath his scratchy wool blanket.

As fiddle music wafted over from the barn dance, he opened one of James's pamphlets. Written by a member of the London Yearly Meeting, it opposed smallpox vaccinations, maintaining that disease could bring people near to death and trigger recognition of the vanity of earthly pursuits. Daniel smiled as he contemplated the role of epidemics in spiritual conversion. Maybe all he needed finally to achieve illumination was a good case of smallpox.

He laid the pamphlet aside and picked up a newspaper from Norfolk. After learning about the slide of tobacco prices in the Northern Neck, he turned the page and saw more ads for fugitive slaves. As he scanned the notices, his eyes were caught by a reward that was twice as high as all the others:

$50 REWARD: Ran away from a forge near the Pamunkey River on the 23rd July last year, a bright mulatto named Tom Hill. Six feet tall with bushy hair, he is missing half his left ear and one top eyetooth. An accomplished blacksmith, he was last spotted lurking around the plantation of Hayden Redmond in York County. It is expected he will persuade his "wife" Nan and their young son and daughter to leave with him on a northbound ship from Norfolk.

Tom Hill is fair enough to pass for white and can read and write well enough to forge freedom papers. All masters of vessels are cautioned against carrying him to sea. He is very tricky and plausible and coaxing when seeking favors.

Any person apprehending him, committing him to jail, and notifying me so that I can retrieve him will receive the above reward. Please note that Hayden Redmond is also offering $25 each for the capture of the wench Nan and her two children, a boy of six and a girl of five. Nan is dark-complexioned with smallpox pits on her cheeks and forehead. Signed: Randolph Hill.

Beneath this was a boxed proclamation signed by two justices of Lancaster County, Virginia, stating that if the above-mentioned Tom Hill did not return to his master, "any person may kill and destroy said slave by such means as he or they may think fit, without accusation of any crime for so doing." Below this, Randolph Hill offered a reward of $100 for Tom's severed head.

Daniel lay completely still. Finally forcing himself to reread the ad, he realized that Tom Hill was the Couchtown blacksmith now known as Ben Jones. The missing tooth and torn ear were too much of a coincidence. Daniel was teaching his fugitive children, Sampson and Rebecca, to read and write. Ben—or Tom—was now worth more dead than alive. But did Ben know this? While a fiddle reel romped through his window, Daniel blew out his candle and lay in the dark. Slowly he understood that if Ben should be unaware of the danger he was in, Daniel was obliged to tell him.

Walking down the street to the trading post the next morning, Daniel spotted the two seedy men from the ferry dock standing outside Ben's smithy. The one in the floppy black hat peered through a crack between the shutters, while the other fumbled with the iron bar fixed across the door. Daniel stopped and stared at them. Once they noticed him, they turned and strode down the street.

Reaching his classroom, Daniel discovered that Sampson and Rebecca were absent. The other children reported that their father was sick and had not wanted them to come to town without him. Distracted with worry, Daniel assigned each child a partner to whom to recite addition tables.

He took Abner aside and asked, "How do I reach that mountaintop where Ben Jones lives?"

"You mean Mulatto Bald?"

"Is that what it is called? Well, how do I get up there?"

Looking at Daniel curiously, Abner gave him directions.

"Can I ride my horse?"

Abner shook his head. "It's way too steep. Almost a cliff."

"Will you mind the class? Once they finish their addition tables, they can practice their letters on their slates."

"Sure. But are you going to all this trouble just because Sampson and Rebecca didn't come to school today?"

"No. There is something I need to tell Ben."

"Well, be careful, Daniel. They don't much like strangers up on Mulatto Bald."

Serenaded by a dozen songbirds that should already have headed south, Daniel struggled up the path that switchbacked across the face of the bluff apparently known as Mulatto Bald. Halfway up, he paused to catch his breath. He turned around and looked down through the tops of the bare trees, the trunks of which were as wide across as a man was tall, to the village alongside the turbulent river. With a stab of regret, he thought about the bustling wharves and carriage-clogged streets of Philadelphia. What in the world was he doing trying to make a life in a place populated by escaped mulatto slaves and renegade half-blood Indians—and expecting Abigail and their future children to do so, too? He had often stood on the wharf in Philadelphia during his lunch break from his father's warehouse and watched the ships being unloaded—trunks of mahogany from South America, teas and spices from the Far East. The sailors had represented every population on the face of the earth. Sometimes Daniel had longed to pack a duffel bag and go with them on their journeys to exotic foreign lands. But now that he was actually living in such a foreign land, he sometimes longed to pack up and go back home to Philadelphia, where he understood what was going on and why.

Sighing, Daniel dutifully resumed his climb. Once he reached the top, he headed down a path across the grassy, treeless plateau. Every so often he passed a cabin surrounded by stubbled gardens and rickety sheds. A hound bayed at him and was joined by a chorus of plaintive howls all down the ridge.

An old man with a grizzled beard came inching along the pathway, supported by a gnarled cane carved to resemble a rattlesnake. Greeting him, Daniel asked which house belonged to Ben Jones. The man studied him mutely.

"I'm Daniel Hunter," he explained. "I teach Sampson and Rebecca down at the trading post."

"Oh yeah, you're that schoolteacher man." A relieved smile curved the lips that caved in over his ravaged gums. "Second cabin on the right."

Daniel passed through a scrolled wrought-iron gate, probably a product of Ben's forge. In the front yard a black and white rooster was strutting and crowing, trying to shield his hens behind his bravado. Arriving at the door, which had iron strap hinges, Daniel knocked with a heavy knocker shaped like the letter S.

Sampson peered around an outside corner of the cabin. "It's Mr. Hunter," he called to someone behind him. He waved solemnly at Daniel.

"Is your father sick?"

The front door opened. Ben stood there, his bald head gleaming in the sunshine. The ad mentioned "bushy" hair, but he was no doubt trying to alter his appearance. Unfortunately, the deformed ear and missing eyetooth were indelible.

"Naw, I ain't sick. I just ain't working today. You come all the way up here just from worry about my health?"

Behind him stood his wife. And yes, she did have smallpox pits in her cheeks and forehead. She smiled politely, but she seemed upset.

"Can we walk down the path?" asked Daniel. "There's something I need to tell you in private."

As they strolled along, Daniel asked, "Do you scale that trail every day? No wonder you look so fit."

"Some days I don't hardly have enough strength left to make it home."

"Why roost up here among the buzzards then?"

"When we arrived, all the good bottomland was took. At least when they start carrying on about Virginia and North Carolina and Tennessee, and deeds and warrants and all like that, we don't have nothing to worry about. Don't nobody but us want this rocky cliff top."

"I saw those two men at your forge this morning," Daniel blurted out, unable to endure any more of the pointless pleasantries that seemed so crucial to southern people in their social interactions.

Ben walked on in silence.

"Look, I know that they're slave catchers, Ben. And I also know that your real name is Tom Hill."

Ben's face froze.

"Here." He handed Ben the ad torn from the *Norfolk Gazette*.

Ben scanned it, confirming what the ad maintained—that he could read.

"Are you aware that you've been outlawed and are now worth more dead than alive?"

Finally Ben spoke, his voice emotionless. "I knew they was after me, but I didn't know nothing about being outlawed. And I didn't know they was after Nan and my children, too."

They walked to the end of the ridge, where a flat limestone table rock overhung Silver Valley. Wheat-colored fields stitched with split-rail fences lay below them like sewn-up wounds.

Ben murmured, "Funniest part is, he's my father."

"Who is?"

"Randolph Hill. The one who will pay more for my head than for my whole body."

"Your father?"

"My mother was one of his cooks."

They sat on the rock, and Ben spoke about growing up playing and studying with his father's white children. Once they were teenagers, Tom and a daughter fell deep into puppy love. They didn't know they were brother and sister. They didn't even know that he was Negro and she was white. Or at least they didn't know what that meant. Tom's mother persuaded his father to lease him to a blacksmith in another county so he could get over his forbidden infatuation and learn a useful trade.

His mother lived long enough to see him happily married to Nan, a slave on a farm near the forge. But once they had two babies, her master sold her and her children to a planter in York County, several hours' walk from Tom's forge.

Tom kept running away to visit them, and the blacksmith kept dragging him back. Finally, the blacksmith announced that since Tom didn't know how to keep his pecker in his pocket, he had hired the sheriff to cut off his balls, like they did to bulls or stallions that insisted on straying. Tom replied to the blacksmith that he had better talk to his owner first. The blacksmith replied that he already had and that Randolph Hill had agreed to this solution to Tom's roaming ways.

When the sheriff arrived, he nailed Tom's ear to a post to keep him still. As the sheriff approached with his glinting knife, Tom jerked loose and ran, leaving half his ear behind. He didn't stop running until he reached Norfolk, where he forged freedom papers and found a job on the docks. On his days off he sneaked out to Nan's cabin.

Meanwhile, he tried to locate a ship captain to transport his family up north. One agreed to take Tom, since he could pass as a white deck hand. But when Tom brought up his wife and children, the captain backed out. Another captain had just been hanged for aiding fugitives.

Finally, Tom, Nan, and their children fled to a swamp south of Norfolk. Tom shod horses and repaired guns for a gang of runaway slaves who survived by robbing travelers. Then he heard about the Squabble State, where people of color could reportedly find land and other people like themselves. They headed west, traveling by night and hiding from the patrollers during the day.

"The only thing I hadn't figured on was how much my father hates me," concluded Tom, as they watched a red-tailed hawk spiral down toward a rodent scurrying across the field below. "I thought if I left, he would just let me go. But now he's got me trapped on top of this ridge, with no way off except to jump."

"I know a way out, Tom. If you will trust me."

"I reckon I already do, Daniel. I just told you my entire life story. Besides, I ain't got no other choice, do I?"

"All right. Just lie low for now and let me work this out."

Tom seized his hand. "I don't know why you're willing to help me, Daniel. I guess you're just a good man. You must be, to spend your days teaching little children. But I thank the Lord for you."

Descending the trail, Daniel wondered what he had gotten himself into. He knew he had sounded confident to Tom, but that was not how he felt inside. When he offered to help, he had intended to raise money to cover the reward and pay off the slave catchers. But he now realized that anyone evil enough to be a slave catcher would merely accept that bribe and continue to pursue Tom. And if those two bloodsuckers departed, others would no doubt replace them, like a nest of ground hornets. Even if Daniel could persuade James to travel to the Northern Neck to purchase Tom from his own father, Tom would probably be beheaded by some other greedy slave catcher before James ever got there.

What kind of man was this Randolph Hill who would condemn his own son to a lifetime of flight and terror? Clearly, he was a man desperate to erase all evidence of his own wrongdoing.

Daniel stood inside the doorway of the barn that had once stabled the packhorses of the Tidewater traders. Now it served the town as a dance hall. In inclement weather it also hosted revivals. So you could sin here one night, and then repent the next—provided you could ignore the evangelists' admonitions that a praying knee and a dancing foot didn't belong on the same leg.

He watched Gideon Martin play the banjo, a faint smile on his lips as his fingers flew in counterpoint to his twin brother Elijah's fiddle bow. The dancers were stamping and pawing the packed earth, and swaying their heads as though sporting huge racks of antlers.

Abner was being swarmed by half a dozen young women in calico dresses. His red hair was parted in the middle and slicked down with pomade. He wore a black and white checkered vest. In the eyes of these country lasses, he was a sophisticated village merchant.

His younger brother Isaac, towering over the others like a timid giant, stood alongside Abner, studying his behavior as though trying to pick up some pointers.

But Daniel was searching for Joshua. He finally located him, standing alone in his buckskins with one foot propped against the wall, his straight black hair falling into his translucent blue eyes. Daniel walked over to him, and he nodded a forlorn greeting.

"Not dancing tonight, Joshua?"

"I don't dance."

"Me, neither. Looks like fun, though."

Joshua grunted. By the entrance Daniel spotted the two slave catchers. They were inspecting the crowd, no doubt looking for Tom Hill.

"Who are those two?" Daniel asked, to find out how much Joshua knew.

"They turn up in Couchtown every few months, looking for runaway slaves so they can claim the rewards. They always try to get the girls to dance with them, but won't a one of them pay those two any mind. One of these days they'll go back home to the coast in wooden boxes."

"How come your family doesn't own slaves?"

Joshua spat into the sawdust. "Slavery is a rich man's sport. The more slaves you own, the richer you get. But my father says he prefers his poverty."

"Would you help a slave escape?" Daniel tried to conceal his relief at perhaps having found an ally.

"If I got the chance. But we don't have many up here, thank the Lord. Most farmers is too poor, and the land is too rocky to grow anything but more rocks. Only slaves in these parts are five women who live in the middle of the forest with Frederick Reeves. Folks say they chase down deer for his dinner, bare-handed and bare-breasted."

Daniel blanched at this intriguing image. "I need to ask you something, Joshua. You can refuse to help me, but you have to promise me not to talk about it to anyone else."

Frowning, Joshua studied him for a while. "Go ahead, Daniel.
Whatever it is, I'll keep my mouth shut. And for those of us who can't
write, our word seals our deals." He gave Daniel an ironic smile.

Daniel told him about Tom Hill's situation. He also inquired
about the cave at the head of Silver Valley, though he didn't admit to
having first heard of it while eavesdropping on Joshua and Mrs.
Reeves as they discussed Joshua's star-crossed romance with the
young woman from Tocaru.

Joshua agreed to lead Tom's family to the cave. Whether they
hid until the slave catchers left, or traveled through the cave to the
Great Warriors' Path that led north to the free states, would be Tom's
decision.

"Either will be dangerous," warned Joshua. "There are all kinda
laws and stuff. But I'll help him if I can. Ben, Tom, whoever he is—
he's a good man. And even if he weren't, don't nobody deserve to be
treated like that. I know what it's like to be hated for the color of your
skin. Though in my case, mine's too pale."

5

Baptism by Fire: November 1837

Joshua and Daniel followed the trail down Silver Valley by the light of a lantern Joshua carried in one hand. They skirted a marsh where some hunters were hunkered down on the shore, fishing for snapping turtles with trotlines baited with chicken gizzards stretched across a span of open water.

"What is that?" Daniel asked Joshua as the trail passed below a high mound overgrown with a tangle of vines and bushes.

"They say the bones of the ancients is buried there."

"Who are the ancients?"

Joshua shrugged. "Our ancestors, I reckon."

"Were they Indians?"

"My papaw used to say they was Porterghee Indians. But I don't know nothing about it."

They scrambled across tumbled rocks that looked as though they had been vomited from the craw of a cave that opened partway up a hillside. Its entrance, large enough for only two men abreast, was concealed by ledges of limestone. They sat on a boulder still warm from the afternoon sun. An owl hooted in the woods. Joshua's head swiveled steadily as he scanned their surroundings to make sure no one had followed them out from town.

Daniel was trembling in spasms. He wasn't cold, so he realized he was scared. The thought of a confrontation with those seedy slave catchers who were prepared to lop off Tom Hill's head terrified him. He glanced up at the night sky. The intensity of the stars was startling. Smoke and city lights obscured the night sky in Philadelphia. But here in the mountains the stars sparkled like crystal.

Joshua pointed out four silhouettes of people moving slowly across the ridge that descended from the table rock at the end of Mulatto Bald down to the floor of Silver Valley.

"I used to play in this cave with my brothers when we was little. One of us would hide and the others would search for him. Not so easy in the dark."

"You wandered around that cave in the dark?"

"At first we used pine knot torches. Then we decided to pretend we was blind. Your other senses take over when you can't see. Clay smells different from limestone. There's a river in there, so you can tell where you are by how it sounds. We memorized the paths by the way they felt to our feet."

Daniel shook his head, thinking about what a protected childhood he had led. His parents would never have let him wander around a cave in the dark. They had raised him like an exotic plant in a steamy solarium, overseeing his every move to guarantee his safety. He was glad they couldn't see him now.

As the silhouettes drew near and transformed themselves into people, Daniel and Joshua greeted Tom, Nan, Sampson, and Rebecca, all dressed in what appeared to be every item of clothing they owned. Each had a bundle strapped to his or her back. Tom carried a rifle and wore a sheathed knife on his hip. Nan's pitted face was tense with anxiety, but the children looked merely sleepy. They smiled shyly at Daniel.

Once inside the cave, Joshua turned up his lantern flame as they entered a huge cavern that opened up overhead like the dome of a cathedral. They passed columns of quartz along one wall that looked like milk frozen in mid-spill. Then they headed down a narrow chute as the roar of the underground river grew louder. Emerging into a rock chamber that featured row upon row of rose-colored cones and hourglasses, Daniel spotted a wall to one side that soared overhead, well beyond the flickering lantern light. On it were painted in red, black, and ocher many different species of animals, some pierced with spears or arrows launched by tiny stick-figure hunters.

"Sweet Jesus," muttered Tom, "someone must have been living down here."

"Indians," said Joshua. "In days gone by. My papaw used to claim that painting their prey on that wall was a ritual to guarantee a successful hunt."

After trekking through the darkness for what seemed to Daniel like half the night, they finally emerged partway down the westward flank of a mountain. A wide valley spread out below them in the sparkling starlight. In the distance a hound bayed. A hint of wood smoke floated on the breeze.

Joshua handed Tom a map he had sketched and pointed out various markings on it in the lantern light. All his life Joshua had hunted in these mountains and valleys, sometimes for weeks at a stretch, so he had been able to indicate caves for sleeping, springs, trail markers, and a few cabins where friends of his lived who would help Tom. Daniel had written down Joshua's estimates of the number of days required for the different segments of the journey. The route paralleled the one down the Shenandoah that Daniel had traveled from Pennsylvania. But it remained along the ridge tops bordering Kentucky and Virginia, where few wayfarers ventured.

"Travel in the dark by the stars and sleep well hidden when it's light," advised Joshua. "Keep the Shenandoah Valley on your right and you can't get lost. Watch out for panthers at night, and bears and snakes during the day. If you can't find a cave to sleep in, go into the middle of a canebrake and sleep there. Hide if you see someone coming. If they discover you, shoot first. Most will be natives or longhunters. Lots would help you, but a few would turn you in for the reward. Or would sell you as slaves farther south. Or would kill you for your gear. And it ain't no way to tell in advance who would do which, so you need to shoot first and wonder later."

As Daniel listened to these instructions, he was chilled to realize that this really was the code of his adopted homeland. It was appalling to someone raised by pacifists, but he had to ask himself if he would prefer to have Tom and his family killed or re-enslaved instead. Perhaps it was true that in the real world, outside of Philadelphia meeting houses, you had to fight fire with fire. Was it really possible to disarm ill-intentioned people by treating them as you would wish yourself to be treated, as his elders had always insisted?

"Don't fret about us, Joshua," said Tom. "We've already crossed Virginia on foot, from the seacoast to the mountains."

"So I reckon you'll be fine then."

Daniel handed Tom a folded letter and all the bills and coins he had been able to collect. "When you reach Philadelphia," he said with more optimism than he felt, "go to my parents' house. Their address is on this letter. Give it to them, and they'll help you."

"Thank you," said Tom in a tight voice, shaking hands with both men. He withdrew some papers from a leather pouch at his waist and handed them to Daniel. "These are the deeds to my forge and my land on the bald. I didn't tell nobody we was leaving, so our furniture and animals is all up there at our cabin. If either of you wants them, they're yours. Because I don't reckon we'll pass this way again."

Daniel and Joshua watched in silence as the four descended toward the valley along a creek that emptied into the Holston River. There, they would find the Great Warriors' Path, deeply rutted by the feet of generation upon generation of hunters and traders, refugees and warriors—fighting or fleeing, seeking safety or excitement, love or gain or glory.

"Do you want any of these?" asked Daniel, holding out Tom's deeds to Joshua. They stood at the fork in the Silver Valley pathway where they would separate, Daniel returning to town and Joshua to his parents' stone house at the foot of the valley.

"I don't reckon so. Me and my wife aim to settle near her parents at Tocaru."

"I didn't realize you were married."

"We keep it quiet. She's Indian. Some don't approve."

"But did you not say that some of your ancestors were Indians?"

"It's her people who don't approve. They claim it's half bloods who've signed the treaties selling off their land to the government, to parcel out to settlers."

"Where will the Indians go?"

"That's what they're wondering. Somewheres out west, I reckon."

As Daniel headed toward town, he thought about the fact that he had just broken a law by helping escaped slaves. He had never knowingly broken a law in all his life. And apart from worry over the fate of Tom's family, he was delighted. He liked the notion of himself as a good boy gone bad—a Robin Hood of the Blue Ridge. He smiled whimsically. What would Abigail say? Her father didn't approve of breaking laws, but maybe she would be titillated to have an outlaw for a fiancé. It was hard to say what she was really like beneath her whalebone corset and behind the stalwart beliefs she, like he, had imbibed since infancy from her pious parents.

Mrs. Reeves was seated by her fire when he got in. She looked amused. "So you're finally out enjoying your fast-fading freedom?"

"Just working late," he improvised.

"I'm not an old woman for nothing. I know all about how men sneak around after dark, searching for women to warm them at their fires."

Daniel laughed. "Believe what you please, Mrs. Reeves. To tell you the truth, I have always wanted to be that kind of man."

Mrs. Reeves clapped her hands. "We'll have you buck dancing in no time, Daniel!"

"What is that buck dancing, anyhow? I saw it the other night at the barn dance. All that thrashing around. They looked like converts at a revival."

"It was a ritual Cherokees performed to prepare for the hunt. Some traders borrowed it for their own entertainment."

"We white people have taken everything, have we not? Your women, your rituals. Joshua told me that even the Cherokee homeland is now being taken."

"Yes, some self-appointed Cherokee leaders signed a treaty exchanging this land for land out west."

"Does that include your children's farms? Or the Martins'?"

"No one knows. There've been so many treaties, all of them broken, that we've lost track. So we make believe that it doesn't include us. Until the soldiers come with their guns to round us up."

As Daniel headed for school the next morning, he discovered that the door to Tom's forge had been chopped open during the night. Entering the building he supposed he now owned, he found tools strewn across the puncheon floor. He replaced them on their shelves. When he returned to the street, he glanced up toward Mulatto Bald and discovered a graceful plume of black smoke fanning across the crisp blue sky.

Running to the store, he found Abner and explained that an emergency required him to cancel class.

"Is there something I can do?" asked Abner.

"Please tell the children to come back tomorrow."

Daniel ran from town to the base of the bald and then clambered up the boulder-strewn trail, the odor of smoke strong in his nostrils. Reaching the top, he stumbled along the path, gasping for breath.

When he reached Tom's yard, he found only smoldering timbers where the cabin and sheds had stood. The front door with its iron knocker and strap hinges lay half-burned in a bed of dancing flames. A cow sprawled dead in the yard, crawling with sluggish flies.

The old man with the rattlesnake cane came creeping along the path beyond the fence.

"What has happened here?" demanded Daniel, bent over trying to catch his breath.

"Them Joneses done got all burned up. Not no sign of them left."

"Have you seen any strangers around here lately, old man?"

"Only yourself, Mr. Schoolteacher."

Deciding it was better for Tom's neighbors to believe him dead, Daniel took his leave and descended the precipitous path to town.

After climbing the steps to his classroom, Daniel found his door broken open, one board splintered. Within stood the slave catchers, backlit by the window so that their faces were in shadows.

Daniel froze in the doorway. When he and Tom had first met, Tom had promised to do his fighting for him. Where was he now when Daniel needed him? These men apparently knew how to cut off someone's head and probably wouldn't hesitate to do so, slave or not.

"May I help you?" he asked.

"We're looking for two escaped slave children," said the one in the floppy hat.

"Then you have come to the wrong place."

"No, we ain't," said the one with the rusty stubble. "You been teaching two slaves to read and write, and that's agin the laws of the state of Virginia."

Daniel glanced over his shoulder. Abner was behind him, his jaws and fists clenched. At least somebody on his team knew how to fight.

"I do not know what you mean. So I would appreciate it if you would leave my classroom. You have ruined my door."

"We'll leave," said the first one. "But if you don't turn them slaves over to us, we'll be back with the law. They'll shut down this school and ride you out of town on a rail, you damned Yankee nigger-lover."

"Get out!" demanded Daniel, feeling a rage that, unleashed, would compel him to attack these two, despite his having no idea how to fight. It would be embarrassing for all concerned.

They brushed past Abner and stomped down the steps.

Abner entered. "What's going on, Daniel?"

"I just went up to Ben Jones's cabin, and it had burned down. They were nowhere to be seen."

"Are Sampson and Rebecca the escaped slave children those two were referring to?"

"Why would you think that? Those children are no more slaves than you or I."

"Can they really shut down your school?"

"Apparently they could if I were teaching slaves." He realized he had now broken two laws and lived to tell about it—aiding escaped slaves and teaching slaves to read and write.

"Are you?" asked Abner.

"No." Before his arrival in Couchtown, Daniel had prided himself on always telling the truth. But it now appeared that lying was his true vocation.

The following morning Daniel dodged his way down the street through another drift of swine. The mounted drovers were cracking blacksnake whips, trying to keep the hogs off the sidewalks and out of the shops without damaging the tender flesh of their hams on the hoof. Daniel spotted some of his students gathered in the doorway of the trading post, giggling at the huge, snorting beasts as they teetered along on their tiny trotters, like boulders balanced on sticks.

By the time Daniel had laid the slates and chalk on the desks, all his students were present except Rebecca, Sampson, Nathan, Abner, and a girl from Mulatto Bald named Delia. As Daniel waited for them, Abner dashed in and scanned the room.

"Has anyone seen Nathan?"

The children nodded no.

"What has happened?" asked Daniel.

"Nathan has vanished. He was watching the hogs. When I went out to bring him upstairs, he was gone."

"Delia is gone too," said Delia's sister Jenny. "A man took her away."

"You saw someone take her?" asked Abner.

"A man in a funny black hat asked Delia if she wanted to ride on his horse. He picked her up and they rode away. I yelled at her to jump off, but the pigs was so loud she couldn't hear me."

"Did they take Nathan, too?" demanded Abner.

Jenny pursed her lips. "I don't know. They might of. I didn't see."

Daniel pulled Abner aside and explained that the slave catchers had probably taken the two children in place of Ben's two, for whom a reward had been offered in the Tidewater.

"I lied to you about them yesterday, Abner. They are escaped slaves. I was trying to protect them."

"Never mind," said Abner. "I'll ride down Silver Valley and get my father and brothers. Send Jenny up the ridge for her father. We'll meet at the ferry dock. Go get your horse. We need your help."

Daniel dismissed the class, promising that things would soon calm down and return to normal. Then he ran to Mrs. Reeves's barn and saddled up his mare, wondering how on earth someone like himself, who couldn't shoot or fight, could possibly be of any help, however much he might want to be. He rode to the ferry through the piles of manure deposited by the passing swine.

As he waited for the Martins, he asked Luke, the slave who hauled the barge across the river, "Did two men cross earlier this morning? One had lots of whiskers and a slouchy black hat. The other had a short red beard and shifty eyes."

"You mean them slavers? Yes sir, I took them across."

"Did they have two children with them?"

"Yes sir. Them little ones was setting up on those big old horses. Them slavers climbed up behind them, and they took off at a trot. It didn't seem right to me, but I didn't want no trouble. Them slavers will cut a nigger to pieces for even looking at them sideways."

The Martins' horses hurtled to a halt on the landing. Nathan's mother, Galicia, wore leggings and a hunting shirt. Like the men, she had a rifle strapped to her saddle. She looked quietly desperate. As Daniel reported what he had learned from Luke, Delia's father and uncle rode up. They were dark-faced men with closely clipped black beards and hair.

Reuben, Abner, Daniel, and the Martin twins crossed first on the ferry and took off down the river road at a canter. Joshua, Isaac, Galicia, and Delia's father and uncle would cross next and travel the ridge road. The two groups had agreed to meet in the evening where the roads converged.

A grim silence settled over Daniel's patrol as fence posts and farmhouses paraded past. The others were far better riders than Daniel—even Reuben, who had only one arm and must have been at least seventy-five years old. Daniel had rarely cantered in his journeys down the Shenandoah, and back and forth to visit Abigail. He lagged behind so he could grip his pommel unobserved.

As they slowed to a walk to rest the horses, Reuben muttered, "They can't travel real fast with children squirming in their saddles."

Breathing as heavily as his mare from the cantering, Daniel watched a red fox dash across the road and disappear into the woods with a backward glance at the riders. All too soon the run resumed, and it continued all afternoon, broken only by occasional stretches of walking. They covered a lot of distance, but they gained no glimpse of the kidnappers.

As the sun dipped behind a wall of rock and the coral sky began to fade into twilight, they reached the junction. The others were waiting in a clearing alongside a spring. As the newcomers watered their horses, all agreed it was pointless to continue since the kidnappers could easily hide in the darkness. So they gathered brush and built a fire. Warming themselves, they gnawed jerky and listened to the staccato chatter of the night insects.

Daniel rolled up in his blanket, flanked by Delia's father and uncle, who spoke little and rarely smiled. Sleep was slow in coming. He agonized over what might be happening to Nathan and Delia. He hated to think of them feeling afraid or being harmed. His students had become almost as important to him as he imagined his and Abigail's own children would be. This realization alarmed him. This was why all the Quaker divines counseled asceticism. Once you started caring too much for the people and things of this world, the world beyond receded from your grasp. But it was too late. He already cared for these children—so eager to learn, so innocent of the evil that currently gripped them in its talons.

As dawn broke, everyone chewed hunks of cornbread and warmed themselves by the fire. Walking over to the spring that gushed from a hillside, Daniel squatted for a handful of drinking water. The bank had been stamped smooth by the horses' hooves. Half buried in the mud he spotted a chunk of wood. Digging it out with his fingers, he discovered that it was Nathan's toy horse.

"Nathan has been here!" he shouted to the others. "Here is his horse!"

Washing it off, he carried it over to Galicia, who sat by the fire. She took it from him.

"Yes, it's his." She glanced up at him gratefully.

They mounted their horses and resumed the pursuit with revived optimism.

When the sun was directly overhead, the road split again. The right fork entered a broad creek, emerging downstream to wind through a rhododendron thicket. Eventually, it would dead end in a trail that linked the Shenandoah to the North Carolina backwoods settlements.

The left fork veered toward the Tidewater. Galicia's group agreed to ride out the southerly route until it sprouted a shortcut that would return them to the Tidewater trail just below the limestone palisades that separated the Blue Ridge from the Shenandoah. The two patrols agreed to wait for one another at this crossroads.

By mid-afternoon Daniel's party reached the cliff of pale limestone. As they rested their horses, they studied the narrow trail that wound down it into the huge valley. On the road below Daniel spotted two horses. From that height they looked like ants on a forced march. He pointed them out to the others. It was impossible to see if a child sat in front of either rider.

"They're trotting," observed Reuben. "Either those ain't our men, or they don't realize we're following them. But they'll spot us once we head down the cliff. Then they'll take off. Or hide out, one."

Dismounting, they led their horses along the treacherous track, sending showers of pebbles over the edge and bouncing off the boulders below. When they reached the bottom, they mounted and took off at a canter. The riders up ahead were galloping now, their images wavy and distorted by the intervening distance, their backs blocking any view of a child.

As the gap between them narrowed, Daniel yelled, "Those are our men! One wore a black hat just like that!"

Realizing that they couldn't outrun their pursuers, the slave catchers finally reined in their horses and turned around to face them. Daniel saw Nathan. He was sitting in a saddle in front of the man with the red stubble. The man held the blade of a hunting knife against his throat. Nathan's dark eyes were wide with fear. Delia sat on the second horse in front of the man with the black hat, who also held a knife to her throat.

"Papaw!" cried Nathan. "I don't want to ride the horse no more. I want to go home with you."

"Nathan, honey, just sit real quiet-like," said Reuben soothingly.

"Why are you trailing us?" asked the man in the slouch hat.

"Because that there is my grandson you got," said Reuben.

"No, he ain't. Not unless you're a runaway nigger named Tom Hill. And you look like a white man to me."

"I reckon I know my own grandson," said Reuben. "Let them go and we won't harm you none."

The two men laughed harshly.

"And we'll pay you whatever reward you'd earn by turning them in," offered Reuben.

Daniel watched in amazement as Reuben chatted amiably with his grandson's kidnappers, discussing the storm clouds on the western horizon and an acquaintance in common from the slave catchers' hometown on the Northern Neck. Southerners had to be insane, reflected Daniel, determined to observe the social niceties no matter what heinous crime might be underway.

From the corner of his eye Daniel noticed motion. Shifting his gaze, he saw that Joshua and Galicia were slithering on their knees and elbows down from the tree line on the hillside behind the bounty hunters, rifles cradled in the crooks of their arms. He realized that there was a method to Reuben's manners.

"Look here, folks, you can't go around just grabbing anybody's child, hoping to fool some slave owner into thinking you've caught his runaway," continued Reuben in an affable tone.

"We seen them come out from that fellow's school in the trading post and cross the street over to Tom Hill's forge."

"But these ain't the same children," Reuben said patiently.

"Prove it."

"I ain't got to prove that they ain't. You got to prove that they is."

Daniel felt dizzy, wondering if he should warn the two that they were about to die. He was supposed to be opposed to violence. But it was now merely a question of whether two despicable scum or two innocent children would die. Daniel's forehead and armpits turned slick with sweat as he struggled to sort out the ethics of this situation. Where was that blasted inner light of the Quakers that was supposed to be giving him guidance?

The man with the red stubble replied, "The owners don't care who we bring them. All niggers look alike to them."

"My grandson ain't no Negro," said Reuben. "He's a Porterghee Indian just like me. And if he ain't a Negro, he can't be a slave."

"Sure he can. Look at this kinky hair here. Look at this dark skin. It don't matter if he ain't a nigger as long as he looks like one, and he sure as hell does."

Joshua and Galicia lay on their stomachs, legs splayed, elbows propped on the ground to support their rifles, which were now aimed at the two men's backs. In unison they squeezed their triggers. Daniel heard two thuds like faint heartbeats. Each man registered a startled expression before beginning to fall from his horse in slow motion. The twins were off their horses in an instant, knocking aside the knives and grabbing the children.

Elijah handed Nathan to Reuben, who hugged him tightly with his one arm, while Nathan hiccupped with sobs. Gideon handed Delia up to Daniel. Her father descended from the hillside and gently took her from Daniel, into his arms and onto his horse.

Joshua and Isaac draped the two corpses over the riderless horses and lashed them into place. Then they mounted their own horses, and the funeral cortege headed up the hill to bury them in unmarked forest graves.

The others rode slowly back to town with the sniffling children. Daniel had never seen anyone murdered before. He had been a silent accomplice to these murders. Yet Quakers were supposed to abjure murder. His own grandfather had resigned from the Pennsylvania Assembly when it voted for scalp bounties to encourage frontiersmen to kill hostile Delaware Indians. But without today's murders, two children might have had their throats slit or been sold into slavery. Daniel was bemused to find himself thinking that these men were two who had needed killing.

6

The Frost Moon: December 1837

Daniel returned from school one afternoon to discover a black-canopied carriage in the road by Mrs. Reeves's front fence. A slave dressed in what looked like a British Revolutionary War uniform jacket lounged on the driver's seat. He also wore a cockaded hat, knee breeches, buckle shoes, and white stockings. Daniel nodded to him, and he nodded back.

Daniel headed across the yard to the barn. This was the first cabriolet he had seen since Philadelphia. Most people in these mountains rode horses or drove wagons. And he had never before seen such quaint livery. It was hard to imagine a carriage like that bouncing along the winding mountain paths. The horse drawing it appeared so highly bred that her fine ankles would surely snap as she stumbled along among the rocks and ruts. As he positioned a log on end for splitting, he tried to picture the outlandish creature who now sat inside visiting Mrs. Reeves.

Carrying an armload of wood through the back door, he found Mrs. Reeves seated by the fireplace in her front parlor with a young woman in a green velvet dress and a veiled hat with a pheasant feather in its band. The hat was so fashionably unfashionable that it had to have been imported from Paris prior to the French Revolution.

"Mrs. West, may I present my lodger, Daniel Hunter. Mr. Hunter is from Philadelphia. He teaches school at your husband's store. Daniel, this is Mrs. West, who lives at Oak Bluff Plantation along the Sturgeon River."

"Enchanted," she replied with an overly bright smile. "My husband has given me wonderful reports of your school, Mr. Hunter."

"Thank you, madam." Daniel dumped the wood into the box by the kitchen fireplace and dusted the debris from his hide jacket into the fire. "I am pleased to meet you, Mrs. West. Your husband is most generous to let me use his storeroom for my class."

"I so long to visit your beautiful city," she said, sighing. "How could you bear to leave it behind for such a forlorn wilderness as this?"

Daniel smiled politely. "To outsiders like myself, madam, Couchtown possesses a rare peace and beauty."

"A beauty that, I confess, sir, escapes those of us condemned to pass all our days here."

"Do you never travel, madam?" Daniel realized that he hadn't participated in a conversation such as this since his days as a textile importer in the drawing rooms of Philadelphia. It reminded him of why he had left.

"Never. My husband, Mr. West, wishes only to annex all the land that adjoins his. And I am overwhelmed with children—our own and those of our slaves. The living, the ill, the dying, those struggling to be born."

"Well, perhaps once they are all grown...?"

"My only hope, sir, is to live long enough to witness the dawn of such a day." Rising, she said, "But I must rush home to my duties, Mrs. Reeves. I simply wished to contribute our little offerings to your family's harvest feast. We Wests feel such gratitude to your late husband for his years of dedicated service to our enterprise."

Mrs. Reeves nodded in an acknowledgment that seemed to Daniel too frosty for the effusiveness of Mrs. West's sentiments and the generosity of her gifts, which lay piled on the walnut dining table—a salted ham in a cloth bag, some oranges and a pineapple, a caramel-frosted cake, a bag of foil-wrapped toffees.

After seeing Mrs. West out, Mrs. Reeves returned, a scowl on her normally benign face.

"What lovely gifts," suggested Daniel.

"Guilt gifts."

"Oh? Of what is Mrs. West guilty, if I may ask?"

"She herself ain't guilty of nothing. But her husband's parents drove my Roger to his grave."

"Good heavens, what did they do?"

She gestured for him to take his usual chair by the kitchen fireplace. She sat too, and then she explained how the export company in Virginia had blamed her husband for the declining supply of hides, claiming that he had allowed the South Carolinian and French traders to out-bargain him with the Indians. The reality was that the deer herds had been decimated by over hunting, driven by the insatiable demands of all the trading companies on the coast.

One afternoon a young man with hair like corn silk had arrived at the trading post. He announced that he was Adam West, son of the owner—and new superintendent of the post. Mastering his humiliation over being replaced with no warning, Roger invited Mr. West and his wife to dinner at his home. Mr. West declined, citing their exhaustion from their journey over from the Tidewater.

At a meeting in the blockhouse the next day, Mr. West, clad in a broadcloth frockcoat, ordered his buckskinned employees to send their "squaws" and "half-breed bastards" back to their own villages. Taking an appalled Roger aside, he suggested that the Anglican priest who had accompanied him and his wife from Virginia marry Roger and his "concubine." He said that although it was illegal for an Englishman to marry an Indian, the priest was prepared to overlook this irregularity at Mr. West's request.

Roger replied, "My wife and I have been married for twenty-five years now, Mr. West. We have fourteen children, some older than yourself."

"Yet your so-called marriage is sanctioned by neither the Anglican church, nor by the state of Virginia, nor by the United States of America," said Mr. West. "In the eyes of God and the annals of our governments, your children are illegitimate."

Roger stared at him for a long moment before turning around and stalking out.

Several traders departed for their wives' villages, possessions piled high on sturdy mountain ponies. Others sent their distraught wives and children away by themselves to the wives' families in native towns. Some of these men later returned from trips to the Tidewater with new rosy-cheeked wives, who passed their days huddled in a sitting room in the blockhouse, fantasizing about impending Indian attacks and hating their husbands for condemning them to such a wasteland.

One morning Mr. West issued instructions to Roger Reeves for his wife to serve these Englishwomen their afternoon tea.

"So I became the Wests' parlor maid," explained Mrs. Reeves. "And Roger became their handyman. We had no choice. They had replaced Roger as manager without giving him a penny for our old age."

Daniel shook his head. "I am truly sorry, Mrs. Reeves."

"Why? You weren't even borned then."

"They were English by origin, and I, too, am English. But you mustn't imagine that all Englishmen feel contempt for those not so blessed."

"You forget that my husband Roger was also an Englishman. His sole crime in the eyes of the West family was that he refused to renounce me and our children."

"You said the current Mrs. West lives on a plantation on the Sturgeon River. I have never seen a plantation down there."

Mrs. Reeves snorted. "Virginians will call any filthy old sty their 'plantation.' Roger used to say that once a Virginian owns a few homesick Africans to torment, he starts thinking of himself as an aristocrat, and of everybody else as a peasant." She laughed. "One thing you can count on in this life, Daniel: people will never cease to tickle you with their pretensions."

"Well, those guilt gifts look pretty nice to me, whatever their reason."

"Yes, she always brings me a ham during hog-killing season, so I can't complain. Will you join us for our harvest dinner this Sunday? You don't really have no choice, since it will be going on right here."

"Thank you. I would love to come."

Daniel was lying on his bed pondering a line he had just read in William Penn's *Some Fruits of Solitude*: "A good end cannot sanctify evil means, nor must we ever do evil that good may come of it." But how could you know in advance what was good and what evil? he wondered. Your inner light was supposed to tell you, but what if it didn't? Had it been evil for him not to warn the slavers that they were about to be shot? When they might have cut the throats of those children in response? Should he have allowed the children to be killed, assuming that their deaths could be viewed as "good" in some larger scheme he didn't yet understand? The Quaker divines wrote admirable sentiments, but these sentiments sounded hollow to someone in the trenches fighting actual battles.

The shouts of children in the yard made it clear that *his* solitude was at an end. Sitting up, he pulled on his boots and adjusted his collar. Then he shrugged on his jacket and descended the steps to join the Martins and Reeveses, attired in their Sunday best—dark suits, vests, starched collars, and polished boots for the men, and colorful calico dresses and woven aprons and shawls for the women.

Reuben Martin and Mrs. Reeves, the patriarch and matriarch of their respective clans, sat in the wingback chairs flanking the fireplace in the front parlor. Each new arrival, even the toddlers, came first to pay them respect before seeking out their peers. Some adolescent boys and girls, uncertain whether they belonged with the children or the adults, flirted awkwardly by the front windows.

After shaking Reuben's hand, Daniel headed for the back door. He spotted Barbary Martin, her lank gray hair framing her chubby, cheerful face. She was organizing the placement on the long walnut table of the dishes the women had brought.

Although the day was cool and the sunlight weak through the winter trees, gangs of small children roved the yard and invaded the barn, annoying the cow and chickens with wild chasing games and swan dives from the loft into the haystack down below. Several of Daniel's students waved to him, and he waved back.

Daniel joined a cluster of men squatting on their haunches near the road, their forearms resting on their thighs. Some were Martins and Reeveses whom he'd never met. Everybody in this area seemed to have a dozen children or more. Their family farms got chopped into smaller and smaller chunks with each generation. This was why people were always trying to push the Indians off their land. It might be easier and more just if they limited themselves to only a couple of heirs apiece.

Joshua Martin had one knee raised to support an elbow, so he could prop his chin on a fist. These men spent their days outdoors, far from furniture, so they had learned how to be their own armchairs. They seemed comfortable in these contorted poses, drawing on pipes or chewing tobacco. But Daniel lowered himself into such a squat with dread. His thigh muscles, still strained from the horseback pursuit of the slave catchers, screamed with pain.

Achieving a tenuous balance, Daniel scanned the faces of his companions, most bearded and shadowed by wide-brimmed black hats. He felt at home amid this Quaker black, even though his own clothing was an undyed wheat color that made him stand out in this group like a cat among dogs.

The last time he had seen several of these men had been the afternoon they had murdered the slave catchers. He had been waiting for someone to cart him off to the gallows, but so far nothing had happened. It was as though a boulder they had hefted into a pond together had stirred no ripples—or rather, had stirred ripples only within his own heart.

Joshua was saying, "At the trading post near Tocaru this week, Mr. Grayson told me the Cherokees have to be off their land by early this summer."

Elijah spat tobacco juice into the dirt and said, "But that's been their land for as long as anyone can remember."

"Not no more, it ain't," said Abner, attired in his checked vest, his red hair slicked back. "They done sold it."

"They never sold it," insisted Joshua, his pale eyes ghostly in the weak winter sunlight. "Them federals got a few mixed-blood chiefs to trade their signatures for land out west. Sixteen thousand ordinary Cherokees have signed a petition saying that those chiefs don't speak for them and they want to stay right here."

"Where does that boundary line run?" asked Peter Reeves, Mrs. Reeves's eldest grandson, a small, wiry man who was captain of the Couchtown militia and a justice of the peace.

"Just this side of Tocaru," replied Joshua.

"Well, thank the Lord for that," muttered Peter. "At least it doesn't include our farms."

"I'm going with them," announced Joshua.

"Going where?" asked Abner.

"Out west, I reckon."

Abner stared at him. "How come you to do that, Joshua?"

"I married a Tocaru woman. We're having us a baby."

Nobody said anything for a long time as they all digested the significance of this statement. If you married a woman in one of the Cherokee towns, you were adopted into a clan and became Cherokee yourself. You went wherever they went. Or wherever they got sent.

Finally Abner replied, "Well, that's all right, then." He extended his hand. When Joshua clasped it, Abner tried to pull him off balance.

Everybody laughed. Peter Reeves uncorked a small wooden cask and passed it around. Each man toasted Joshua before taking a sip.

All too soon the cask reached Daniel. Taking a cautious sip, he felt the clear liquid sear his mouth as though he were a flame swallower who hadn't mastered his craft.

To avoid further sips, Daniel struggled to his feet and limped inside. He waited by the laden table for his eyes to adjust to the dim light. Once they had, he spotted Galicia behind the table, carving Mrs. West's giant ham. She wore a long dress of blue calico, topped by a homespun apron. On her head was a kerchief of the same blue fabric, knotted in back beneath her bundle of curly black hair. He recognized from dinner at her home the dull red stone that hung around her neck on a rawhide thong. With a start Daniel realized that the hands deftly slicing the meat each had an extra thumb.

Galicia glanced at him and then turned her head aside. Daniel struggled to understand how a woman who could so calmly shoot a stranger in the back could duck her head like a timid child when confronting an accomplice to her crime.

She looked up, and her eyes met his. He was aware only of the thick black eyebrows and long lashes, the cocoa-colored irises, and the dilated pupils. The din in the room around them grew muffled.

"Mr. Hunter?"

"Yes?" He couldn't stop staring into those pupils, which were like shafts leading to an underworld where good and evil were so intertwined that you couldn't separate them.

"I sure do appreciate you helping us get Nathan back the other day."

"I am just glad he and Delia weren't hurt."

"I wanted to ask if you would learn me how to read and write."

"Yes, of course. Would you like to join my class at the store?"

"I can't come during the day. I got to help my mama on the farm. But I was wondering if I could have a quick lesson whenever I come to town to pick up Nathan."

Daniel did Mrs. Reeves's chores in late afternoon. But he figured he could postpone them for a little while. He wanted more adult students so that word would spread that reading wasn't just for children. After making a plan to work with Galicia the following afternoon, he watched her walk back to the kitchen, her hips swaying beneath the calico skirt.

Daniel woke up abruptly on his lumpy cornhusk mattress. The full moon was perfectly framed by the small gable window at one end of the loft. He studied the ivory globe, mottled with shadows. Mrs. Reeves had told him the Cherokees called this month's full moon the Frost Moon. He had hardly ever noticed the moon in Philadelphia, much less observed it closely enough to give it a new name every month.

He heard the lonesome howl of a wolf from the hemlock forest at the edge of town. Mrs. Reeves had explained that herds of deer sheltered in those boughs on winter nights, and wolves dined on those too young or old or ill to escape their assaults. This was the time of night Mrs. Reeves called the Hour of the Wolf, when babies were born, old people died, and those in between regretted the past and feared the future.

All of a sudden Daniel pictured the startled expressions on the slavers' faces as they fell slowly from their horses. Where had they gone, those horrible daylight personalities who had stalked fleeing fugitives for fun and for profit? According to his Philadelphia meeting, even these men would have harbored an inner light that was God. This light was supposed to link a man to every other person on earth and prevent him from harming them, because to harm others was to harm oneself. The slavers had ignored this light. Were their startled expressions as the life force flowed out of them because they were suddenly flooded with the light they had denied? Or was the shock on their faces evidence that this light, renounced by them, was now renouncing them in turn—and relinquishing them to everlasting darkness?

Shivering both from the cold and from distress at not knowing the answers to these questions, Daniel reached down to the pile of books on the floor beside his bed and grabbed one by James Naylor. The book fell open to one of his favorite passages. He read, "Art thou in the darkness? Mind it not, for if thou dost, it will fill thee more. But stand still and act not, and wait in patience until light arises out of darkness to lead thee."

Calmed by these familiar words, Daniel watched the Frost Moon out the gable window and listened to the howls of the wolves feasting on fawns in the hemlocks until the book drooped in his hands and he fell asleep.

Galicia was wearing her blue calico dress and headscarf, plus a wool shawl dyed in stripes of yellow and red. Daniel was beginning to overcome his horror of dyed cloth, having realized that women here in the mountains did the dyeing themselves with plants and roots gathered from the forest. The deadly dye vats of South Carolina were not involved in these beautiful muted colors.

As Galicia sent Nathan downstairs to help Abner count pelts, Daniel realized that Abner had always taken Nathan home from school in the past. Galicia hadn't previously come to the trading post to pick him up herself. Furthermore, both Abner and Nathan could have taught Galicia what they were learning without her needing to see Daniel in person.

Bewildered, he placed a slate and chalk on her desk. She cast him that look of hers, so intriguingly bold and bashful, both at once.

"I guess your husband must be proud that his wife and son will soon know how to read and write," Daniel commented.

She lowered her eyes. "Got no husband."

"Oh, excuse me. You are a widow?"

"Nathan's not got no daddy, if that's what you're asking." She fixed him with a sullen stare. "He has a daddy, but not one who cares to claim him."

"He is a fine boy." Daniel was chagrined to realize that Galicia was an unwed mother and that Nathan was apparently illegitimate.

"Yes, my Nathan is a very fine little boy." She glanced up at him with a touch of belligerence.

"Well, let us get started, then." Daniel picked up the chalk and placed it in Galicia's fingers. As he struggled to position it in relation to her extra thumb, he realized that his palms were clammy. Her eyes shifted from their tangled hands to his face. He felt a sudden urge to lower his lips to hers.

Straightening, Daniel walked back to his desk. He picked up his slate and showed her how to form an A. As she copied his marks, he reminded himself that he was engaged. He was supposed to want to kiss Abigail, not Galicia. Tom Hill's escape and the murder of the slave catchers must have undermined his belief system even more than he had realized. If you had broken two rules, maybe it seemed easier to break more, just as Galicia herself had apparently already done.

Nathan appeared in the doorway. "Mama, Uncle Abner says to tell you it's time to head on back home now."

As Galicia stood up, Daniel said, "Take that slate and chalk with you, Galicia. Practice your A, and then get Nathan and Abner to teach you some more letters. If you have any problems, you can come see me any time."

"Thank you. I promise I'll keep them safe." She slid the slate into her apron pocket. Her voice sounded subdued. Was she disappointed that he had so abruptly canceled her private lessons? She walked out without looking at him. He felt relieved to have resolved his momentary temptation. She was, after all, a murderer, however he might try to rationalize it.

A couple of weeks later, as his students careened down the steps from the classroom, Daniel looked up from his desk to find Galicia standing in his doorway in her blue calico dress, which appeared to be the only one she owned. To his dismay, his heartbeat lurched, as it did whenever he saw her nowadays, which was often, since she seemed to need help with her letters every other day.

"Just can't seem to get them R's." She sat down at a student's desk.

He picked up a slate, walked over to her, and slowly printed an R in three steps.

As she copied his marks, he said, "Galicia, I will be gone for the next few weeks. I'm about to head down to the Shenandoah for the holidays."

"I had hoped you might could join my family for Christmas."

"I would have loved to."

"Why not change your plans, then?"

"I am going to visit my fiancée," he forced himself to confess.

After a long silence Galicia said, "I didn't realize you're engaged."

"Yes. To the daughter of some friends of my parents. She and I are both Quakers."

"Do you love her?"

Daniel was shocked into silence that she would ask him such a question.

"If you ain't sure, then you don't. So why are you marrying her?"

"I did not say I don't."

"You didn't say you do either." She smiled faintly.

He decided to be as blunt with her as she was being with him. "Maybe I hesitated because I did not want to hurt you."

"Why would it hurt me to know that you love the woman you're about to marry? Ain't that the way marriage is supposed to work?" Her gaze met his.

He wondered if he had misread the situation. The notion that she might not be interested in him as a man perturbed him. And the fact that it perturbed him perturbed him even more.

"I'll have learned all my letters by the time you get back." She sounded indifferent as to the target of his affections.

"Good. And I hope you have a pleasant holiday," he said, somewhat huffily.

She laughed. "Schoolteachers have holidays. Storekeepers have holidays. But farmers and housewives and mothers don't have no holidays, and I'm all three at once."

Galicia stood up and gathered her belongings. Watching her, Daniel reflected that she had already taken one man without the sanction of marriage. Would she take a second? But if he should succumb to her allure, he would be trapped. Her brothers would force him to marry her. And if he refused, he would have to leave town. And if he did succumb, his relationship with Abigail would be finished. Still, Galicia was standing right here in front of him, and Abigail was two days away.

As Galicia headed out the door, he was appalled by these thoughts. He needed to rein in his dangerous fantasies once and for all. He was poised on the brink of total depravity.

Daniel's journey to the Shenandoah was a reluctant one. Each step toward Abigail now represented a step away from Galicia, and Daniel was disturbed by this further proof of his growing attraction to Galicia, as though he were a nail who had unwittingly strayed too close to a magnet and was now unable to back away.

The Perkinses were surprised to discover him on their doorstep several days early. He explained that he had closed his school sooner than planned. He didn't tell them why. After escorting him to the guest room, Abigail handed him a stack of letters from his parents, stroking his hand with her fingertips and smiling at him with infinite promise.

Daniel unpacked and cleaned up. Then he lay on the bed to read the letters. In one, his parents expressed their delight at his marriage plans. As a wedding gift they offered Daniel and Abigail round-trip tickets on a ship from Norfolk to Philadelphia. Calculating that such a journey would require a month or more, Daniel realized that he couldn't bear the thought of being away from Galicia for that long.

Shaking himself like a wet dog, Daniel returned to his mother's letters. A more recent one informed him that Tom Hill and his family had arrived in Philadelphia and were now en route to Halifax, Nova Scotia, on a ship owned by one of Mr. Hunter's London business associates.

At dinner Daniel told the Perkinses the Tom Hill story. All three looked at him admiringly, despite the laws he had broken. He skipped the coda concerning the murder of the slavers because he had begun to regard the Perkinses as unworldly people whose innocence had to be protected. They condemned violence without allowing for the possibility that it might sometimes be necessary in order to prevent a greater violence. Vera had ridden alone and unarmed through Shawnee territory during Tecumseh's War. Daniel had always been told, and had believed, that God had protected her. But recently he had begun to wonder if she had just been lucky.

James and Vera tactfully ascended to their bedroom after dinner, abandoning the parlor and its blazing fire to the young lovers. Sitting side by side on the settee, they gazed at the flames. Daniel fought not to picture the Martins' walk-in stone fireplace, with Galicia, Nathan, and her brothers crowded around it.

Abigail said, "Daniel, thou art distracted."

He looked at her, startled to be so easily decoded. "It is just that I abhor the two years we must wait before we can be as one. If we are to be blessed with children, I prefer to pursue this goal as soon as possible."

Abigail blushed. "Yet our elders insist that anything worth having is worth waiting for."

"I feel as though I have already been waiting for you—for thee—for my entire life." He eyed the row of buttons down the bodice of her ebony silk gown, like tiny poison toadstools. "Why not just commence our life together right away?"

"I am glad thou hast waited for me, Daniel," she said softly.

"Could we not marry in the spring?"

"Thou must ask my father. I wish to please thee, Daniel, but not at the expense of displeasing my parents."

As Daniel lay in bed that night, he was alarmed to discover that it was not the buttons down Abigail's bosom that he imagined unfastening, but rather those up the front of Galicia's blue calico skirt.

In the morning Daniel rode with James to the mica mine he had opened in the foothills to the south of his farm, at which he was employing landless whites as well as the slaves the Mulberry Meeting had bought and freed. James introduced him to the foreman, Able McCoy, a burly man with a bushy moustache and piercing black eyes.

As Daniel and James watched McCoy and the workers descend into the shaft with their picks, Daniel said, "James, I have Abigail's permission to ask thee if we might advance the date of our union to this spring."

James looked at him reprovingly. "But Daniel, thou knowest that a waiting period is necessary. Thy carnal desire must recede in order to assure that a more spiritual love remains." He laughed amiably. "Thou art like a horse headed for the comforts of the stable. Thou longs to bolt and must be restrained."

"But I fail to see what is so undesirable about desire."

"If thou wishes to root about like a boar in rut, thou wouldst do well to seek some young woman other than my daughter to join thee."

Meeting James's offended gaze, Daniel fought to master his own resentment. "At least allow me to remain here, James, to work in thy mine or on thy farm, close to the woman I love."

James shook his head. "Thy educational mission among the mountain people is important, Daniel. And thou must prove thyself worthy of such a wife as Abigail. Frankly, I do not admire what I have heard from thee just now."

Daniel lowered his head, feeling frantic. He would fail this test. He was an accomplice to two murders, and he lusted for a woman who was not his intended. He was not, in fact, worthy of Abigail.

At dinner Daniel noticed questioning glances from Abigail. He knew he seemed distant, but his heart was in the process of separating from his body and heading back home to Couchtown—and to Galicia.

To conceal his inner turmoil, Daniel told the Perkinses about the fraudulent treaty the United States government had negotiated with the Cherokees. "Sixteen thousand Cherokees have signed a petition of protest, but the federal government is still insisting that they leave their homeland."

"The property this very house sits on was once owned by the Cherokees," confessed James, his goatee wagging in the candlelight. "Before the arrival of Europeans their territory included this entire mountain region. It feels wrong to be living on their land, even if they did sign it away in various treaties. I struggle daily with this contradiction to my deepest beliefs."

"The United States could once have been a great nation," murmured Vera, her head encased in her translucent white bonnet. "But the way we have dealt with the Indians and the Africans has robbed this country of all that early promise."

In the parlor after dinner Daniel told Abigail, "I approached thy father about a spring wedding. He said we must wait."

She took his hand in both hers. "I am sorry, Daniel. But is our love not strong enough to survive this delay?"

Daniel remained silent as she stroked his palm with her fingertips. "I do not know." If he didn't tell her the true reason for his urgency, there was a faint hope their love might prevail over his baser nature.

Abruptly she released his hand. "If thou knowest not, Daniel, then such a delay is absolutely necessary."

He looked at her profile in the firelight. Her lips were set and her eyes steely. She was as principled as her pious parents. He himself had once been so principled, before his sojourn in the mountains, where life had taken on ambiguities he had never imagined possible. He felt torn in two by passion and duty, by the demands of his body and the admonitions of his brain. Tears flooded his eyes, causing the flames to flow rather than flicker. He closed his eyelids, but the tears seeped through them to trickle down his cheeks.

"Thou art crying."

"I am so lonely up there in Couchtown, Abigail. The nights are long and dark and filled with the howls of wolves and the screams of panthers. I need my wife beside me to give me the strength to endure it."

"I am not yet thy wife."

He wished she could simply take him in her arms and kiss away his doubts and conflicts. She could pity oppressed Africans and Indians whom she had never met, but not her own fiancé who sat suffering by her side.

Struggling for manly composure, he said, "No doubt the months until we can be as one will pass more quickly than I now imagine."

And his days with the Perkinses did soon settle into a soothing routine of work, meals, reading, and meditation by the parlor fire. At first he had to struggle mightily during the periods of silent sitting to prevent his thoughts from drifting to the way in which Galicia's hips swayed in her calico skirt as she walked. But gradually Daniel's thwarted lust faded, and his faith in his and Abigail's shared future revived.

After New Year's, as he turned his mare's head toward the towering mountains, Daniel felt as his namesake must have upon entering the lions' den—only he now knew that the lions lurked within himself. He had learned how to tame them during this visit with Abigail, and he would now keep them safely behind bars back in Couchtown.

7

Seedbeds: April 1838

Daniel's mare plodded alongside the Otter Creek down the cart path that led to the Martins' farm at the foot of Silver Valley. The forests on either hand flared with ivory, coral, and purple blossoms. Spring had exploded like a fatal fever. Daniel had closed his school for the planting season.

A few of the Martin brothers were helping him convert Tom Hill's forge on the main street of Couchtown into a house for Abigail and himself after their wedding. He would have only to cross the street to get to his classroom at the trading post.

In return, Daniel was working on the Martins' farm. The other Martin brothers had their own business to attend to. Abner was busy at the store. Joshua was building a cabin near Tocaru for his wife and baby. Once the child was born, Joshua's wife's family had finally relented and accepted him. Reuben had had some "spells" and now spent most of his time in a rocking chair on the porch, surveying the flocks and fields he could no longer tend. The twins, Gideon and Elijah, who were married to twin Reeves sisters, lived in cabins in the meadow most distant from their parents' house. The twins and their many double-first cousin children worked the fields that stretched below the mouth of the cave and alongside the marsh over which the ancient burial mound loomed.

That left Isaac, Galicia, Barbary, and Nathan to run the main farm. Hired men were in short supply during planting season. The Martins couldn't afford slaves, and they opposed the practice in any case. So Daniel, however inept at farm chores, would have to do. He already ached all over from planting Mrs. Reeves's kitchen garden and from helping to transplant the Martins' tobacco seedlings. But it seemed a healthful ache, one that promised new muscles and improved posture. The best part was that he was so exhausted by day's end that he fell into a dreamless sleep that allowed no room for fantasies about faceless women with loose limbs and looser morals.

Abigail wanted to come see Couchtown before their marriage. James and Vera were both too frail now to ride for two days in the mountains, but they didn't want Abigail to make the journey unaccompanied. Daniel was trying to find a time when he could go get her, bring her to Couchtown, and then take her back home. But her parents weren't enthusiastic about their being alone together for that long without a chaperone and encouraged Daniel to continue his visits to them as he was able. This suited Daniel fine because he wasn't too confident about his behavior if left alone with Abigail for several days unsupervised. To be a young man with no acceptable outlets for the urges normal to a young man was not a fate he would wish on his worst enemy, if he had one.

Passing a rail-fenced pasture owned by Peter Reeves, Daniel spotted a bay stallion mounting a piebald mare. She struggled to buck him off as he diligently pumped her full of seed. Across the fence from the horses, a low-slung black bull with swollen testicles bellowed at bored-looking Holsteins. A buzzing swarm of bees had clumped like a burl on the branch of a dead oak on the creek bank. All nature appeared to be involved in a plot to remind him constantly of the act of procreation that he himself wasn't yet allowed to perform.

Daniel smiled, remembering that Galicia would be serving him lunch. He had learned to enjoy her presence without wanting more. In less than eighteen months, he and Abigail would live in the renovated forge in Couchtown. No doubt his path would cross Galicia's now and then, and perhaps his heart would still misfire and his palms prickle. But that was all there was—or ever would be—to it. He had negotiated a truce between his higher and lower selves. The only fatality had been his burgeoning fascination with Galicia, which he had buried in an unmarked grave deep in his heart. He thought she sometimes looked at him reproachfully. But he knew this was the only sensible course for them both.

Upon reaching the Martins' yard, Daniel stabled his mare, picked up his burlap seed sack, and ambled out to the cornfield, where Gideon was already plowing behind the lop-eared mule. Isaac, Elijah, Nathan, and several of the twins' sons whom Daniel couldn't tell apart were scuttling like crabs along the furrows, inserting and tamping down kernels from their sacks.

Slinging his bag over his shoulder, Daniel stumbled through the clods beneath the morning sun as moisture steamed from the freshly turned earth. Flocks of rust-breasted robins hovered overhead, poised to swoop down and peck up insect eggs or to drag exposed worms wiggling from their upended burrows.

When the sun reached its apex, all the men and boys were soaked with sweat. Hobbling the mule in the shade by the pasture's edge with a nosebag full of oats, they removed their seed sacks and headed back to the house. After splashing themselves cool and clean at the well, they went inside to a table loaded down with baked ham, fried chicken, roasted venison, half a dozen vegetable dishes, cornbread, and three varieties of fruit cobbler oozing with thick yellow cream.

Barbary, Galicia, the twins' wives, Anna and Hannah, and some of the twins' daughters served the men and boys, standing behind them and replenishing their plates as bare spots appeared. The women would eat whatever was left over once the satiated males moved out to the porch for a smoke and a nap.

As he sprawled on the sagging porch floor with an uncomfortably full belly, Daniel reflected that he loved this hard manual labor. By dusk the cornfield would be planted. Come autumn, the corn, dried on its stalks, would be harvested. All winter long the Martins would eat breads and stews concocted from it. In spring they would drag out the mule, braying protests, and start all over again. He looked forward to the day when he, like the Martin sons and grandsons, would know every dip and rise of these fields as intimately as his hands would then know the landscape of Abigail's body.

Daniel opened his eyes to discover Galicia sitting on the floor beside him, back against the wall, her legs stretched out before her.

She wore the loose homespun dress she always slipped on when she joined them in the fields after lunch.

Smiling, he murmured, "Delicious dinner, Galicia."

"I make special dishes when I know you're coming," she said in a voice lowered so that no one else could hear.

"Thank you." He felt the familiar catch to his heartbeat, like a horse stumbling in mid-trot.

She smiled at him, her eyes the rich brown of a newly turned furrow.

Back in the cornfield, the women destroyed the careful rows the men had sown, surrounding the corn kernels with those of beans, squashes, gourds, pumpkins, and sunflowers, shaken from their apron pockets and stamped into place by their bare feet.

In the golden light of late afternoon, they all jumped into the Otter Creek fully clothed. Some otters lounging on a sun-struck log slithered into the water and disappeared downstream. Nathan splashed Daniel and pushed down on his shoulders to dunk him, while Daniel struggled to throw him off his back. He noticed Galicia watching their scuffle with a wistful smile, and he felt a moment of sadness. If he were not committed elsewhere, he would have liked nothing better than to be the father Nathan had never had and wanted so much.

At the house they supped on lunch leftovers on the porch floor, cooled by their damp clothing. Gideon and Elijah serenaded them with a mournful banjo and fiddle duet called "The Banks of the Bloody Otter" about a girl who cut out her boyfriend's heart while he slept and fed it to the dogs because he had married someone else. As Daniel's stomach turned at the gruesome details of the boy's death, he made a mental note that these people took their love matches seriously. Forgiveness was not a quality they admired or even considered. Thank God he had had the good sense to renounce Galicia before they had gone too far to turn back. She hadn't hesitated to shoot a man who had harmed her son. Who knew what she might do to a man who harmed her heart?

As Daniel tried to summon the energy to get up and ride back to Couchtown, Barbary said, "Why not stay here tonight, Daniel? Joshua is over at Tocaru, so his bed is empty. That way you won't have to get up so early in the morning to get back over here."

"Mrs. Reeves will wonder where I am." He glanced at Galicia, who was studying a hound in the yard that simultaneously gnawed a hambone held in his front paws and scratched at a flea with a rear leg.

"Mrs. Reeves will realize that you stayed here with us," said Barbary.

"Good idea," said Abner, who had just arrived from the store. "It's decided."

Daniel wondered if they could really be unaware of his former attraction to Galicia, or whether they were all committed to destroying the barriers he had so carefully erected between the two of them. But he was too fatigued for anything but sleep, probably too fatigued even to make it back to Mrs. Reeves's without falling off his horse from exhaustion, so he acquiesced.

As dusk faded into night, stars popped out above the cliff in which the cave mouth yawned. The yard filled with tiny flares from fireflies that floated on languid currents of damp air off the creek.

The others drifted away to their cabins or their beds, until only Galicia and Daniel remained on the porch. Daniel sprawled supine across the floor, already half asleep. Galicia was leaning against the wall with her legs drawn up to her chest. Down in the creek bullfrogs and peepers sang their syncopated harmonies in bass and treble. From some distant ridge a panther screamed. Daniel's mare snorted in her stall, and one of the hounds offered a token bark.

Galicia unfolded her legs and stretched them out straight. Then she lifted Daniel's head with both hands and scooted sideways so her lap could be his pillow. From within the house came the sighs and snores of bone-tired slumber. Daniel clasped one of Galicia's bare feet in one hand. The sole was as tough and cracked as old leather. This was probably what it felt like to have a sister. Neither of you worried about being sweaty and dirty and too tired to talk.

Lying there with his eyes closed, Daniel inhaled the musky scent of Galicia's sweat. Then, as though in a trance, he turned on his side to face her. She cradled his head against her abdomen and stroked his hair. He could hear her heart pounding in tandem with the crickets. He felt blood rush to his face. His scalp prickled under her fingertips. He realized Galicia was no sister to him. All his notions of renunciation were nonsense. He was done for—and willingly so.

Pushing himself up with one arm, he paused to consider the grisly fate of the young man whose heart had been hacked out of his chest and fed to the hounds for unfaithfulness. But Galicia's breasts were pushing against his chest, and his alarmed brain switched itself off just when he needed it most. Their lips met, and he and she fell on one another with the fervor of lost travelers who had finally found the trail back home.

Later, they lay amid a jumble of disheveled clothing, their sweat chilling them. Galicia whispered, "I'd thought you didn't want me like this, Daniel."

"I've been a fool. I've known for a long time now that you are meant for me, as I am for you." As he said this, it felt truer than true to him, whatever the consequences. Was this sudden conviction the gift of his inner light, which had so stubbornly refused to guide him until now? Or was it the result of the absence of that light, which had allowed him to sink into a quagmire out of which he would now be unable to drag himself?

8

Soldiers' Joy: June 1838

The cornstalks had grown high, and the Martins' huge field had turned into a riot of climbing bean vines, sprawling squash plants, and nodding sunflower blossoms. Galicia and Daniel ate lunch every day in a small clearing in the middle of this patch. She brought food from the house in a basket she had woven from marsh grass and spread her red and yellow shawl on the dirt for their picnic and nap.

One afternoon as they dozed in the shade, Daniel asked, "Who is Nathan's father?" He was trying to imagine how a man could turn his back and walk away from a woman as kind and loving and passionate as Galicia, especially if he had known she was carrying his child.

Galicia said nothing.

Daniel rolled over so her eyes couldn't avoid his. "You don't have to tell me if you don't want to."

"There's nothing I wouldn't tell you now, Daniel. It's just that I sent my memories of that other one away. That lying hog drover don't hardly even exist for me no more. I've made myself all fresh and clean and new for you."

Emerging from their love nest as the shadows lengthened, they spotted Joshua riding up to the house, bareback on an Indian pony, dressed in a loincloth, leggings, and moccasins. He slid off the pony and greeted his family, who still lounged on the porch since their lunch break. Galicia ducked inside the house with the basket while Daniel assumed a squat alongside the other men. He wondered what Galicia's brothers and parents thought about the lunchtime naps in the cornfield. Nobody ever said a word. Probably they had more important things to worry about now that the Cherokees were being forced off their land.

Joshua was saying, "...so them soldiers rounded up the Cherokees who hadn't turned themselves in. They've herded them into stockades along the river down in the valley, like big cattle pens. It's too hot to travel out west now, so they're just setting there in the dirt, baking in the sun. A few babies and elders die every week from bad water. The soldiers rape the girls at night. Now and then, a warrior escapes and heads for the hills."

"What's going to happen to you all, Joshua honey?" asked Barbary anxiously. She sat beside Reuben in a rush-seated rocking chair identical to his.

"Them soldiers keep posting notices at the trading posts, ordering us to come down to the stockades. We're hoping if we just ignore them, they'll give up and go away."

"Son, you don't have to put yourself through this." Reuben gestured expansively with his sole arm. "Bring your wife and child here. We have lots of room for a new cabin and crops. You and your wife are our family, just as much as you're Tocaru."

"You know how they are at Tocaru, Papa. If you marry one of their daughters, you're part of her mother's household, and that's that."

"Well, bring the whole bunch up here then."

"I may have to before this thing is over with."

Toward evening Daniel returned to Couchtown, hoping by passing an occasional night at Mrs. Reeves's to conceal his and Galicia's liaison from her. As he entered her kitchen, she said, "Well, well, if it ain't my wayfaring boarder." She didn't sound happy.

David felt guilty. He had been neglecting her chores, with which he paid most of his rent. "I'm sorry I've been gone so much, Mrs. Reeves." He plopped down in his usual chair. "It's a busy time out at the Martin place just now."

"So I hear. You look right peaked, Daniel."

"Yes, farm labor is pretty grueling. Especially for a city boy."

"Especially when you got to plow all night long, too."

David realized she was teasing him. "So you already know about Galicia and me?"

She laughed curtly. "No one in these parts has ever kept a secret longer than a week."

He shrugged comically.

"What do you aim to do, Daniel—marry your Quaker miss like you planned?"

"I don't know."

"If you don't know, then I want you packed up and out of here by next week."

He looked at her, startled by her ferocity. "I thought you were always urging me to sow my wild oats, Mrs. Reeves?"

"Sow your damned oats with a woman who aims to sow hers as well. Galicia has already had her heart broke once—by some sorry hog drover who promised to come back for her. If you mean to break her heart a second time, don't think of me no more as your friend or your landlady."

"Either way a heart gets broken. And Abigail is from my own world."

"Not no more she ain't. You left that world behind the day you started messing around with Galicia in the corn patch."

"But she has been messing around with me, too."

"She ain't the one who's engaged to someone else. Galicia is free to mess around. You're the one trying to take everything and give nothing."

"But I did tell her I'm engaged."

"Everyone thinks from the way you've carried on with her, almost in public view, that you've done broke that off."

"My parents would never accept Galicia as my wife."

"I thought they was thrilled to death that you was aiding us illiterates, mired down in our ignorance up here in the mountains?"

"Aiding, yes. Marrying, no." If he married a woman who was not a Quaker, he would be expelled from the faith and his parents would be chastised by their meeting.

"Fornicating with, yes. But marrying, no?"

Daniel frowned.

"It's all right to do it, just not to say it?"

"All right. I was wrong. I am wrong."

"Yes, you were and you are," she agreed. "How do you mean to put it right?"

"I guess I have to choose."

"Yes, *you* have to choose. Not your mama, not your papa, not your Quaker folks back in Philadelphia, but you. Which woman do you want to sleep next to every night? Whose eyes do you want to look into when you wake up in the morning? Which woman do you want to make babies with, and tell your troubles to, and grow old and sick with?"

"Galicia." The consolation of being a Friend seemed feeble compared to the consolation he had already found in Galicia's arms.

"Then you need to travel down to the lowlands, get yourself free from that other one, and give yourself to Galicia for real. Or else you need to get out of my house and out of this town, and set Galicia free to love a man who loves her back. And if you're going, go fast, because her brothers wouldn't care a bit to kill you after what you've done to her."

Feeling like a kicked cur, Daniel stumbled up the steps to bed. Mrs. Reeves was right: he could marry Galicia, flee, or die. He had already witnessed the ease with which the Martins served up their own style of justice. And it could just as well be turned on a two-timing Yankee fornicator as on two kidnapping slave catchers.

In any case, it was Galicia he wanted, he finally acknowledged to himself. But he dreaded confessing this to Abigail, to her parents and his, and to both their meetings. He could no longer pretend to measure up to the lofty standards of the Quakers. But the circuit riders of the Blue Ridge and the holy men of the Tocaru would not fill the void that would be left behind. Of course, the inner light of the Quakers had never really filled his void either. Only Galicia had ever salved the echoing emptiness within himself, and he vowed to do whatever he could to make sure she always would.

Daniel lay on his back, watching through a gap in the cornstalks as a lacy cloud drifted past overhead, like a tuft of milkweed on an autumn breeze. He had been explaining to Galicia, who lay beside him, that he needed to travel to the Shenandoah to break off his engagement.

"I'm afraid," she admitted.

"Afraid of what?"

"Afraid you won't come back to me. Like that other one."

"But the woman I love is right here beside me."

"When you see her, you might decide she's the woman you love. After all, you loved her first."

"I don't think I ever really loved her. I was trying to please my parents and her parents and our church."

"Your elders and preachers is important people to please. And breaking off with her will displease them."

"But to give you up would displease *me*."

They heard a tattoo of cantering hooves coming down the path by the creek. Standing up and peering through the stalks, Daniel spotted Joshua racing along the Otter Creek, the sunlight through the branches playing across his muscled shoulders, which had baked mahogany in the sun.

"It's Joshua," he told Galicia. "We had better get back to the house and find out what's going on."

Approaching the yard, they saw Joshua gesturing urgently to those who sat on the porch.

"What has happened?" Daniel asked Isaac. Isaac was nearly as tall sitting on the floor as was Nathan standing beside him.

"The troops came for the Tocaru," Isaac explained. "Joshua has hidden his family in the cave at the foot of our valley. He thinks the soldiers will come here looking for them. We're trying to decide what to do."

"Can they round you all up, too?" Daniel was terrified by the thought of Galicia's being taken away from him. Was he prepared to go wherever she might get sent?

"I don't think so," said Isaac. "We're outside the most recent boundary line. But they can order us to hunt down those who've escaped."

"So you muster," concluded Reuben from his rocking chair. His voice was soft and weak compared to the way it had sounded that evening nearly a year ago when he had first recounted his tale of King's Mountain to Daniel. "You wander around pretending to search till them federals get fed up and go away."

"Good plan," said Joshua. "I'll go back to the cave now. If the soldiers find the entrance, you all make a lot of noise. I'll move my family around the cave while you pretend to search it."

"How did you escape the soldiers?" asked Daniel.

"I was fishing," replied Joshua. "I heard some shouts. I ran over to my wife's aunt's cabin. She was scattering corn for the chickens while some soldiers in dark blue uniforms waited on her to finish. Then they marched her and her husband and children down the road. I raced home and persuaded Whippoorwill's mother to clear out fast. They want me to go back down to their cabins and lead Whippoorwill's brother's family up here to the cave if they haven't been taken to the stockade yet."

"Be careful, Joshua," pleaded Barbary from the doorway. "The soldiers could arrest you, too, and ship you out west. You look like one of them now."

"Mama, I *am* one of them."

Barbary nodded resignedly. "I know, honey. Do you all have enough food there in the cave?"

"Just what we could grab as we ran."

Barbary and Galicia went inside and returned with a couple of sacks, which Joshua strapped across his horse before jumping on and cantering back up the valley. Gideon and Elijah went into the house and returned with their instruments.

"Good idea," said Reuben. "We need to act normal-like while we wait on them federals."

The twins played "Soldiers' Joy," a reel Daniel had heard them play at the dances in the stable behind the trading post. They all clapped and tapped their feet and tried their best to pretend everything was going to be all right.

By late afternoon half a dozen men in blue uniforms with cartridge belts across their chests sat on their horses in the yard, asking Reuben for permission to set up camp in the sheep pasture. He consented. Then, to Daniel's astonishment, he invited the soldiers to clean up and come for supper.

The soldiers crammed together on the benches around the long dinner table and watched their plates being filled by the women who stood behind them. The captain wore a uniform jacket with epaulettes and gold buttons. In his clipped Yankee accent he asked Reuben if he had seen any stray Indians that day.

"Ain't seen a one," Reuben assured him. "And I been setting on my porch all day long."

"Who's the head of the militia around here?" asked the captain.

"Fellow name of Peter Reeves who lives on down the road toward Couchtown," said Reuben.

"Tomorrow I need you to send someone to order him to muster his men and help us search this valley for some renegade Cherokees who are trying to escape going west."

"Yes sir, I'll do it," said Reuben. "But I can't say as I blame them Cherokees none. This was their land long before any settler ever laid eyes on it."

"Well, I know lots around here feel that way," said the captain. "But it's really for their own good. Their new territory out west is teeming with game. And they'll be safe from these squatters back east who are always trying to steal their land."

"You might could say we oughta ship them squatters out west instead," said Reuben.

The soldiers laughed as though Reuben had intended a joke. No Martin smiled.

Daniel watched a red-faced soldier with a belly like a dark blue melon put his hand on Galicia's buttock as she served him corn pudding. She dumped a steaming ladle of the pudding on his other hand, which lay alongside his plate. He yelped.

"Sorry." She raised one eyebrow at him in warning.

Daniel smiled. She knew how to take care of herself. He felt proud knowing she was his woman. Or nearly so, assuming he had the courage to get himself free from Abigail when he visited her the following week.

After dinner all the men gathered on the porch as the sun sank behind the cliff in which the cave mouth gaped. Luckily, jutting ledges camouflaged it from those who didn't know it was there. Reuben sent Isaac to fetch applejack from the root cellar, and they passed the wooden cask around the porch.

Daniel noticed that the Martins were only pretending to drink, so he gratefully did the same. Once the soldiers had finished off the entire cask, Reuben sent Isaac to the cellar for a second one, which the soldiers also consumed. Then they stumbled off the porch, singing some song involving a woman with raven black hair. They wove back to their tents in the pasture, crawled inside them, and were not heard from again.

In low voices the Martins discussed whether they needed to warn Joshua of the soldiers' arrival.

Isaac cupped his hands and called into the darkness like a hoot owl. He was answered with a similar call. "He's out there," said Isaac. "He knows they're here."

Reuben said to Gideon and Elijah, "You and your families had better sleep here tonight, boys. Load up your guns and prop them by your beds. We'll do whatever we need to, to protect Joshua's family."

Daniel lay in bed alongside Nathan, two loaded rifles leaning against the wall. He prayed he wouldn't have to use one. He prayed that if he did, he wouldn't kill anyone. He prayed that if he did kill someone, it wouldn't be a Martin by accident. It was one thing to have witnessed a murder, but something else altogether to participate in one. It was a skill he was still happy to lack.

The next morning the captain came to the house, squinting in the sunlight. With a grimace, he declined Barbary's offer of a plate of ham gravy and grits. "That applejack packs a punch," he said weakly.

"Don't it just?" said Reuben.

"Sir, I'm heading out to muster the militia," Gideon announced to the captain. "Where should we meet you at?"

"Just carry on by yourselves," croaked the captain. "Bring any Cherokees you capture to the stockade south of Grayson's Trading Post. There's a cash reward for every one you deliver."

"Yes sir, we'll get right on it. It would sure be great to have that reward!" said Gideon, saddling his horse. He added, "Sir, my brother Elijah here could guide you to some likely hiding places around this valley. We know it like the backs of our hands."

"Good idea," said the captain unenthusiastically.

As the hung-over soldiers followed Elijah up the path by the creek in a cloud of dust, the Martins stacked their rifles on the porch floor along with their powder horns and shot pouches. Daniel followed them to the stable, where they all saddled their horses, led them out into the yard, and tied them to the fence.

Everyone sat back down on the porch and watched in tense silence as the dust cloud wandered aimlessly around the valley. It paused by the abandoned Spanish silver shaft before continuing along the trail that ran through the twins' main pasture below the cave mouth. Then the patrol struggled up the rocky hillside to the rim of the bowl and passed over it into the next valley.

Daniel joined the Martins in jumping to his feet. They all shook hands and slapped shoulders and laughed out loud, relieved that their guns would not be needed for the present.

9

The Wilderness Road: July 1838

Once Luke had lashed the barge to its posts on the far riverbank, Daniel handed him a coin as usual and led his mare onto the landing. Mounting, he waved to Luke and turned toward the Shenandoah. As he rode, he felt a churning in his guts when he thought about his upcoming confrontation with Abigail and her parents. Maybe he could just camp out under his favorite rock ledge on the way down and then head back to Couchtown, pretending to have ended his engagement. If he never visited the Perkinses again, surely they would get the picture without his having to endure their contempt in person. Unlike the Martins, the Perkinses would not harm him physically for his perfidy. But their scorn would probably hurt him more than a knife carving out his heart.

Pulling in on the reins, he sat motionless, listening to a catbird call in the woods as the sun scorched his head and shoulders. Did he love Galicia enough to undergo this ordeal? He scarcely noticed her exotic olive complexion, her extra digits, or her poor diction anymore. But what would his parents think if they ever met her—and her illegitimate son? Would they support his choice, or would they go along with their meeting in scorning him for having picked an unbeliever for his mate? Or should he sever his ties to his parents so that they need never meet her? Was he prepared to defend Galicia's family to the death, and, like Joshua, to follow them into exile out west? Deciding reluctantly that he was, he clicked his tongue at his mare and resumed his journey along the route that was becoming as familiar to him as Chestnut Street in Philadelphia.

Two days later, Daniel's heart sank when he saw Abigail's face light up as she opened her door to find him standing before her. He had dared to hope that her enthusiasm for him might have flagged in his absence, just as his had for her. Taking both his hands in hers, she squeezed them with a fervor that left him cold. His senses had become attuned to a full-bodied passion and were no longer piqued by her teasing caresses that promised much but led nowhere. She wanted endlessly to sip the champagne of new love and inhale its intoxicating bubbles, but he had already experienced the relief of quenching his thirst with deep gulps of cool, clear water.

Daniel was delighted to learn that Abigail's parents had gone to Mulberry Courthouse for the day. Perhaps he could perform his grisly task and depart before their return. The two of them sat down opposite one another in the parlor.

"I cannot stay," he announced.

She frowned. "But thou hast just arrived, Daniel."

"I need to return to the mountains this afternoon."

"Then why hast thou come?"

"Abigail, I wanted to tell you—thee in person that I must end our engagement."

She looked as startled as a chicken with a newly wrung neck.

"I cannot marry thee, Abigail, for I am not worthy of thee."

She said nothing.

"Thou wilt find a man far finer than I."

"Who is she?" demanded Abigail.

Daniel remained silent.

"Who is she?"

"I have come to realize that thou wouldst not enjoy life in the mountains," tried Daniel.

"Who is she?"

"Because there is nothing to do up there and nowhere to go."

"Tell me who she is," Abigail snarled, her shock yielding to outrage.

Daniel lowered his head. "She is one of my adult students." *And the unwed mother of one of my child students*, he managed not to add. His fascination with Galicia made less sense here in the lowlands.

"What does she possess that I lack?"

"Nothing. Thou art a truly wonderful woman, Abigail. Beautiful and kind and smart."

"Then why dost thou love me no longer?" she wailed.

"I was unable to fulfill the waiting period. It is fortunate that everyone insisted we wait because that wait has exposed me for the reprobate that I am."

"Thou hast had carnal relations with this woman!"

Daniel nodded shamefacedly.

She began to unbutton her bodice. "This house is empty. My parents will not return until evening. Thou mayest also partake of carnal relations with me. Then thou canst merely cast off thy mountain whore, and we will say no more about it."

Daniel's mouth fell open, both at Abigail's use of the word "whore" and also at the sight displayed before him. The tops of her breasts were popping out of the corset cups that cradled them. Daniel gazed at them with alarmed desire. "I cannot," he muttered unconvincingly.

She strode over to him and sank down on his lap, taking his head in her hands and gluing her lips to his. The next thing he knew, his hands were ripping her bodice open even further, hurling her tiny mushroom buttons across the parlor.

Abigail shook him awake as he lay sleeping on the Oriental carpet. "Hurry, Daniel! We must clean up and dress before my parents' return."

Slowly he sat up and stared at her as she loomed over him, naked in the waning golden rays through the parlor window. "Art thou all right?" he asked dazedly.

She blushed. "Far better than all right, my wicked little beast."

Daniel struggled to smile. As he crawled around the carpet on chafed knees collecting her buttons, his thoughts strayed to Galicia, suckering tobacco, lonely for his touch in the corn patch. Then he pictured her muscular brothers and their rifles that never missed. What would be the least painful way to kill himself? Stones in his pockets and a midnight dip in the Sturgeon River? A rifle barrel caressing his faithless lips? A swan dive from the limestone palisade that separated the mountains from the lowlands?

He mounted the steps to the guest room, clutching his tangled clothing, feeling betrayed by his own body. But for it, he could have been leading a quiet, dignified life as a mild-mannered Quaker schoolmaster. Instead, his body's lugubrious machinations had condemned him to suicide, homicide, bigamy, or emigration.

Daniel and Abigail, washed and dressed, sat opposite one another in the parlor, awaiting her parents.

"Abigail, I cannot marry thee," he announced bravely.

"But thou already hast, my darling." She smiled as smugly as a gladiator with a lion hooked by his gaff. "Thou hast sullied my purity. No other man would have me now."

"But that is what thou wished."

"Yes, and so didst thou. And we accomplished this together. And now we are one. Perhaps even now thy child is sprouting within my womb."

Daniel blanched. "But what if I love another?" he asked meekly.

"Thou wast, and art, engaged to me. Thou wast not hers to have. Obviously, thou must now get rid of her."

Just then Abigail's mother entered, untying and removing her translucent bonnet and patting her silver hair into place. "Ah, Daniel!" she exclaimed with uncharacteristic exuberance. "We spotted thy mare in the yard. What a lovely surprise."

That night, once her father was snoring so loudly that his bedroom door shuddered on its hinges, Abigail arrived in the guest room. Daniel watched helplessly while, in a moonbeam through the branches outside the window, she shrugged off her starched nightgown and slipped under his covers.

When Daniel reached the turnoff on the trail to Couchtown, he wondered if he should just continue straight ahead. That route would cross the Holston settlement in Tennessee before merging with the Wilderness Road to veer north through the Cumberland Gap into Kentucky. Once there, he could head due west to the Missouri territory. He had heard of men who had done this to escape unhappy marriages, debts, or crimes.

Instead, Daniel turned toward Couchtown, trying to decide whether he preferred a woman in bare feet and a homespun dress or one who wore shoes from Rome and dresses from Paris. Now that he had witnessed the delirious paroxysms of which Abigail's doppelganger was capable, he was no longer quite so willing to let her go. In fact, relinquishing either woman now seemed as out of the question as did having both of them. He was in a wagon headed for a cliff, powerless to stop the horses or to alter their direction. Something, he bravely assured himself, would happen to rescue him from this calamity, which was approaching as implacably as a tornado funnel on the far horizon. Like a case of smallpox, if this disaster of his own making didn't force his inner light to at last ignite and offer him some help, he didn't know what would.

During their reunion in the cornstalk arbor, Daniel asked Galicia to marry him, just as he had promised he would before his departure for the Shenandoah. She accepted with a quiet joy that increased his mounting self-loathing. Determined not to add a lie to his proliferating pile of sins, he didn't mention Abigail, leaving Galicia to draw her own mistaken conclusions about their alleged split. If he married Galicia right away, he could solve his immediate dilemma of remaining in Couchtown without being butchered by her brothers. His trial period with Abigail would end in eighteen months, and maybe one of the three of them would have died by then. If not, he could always gallop his mare up the Wilderness Road into the setting sun.

When Daniel and Galicia arrived back at her parents' house, a grim Joshua stood on the porch, down from the cave where he and Whippoorwill's family were still hiding. He was telling the others some news. Daniel and Galicia exchanged glances, silently agreeing that it was the wrong time to inform her family about their impending nuptials. Galicia went inside with their lunch basket while Daniel assumed a squat on the porch.

He listened as Joshua described his trip to Tocaru to lead Whippoorwill's brother Panther to the cave: "Before I reached their cabin, I spotted them being herded by some soldiers along the path down to the river. Panther's wife was carrying their baby, who was screaming. She offered him her breast, but the federals was driving them too fast. So she plopped down, lifted her blouse, and started suckling him right there in the middle of the path.

"A soldier yelled at her to get moving. She doesn't speak English, so she didn't know what he'd said. He poked her in the shoulder with his bayonet. Her blouse ripped open and she started bleeding. She jumped up, dropping the baby. His head hit a rock and split open.

"She howled like a madwoman. Panther and two of their sons grabbed rifles from the soldiers and started stabbing and shooting them. The captain galloped away down the trail. The mama scooped up that poor little dying baby, all soaked with blood. They climbed on the dead soldiers' horses and took off up the path toward the forest.

"I took off, too. I figured the captain would round up more troops and come back for the soldiers' bodies. Then they would track down Panther and his family and shoot them on the spot. I wondered if I should follow them and lead them back up here. But in the end I didn't."

Reuben shook his head sorrowfully. "That was the right decision, son. Them folks is done for. But the rest of you stands a chance."

"Well," said Joshua, "if them federals don't catch Panther right quick, they won't stop looking until they've rounded up the whole bunch of us."

"I would purely hate to see them caught," said Reuben, "but it would be best for the rest of you."

Joshua's face contorted. After a silent struggle, he regained his usual impassivity. "I went back to Panther's cabin to try to salvage some of his possessions. A bunch of men was already there, so I hid in the woods and watched them burn down the cabin. Then they took shovels and dug up some graves out back and collected jewelry from the skeletons. They stuffed Panther's chickens and his feed corn into sacks and put the sacks on the backs of his horses and cows. Then they drove the livestock down the road, laughing and singing. I wanted to kill them, but I knew I'd get myself killed as well, and then my wife's family wouldn't have no one to protect them. So I just reburied the bones of Panther's kinfolks and came on back up here."

No one said a word. Daniel saw that Barbary's face was wet with tears.

Friends and relatives crammed into the downstairs of Mrs. Reeves's house to watch Peter Reeves, Mrs. Reeves's grandson who was a justice of the peace for Couchtown, marry Daniel and Galicia. The overflow peered through the windows from the front yard, where a long table heaped with food was waiting.

Afterwards, some ate while others danced in Mrs. Reeves's barn. Gideon's and Elijah's tireless fiddle and banjo jigs and reels inspired stamping, clapping, and whooping as vigorous as the contortions of the newly saved at Reverend Foster's revivals. The cow and the horses watched, astonished, from their stalls, and the alarmed chickens flapped up to hide in the loft.

Isaac came up to Daniel as he stood at the edge of the dance floor watching Galicia dance with Peter Reeves. He slapped Daniel on the back, nearly knocking him over. "Congratulations, brother! Some of us had a wager, and thanks to you, I won it."

"What was the wager?" Daniel looked up at his giant brother-in-law.

"Most bet that since you had already drunk the milk, you'd never buy the cow. But I said you wasn't like that sorry hog drover— sucking Galicia's nectar and then claiming he wasn't no bee. I said you would do right by my baby sister, or you'd have to carve yourself a new pecker out of wood."

Daniel blanched. Then he reminded himself that he had over a year to either find a solution to his secret double-dealing or to leave town.

Isaac dragged him out amid the dancers and demonstrated how to buck dance. As Daniel copied him, pawing his feet and hefting his rack of imaginary antlers, he remembered that Quakers weren't supposed to dance. Then he realized that he wasn't a Quaker anymore. He had made choices that had turned him into a pariah in their eyes. As much as he had enjoyed thinking of himself as a Robin Hood of the Blue Ridge, the reality of being forever cast out from the faith of his fathers filled him with despair. He had now left behind his homeland, his parents, and his faith. He only hoped this new life with Galicia would be enough to take their place.

Daniel leaned against a post, trying to catch his breath. Joshua came up to him. "Good job, Daniel. You're a natural-born buck dancer."

"Thanks," gasped Daniel.

"Once you're finished honeymooning, I need to ask your help."

"What is it? You know I'll do anything I can for you, Joshua. You certainly didn't hesitate to help me with Tom Hill."

"Folks tell me there are some new signs up at Grayson's Trading Post near Tocaru. I think they say something about Panther's escape. But nobody down there can read. And we can't ask Grayson because he's done gone west with his Cherokee wife and children. Would you go down there and read what they say?"

"Yes, I'll go as soon as I can, Joshua. I know Galicia will agree."

Daniel and Galicia passed their wedding night in his narrow bed at Mrs. Reeves's house because they hadn't had time to move into the new quarters in Tom Hill's former forge that Daniel had been readying for Abigail. Both were so exhausted that they merely slept on the rustling corn husks, quietly commencing their legal love life at dawn while Mrs. Reeves and guests from afar slept downstairs.

As he lay there afterwards, watching a beam of sunlight through the gable window, he reflected that lovemaking with Galicia flowed naturally from who she was—quiet, direct, and intense—whereas Abigail transformed into a stranger the opposite of her demure everyday self—athletic and energetic. Both were completely thrilling for him after a lifetime of deprivation. With Galicia he dove deep to explore underwater caverns. With Abigail he was swept over a waterfall, clinging for dear life to a raft of bucking flesh. It was impossible for him to have both, but he couldn't give up either. He knew he was lost in the grip of lust, and he didn't care anymore. He would just enjoy his sins for as long as he could get away with them.

Following Joshua's map, Daniel crossed three mountains on a deeply rutted track blazed by ancient herds of buffalo heading to a salt lick. Ancestors of the Martins and the Reeveses had traveled this same path with trains of laden packhorses to Indian villages in the valley beyond. Daniel covered the distance more quickly than they because he rode his horse rather than leading her. Occasionally his horse was able to trot on short stretches of level path, as horses with heavy packs would not have been able to do. But even so, it took him two days of winding along the mountain crests, high above the valley floor, before he reached the turnoff to the steep-walled canyon where Grayson's Trading Post nestled.

As the sun disappeared beyond the farthest edge of the broad valley below, Daniel built a fire, ate beef jerky, and went to sleep in his blanket roll. He awoke at dawn, feeling odd. Slowly he opened one eye. Only inches from his nose he saw a copperhead coiled on the ground, staring at him. He closed his eye and remained completely still, silently begging the snake to spare him.

When he at last dared to open his eyes again, the snake had vanished.

As he packed his gear, Daniel tried to figure out what this visitation meant. In Quaker eyes the copperhead was evil, like the serpent in the Garden of Eden, perhaps a warning that his current state of unrepentant sin would get him expelled from the realm of God's grace.

But those around Couchtown regarded snakes with a wary reverence. Their habit of slithering into small openings in walls of rock suggested that they had privileged access to the underworld. If a Martin came across a snake while plowing, he picked it up by its neck and deposited it in a safe spot. Did the snakes consider Daniel a Martin now, to whom they could reveal themselves without danger? He felt moved by this interpretation as he mounted his horse and headed down the trail. He guessed he liked being a Martin more than he missed being a Quaker.

Two hunters in leather shirts and leggings were watering their packhorses at a muddy mire next to the trading post, a one-story chinked log structure. Its door and windows were boarded shut. Nailed to a post beneath the porch roof was a sheet of newsprint. Once he got near enough, Daniel could see that the type was Cherokee.

"Do you all know what this says?" he called to the hunters.

"Can't read a lick of Cherokee nor English, neither one," replied the nearer of the two. He was trimming his shaggy beard with his hunting knife. The results were alarming.

"I thought the Cherokees had all been sent out west," ventured Daniel, feigning ignorance in order to gather information.

"They's some still lurking around these parts."

"Did you hear about the ones who killed those soldiers?" asked Daniel.

The trapper nodded, frowning as he sawed at his whiskers with what appeared to be a very dull knife.

"Did they ever catch them?" asked Daniel.

"Yeah, they caught them."

"No, the federals didn't catch them," said the other one, appearing from behind the horses. "Some Cherokees who farm outside the treaty land caught them. Shot them dead. They had to or else them federals would have kept searching and found all the others hiding out in these mountains."

"Are many hiding out?" asked Daniel innocently.

"More than them federals know about."

"Did they kill that whole family?"

"Just the father and two grown boys. The women and children got took to the stockade on the river. They'll send them out west when the weather cools."

The one trimming his beard was cross-eyed from inspecting his handiwork without a mirror. "I don't care what nobody says: I've hunted many a day with them Indians, and you won't find no finer folks."

"Naw, it ain't a bit right. It don't make no sense at all," said the second man as he used the tip of his knife to pick out the mud and pebbles packed in his horse's hooves. "God's honest truth is that most whites around here is part Indian, even though they all claim to be Scotsmen or Irishmen. And most Indians is part white, from their dealings with the traders in days gone by. Except for them traditionals way back in the wilderness who don't never meet no one but each other."

"I can hear by your voice that you ain't from around here. Where do you hail from?" the first man asked Daniel.

"Philadelphia originally. I'm teaching school in Couchtown."

"That a fact? I might come to your classes sometime. I always did want to know how to read."

"Stop in whenever you're in the area. My classroom is at West's Trading Post."

"I might just do that one of these days."

"Where are the soldiers now?" asked Daniel.

"They're all down guarding them stockades on the river. They say any Indians they ain't caught yet can just stay put."

Daniel forced himself not to grin.

"How come you to be so interested, young fellow?"

"Some of my students are half bloods," he improvised. "I've been worried about what's going to happen to them."

"If they live up near Couchtown, I'd say they're safe now."

"Well, that's the best news I've heard all week."

"Happy to oblige."

Daniel waved goodbye and started back up the steep path. Partway up, his light-hearted mood at knowing the Martins were now out of danger evaporated. He realized that he would have to tell Joshua that Panther and his sons had been killed and that Panther's wife and daughters were in captivity, pending deportation. Furthermore, he could no longer insulate himself from the knowledge of this awful crime being committed by his fellow countrymen, as white settlers raged like floodwaters into these ravaged coves and blood-soaked valleys.

His faith had taught him to focus on performing good deeds, promising that evil ones would thus wither away from lack of nourishment. This brave belief didn't appear to be in operation in these mountains, as soldiers forced Cherokees off their farms and herded them into stockades. Evil was currently flapping its wings and crowing its victories from the ridge tops. All Daniel wanted at the moment was to join the Martin brothers in attacking that stockade by the river and freeing Panther's wife and children. But the Martins would kill a few soldiers and then get killed themselves, and nothing would change. So what was the point?

Daniel tried to banish these murderous thoughts by meditating on a George Fox quotation that used to bring him peace in his days on the docks of Philadelphia: "Be still and cool in thy own mind and spirit, from thy own thoughts." But here in these tortured mountains, with thousands of innocent people being hunted down and caged like wild animals, this advice seemed pretty puny.

10

Squatters: October 1838

Daniel sat on the Martins' porch, watching Nathan chase the chickens around the yard. Nathan kept mimicking their squawks and awkward evasions. The black and red rooster, poised on a collapsing stone wall, studied Nathan as though planning his attack.

"Nathan, you'd better leave those hens alone," called Daniel. "That rooster is fixing to tear you to pieces."

Galicia patted Daniel with one hand. "No point in wasting your breath, honey. Just let him find out for himself. A rooster attack is a lesson you don't never forget."

"But why let him get hurt if you can prevent it?"

"Well, not everbody likes to preach and teach all the live-long day." She smiled tolerantly.

So close were Daniel and Galicia now that he was startled to be reminded that they were from such different worlds. His parents had raised him like a new shoot on an espaliered fruit tree, which had to be bent and shaped and pruned to fit some overall design. But Galicia let Nathan run free, indulged in his every whim. Her sharpest reproach took the form of a mild mockery, and the concept of physical punishment for his misbehavior left her gaping with disbelief.

Checking to make sure Reuben was asleep in his chair, Daniel reached over and stroked Galicia's belly, swelling beneath the folds of her homespun dress. They didn't know whether she had conceived before or after their marriage. Most first babies in Couchtown were "premature." Nobody seemed concerned or even interested. This tolerant attitude toward the weaknesses of the flesh was a relief to

Daniel after the system of group surveillance under which he had
grown up. Unfortunately, this tolerance didn't extend to marital
infidelity.

Daniel could hear the steady pounding of mauls and axes in the
woods across the pasture. Joshua and his Cherokee family were
building several cabins, their quarters and land near Tocaru having
been seized by squatters during their sojourn in the Silver Valley
cave. To have challenged the interlopers would have drawn
dangerous attention to themselves without, in any case, recovering
their property.

The previous week, Daniel had traveled with Joshua for two
days down to the stockade on the river that held Joshua's wife's
sister-in-law, nieces, and nephews. Word had it that the westward
trek was about to begin, and his wife's mother wanted Joshua to bear
silent witness for them all and to bid their kin farewell. Mrs. Reeves
asked the same of Daniel. Her older sister Wren and several of her
nieces and their children were also being held at the stockade and
would go west with their tribe. Mrs. Reeves was too infirm for the
demanding journey, so Daniel had agreed to stand in for her.

The morning for the prisoners' departure was gray and chilly.
Joshua and Daniel sat on a cushion of pine needles at the edge of a
forest atop a cliff above the river and watched in a steady drizzle as
the soldiers in blue uniforms herded the Cherokees like cattle, poking
and prodding with their bayoneted rifles, dividing them into group
after group of several hundred or more. Each group was headed by a
respected chief or preacher or trader, many of whom Joshua pointed
out to Daniel. Several were white men who could have stayed in
these mountains, but refused to. Some were slaves who had no choice
but to leave with their owners. The prisoners traveled in Conestoga
wagons drawn by teams of draft horses, in carts pulled by oxen with
huge curving horns, on horseback, on foot, surrounded by livestock
and by the dogs that had escaped being eaten in the stockade. It took
hours for the different groups to unscramble themselves and set out
along the westward path.

One of the last groups to leave, lead by a Moravian missionary,
started singing: "Guide me, O Thou great Jehovah, / Pilgrim through

this barren land. / I am weak, but Thou art mighty. / Hold me with Thy powerful hand." Other groups ahead of them on the trail picked up the refrain. Soon the river valley above which Daniel and Joshua perched was filled with the harmonies of this hopeful hymn. Daniel and Joshua looked at one another. Joshua's face was contorted with anguish.

The wail of a cicada lent a note of sadness to what otherwise seemed to Daniel a day of mellow fruitfulness, one warmed by sunlight slanting through a crisp blue sky onto the porch where he sat with Galicia and Reuben. He wondered how it was possible to feel so despondent and so happy, both at once. It seemed almost obscene for him to be experiencing such happiness while the Cherokees were undergoing such hardships. But there it was.

Galicia loved their home in Tom Hill's forge, with its new puncheon furniture and floors. She spent a lot of time with Mrs. Reeves, doing her chores now that Daniel was no longer her boarder. But she missed her parents, so she, Daniel, and Nathan stayed with them most weekends. Galicia aided Barbary in the kitchen, and Daniel helped Isaac around the farm. Reuben mostly dozed on the porch nowadays, awaking only to recite his account of the Battle of King's Mountain to anyone patient enough to listen.

The corn and tobacco had been harvested. Daniel would soon cancel classes and accompany the tobacco wagons to the landing below the Sturgeon River falls, where the crop would be loaded on flatboats for shipment to the coast. He would return to Couchtown via the Perkinses. With a baby on the way, his game of deceit was up. He needed to face the consequences of a genuine split with Abigail. He only prayed that she, too, wasn't already carrying his child. What in the world had he been thinking? His bigamous behavior now seemed to him not only immoral, but possibly insane. His overindulgence in sexual pleasures may have resulted from a lifetime of enforced chastity, but he now felt fulfilled by Galicia in every way. Abigail would have to accept this and find another man who could fulfill her similarly.

A man rode into the yard on a bay gelding. He wore a frockcoat, dusty from the road, and a planter's wide-brimmed straw hat. His saddlebags bulged. A rifle was strapped to his pommel, and a bedroll hung across the horse's haunches.

Daniel stood up. "Can I help you, sir?"

"I reckon so," he said affably. "The name is George Hale, and it appears you folks is living on my land."

Reuben stopped snoring to inspect the newcomer through half-opened eyelids. Nobody said anything, except for the cicada, which wailed mournfully from the dead oak on the creek bank.

"What makes you believe this land is yourn, Mr. Hale?" asked Reuben, using his one arm to push himself upright in his chair.

"I bought it offen this fellow, who bought it offen another fellow, who was give it for fighting the Creeks at Horseshoe Bend."

"Well, I fought at King's Mountain," said Reuben amiably. "That's why I ain't got but one arm here."

Daniel braced himself for the saga of King's Mountain, but Mr. Hale failed to bite, asking instead, "Did they give you a warrant for this land for your service in the Revolution, sir?"

"Naw, this land was mine long before that."

"Do you have your papers?"

"Don't need no papers. Anybody in these parts will tell you that my people has farmed this land since ancient days."

"Sounds like you're some kind of Cherokee or something. Well, the government done bought this land offen your tribe three years back. You're supposed to be headed out west by now, sir."

"I ain't no Cherokee, I'm Porterghee," said Reuben.

The man laughed unpleasantly. "If you ain't an Indian and you don't have no papers, then what you is, is a squatter."

Daniel glanced around for a rifle. Realizing what he was doing, he was astonished. After a lifetime of pacifism, he was apparently a Martin man now.

"How can I be a squatter on my own damn land?" demanded Reuben.

"I'm telling you as polite as I can, sir, that it ain't your land. Hit's mine, and you folks has got to get offen it."

"Where would I go? I'm an old man. I done been right here my whole life long. And my father before me. And his father before him."

"Have you got children?"

Reuben nodded.

"Well, go live with them, why don't you?"

"They are all living right here on this farm," Reuben explained.

"Well, I'm real sorry, sir. But they'll have to go, too."

Reuben stared at him disbelievingly.

"Look," said the man, shifting uneasily from one buttock to the other in his saddle, "I'm trying to give you all a break here. I could be charging you back rent for all the years you been farming my land for free."

Deciding enough was enough, Daniel broke rank and jumped in. "Mr. Hale, do you have a deed to prove what you are saying?"

"Sure do." He slid down from his horse and rummaged around in a saddlebag, extracting some papers. Walking up to the porch, he handed them to Daniel.

Daniel skimmed the spidery handwriting and realized that what Mr. Hale claimed was true. The plat showed landmarks such as the road along the Otter Creek, the deserted silver mine—even the Martins' house, which was labeled "stone ruin."

"Where did you get this?" Daniel asked.

"Down at the land office at Mulberry courthouse."

"Well, I need to go down there and ask some questions."

"My wagons and my slaves are already headed this way."

Reuben blinked. "I don't want no slaves on my property."

"Sir, like I been saying, this ain't your property."

"That remains to be seen, Mr. Hale," snapped Daniel. "Meanwhile, you would do well to stay off it, sir. Mr. Martin here has five sons who can, every one of them, shoot a hole through a coin tossed into the air."

"That's a fact," said Reuben. "Seem like I can't do nothing with them boys. They's always shooting somebody."

"I'll go," snarled the man, "but I'll return with some armed sons of my own, and you better be fixing to clear out by the time I get back."

"Let's all just calm down," suggested Barbary, standing in the doorway in her striped apron. "Daniel will go down to the courthouse and get this straightened out. Nobody needs to shoot nobody. I am sure it's all just a big misunderstanding."

The man nodded and mounted his gelding. "All right, ma'am. I'll put up at the hotel in town until my wagons arrive. You all can reach me there once you've checked the records and learned that what I'm telling you is the truth."

The next morning Daniel left Galicia and Nathan with her parents, posted a sign on his classroom door suspending classes until further notice, and crossed the river on Luke's ferry. He headed down the road toward Mulberry Courthouse as fast as his mare and his thigh muscles could manage.

Reaching the county seat the following afternoon, Daniel stabled his horse and crossed the street to the red brick building in which he had witnessed the slave auction. After several wrong turns and trips up and down staircases to nowhere, he finally reached the basement room that housed the deed books. A pasty-faced clerk in sleeve garters sat in a cobwebbed corner, copying a document on the desk before him by the feeble daylight filtering through a tiny window near the ceiling.

"Excuse me," said Daniel.

The clerk looked up, appearing annoyed.

"Could you please tell me how to look up something in these deed books?"

The clerk gave him instructions as convoluted as directions to the location of the Holy Grail. After perusing the huge leather-bound volumes for a couple of hours, Daniel was finally forced to admit that Mr. Hale's claim seemed authentic. George Hale had bought the farm that Couchtown thought of as Reuben Martin's from a Josiah Marsh, who had in turn purchased it from a Uriah Gray, who had received a warrant for it as payment for fighting in the Battle of Horseshoe Bend in 1814. It had already been surveyed and the plat had been registered with the land office.

Straightening his notes, Daniel stood up and went over to the clerk. "Excuse me again."

The young man looked up, a corner of his mouth twitching with irritation. Daniel recognized the attenuated handwriting on the document before the clerk as that on Mr. Hale's deed.

Daniel described the Martins' situation. "In such a case," he concluded, "could the family living on the land claim it as their own, based on many years of prior possession?"

"Why didn't they register it here and obtain a deed?"

"They don't read or write. They never realized they needed a deed. They've farmed that land for many generations."

"Which are they, then—Indians or squatters?"

"They say they're Portuguese," said Daniel.

"Portuguese in the Smokies?"

"They say their people came across the ocean a long time ago."

"All that mumbo jumbo is just an attempt to hide the fact that they're either Indians or Africans," explained the clerk. "Half bloods or mulattos. Free people of color. Happens all the time around here."

"Perhaps," said Daniel, struggling to remain polite.

"Would you like to hear what the law books have to say about free people of color testifying in court?" He took a fat volume from the shelf behind him and flipped through it. Clearing his throat, he read, "'No free colored or descendant of a free colored to the fourth generation shall be deemed a competent witness in any court of this state to which a white person may be a party.'"

"But I don't understand. Is a 'free colored' an Indian or an African?"

"Either. Both. Both together. Mixed breeds."

"So a free person of color can't testify against a white man, even when he's been wronged?"

"Correct."

"But that's outrageous."

"Perhaps, but it's right here in black and white. So to speak." The clerk smiled whimsically.

"So if my friends are free coloreds, they have no recourse?"

"No legal one. Perhaps they should have seized the chance to sell their improvements here and start over again out west."

"But this is their home," snapped Daniel.

"It's not my fault. I don't like it any better than you do."

"If nobody likes it, who set it up this way? Why do we allow it to continue?"

The clerk shrugged and gazed wistfully at the document he longed to get back to copying.

"Well, I don't think they're free coloreds, in any case," temporized Daniel. "They look just the same as their white neighbors. They vote in elections. Some have married into the families of Irish and Scots settlers. Their children go to school with white children."

"I guess they're white, then. But they're still squatters."

"Squatters on their own land?"

"I don't write the laws, sir. There's nothing I can do about it."

All of a sudden, Daniel wondered if his and Galicia's marriage was legal. If she should be classified as free colored, she couldn't marry a white man, and the child in her womb would be labeled illegitimate. Peter Reeves had signed their marriage license with no questions asked about their races. Of course Peter had a Cherokee grandmother himself, so maybe he dealt with such issues by ignoring them.

Fumbling through some documents in his saddlebag, Daniel extracted the marriage license. Handing it to the clerk, he tried to sound casual when he said, "By the way, sir, could you please record my marriage?"

The clerk studied the license carefully, as Daniel's scalp prickled with fear that he might find something suspect. Instead, the clerk took another huge leather-bound volume off the shelf behind him, flipped through it, and copied the information off the paper and into his book.

"Congratulations," he said as he returned the license to Daniel.

The stable owner brought out Daniel's mare, which nudged him with her nose. He patted her soft velvet muzzle. Then he mounted and headed down the main street. Although the Martins' dire plight and that of the Cherokees made his convoluted love life seem trivial by comparison, he decided to return to Couchtown via Abigail's. He was determined to become an honest man, whatever the price. It was past time for him to grow up.

As his horse plodded along the road toward the Perkinses', seeming as reluctant as her rider to make the trip, Daniel brooded about the Martins' situation. It appeared there was nothing to be done—short of murdering Mr. Hale and burying his body in the forest, as they had done with the slave catchers. He now understood why the Martins sometimes took justice into their own hands—it was the only way to achieve it if your skin were a shade too dark.

The Perkinses' house appeared on the horizon, a spiral of smoke rising from the stone chimney. The sun was setting, and Daniel was chilled, all the more so recalling the reason for this visit.

Abigail and her parents had just sat down to supper when he knocked. Thrilled to see him, they ushered him inside, sat him at the dinner table, and served him a steaming plate of chicken and dumplings. As they ate, he explained the purpose of his trip to the Mulberry courthouse and the sad outcome of his afternoon's research.

"But how wonderful thou art, to work so hard to protect thy new friends," exclaimed Abigail, gazing at him admiringly.

Daniel drew a deep breath, knowing now was the time simply to state that his real reason for helping them was that he shared their fate through his unborn child. But as he steeled himself, Abigail ran her foot beneath his trouser leg and stroked his calf with the supple leather sole of her slipper. He found himself choked into silence by sudden desire.

"Hast thou heard of this new sect up north called the Church of Jesus Christ of the Latter Day Saints?" asked James, a twinkle in his eyes.

Daniel shook his head, trying to keep his face impassive now that Abigail's caressing foot had reached his lap. Yet her demeanor from the abdomen up, as she sliced her chicken and minced the morsels behind closed lips, displayed only placid propriety.

"They call themselves Mormons, and the men style themselves after the Old Testament patriarchs," explained Vera. "They believe they each merit more than one wife."

"I fear they will find themselves in jail rather than in heaven," quipped James. He and Vera laughed indulgently at the quaint foibles of their fellow human beings who had the misfortune not to be Quakers.

Daniel gagged on a bite of biscuit. As he sipped his water and struggled to regain his composure, James and Vera murmured their concern.

After dinner Daniel and James discussed the Martins' quandary by the parlor fire. James speculated about raising funds to buy the land from Mr. Hale, and Daniel felt his first glimmer of hope. But this glimmer was extinguished once James began to calculate the cost involved, and the greater importance of using available funds to free slaves.

"After all," James concluded, "although it is appalling that thy friends may lose their land, at least they are still free to move elsewhere."

"Yes," said Daniel, "but they have no money with which to buy new land, and—"

"Daniel," Vera interrupted, "I can read the exhaustion from thy trip in thy face. We must allow thee to retire and resume this discussion in the morning."

Grateful not to be left alone in the parlor with Abigail, Daniel mounted the steps to the guest room. Undressing, he fell into bed and was soon fast asleep.

He awoke to discover Abigail slipping between his sheets as her father's snores shook the rafters.

"My clever darling," she murmured, her hands stroking his chest. "Thou missed me as much as I did thee, and thou invented a way for us to be together again."

Still half asleep, he murmured, "I can't do this, Abigail. I love my wife."

"I love my little husband, too."

"But I'm too tired," he whimpered.

Placing her hand over his mouth, she rolled atop him and moved up and down like a cavalry rider on a forced march.

The next afternoon as he rode toward home, Daniel wondered if his parents would give him the money to buy the Martin farm. But at some point he would have to confess to them that his concern for the Martins was not simply disinterested charity. They had taught him that all people were equally valuable vessels for the inner light. Would they stand by him once they learned that he had put their beliefs into practice by marrying a woman with twelve fingers and olive skin? A woman who was mother to a son born out of wedlock? A woman who had shot down a slave catcher in cold blood? A woman now pregnant with his first child and their first grandchild? Or would they disown him as a son and join forces with their meeting in renouncing him as a Quaker?

Daniel reached the junction with the Couchtown cart path. The branch that led to the Wilderness Road stretched before him, beckoning him as the route to Canaan must have Abraham. Could he perhaps persuade Galicia and Abigail to accept one another as co-wives and follow him up that trail to a land where all three could cohabit in connubial bliss?

Despair settled over him like a roosting crow. The Martins were losing their farm, and he could do nothing. Galicia was carrying his child, and Abigail might soon be—and it seemed he could do nothing to curb his desire for both of them. Despite his self-flattering delusions during his years as an upstanding Quaker, he now knew that he was nothing but a sin-soaked mortal, as lost to lust as any Mormon patriarch. Worst of all, he was savoring every second of it.

Daniel and Galicia arrived at Reuben's house to find him and her brothers sitting on the porch, silently watching Mr. Hale's half-dozen slaves dig a foundation hole in the sheep pasture, supervised by an overseer on a horse with a rifle in his saddle holster. The Martins nodded glumly to the new arrivals.

Daniel helped Galicia down from the cart he had acquired as tuition for the wheelwright's son. Galicia's belly was so heavy that she could no longer mount a horse. They had concluded that they must have conceived this baby before their marriage, sometime in early summer under their arbor in the corn patch. Galicia lumbered inside to find her mother while Daniel hunkered down on the porch.

"What did you learn at the courthouse?" Reuben asked from his rocking chair.

Daniel shook his head. "Hale appears to own this land."

Reuben looked thunderstruck. "And they ain't nothing we can do about it?"

"We could buy it from him."

"Buy my own farm from some stranger? That don't make no sense."

Daniel shrugged. "It appears the only solution left."

"I got no cash. We'll make some offen the tobacco, but not much."

"I might be able to find some," said Daniel. His parents' meeting might help, at least until they learned that he had both an infidel wife and a Quaker mistress.

"Ask Hale then," muttered Reuben.

"We can run them off, Papa," Isaac assured him.

The twins muttered agreement.

"But if you don't get a deed," warned Daniel, "Hale can just sell the land to some unsuspecting settler from far away, who will then arrive to claim it."

"How can we get us one of them deeds?" asked Reuben.

"You have to register at Mulberry Courthouse with a bill of sale from Mr. Hale."

"Hell, it's my own damned land," moaned Reuben. "I didn't never sell it to nobody, and now I got to buy it back?"

"It doesn't make any sense to me either," said Daniel, "but I think it's what we need to do."

"I'll drag that damned Hale fellow down to the judge and prove that my family has always owned this land," announced Reuben.

Daniel sighed. "They might not accept your word against his, Mr. Martin."

"Why the hell not?"

"Because he's British and you're a Portuguese Indian," Daniel temporized, trying to state this ugly scenario as gently as possible.

"You have to be British to get justice in this country?"

"These days you do," Daniel assured him.

"But I thought I lost my arm to help get us free from them thieving British."

Daniel found Mr. Hale eating lunch in the dining room of the Couchtown Inn at a long table occupied by trappers and drovers. The stench of unwashed bodies and soiled leather clothing competed with the aroma of roasted meats and freshly baked breads and pies.

Hat in hand, Daniel introduced himself to Mr. Hale as the town schoolteacher. "We met the other day at Reuben Martin's house."

Nodding, he invited Daniel to sit. "Would you like something to eat, Mr. Hunter?"

"No, thank you." The competing odors had destroyed his appetite. In any case, Galicia had lunch waiting for him at the forge.

"Well then, what can I do for you, Mr. Hunter?"

"I'm here to ask what you'd take for the Martin farm, Mr. Hale.

He smirked, a forkful of green beans halfway to his mouth. "It ain't the Martin farm, son. It's the Hale farm."

"Well, what would you take for it, sir?"

"Wouldn't take nothing for it. That's where I aim to live out my days. I paid plenty for it, and it's mine."

"No amount of money would entice you to leave?"

He shook his head emphatically.

"Do you know what might happen if you don't leave?" asked Daniel.

Mr. Hale laid his still-loaded fork on his plate and looked at Daniel. "Are you threatening me, son? Because if you is, you should know that I have sons with guns, too. They'll be along directly. As will several of my neighbors from up Lunenburg way who have bought land all down Silver Valley—and we sure as hell aim to claim it."

"Doesn't it bother you, Mr. Hale, that the Martins have been living on that land for many generations?"

"You seem like a bright enough fellow." Mr. Hale leaned back to stretch out his legs. "I can hear you're not from around here. How come you to get mixed up with that pack of mongrels?"

Daniel frowned. "The Martins are the finest people I've ever known, Mr. Hale. I'm honored to be their friend and kinsman."

"Well, if I was you, young fellow, I'd take myself right back up north and stop meddling in things I didn't understand."

Daniel stood up, his hands knotted into fists. "Thank you for your time, Mr. Hale."

As Daniel walked out the door and across the plank porch, he felt so helplessly infuriated that he almost burst into tears. He might have punched Mr. Hale in the face, if only he had known how to do so without breaking his own hand. He spotted Nathan and some other students eating sandwiches along the curb outside the trading post. Waving to them, he headed down the street to his house so he could tell Galicia the bad news before returning to his classroom.

Finding her stooped inside the walk-in fireplace, stirring a stew in a cast iron pot that hung over the fire on a crane, he grabbed her shoulder. "Be careful, Galicia. Don't fall into the fire."

She turned to look at him. "I've managed not to fall into the fire for many years now without your help, Daniel."

"Yes, but you never had my baby hanging off the front of you. I don't want anything to happen to either of you." He took her in his arms. Leaning over her belly, he nibbled the side of her neck.

"What did that man say about our farm?" asked Galicia.

Daniel shook his head and recounted the conversation with Mr. Hale.

"What will my family do? Where will they go?"

"I don't know." He plopped down at their dining table and buried his head in his hands. "I need to think this through."

Galicia brought him a bowl of the stew, and he ate it in silence, running through various dead-end scenarios in his head. The Martin brothers had the only viable alternative—to shoot that whole bunch of interlopers flooding into Silver Valley from Lunenburg and bury them in the woods. It was the only way to ensure that justice prevailed.

Realizing what he had been thinking, Daniel shook himself. Apparently once someone stepped over the line and accepted acts of violence against others, as he had the deaths of the slavers, the floodgates opened and he had no qualms about more killing as a solution to his problems. But, although he was no longer a Quaker, violence still appalled him. He needed to find another solution for the Martins that didn't involve bloodshed.

He got up and retrieved the leather satchel in which he kept his valuables. Removing Tom Hill's deeds, he studied them in the light through a front window.

Beneath Tom's signatures were the words "a free man of color," written in the familiar spidery handwriting of the clerk at Mulberry Courthouse whom Daniel had already met. He realized he needed to get these deeds reissued in his own name before some would-be settler claimed both the forge in which he and Galicia now lived and Tom's land on Mulatto Bald. If someone could prove that Tom was actually an escaped slave, these deeds would be worthless.

All of a sudden it hit him: the Martins could move up to Tom's land on the bald. It wasn't as level as their fields in the valley, and the soil wasn't so rich. But at least they would have somewhere to go. The bald was so inaccessible that newcomers wouldn't be eager to contest them for it. In any case, if Daniel could get the deed reissued in his own name, he himself, as a white man, could fend off any new claimants. Nobody needed to die.

Despite all the upheaval with Mr. Hale, the Martins still had to haul their tobacco out of the mountains before snow clogged the roads and autumn rains turned the river below the falls into a torrent. So they rented Peter Reeves's ox cart, and Daniel helped them load it with the bales of dried leaves from the curing barn. They also loaded up their own mule-drawn wagon.

Managing to cross the Sturgeon without capsizing Luke's ferry, they headed for the wharves and warehouses at the foot of the falls, riding their horses alongside the straining mules and oxen. They circumvented the limestone palisade overlooking the Shenandoah by detouring north and then circling back around to the landing below the crashing waterfall.

A buyer from the coast inspected leaves from each bale and paid them more than they anticipated. They cheerfully unloaded the bales on to the flatboat that would carry them to the coast for shipment to England.

While the Martin brothers headed back to Couchtown, Daniel rode to Mulberry Courthouse. Finding the clerk in his sleeve garters still copying documents in his cobwebbed corner, Daniel greeted him like a long-lost friend.

"What can I do for you, sir?" asked the clerk, pleased by this unprecedented warmth from a member of the public.

Daniel laid Tom's deeds on the desk, signature pages first. He pointed to Tom's scrawled notation: "Sold to Daniel Hunter, 30 Oct., 1837."

"Could you please reissue these deeds in my name?" He struggled to sound more confident about this transaction than he felt.

The clerk picked them up and read them line by line. Finally he said, "Was he a big tall fellow with a bald head and only half an ear on one side?"

Daniel nodded, wondering if he had figured out that Tom was actually an escaped slave.

"Mr. Jones failed to notarize his sale to you."

Swallowing, Daniel said, "He got called up north to a new job. He had to go quickly. We didn't have time for all the necessary steps."

"Why did you wait so long to register these yourself?"

"Frankly, I forgot." Daniel felt his palms turn clammy. "I was busy getting married and renovating Mr. Jones's forge as a house for my new bride." He forced himself to be as mindlessly chatty as any southerner. "Then I had to help my in-laws harvest their tobacco...."

The clerk cast him a jaded look, and Daniel fell silent.

"Well, normally I'd need some proof that the seller, as a free man of color, really was free. His emancipation papers, for example."

"Oh, he was free, all right. He ran a thriving smithy up in Couchtown, and he farmed up on that ridge. Look, that's your handwriting, isn't it? 'Free man of color.' You wrote that yourself, so he must have shown you his papers."

The clerk studied the writing, scratching his head. "I can't remember. I guess I must have seen his papers or I wouldn't have written that. Give me a few minutes, though. I need to look at the deed books to see if anyone else has registered a claim for the same properties."

Daniel sat down, hat in hand, and watched the clerk rifle the pages of the thick volumes with as much familiarity as a jackleg preacher thumbing his Bible. He slammed a final volume shut, sending up a cloud of motes that danced wildly in the dim cellar light.

The clerk walked over to a large map on one wall and traced various lines on it with his fingertips. Daniel felt like a patient waiting for a doctor to diagnose a disease.

Finally the clerk turned around to face him. "These deeds appear free of encumbrances."

"Thank the Lord."

"You can thank the Lord, or you can thank the lay of the land. Here, let me show you."

Daniel rose and walked over to the map. The clerk pointed out a shaded area. "This is what they call Mulatto Bald. Here is your property. It was deemed so precipitous that it was never surveyed or included in grants made to soldiers after Horseshoe Bend, the way the land in Silver Valley was."

"The entire unshaded area is unclaimed?"

"That's right."

"If it's so worthless, will you include it in my deed?" asked Daniel, with a smile meant to be winning.

The clerk stared at him. "Why do you want it? It's nothing but a skullcap of rock, according to this map."

Daniel regarded the clerk for a long moment. He seemed a decent sort. Maybe the simple truth would sway him toward an act of mercy. "Do you remember me from before? I told you about my friends whose land had been granted to someone else because they didn't realize they needed a deed." Daniel pointed out the Martins' farm in Silver Valley on the map.

"Yes, I remember now. I knew I'd seen you before."

"Well, these people are being forced off their farm, and I want them to be able to move to this land on Mulatto Bald. It's a large family—thirty people or more. Several households."

The clerk considered the situation for what felt to Daniel like several hours before replying, "I might as well deed it to you. No one will ever know the difference. And if they do, both you and I will deny it."

Daniel nodded.

"You've never seen such a mess as we're in around these parts. The English king gave this region to various supporters, who made overlapping grants to settlers. Then, after the Revolution, the American government bought it by treaty from the Cherokees and unwittingly assigned it to both Virginia and North Carolina because the survey of the state line was inaccurate. Both states gave warrants to soldiers for the same properties. And many Cherokees who opposed that treaty refused to leave. Then squatters moved in and claimed the same land by right of habitation. That's why they call it the Squabble State. It will take centuries of court cases to unravel it all. Meanwhile, your friends might as well make themselves at home up on that ridge that nobody else appears to want."

Standing by the steps, Daniel held out his hand to the clerk. As the clerk shook it, Daniel said, "Thank you, sir. You're a good man."

"I try to be, but it's not easy these days. You wouldn't believe the greed and deceit I deal with every day of the week. I'll write up these deeds today. You can stop by to sign and notarize them tomorrow. That should fix up your friends, for a while at least."

Limp with relief, Daniel retrieved his mare from the stable. As he mounted, he was seized with dread to remember that he still had unfinished business. He needed to tell Abigail and her parents the truth about himself. He had been behaving like the lowest of rapscallions. But now that he was about to be a father, he was determined to assume the mantle of adulthood, which required him to protect and provide for his loved ones—and to forsake all other distractions. And however delirious their sexual interludes might have been, Abigail was merely one such distraction.

When Daniel knocked, James answered, looking both pleased and chagrined. Ushering Daniel into the parlor, James said heartily, "Look who's here to visit us, my dear!"

Vera looked up from her worn Bible, her face drawn and her smile forced.

"Where is Abigail?" Daniel sat in his usual chair.

James sat, too. Neither parent replied.

"Is she already in bed?"

"Daniel," said James, "I have some awkward news for thee."

"Is she ill?"

"No, not physically."

"What's happened?" With a flash of horror, he wondered if she had become pregnant and killed herself.

"Abigail has gone," said Vera.

"Gone where?" Had she been sent away for the birth of his child? Had she fled so her parents wouldn't have to know about it?

"We know not," she said.

"All by herself?"

"Abigail has run away with Mr. McCoy, the foreman from my mica mine," admitted James.

Daniel's mouth dropped open. He pictured the muscular man with the bushy moustache he had watched descend with his pick into the mineshaft in the hills to the south of James's farm.

"We did not know how to contact thee in Couchtown," said James.

"Or, frankly, what to say if we had." Vera's lined face flamed with shame.

"We hoped if we waited, she would return. But several weeks have now gone by," said James.

"How did this happen?" asked Daniel.

"Mr. McCoy had nowhere to live," said James. "We offered him the loft of our barn. We had no idea that he would thus repay our hospitality. But it is Abigail of whom we are most ashamed. Evidently, she sneaked to the loft at night while we were sleeping."

"Indeed," murmured Daniel, striving for a note of shock.

"One night we found her bed empty, and we discovered her lying, unclothed, with Mr. McCoy, who was also unclothed. I fired him and ordered him to leave. He left, but Abigail went with him."

Vera stood up unsteadily and took a white envelope off the mantle. Handing it to Daniel, she said, "She left a letter for us and another for thee."

Daniel ripped open the envelope. Unfolding the single page, he read, "Darling Daniel, My parents will no doubt have told thee of my betrayal. Please believe that I do not intend my behavior to be such. But I can no longer tread the narrow path laid out before us by our parents and our faith. Thou opened for me the door to passion. Having passed through it, I cannot now turn back. I must travel whithersoever it leads me.

"Thou must not grieve too long for our lost love. Thou wilt find a woman to love thee as dearly as I have done. Perhaps it is not too late to reconcile with thy woman in the mountains. Thou art a fine man, brave and true, and I will guard my happy memories of thee with a deep and abiding love and respect. Go always with God, A."

Realizing that James and Vera were watching, Daniel assumed a somber expression and said, "I don't know what to say."

"They were last spotted on the trail that leads to Kentucky, perhaps headed for the Wilderness Road," said Vera. "Might thou wish to pursue them and bring her home and restore her to her senses?"

Daniel tried to make his sigh of relief sound pathetic. "Abigail must follow her heart, Vera. I would never wish to marry her if she loves another."

James replied, "Thou art as reasonable and as generous as always, Daniel. I wish we could say the same of our errant daughter."

"As a favor to me, I ask that thou not thinkest badly of Abigail. I myself do not."

"Let us sit together in silent communion," suggested Vera, "wishing Abigail safe and happy, and thanking the inner light for guiding Daniel so evenly through his pain and turmoil."

Closing his eyes and lowering his head, Daniel felt nothing but astonishment to have emerged from the chaos he had created looking like the one who had been wronged. If he had previously doubted the existence of a merciful God, he did no longer.

Daniel helped the Martins load their household goods into their wagon. Then the mules hauled it up the path along Otter Creek, past the post and beam framework for Mr. Hale's new house, around which his slaves and his sons were swarming like bees.

Daniel was glad he had insisted on taking Reuben and Barbary in to town to stay with Galicia as she nursed her swollen ankles so that they wouldn't have to witness this sad exodus from their ancestral home. Since the Martins were losing their land anyway, he wondered if they might not have been better off going out west. At least they would have had their tribe for consolation. Then he remembered that the Martins weren't really Cherokees. They were neither fish nor fowl, neither white nor Indian nor African, most probably all three at once. The only people who accepted them were others like themselves—and the occasional white misfit like himself, who no longer belonged anywhere either.

Farther up the valley Joshua and his Cherokee family were waiting alongside their recently completed cabins, their sturdy horses piled high with their belongings. Although refugees for the second time in a few months, they stood silently, their impassive faces masking their pain. *They* might be wondering if they shouldn't have followed their kinsmen to new pastures out west. But it was too late for regrets. The wagon train had already departed, and they had chosen to stay behind with the looted graves of their forebears.

At the foot of the valley the Martin twins, their twin wives, and their crowd of double first cousin children piled into wagons with all their belongings, turned their backs on their cabins and outbuildings, and joined the throng moving slowly up the road.

The path up the front side of Mulatto Bald was too steep for horses or wagons, so the caravan headed along the trail that passed the turtle marsh and the ancient burial mound. Skirting the cave mouth, they mounted to the rim of the bowl and retraced in reverse the route that Tom Hill's family had followed the night of their flight down from the bald and through the cave to the Great Warriors' Path. The trail sloped gradually upward to the table rock along one side of the treeless plateau.

Finally reaching the top, Daniel assembled the three dozen people and explained, while Joshua translated his words into Cherokee, that they could build anywhere from the table rock to a large chestnut tree just past the charred ruins of Tom Hill's cabin. But he wanted to preserve the far side of the bald, which he now also owned, for those already living there.

Leaving their wagons and pack animals for Daniel to guard, the families fanned out along the ridge to identify camping sites for that evening. They could pick their cabin sites in the morning light. Daniel and Joshua had aided Tom Hill. Now Tom, whom he hoped was living in freedom in Nova Scotia, was unwittingly repaying the favor.

Daniel stood atop the table rock, the patient pack animals waiting below him. He had helped Tom Hill's family escape slavery, but millions more remained in bondage. He was helping three dozen Cherokees and mixed-blood people remain in their homeland, but sixteen thousand more had been driven out at gunpoint. He hadn't accomplished much, but it wasn't nothing either. And maybe a few small acts of kindness were the best that one person could hope to achieve in this troubled world. Even if the Quakers preferred not to claim him anymore, he realized that he remained one with them in his deepest beliefs.

He looked out across Silver Valley to the cave in the opposite cliff. Its mouth seemed to grimace at the fate of the Martin family, whose ancestors had found safety and shelter within its cavities for generations. But the longer Daniel studied that jagged maw of stone, the more he imagined that he saw the faint hint of a smile around its ragged edges. That cave had been there for millions of years. In times of trouble it would continue to shelter and protect these people—*his* people.

PART III

PASSING FANCY

1

The Ringer: August 1909

The Eagles' ringer from Mulatto Bald was long and lean, and he wound up like a coiled spring to pitch. The ball glided across the plate with a last-second hop, like a sapsucker in flight. The shortstop for the Couchtown Panthers swung at thin air.

The crowd stirred irritably, as though it were bad sportsmanship for the Eagles' pitcher to have been born both six-fingered and ambidextrous. Some said the extra finger allowed him to put a mysterious spin on the ball. And the way he switched his pitching hand back and forth from right to left unnerved even Galicia's brother Matthew, who had the highest batting average of all the Panthers.

Galicia sat on the plank bleachers between her younger sister Louisa and her best friend Rachel, sad that her hometown Panthers were being trounced, but fascinated at last to lay eyes on the infamous Will Martin. His strange hands reminded her of the six-toed paws on the feral cats in the shed behind her house. She wondered how he got his battered glove to fit.

Everyone said Will Martin was wild as a trapped hawk. He was rumored to have fathered a child with Palestine Sanders, whose family farmed down the back side of Mulatto Bald. Talk had it that she had recently been shipped off to marry a middle-aged widower in the next county.

The Eagles came to bat. Will stood at the plate in his faded overalls and sleeveless undershirt, his tanned biceps rippling as he tapped the dirt from the sole of one high-topped work shoe with his bat. After a couple of practice swings, he watched calmly as two fast balls, both high, whizzed past him. The third pitch was an arcing slow ball. He swung the bat as though scything hay. Galicia saw the ball coming, but she ducked too late.

When she next opened her eyes, Will Martin was kneeling beside her, stammering apologies. He had a large crooked nose, eerie blue eyes, and unusually long earlobes. The black hair escaping from his cap was as coarse and glossy as a horse's mane.

"I'm all right. Really," Galicia insisted. "Please go on with the game."

Rachel and Louisa, each holding one of Galicia's elbows, walked her slowly up Main Street, past her father's store with the sign out front that read "Hunter's Five and Dime." A lump was erupting in the middle of her forehead, like a unicorn horn. They turned in at her sidewalk and passed the plaque that read "The Old Forge, est. 1835." Her parents sat on the screened back porch, sipping iced tea and playing Set Back with Alan and Wilda West.

"Who won, honey?" her father called as Galicia headed for the stairway, through the oldest part of the house, which featured heavy beams overhead, a worn puncheon floor underfoot, and a huge stone walk-in fireplace with a wrought iron cooking crane.

"I left before it was over. But the Eagles were way ahead."

"Oh dear," sighed her mother. "There'll be no living with Matthew Hunter this evening."

The next morning Galicia discovered a purple egg between her eyebrows. Her mother gasped at breakfast when she saw it. But Galicia was a tomboy who had a long history of falling out of trees and into creeks. She once rode her pony beneath the backyard clothesline and sported a choker of bruises for weeks. She didn't want anyone blaming Will Martin for her latest injury. Though why she cared she couldn't have said.

At least her father had one virtue, reflected Galicia as she sat atop a tall stepladder sullenly rummaging through a box of sewing supplies: he didn't play favorites. He worked both Matthew and herself like lop-eared mules. After poking the bruise between her eyes with his fingertips, he set her right to work on a stock inventory.

In June Galicia had graduated as valedictorian from Couchtown High School. Her father had promised that if she would work at his store for a year and save her wages, he would pay her living expenses the next year at the Leesville Teachers' College, where she had applied for and received a scholarship. He was planning to turn the store over to Matthew. But Galicia preferred teaching anyway. She had enjoyed tutoring the younger pupils at school and had decided to emulate her father's grandfather, Daniel Hunter, a Quaker from Philadelphia who had opened Couchtown's first school back when the Five and Dime had been a log trading post. Her father remembered his grandfather as usually holding a book in one hand, and Galicia supposed she had inherited her love of learning from him. Some of his worn leather-bound Quaker books sat on a shelf by the forge fireplace, and she loved to take them down and read quotes by William Penn and James Naylor and George Fox that her great grandfather must have read, too.

On a chain around her neck Galicia wore a pendant that had belonged to Daniel Hunter's wife, Galicia, for whom she had been named. When she had asked what Galicia meant, her mother replied that it was probably just a pretty Hunter family variation on Alicia. On the world map in the school library, Galicia had once found an area in northern Spain called Galicia and had asked her parents if there were any connection to her name. But they had assured her that her ancestors were British, not Spanish.

The pendant was a jagged black pebble with dull reddish veins, which someone must have picked up from a creek bed. But she liked it all the same. It made her feel connected to those unknown ancestors, who had evidently valued education as much as she did. They were her allies while she lived among the Philistines of Couchtown, who cared only about the score of the latest ball game. She sometimes wondered if she had been abducted at birth from some sophisticated urban center.

Glancing down from her ladder, Galicia spotted Will Martin wandering among the counters, his hands stuffed into his overall pockets.

"Can I help you?" she called faintly.

Looking all around the store, he spotted her near the ceiling. His face relaxed into an amiable smile. "Hey there, I wanted to find out if you was okay. I guess you must be, or you wouldn't be setting up there on no ladder. I swear, girl, you look like an angel straight from heaven!"

Galicia climbed down. When she reached the floor, she found that he towered over her. She felt a shiver of excitement to be alone with the boy from Mulatto Bald whom all the other kids were talking about. The girls discussed his swarthy good looks, and the boys his ambidextrous pitching and batting skills.

"Lord!" he exclaimed, inspecting the purple knot between her eyes. "I really beaned you good, didn't I? I sure am sorry."

"It's not like you did it on purpose." She added with a coy smile, "Did you?"

He smiled back. "I wouldn't never hurt a flea iffen I could help it."

She struggled not to grimace. His double negatives were definitely hurting *her*. There was the language you learned in school, and the language most in Couchtown actually spoke. Galicia usually made it her mission to correct this patois. But Will's grammar was so atrocious that it left her speechless. "Who finally won?"

He shrugged modestly.

"You sure can pitch."

"But my hitting could use some help, right?"

Both laughed nervously.

"I'd like to make it up to you," he said. "I've got a notion to buy you an ice cream soda."

"I don't hold it against you that you hit a foul ball, Will. It's my fault that I didn't duck when I saw it coming. I've always been a little bit clumsy that way." The fact that she was blushing made her blush even more. She wondered if he noticed.

"Well then, can I buy you a soda just because I want to?"

She studied him, her stomach fluttering like a moth circling a Roman candle on the Fourth of July. Will, with his sly blue eyes and easy grin and dark hair hanging in his eyes, was the kind of boy mothers warned their daughters about. His crooked nose was probably the result of some drunken brawl. Everyone said those people up on Mulatto Bald guzzled moonshine as though it were water and then fought each other just for fun. If the rumors were true, Will had already had carnal knowledge of at least one girl—and had refused to accept responsibility for the outcome. If Galicia should succumb to his charms, which smacked you in the face like a line of wet laundry, she might never make her escape to the teaching college at Leesville. She would be stuck in Couchtown for the rest of her life, raising Will's babies by herself, while he played bush league baseball all over the state of Virginia. Realizing where her thoughts had just led her, she blushed again.

But it was time for her break, and her father was out back with the teamster who had hauled salt for the autumn hog slaughter over the mountain from Saltville. So Will sat in a booth while Galicia fixed chocolate sodas. They sipped them through paper straws, both tongue-tied.

"Are you going to that revival this weekend?" he finally asked.

She nodded.

"Me too. Is your family hard-shell or soft?"

"Soft."

"My uncle is a hard-shell preacher—name of John Calvin Martin?"

Galicia nodded, recalling the jackleg lunatic who paraded down the main street of Couchtown every Good Friday, dressed in a white bathrobe and dragging a large wooden cross draped in purple gauze.

"But I'm soft-shell myself," he added.

"Is your family upset about that?"

"Naw, cause I ain't told them yet." He laughed. "But if heaven is full of them hard-shells, I wouldn't want to be up there anyhow."

"It doesn't make sense that you would have to be Baptist in order to be saved. What about all those Hindus who never even heard of Baptists?"

Will nodded. He was sipping his soda without steadying the straw with his fingertips. His hands remained under the table. He had probably been teased a lot about his extra fingers. A few other people around town had them. Everyone said you inherited them because your parents were brother and sister, or father and daughter, or double-first cousins.

"I reckon I better go." He slid out of the booth and unfolded like an upended accordion. "My boss is out back yakking to your daddy. Meantime, I got to unload all them sacks of salt." He laid some coins on the tabletop. She tried to return them, but he refused.

"Well, thank you for the soda, Will. And for the apology, which really wasn't necessary."

"Maybe I'll see you at that revival?"

"Maybe so." She was afraid her smile probably looked as bashful as she felt.

Galicia's father walked in. He and Will nodded in passing.

"What did he want?" asked her father as he straightened his omnipresent bow tie.

"To apologize for hitting me in the forehead with his pop foul."

"Well, get a pail of soapy water and wash down that booth."

Galicia stared at him uncomprehendingly.

"If anyone knew we had table-served someone from Mulatto Bald, I wouldn't have a single customer left."

"But Will is very nice, Daddy."

"Darling, wolf pups will always grow up into wolves. Those ridge Martins would as soon shoot you as look at you. During the war they bombed railroad bridges, dodged the draft, and hid escaped Yankee prisoners. Why, one winter a gang of them broke into this very store and looted it bare, while my great-uncle Abner, who owned it then, was off defending the Confederacy."

"But that's ancient history, Daddy. It's got nothing to do with Will."

"Well, if I ever catch you talking to him again, you can just kiss teachers' college goodbye. Trust me, honey, that boy has got bad blood. I don't want you mixed up with any of those Martins from Mulatto Bald."

As Galicia scrubbed the wooden booth, she paused now and then to glare at her father as he wrote up the salt transaction in the ledger, certain now that he couldn't be her real father. How could he treat his own customers as though they were barnyard beasts that needed to be cleaned up after? She had to get out of this town before she became as narrow-minded as everyone else who lived here.

Will stood on the preaching platform inside the wooden revival shelter in the woods outside of Couchtown. He was singing baritone with his brother Silas and two of his cousins, sons of John Calvin Martin.

"Are you washed, in the blood,
In the soul-cleansing blood of the Lamb?
Are your garments spotless? Are they white as snow?
Are you washed in the blood of the Lamb?"

His uncle John Calvin, dressed in an ill-fitting suit, with hands folded neatly at chest level, intoned above the song: "Don't you hear it in your hearts, folks? That still small voice summoning you to your heavenly home? Just like a shepherd will herd his flock back to the fold when darkest night begins to fall. Inside that fold is food and warmth. Outside, wolves is howling, lurking, watching, waiting to rip you limb from limb. Come into the safe haven of our Lord Jesus Christ here tonight, friends. Let Him nourish you and protect you...."

As several overwrought townspeople staggered to the podium, Will searched through the forest of upraised arms that were swaying to the music like tree branches in a windstorm. Their palms were outstretched as though they were warming themselves at the flame of John Calvin's scorching faith. Will finally located Galicia, standing halfway back on the right, flanked by the same two girls who had been with her at that ball game when he had beaned her between the eyes. She looked cute in her green gingham dress and pigtails with matching ribbons. Directly behind her stood her brother Matthew and several other Couchtown Panthers, their girlfriends beside them.

With satisfaction Will realized that Galicia didn't have a date. A new girl was the only thing that might help him get over Palestine. She had ordered him to find one, and he had been trying his best. But so far it hadn't worked. The only girl he wanted was Palestine, but he couldn't have her now that she had married that sorry old man in the next county.

Will thought Galicia was watching him sing, so he tried to catch her eye. But she turned her head aside. He missed a couple of notes. Silas nudged him with his elbow. He struggled to get back on key, but his pleasure in the close harmonies had evaporated. He had thought there was a spark between Galicia and himself as they drank sodas that day at her father's store. But she must have realized, as people in town always did, that he was nothing but a Martin from Mulatto Bald.

Will trudged up the rutted trail toward home in silence, the young people ahead and behind him cutting up and teasing one another like always. He had known them his whole life. They had played Kick the Can through the tepid summer nights of childhood. They had attended the mission school on the mountain and played on the sports teams together. When they got older, the boys fought over the girls in the dirt playground.

Will's fights, though, had concerned his extra fingers. Everybody knew that he and Palestine belonged to each other. As small children they had met at a laurel cove midway between their houses, where he had strung her necklaces of scarlet haws and woven her headdresses of oak leaves, cardinal flowers, and ferns. She had braided him bracelets, necklaces, and crowns from honeysuckle vines. They had pretended he was a king and she was his queen.

As they grew older, it had seemed natural to explore each other's changing bodies. They had not even realized they were sinning until everyone told them so last spring when Palestine's belly began to swell. It was hard to see how something that felt so right could be so wrong, but apparently it was. When he called on her parents to ask to marry her, they refused. They said that with no father—and with a mother, a grandmother, and several brothers and sisters to support with his job at the lumber camp—Will couldn't keep up a wife and child as well. They shipped Palestine off to marry a distant in-law whose wife had just died, leaving a passel of children in need of a mother. But the real truth was that they didn't want their daughter marrying a Martin boy.

Several times Will had crossed the ridge into the next county and spied on Palestine from the woods. Lying on a cushion of pine needles, he had watched her scatter grain for the chickens outside a dingy white farmhouse, surrounded by squabbling children, her belly growing rounder every week. He felt that the torments of hell his uncle J.C. was always carrying on about would have been nothing compared to the pain of watching the girl he had loved all his life belong to some ugly old man.

When Palestine had visited her parents last month, she sneaked out to meet Will in the cove where they had once built huts from branches and pretended they were husband and wife. Her shiny auburn hair had gone dull, and her waist had vanished to make room for her baby. *Their* baby. He told her about his new job driving a salt wagon between Saltville and Couchtown. It paid twice what the lumber company had paid. He begged her to come live with him in his mother's cabin. He could eventually build them a cabin of their own. She replied that her parents would never speak to her again, which she wouldn't be able to bear. And besides, she had grown fond of her stepchildren.

"And of that awful old man, too?" demanded Will.

"It's not like with you, Will. We don't hardly ever do that thing you and I used to do. But he's good to me and has promised to help me raise my baby. You and I need to let each other go, or we'll only be unhappy."

"I'm already unhappy. And that's *my* baby as much as it is yourn!" He placed his hand atop her belly.

"You'll soon find some other girl to love you like I do."

"I don't want no other girl."

"But I want you to find one, Will. And you know that you always do what I say."

They lay down together one last time on a bed of leaves, bathed in the copper light from a low-slung moon. Afterwards, they sobbed goodbye in each other's arms.

When Will reached home after the revival, his grandmother was still awake, sitting by the stone fireplace wrapped in a brown and orange afghan she had knitted before her fingers seized up. She called her affliction "the Arthur-itis" and claimed that Arthur was the only man in her entire life she had not been able to get shet of. Her leathery brown face was stretched so taut over her high cheekbones that she resembled one of those mummies from the Egyptian pyramids. His mother was stringing a basket of yellow beans for drying. The younger children lay asleep in a twitching heap in the corner bedstead. Will plopped on the bench before the fire.

"How did it go, son?" asked his mother.

"Fine. Lots got saved. Uncle J.C. seemed real pleased."

A storm was on the way, and the wind shook the windows in their frames.

"Momma, why do they hate us so bad?" asked Will.

"Why does who hate us?" She looked up from her beans.

"Everbody."

"I don't know nobody who hates us."

"Stop it, Arbutus!" snapped his grandmother. "The boy is asking you a true question. You owe him a true answer."

His mother sighed and said nothing.

Will said, "They sent Palestine away because I'm a Martin. And them folks in town always turn their noses up at me. But I ain't never done nothing to none of them."

His grandmother spat tobacco juice into the fireplace, where it sizzled in the embers. "They've hated us since time began, Will-Usdi."

He braced himself. The grown-ups called him Will-Usdi to soften it when they were about to tell him something bad. Supposingly, it meant "Little Will" in Cherokee.

"They chased us out of the Smokies, where we had lived since them peaks first poked up from the mud," said his grandmother. "Then they run us out of Silver Valley, up onto this skull of rock. Then they cut down our forests and crushed the life out of our men folks in their timber camps. They wouldn't give us no salt to cure our hog meat with when we was starving to death during that there war. And then them Secesh soldiers shot down half a dozen Martin men in cold blood just for taking the salt that was due them. If that ain't hatred, Arbutus, then I don't know what is."

"But why?" asked Will.

After a long silence his grandmother replied, almost inaudibly, "Some says half breeds don't deserve no better."

"Is that what we are?"

She shrugged. "To tell you God's honest truth, Will-Usdi, I don't rightly know. We got this skin that's too dark for the whites and too pale for the coloreds. Neither one wants us at their schools or in their churches. My grandpaw used to claim we was Porterghee Indians."

"What's Porterghee?" asked Will.

"I don't have no idea."

"The Lord give us this cross," insisted his mother. "But He also give us the strength to carry it."

"Well, that ain't how I see it, Arbutus," growled his grandmother. "I say since you got to one day die, boy, die like a damned dog, with your teeth in your enemy's throat."

Will nodded doubtfully. His grandmother was always saying bloodthirsty things like that. But Uncle J.C. claimed God wanted His people to turn the other cheek like His son Jesus Christ had done on that cross on Good Friday. How was Will supposed to know who was right?

They sat listening to the wind whistle down the chimney.

"Funniest part is," said his mother, "we're kin to lots of them folks down in town."

"Like who?" asked Will.

"Like the Hunters at the Five and Dime."

"How are we related to the Hunters?" He felt his heart lurch like a stumbling horse. He had heard rumors of being related to the Hunters all his life, but he had never had reason to pay them much mind until now. Maybe Galicia knew they were cousins and couldn't date. Maybe that was why she wouldn't look at him at the revival, and not that he was a Martin.

"I disremember how," said his mother.

"A Hunter man married a Martin woman, name of Galicia, back in Removal days," confirmed his grandmother. "She was a sister to

Abner Martin, who ran the store for the Wests. My uncle Joshua was their brother. So was my daddy, name of Isaac. They called Uncle Josh the Pilot of the Blue Ridge because he led so many escaped Yankee soldiers through that cave up in Silver Valley and across the federal lines into Kentucky. They say he hated slavery and did everything he could to stop it. But he wouldn't join anyone's army.

"My grandpaw, the father of Abner and Joshua and Isaac and Galicia, was named Reuben. He died before I was borned. They say he lost an arm fighting to get shet of the British. He used to farm down in Silver Valley before they pushed him up onto this bald. His daddy Zachariah was an Indian trader, and so was his daddy before him, name of Joseph, and...."

Will yawned. He had heard this litany his entire life. It was like when Uncle J.C. read from Exodus about who begot who. All of a sudden it struck him that his grandmother's aunt was named Galicia, the same as Galicia Hunter in town. Maybe it was more than a coincidence? It wasn't a name you heard very often.

Will stood at the plate eying the left-handed pitcher the Panthers had dragged in from somewhere over in North Carolina. So far this new guy had a perfect game going, but Will intended to put a stop to it. He had spotted Galicia in the bleachers and knew she was watching him. Partly to show off for her, he moved to the other side of the plate so he could bat left-handed.

The pitch streaked toward Will with a slight curve to the outside corner of the plate. He swung. The ball flew toward right field. As Will rounded the bases, the coach waved him home and he realized he had hit a homerun. Passing third, he glanced toward the bleachers, caught Galicia's eye, and lifted his cap to her. He noticed only that her hair was shining auburn in the afternoon sun, just like Palestine's used to.

After the game Will sauntered in Galicia's direction, trying to act casual, as though his running into her was an accident. He turned his head toward her and made his expression look surprised. "Hey there, Galicia. How's it going?" he asked in a tone meant to sound politely indifferent.

"Just fine, thank you." Her cheeks turned the color of her sunburned nose. "Nice game, Will."

Will thought this blush might be a good sign. "Thanks. Say, I'm headed your way. Can I walk you home?"

She whispered something to the two sidekicks who always seemed to be with her and then agreed. The other two crossed the street, giggling and whispering. Galicia turned aside to scowl at them.

As Will and Galicia strolled along the sidewalk to the whining of cicadas in the hot afternoon sun, Will said, "My momma says we're some kinda kin to you all."

"Oh, I don't think so. Our people were Quakers from Philadelphia."

"Well, maybe not, then."

"How?" She realized too late that she might have hurt his feelings by not wanting to be related to him.

"My grandmaw said her aunt, a Martin woman named Galicia—just like you—married a Hunter man back when your daddy's store was a trading post."

"I don't know. I'll have to ask my parents." She was disturbed to think this might be true because you weren't supposed to get a crush on your own cousin. But no one in Couchtown could date otherwise, since most were cousins from one direction or another. Still, it was one thing to sip a soda with Will Martin or to walk home from a ball game with him, and something else again to be related to that brawling bunch up on the bald.

Still, Will had started to remind her of Heathcliff in her favorite novel, *Wuthering Heights*, with his dark, brooding good looks. It would take a girl as wild-spirited as he was to tame him. But Galicia wasn't sure she was up to the task.

Reaching her front door, Galicia started to invite Will inside for iced tea. But then she remembered her father's telling her to stay away from Will or to forget about teachers' college. She bade him a quick goodbye and ducked through the doorway, hoping he would leave before anyone saw him there. If the neighbors did see him, maybe they would think he was the yardman. He looked like one in

his faded overalls, undershirt, and work shoes. But who ever had a
yardman whose tanned muscles rippled like a Greek god's?

As Galicia buttered her cornbread at supper that night, she
asked, "Is it true that we're related to Will Martin?"

"We're related to Will Martin?" asked Matthew. "That's so great!
I'd love to play ball like him. Did you see that left-handed homer he
hit today?"

"Certainly not!" exclaimed her father, laying his fork on his plate
with a clatter. "Where on earth did you hear that we're related to Will
Martin?"

Her mother looked perplexed. "But Harry, wasn't your
grandfather Hunter's wife a Martin? The woman we named Galicia
after?"

"That's a different Martin family from those up on the bald,"
insisted her father. "Galicia Hunter was a sister to Abner Martin, who
managed the trading post for the West family. Abner married one of
the West daughters and organized the first Confederate cavalry unit
from Couchtown. They rode with Jeb Stuart. When Weaver County
was set up after the war, Abner was elected the first clerk of the
county court.

"His father Reuben lost an arm fighting for the British at King's
Mountain. Reuben owned a thousand acres down in Silver Valley on
a land grant from the English king, James the Second. Those Martins
were a fine Cavalier family from the Virginia Tidewater. God only
knows where those trashy Martins up on Mulatto Bald came from."

Galicia felt relieved to know that she and Will were not cousins
after all. At least their babies might not be born with twelve fingers.
Then she blushed to realize that she had just been speculating about
making babies with this long-lobed delinquent whom she scarcely
knew and was supposed to be avoiding.

2

Leesville: October 1909

Will held the reins loosely, slapping them against his teams' backs now and then to keep the horses plodding along the winding dirt track. He had just picked up some bales of tobacco from the Hale farm at the foot of Silver Valley, which he would deliver to the railhead at Independence this afternoon for shipment to Richmond. After spending the coming night in the rail yard, rolled in a blanket beneath his wagon, he would load merchandise at a warehouse and then head over to the Saltville general store.

Above him yawned the mouth of the cave through which his grandmother's Uncle Joshua had led escaped Yankee prisoners to the Federal lines in Kentucky. Joshua and five others had been shot to death there at the entrance, which was heaped with tumbled stones and hidden behind limestone ledges.

Will had heard this story so many times that he could almost picture the overcast winter afternoon, with snow having drifted deep down the valley and frozen to a sheen of blue ice on the bald. That winter had been the coldest in living memory, and the growing season the previous summer the shortest. The corn crops were sparse and had been raided repeatedly by deserters from both sides. In addition, General Lee had sent several dozen exhausted cavalry horses from the battlefields of Virginia to Silver Valley for recuperation, and the Home Guard had requisitioned corn to feed them from every farm in the area.

When it came time for the hog slaughter, Abner Martin at the trading post had refused to sell the families on Mulatto Bald their allotment of salt. Some said he didn't have any salt because the Federals had closed the route to Saltville. Others insisted he wanted to punish those on the bald for their Union sympathies. Still others maintained that Abner was riding with Jeb Stuart in the Shenandoah Valley that winter and had no idea what was happening back at his store. Whatever Abner's role, those on the bald had no salt with which to cure their butchered hogs, their only sustenance until wild greens sprouted in the spring.

So Joshua Martin led six other men, including his two teenaged sons, to the trading post run by his brother Abner. They kicked down the door, placed their money on the counter, and loaded sacks of salt from the storeroom onto their packhorses.

Abner's wife, Martha Ann, a daughter of the Mr. West who then owned the store, lived upstairs with their two children. Awakened by the commotion, she came down in her robe and begged the men to leave. Someone yelled at Martha Ann that the Secesh would all go straight to hell, led there by General Robert E. Lee himself. Joshua warned him not to talk that way to his sister-in-law and ordered him out of the store.

The next week Martha Ann came down with pneumonia. A few weeks later she died. When Abner got home on compassionate leave, gaunt with grief, he vowed to arrest those he held responsible for her death, including his brother Joshua. He led the Home Guard of old men and young boys up the steep trail to Joshua's house. Every man on the ridge had fled, as they always did whenever the Guard came prowling around looking for draft dodgers and deserters. Joshua himself often hid in a pit he had dug beneath a boulder in the woods below his house.

Joshua's wife, a Cherokee named Whippoorwill, spoke little English and understood only that the Guards were looking for her husband and that they were angry. When she refused to say where he had gone, Abner commanded his men to hang her by the neck from an oak branch in the front yard, while her children cowered in the doorway. As she began to gasp and gag, he ordered them to cut her down.

Once she had caught her breath, she again refused to reveal Joshua's whereabouts. So Abner instructed his men to string her back up. Watching her struggling body lift off the ground, he was heard to mutter, "All right, Joshua, looks like it's your wife for mine."

A small boy ran out from the house and began to pummel his Uncle Abner's thigh with his tiny fists. Abner's sergeant grabbed the boy's ankles in one hand and held him upside down. He spat and writhed and cursed like a tiny demon as the soldiers once more hoisted his mother into the air.

After four such sessions, Whippoorwill's face was purple, and her swollen tongue was lolling from her mouth. Her distraught daughter screamed from the doorway that her father had gone down to the big cave in Silver Valley.

Abner knew that cave nearly as well as Joshua did, since they had played there as boys. Providing his troops with lanterns, he stationed guards at Joshua's favorite hiding places and at the pathways to the exits. Then he and his remaining men tracked Joshua through the echoing caverns as though he were the mythic fourteen-point buck.

Meanwhile, Joshua's group, having already burnt up their pine knot torches, had roped themselves together and were stumbling along in the dark in the belly of the cave. For many hours Joshua led them along ledges, down narrow pathways, and back and forth across the icy river as light from their pursuers' lanterns approached and receded. Shivering, starving, and exhausted, they finally voted to surrender. They urged Joshua to escape on the path that stretched through the cave to the Holston Valley. But he refused, probably believing that if he turned himself in, Abner would at least release Joshua's sons.

"You all should of give us our share of that salt," Joshua muttered to Abner, as the Home Guard collected his men's rifles and bound their hands behind their backs in the wavering lantern light, which played across a high rock wall where some ancient Indian hunters had painted effigies of their intended prey. A vast herd of elks, buffalos, panthers, wolves, deer, and waterfowl were being shot at by stick figure hunters with drawn bows. "Then there wouldn't have been no trouble."

"Josh, the troubles between you and me go far beyond a sack of salt," Abner was heard to reply.

Abner's men marched their prisoners out into the daylight. Some say Abner himself gave the signal to shoot. Others say he was as appalled as Joshua when bullets began to fly. Still others insisted that Joshua's men fired first, with the Home Guard responding in self-defense. Though how Joshua's men could have fired first with no weapons and their hands tied behind their backs was still a topic of discussion on the bald.

Whatever the truth, when the smoke cleared and the shouting ceased, the Pilot of the Blue Ridge lay dead, his two sons dead by his side. His four comrades, all slain but the one who lived to tell the tale, sprawled behind him in the scarlet snow, while a red-tailed hawk wheeled overhead with a shriek that was almost human.

The autumn rains had been holding off, and the Sturgeon River was so low that Will crossed the ledges at the ford with dry hubcaps. Upon reaching the crossroads where different cart tracks led southeast to North Carolina and west to Kentucky, he headed north toward Independence. Alongside his route ran the abandoned rail line the timber company had laid to haul the logs cut off the mountains around Couchtown. The hardwood had been shipped to a furniture factory in North Carolina and the softwood to a pulp mill in Leesville.

New growth had concealed the tangles of brush left from the clear cutting. But some hillsides were so ravaged by deep gullies down to the bedrock that they would never again produce anything but rivulets of orange mud.

A man had to do whatever work he could find to feed his family, Will reflected. But he imagined how his own father must have felt as he chopped down the forests that had sheltered the game he had hunted all his life. On Sunday mornings in the little frame church on the bald, Uncle J.C. used to warn the timber crews that by destroying the forests left to them by their ancestors, they were trading their immortal souls for pots of soup beans. But on Monday mornings J.C.

was out there felling trees with the rest of them, vying for his own pot of beans.

Uncle J.C. had described the accident that killed Will's father so often that Will felt he had been there, too, that afternoon when the splash dam broke open and tossed like matchsticks the huge tree trunks piled up behind it waiting to be floated downstream to the railhead. Fourteen men were killed by the ricocheting logs. His father's body had been mashed up so bad that his mother had insisted the coffin stay closed at his funeral. Will had seen him, though, before the lid was nailed shut. Although his mother and grandmother had tried to clean him up, one side of his head was bashed in like a rotten pumpkin. One arm lay loose in his suit coat, out of its socket, limp as the limb of a rag doll. The tall, strong man Will had thought of as his protector throughout his childhood was gone.

Will was twelve at the time. In compensation, the logging company had hired him as a trimmer for twenty-five cents a day, sunup to sundown, six days a week. The grown men chopped down the huge first-growth poplars, chestnuts, black walnuts, oaks, and evergreens with ax blades they whetted to razor sharpness every evening. Then the boys who were replacing dead fathers hacked the branches off the trunks. The mules skidded the stripped trunks down the hillsides to the creeks that carried them to the splash dams.

Never having spent much time off the bald, Will was embarrassed when loggers from the lowlands snickered at his extra fingers. So one day he had decided to cut them off. Positioning a finger on a fallen log, he raised his ax with his other hand.

Just then Uncle J.C. came along. "What you doing there, Will-Usdi?"

"I'm gonna whack off these infernal fingers."

"I don't believe I would do that. They would bleed right smart and might could turn into the gangrene. You might could lose your entire arm, and maybe even die."

Slowly Will lowered the ax.

"You know, son, they's a man in First Chronicles had him six fingers on each hand and six toes on each foot—twenty-four digits in all. Yet he proved himself a hero in the battle of Gath. The good Lord made you like you is on purpose. You just got to figure out what that purpose is."

Will looked down at his hands, which now rested on his thighs, interlaced with the reins from his team of plodding horses. Even after a lifetime of living with those fake fingers, he still found them disgusting—flimsy splinters of bone, like the tips of baked turkey wings. But the night before Galicia left for the teachers' college at Leesville, she had sneaked out to tell him goodbye in the shed behind her house. She took his hands in hers and kissed each finger, including those ugly ones he had always hated. How could he help but love a lady like that? And Palestine was right, like always: now that he loved Galicia, he didn't hurt so bad over losing Palestine.

Will departed from Independence at dawn, his wagon bed crammed with barrels of goods for the Saltville store. Barring a broken rim as he negotiated the rutted path through the pass near the Continental Divide, he would reach Saltville by late afternoon. He would unload the barrels at the store and stable his horses. Then he would put on the white shirt and wool trousers he wore to church and hop the evening coal train up the valley to Leesville, where he would visit Galicia in her dormitory until time to hop the midnight freight train back to Saltville.

Galicia had written that her building was locked up after supper. But he would find a way to reach her. She was terrified of getting caught and kicked out, but she had not forbidden him to come. He smiled, knowing that she must have it near as bad as he did. Love forced you to do all kinda scary stuff you wouldn't never try if you was in your right mind.

Swaying on the seat as the wagon lurched from rut to rut, he wondered what would become of Galicia and himself. Her father had sent her to Leesville a year ahead of schedule, hoping that her interest in Will would prove a passing fancy. Would Galicia give up her family for him if she had to? Palestine had not. If Galicia would, was he selfish enough to let her do it?

"Hell, yes!" he shouted to no one in particular. The horses twitched their ears. He realized he was actually happy, for maybe the first time since Palestine got sent away.

Galicia sat at a round oak table with four other students and two teachers, their empty dessert bowls on saucers before them. Opposite her was Miss Woodward, who had come south from Boston. She wore a skirted suit and a silky white blouse with a high neck. At her throat was a cameo on a black velvet ribbon. Her strawberry blond hair, piled atop her head like a puffy cushion, was held in place by pins of carved ivory. She and the other teacher, Miss Burton, who was from Philadelphia, were discussing whether marriage was a desirable state for a woman.

"Marriage usually brings children," observed Miss Woodward. "And children confine one to the home. Susan B. Anthony accomplished so much for women's suffrage only because she remained single."

"Not necessarily," insisted Miss Burton, whose tiny frameless glasses looked as though they were about to slide off the tip of her nose. "Think about Elizabeth Cady Stanton. She bore seven children, did she not?"

"Yes, but Anthony had to baby-sit them so that Stanton could get her speeches written!"

The two teachers laughed. Galicia laughed, too, although she didn't know who those women were and had never heard women referred to only by their last names. Nor had she ever heard two women argue with one another, yet seem to enjoy it. Her mother had always insisted that good manners required you to appear to agree with someone, even if you found their opinions ridiculous.

"All right, ladies, back to work," announced Miss Woodward, pushing herself up from the dining table with her fists.

As Galicia sat at the desk in her room trying to concentrate on Latin conjugations, her thoughts kept straying to Will. Would he really ride the train to Leesville that night? If so, how would he get up to her third-floor room? The weaker part of her longed to see his olive face and crooked nose and to feel his lips nibbling the curve of her neck. He was her Heathcliff, her wild mountain boy, who had ignited desires she had never known she had.

But the finer part of her hoped he would not come. She had always assumed that marriage was a woman's lot. But Miss Woodward was unmarried, and she seemed perfectly happy and fulfilled. If Galicia truly wanted to teach, maybe she needed to avoid men and all the domestic shackles that came along with loving them.

Besides, she was beginning to feel at home here in Leesville. Her dorm was housed in a turreted stone mansion that looked like a castle in the fairy-tale books of her childhood. It had been built by the owner of a shoe factory who had died childless, leaving his house to the Presbyterian church for a school in which to train teachers from the "disadvantaged" regions of Virginia.

In his opening-day address, the president of the board, a corpulent man with a gold watch chain draped across his expansive pin-striped vest, had informed the students that graduates of the training school were expected to return to their hometowns and work to uplift their own people. Galicia had not known until then that Couchtown was disadvantaged. But she realized that Miss Woodward had been studying her gingham dresses and pigtails with gentle pity and subtly instructing her in how to walk and talk, how to dress and fix her hair. And now Galicia wondered if Will—with his worn overalls, his atrocious grammar, and his deformed hands—could ever fit into her stimulating new life here in Leesville.

Glancing out the window, she discovered that a full moon was bathing the sculpted bushes in the yard below in a pale ivory glow. Just then a head popped up behind her windowpane, like a gypsy jack-in-the-box. Will winked at her and grinned, and she felt her misgivings about him evaporate like fog in morning sunlight.

Jumping up, she ran to the window and heaved it open. Will had shinnied up a drainpipe and was now clutching her granite sill with his strange hands. He pushed himself up and rolled through the window opening onto her carpet. Terrified that someone would come to investigate the crashing noise, Galicia grabbed her desk chair and wedged it beneath the embossed bronze door handle. With relief she saw that Will had changed out of his overalls. If they got caught, at least he would look somewhat respectable, even though his white shirt was wrinkled and dirty from his hours in the boxcar.

Will got up and closed the window. They went into each other's arms and exchanged prim kisses. Then Will held her out at arm's length and inspected her striped black skirt and ivory silk blouse, hand-me-downs from Miss Woodward, and the soft nest of auburn hair perched atop her head, its coiling tendrils framing her face.

"Lord, girl, I don't hardly recognize you."

"How do you like my new look?" She turned so he could inspect her.

"I like it. But I liked the old look just fine, too."

"I'm still the same person," said Galicia, trying to convince them both. She led him over to sit on her narrow bed. "So tell me everything you've thought and done since I last saw you in our back shed that night."

He laughed and reached out for her.

"No." She slapped his hand. "Behave like a civilized human being and talk to me, Will Martin."

"But the train back to Saltville leaves in two hours," he groaned. Then, pulling himself together, he obligingly told her about his trip by wagon over the Blue Ridge and the one by boxcar up the valley from Saltville. And he listened as she told him about her courses and about her new idol, Miss Woodward.

"Have we talked enough yet?"

Smiling, she said, "You've been very patient, Will. Now you may have your reward."

She turned toward him, closed her eyes, and tipped up her chin. As they kissed, she struggled to steer his roving hands to safe areas. She knew from a medical text at the school library that the only sure way not to have a baby was to keep him outside her clothing, and she was determined that that was where he would stay. Judging from the fate of poor Palestine Sanders—about whom Will had not yet spoken—Galicia knew she could not count on any help from Will himself.

3

Palestine: February 1911

Galicia turned to Will, who stood beside her in a long line that wound out of the fanciest house in Leesville, a four-square brick Georgian with two towering Corinthian columns out front. "At least tell me what we're waiting for."

He smiled teasingly. "Have patience, Galicia. I promise you won't be disappointed."

She sighed and raised her hands to adjust the pin that secured her straw hat to her cushion of hair. Will was wearing his new wool suit and the cream-colored silk shirt she had bought him, with his monogram stitched onto the breast pocket. With his tall, slender build, he looked far more sophisticated than the overfed, city-bred men all around them. But she realized that he needed a bowler to complete his outfit. Would he ever agree to wear one? She doubted it.

"Don't you have to get to the clinic?" she asked.

"Don't worry, I'm never late to work. I learned to be on time by hopping all those coal trains up the valley to visit you last year."

Galicia had spent the summer after her first year at the teachers' college working at her father's store in Couchtown. Whenever Will was home from his wagon trips to Saltville, they met in secret late at night in the shed behind her house, while her parents slept on unaware upstairs and the family dogs gnawed the deer bones Will brought to shut them up.

At the end of the summer, Will announced to Galicia that on his last trip to Saltville he had taken the train to Leesville and found himself a job as an orderly at the Robert E. Lee Confederate Veterans' Home. He would live in a room in one of the barracks there. Then the two of them could see each other whenever they wanted without having to sneak around in the middle of the night. Silas would take over Will's teamster job and help Will support their family on the bald.

"Don't you love this house?" Galicia gestured to the Corinthian columns.

"It's all right."

Noting its every detail, Galicia resolved that one day she and Will would build one just like it on a wooded lot down in Silver Valley.

They finally reached the doorway with its leaded glass fanlight and dentate molding. Inside, a Negro in a starched white jacket was seated behind a Chippendale table, taking up the admission fee of a dime apiece.

The line snaked down a hallway to the right. Will and Galicia edged ever closer to the room that housed the mysterious exhibit.

At last packed into a tiled cubicle along with a dozen other townspeople, Galicia studied the white porcelain chair in the corner, with a bowl at its base that was half full of water. A bewhiskered old man in a green velvet smoking jacket, presumably Mr. Wright, the eccentric owner of this house, pulled a chain that hung from the ceiling. With a roar, the water in the bowl swirled like a whirlpool and vanished, only to be replaced by a trickle of fresh water. The spectators buzzed as though watching a magic trick.

The old man explained proudly in a quavering voice, "Water is pumped up from the river and stored in a tank on the floor just above us. Releasing it forces the water in the bowl down a drainpipe that empties back into the river. Soon every home in our great nation will have a flush commode. In big cities like Richmond you are already hard-pressed to find a single outhouse still standing."

The audience applauded. As a new group entered, the previous spectators filed from the room, whispering their misgivings like the nests of curious skeptics that used to huddle at the rear of revivals back in Couchtown.

"I admit that was impressive." Galicia said as she and Will strolled along the cobblestone sidewalk toward the streetcar stop.

"One day we'll throw a party," promised Will, "and smash all our chamber pots!"

Galicia smiled as she climbed aboard the trolley bound for the Virginia Colony for the Feebleminded. "Don't forget to meet me at the reservoir after work," she called to Will, as the car whisked her away on its tracks of steel. It still felt like a miracle to meet Will during daylight hours without worrying about whether her parents would catch them. She wondered if they had figured out yet that Will was now in Leesville, too.

The trolley rattled along a bridge that stretched across the river on cement pylons. Galicia had spent her childhood enslaved by the whims of the Sturgeon River, which had sometimes run so low that the ford was no more than a puddle. At other times, its waters had raged through the streets of Couchtown, tossing the ferry like an autumn leaf and swirling away squawking chickens and bobbing hogs. But you could cross the James River at Leesville any day of the year and stay dry as a drought.

Running up the steps into the dreary brick building that housed the classrooms at the Virginia Colony, Galicia entered the teachers' lounge, where she unpinned her hat and laid it on the closet shelf. Then she unbuttoned and removed her suit jacket and hung it up. After slipping on a pink smock over her long skirt, she picked up her notebook and reader and hurried down the hallway.

Entering the library, she was assaulted by the odor of mildew. The books on these shelves had no doubt been rescued from the musty cellars of area benefactors. She found her students waiting for her around a large oak table, their supplies spread out before them. The boys and the girls at the Colony were kept separate to prevent their passing their mental afflictions on to a new generation. Galicia taught the girls who could already read and write upon their arrival. This practice teaching was required of her before she could graduate in June.

Another intern from the Teachers' College sat at the far end of the library, reading a story to those who would never be literate. Their vacant gazes or incessant rocking gave no indication of whether they understood the story or were even listening.

After greeting her students, Galicia collected their writing assignments and set them to work on a passage in their readers, in preparation for that day's discussion. As she began to correct a homework paper, the glass door swung open. The director of the Colony, Dr. Manning, appeared. He had a pocked face and receding hairline. Behind him stood a rather chubby young woman with pond-green eyes and messy auburn hair.

"Miss Hunter, I've brought you a new student," said Dr. Manning. "Her name is Palestine McClellan."

Galicia did a mental double take at the name Palestine. "Welcome, Palestine," she managed to say.

She signaled to one of the other girls to pull up a chair from the next table. Then she handed Palestine a reader and briefed her on their routine: Each day they read a passage, discussed it, and wrote a draft of an essay based on the discussion. At night the students prepared a finished paper to hand in the next day for correction and grading.

As Palestine intently mouthed the words she was reading, Galicia sneaked glances at her. Palestine was an uncommon name, but surely she couldn't be Will's old girlfriend, Palestine Sanders? After class Galicia would read her file.

As a rule Galicia preferred not to know a student's history. Often they were some variety of criminal, or they had been labeled "moron," "imbecile," or "feebleminded," She liked to remain ignorant of their diagnoses and treat them as she would any other human being. In the absence of crippling expectations from herself, sometimes even the least promising girl would flourish.

Several students had finished the passage and were looking around for trouble. If she left them unstructured for too long, a couple tended to sneak out the door and down the corridor, searching for the boys' classrooms. When she went in pursuit, the others would be ransacking the bookshelves upon her return or wrestling each other beneath the tables. So she asked the group to summarize what they had just read.

After class Galicia walked along the sidewalk toward the administration building past the dormitories, which were dominated by two huge wooden water tanks, elevated on spindly metal supports so that they resembled daddy longlegs. Behind the dorms were the barns and fields where the male patients worked. The female patients worked in the kitchens and the laundry. The disabled of both sexes sat in wheelchairs that lined the corridors of the sex-segregated dorms—some sleeping, some howling, some chatting with one another or waving to passersby.

In the records office Galicia asked the bored-looking secretary behind the counter for Palestine McClellan's file. Sitting down, she opened it and read, "Palestine Sanders McClellan. Place of birth: Couchtown, Virginia." She let the folder droop until it rested in her lap, facing the fact that this Palestine was, indeed, Will's Palestine.

Drawing a deep breath, she skimmed the psychologist's report. Palestine was referred to as a runaway, a vagrant, a prostitute, and "feebleminded." Her husband stated that she would leave their home in the middle of the night and wander the roads until dawn, searching for strangers with whom to copulate. She had already given birth to two sons out of wedlock, one mulatto. The social worker had recommended that her husband commit her to the Colony to keep her away from males until she was no longer fertile. Dazed, Galicia closed the folder and returned it to the secretary.

As Galicia rode the streetcar back to the teachers' college, she tried to decide what to do. Will's childhood girlfriend, reportedly the mother of his child, would be incarcerated at the Colony for some twenty-five years. Meanwhile, what had become of Will's son? Would he be put up for adoption? Could he be the one referred to as "mulatto"? Will was dark-complexioned, but many Couchtowners were darker than he was. Surely no one could claim that he was "mulatto"? The name Mulatto Bald was taken from the old days when escaped slaves and free coloreds used to live up there. But those up on the ridge now were just poor whites.

Palestine had been diagnosed as feebleminded, but it was clear from that morning's discussion that she was just an uneducated mountain girl, no different from most in Couchtown. Yet she would be locked up for two or three decades with women who were completely insane, while Will's son fended for himself.

Galicia wondered if Will would want to know this. She had never yet discussed this early indiscretion with him. Would he try to help Palestine if he knew of her plight? But was she helpable? Probably not. After all, her husband had placed her at the Colony. Therefore, it might be better for Will's peace of mind that he not know about her predicament or that of his son.

But then Galicia wondered if she were merely being selfish. It was safer for *her* if Will didn't know that Palestine was now in Leesville. He might decide to rescue Palestine and their son and make a life with them instead. Was Galicia noble enough to court this risk by telling him? Yet if she didn't tell him and he later found out that she had known, he might be furious with her. And justifiably so. But he might forgive her for having spared him worry about a dilemma that couldn't be resolved.

Galicia thought about how much she loved her current life with Will. On Sundays they attended the Presbyterian chapel at the teachers' college. He donned a blue robe to sing "Come, Thou Almighty King" with the choir. The Presbyterians didn't consider every conceivable human activity or inactivity a sin, as had the Baptists back home. And their services were so dignified compared to the Couchtown revivals, at which unsavory rustics had writhed in the dirt to the accompaniment of gospel quartets bellowing "Washed in the Blood." Even the most "feebleminded" patients at the Colony seemed sane by comparison to Will's preacher uncle, John Calvin Martin.

Will had asked Galicia to correct his grammar and his accent, and he was making good progress at remembering the corrections. He was earning a salary that seemed like a fortune to him after the timber camp and the salt wagon. She would graduate from the teachers' college in June and would soon have a salary as well. Neither had ever uttered the word "marriage," but it appeared that was where they were headed. Or had been until Palestine's appearance in the classroom that morning. Galicia still recalled the warnings about marriage issued by Miss Woodward, who had returned to Boston last year. But she could only conclude that Miss

Woodward had never been in love, or else her misgivings would have evaporated as quickly as Galicia's had.

Will took a shortcut to the infirmary through the veterans' cemetery behind the mess hall. He passed the bronze statue of Robert E. Lee's first horse, Phantom, who had been killed by a cannonball on a nearby battlefield. His fame having been eclipsed by his more renowned successor, Traveler, Phantom lay buried beneath this larger-than-life replica of horseflesh, with its bulging muscles of polished metal. The citizens had used Phantom's burial here as an excuse to change their town's name from an Indian word that meant Ford Where the Black Bears Water to Leesville. Phantom's effigy was surrounded by Civil War-era artillery on carriages, facing outward as though belatedly defending the embattled gelding.

Will spotted a bent old man who leaned on a shovel amid the identical marble tablets that bore the initials, regiment number, and state of origin of each interred soldier. Colonel Combes had led a failed charge at Gettysburg in which almost all his soldiers had been slaughtered. He had gone insane afterwards. Now he was the caretaker of this cemetery, tending his soldiers in death as he had been unable to in life. Will greeted the colonel, who nodded back glumly as he wiped his forehead with a handkerchief.

Will approached the three-story brick infirmary, which had been a tobacco warehouse before the war and a field hospital during it. Now it housed the veterans who were ill or dying. Otherwise, they lived in a dozen rambling wooden barracks that surrounded a treed park in which they strolled or sat or played croquet when the weather was nice.

Even though Will had to empty bedpans and collect soiled linens, he loved his job. Often he watched the doctors operate, and sometimes they let him drip chloroform onto a mask over the patient's nose and mouth. Everyone was amazed that he didn't get woozy when he saw blood and wounds. They didn't realize that nothing could ever faze someone who had seen his own father's corpse, bashed to bits by ricocheting logs. He would like to be able to repair injured people, as he had not been able to repair his own father.

Dennis Freeman, an intern from the Leesville Medical College, was sitting behind the oak desk in the admitting room in his white scrub clothes, playing solitaire. He nodded to Will.

"Pretty quiet today?" Will noticed a male nurse snoring on a stretcher in the corner.

"One ingrown toenail and two cases of tonsillitis," replied Dennis.

Will plopped down in a chair. "Any jobs for me?"

"Not at the moment."

"Tell me, Dennis, what does it take to become a doctor?"

"A strong back and a weak mind."

Will laughed. "Don't you like your profession?"

"Mostly I do. But on slow days like this I start wishing I could work outdoors. I grew up on a cattle farm up the valley, and sometimes I miss it."

"I worked outdoors all my life till now, growing corn, hoeing tobacco, chopping trees, driving wagons. Believe me, it's no picnic. You're too hot or too cold. You're wet to the bone or eaten up by insects. You get poison ivy or cut your foot open with an ax. You get snake bit or—"

"All right, I get your point, Will," laughed Dennis. "Is that why you came to Leesville—so you could work indoors?"

"No, I followed a lady friend up here."

"So you're in love?"

"Yeah, I reckon." His olive face flushed several shades darker.

"Well, enjoy it while it lasts."

"You don't think love can last?"

"It never has for me."

"Well, for me it don't never quit...doesn't ever quit. I had me another girl when I was a kid. She got sent away. I don't reckon I ever will get over her."

"Well, maybe you'd better think twice about leading this new lady on, then?"

"No, I turned the page on that first one. They wasn't...there wasn't any way her and me could be together. So I had to let her go. But that doesn't stop me from loving her still."

"You're a very sensible young man to move on, Will. No point in crying over spilled milk when there's a whole barnful of cows with bulging udders." Dennis cast him a mocking smile before returning to his pyramid of playing cards.

"Dennis, let me ask you something."

Dennis looked up.

"What would it take to remove my extra fingers?"

Dennis blinked. "Why would you want to do that, Will?"

"I get sick of being stared at."

"But you aren't stared at. You keep your hands in your pockets most of the time."

"These damn things embarrass me. Always have. It's like I'm some kinda freak show or something."

Dennis hesitated. "Well, I could ask my surgery professor. It should be an easy operation. But you probably depend on those fingers more than you realize."

"I watch those fellows out there in the yard, some missing an arm or a leg, and they seem to manage just fine. So I keep thinking I would, too."

"I'll look into it for you, Will."

"I sure would appreciate that, Dennis. What do you reckon it would cost me?"

"They most likely wouldn't charge you a penny, as long as you're willing to let a bunch of rowdy medical students watch."

Will nodded.

Will met Galicia by the reservoir on the hillside overlooking Leesville. She was carrying their supper in a straw basket. They strolled out to an Italianate belvedere atop a sheer rock cliff named Lovers' Leap. The legend maintained that a Yankee soldier and the daughter of a Confederate officer had fallen in love. At the time, the soldier was a patient at a field hospital in town at which the girl volunteered as a nurse. When her father forbade her to see him anymore because he was a Yankee, they jumped to their deaths from that very spot, hand in hand. Galicia and Will leaned over the railing and looked down at the boulders along the riverbank, on which the two plummeting bodies had presumably splattered.

"If your father won't let us marry," mused Will, "let's us jump off this cliff together."

Galicia smiled. It was the first time he had mentioned marriage to her, and he seemed to assume that was their goal. "Wouldn't you rather just elope?"

Will turned to look at her, feigning shock. "Did you just propose to me, woman?"

"I guess I did."

He glanced around. "I wish I could kiss you."

"You'd better save it till we get back to my room."

Suddenly shy, Galicia spread a cloth on the grass, worried that she had been too forward. They sat and studied the downtown laid out below them, crosshatched by its proud parade of electric poles and intertwined wires.

"Those lines look like cat's cradles," observed Will.

"Cat's cradles! I'd forgotten all about them!" Galicia was relieved to have a new topic to distract them from her indiscretion. "Did you make them when you were a kid?"

"Lord, we wove those things all day long. With my extra fingers I could make patterns nobody else could copy. I was the envy of Mulatto Bald." He held up his hands and studied them, wondering if amputation might be a mistake. In some ways these stupid fingers had served him well.

"Isn't it strange to think that we lived all those years so close to one another, doing the same things, without ever laying eyes on each other until two summers ago?" asked Galicia.

"We ran in different circles. But I bet we were in the same place plenty of times—like at revivals and ball games and barn dances and the Fourth of July carnival. God just waited to introduce us until He saw that the moment was right."

Galicia loved how Will said simpleminded things so sincerely that they came across as touching rather than silly. She laid out fried chicken, deviled eggs, potato salad, coleslaw, baked beans—all his favorite dishes—which she had assembled in the college kitchen.

As they ate, they watched trains crawl like caterpillars along the intersecting tracks in the rail yards across the river, belching puffs of white smoke. A southbound engine entered the huge roundhouse with a plaintive whistle and soon emerged facing north. Beyond the tracks stretched the red brick factories where shoes, cotton cloth, ploughs, paper, and machine parts were fabricated.

"You know," mused Will, "I could hop a boxcar down there that would carry me north to Alexandria, or south to Bristol, or east to Richmond, or west to Lexington. It would take two days by wagon to reach Couchtown from here, but two days on one of them...one of those trains would carry us halfway across the continent."

"So you say the word 'marry' to me, and then all you can talk about is hopping a train out of town?" She intended this to sound playful, but it came out melancholic instead.

"Is something wrong?" he asked.

She smiled too brightly. "No, everything's fine." She forced herself to tell him amusing tidbits from her day at the Colony, omitting the fact that she had a new student who had once been the love of his life—and was still the mother of his only child.

In return, he told her about his day at the Veterans' Home, though he concealed his discussion with Dennis about removing his fingers. If he went through with it, he wanted to surprise her. As he rambled, he reflected inwardly that Galicia's mood had shifted abruptly from gaiety to anxiety, and he had no idea why. Maybe the idea of marrying him frightened her because it might estrange her from her family.

Will helped pack up the picnic basket, and they strolled along the promenade past the reservoir, which was surrounded by a wrought-iron fence that featured arrow-shaped pickets and acorn-topped finials. The sun was sinking behind the bluff on which the Colony sat, turning the graceless brick buildings and the water tanks on their metal stilts into ominous silhouettes.

At the bottom of the walkway they arrived at the Casino, a white frame pavilion trimmed with elaborate Victorian gingerbread. They joined the crowd of townspeople slowly filing inside.

After ten tedious acts featuring an off-key soprano, housecats in costumes jumping through hoops, two bears dancing the polka, and the testimony of a convicted murderer who had survived his own hanging, Galicia and Will caught a packed streetcar back to the teachers' college.

"Well, that was pretty pitiful," said Will. "But it sure beats those sideshows at the Couchtown carnival."

"I never got to see them."

"Oh, that's right. Girls weren't allowed in, were they?"

"What went on in those tents, Will? None of the boys would ever tell us."

Will laughed. "Well, I won't either!"

"And you expect me to marry you when you have this whole secret life?" Her stomach lurched as she recalled his major secret—Palestine and their son.

"I'll tell you about those shows once I know you better," he promised with a teasing grin.

"You know me well enough to marry me, but not well enough to tell me about some carnival sideshows?" *And about your abandoned child*, she added silently.

"You seem pretty prim to me, girl."

She knew that he was only half-teasing. Her feints and evasions when he was trying to hold her and kiss her annoyed him. But it was for his own good as much as for hers. Though now that she was in silent competition over him with Palestine, maybe she needed a child with him to even the odds....

"If I weren't so prim, there'd be no telling what kind of a mess we'd get ourselves into." Her voice was tinged with her resentment at having to be the guardian of their future welfare—and then being ridiculed for it.

He said nothing else for the rest of the trip. She wondered if he were thinking about the mess he had gotten into with Palestine for want of primness.

After ushering Galicia to her dorm, Will ducked around back and shinnied up the porch post to the roof. Crawling along the shingles, he reached the drainpipe, which he climbed to the third floor. Then he tiptoed along the narrow ledge toward her window. Galicia had acted so strange all evening that he was terrified she was going to back out on him now that he had dared to mention marriage. If she spurned him, maybe he would join a vaudeville troupe as a tightrope walker and go see the world. One thing was certain: he could never go back to Mulatto Bald. Galicia had already changed how he talked and dressed and thought so drastically that he wouldn't fit in there anymore.

But by the time he arrived at her window, Galicia had raised it high. He entered, and they lay on her bed in each other's arms, soon feeling the tension from their unexpressed misunderstandings start to fade.

"I can't wait until we can sleep like this all night long," murmured Will.

"Me either."

"When can we?"

"As soon as I graduate."

"Why not get married now and keep it a secret?" He realized that he didn't want to join a vaudeville troupe. He wanted to lie next to Galicia every night for the rest of their lives.

"I wouldn't feel right using my father's money to stay at school if I were secretly married to you, Will. That's just not an honorable way to start our life together."

"I'm earning pretty good money now. I can pay your way. Your father is going to be furious whether you marry me now or this summer. So why not now?"

"We couldn't live together anyhow."

"Wouldn't they let you live off campus and stay on as a student?"

"I don't think so. They consider married ladies a bad influence on the single ones."

He laughed. "Could you ask them? Please?"

Galicia studied him, stretched out on her bed in his suit and sock feet, pleading like a puppy with his mournful kingfisher blue eyes. Palestine had given herself to him without reservation and would bear the consequences for the rest of her life. No doubt she would do it again if she got the chance.

"Yes, I could ask. But are you sure this is what you want, Will?"

"Yes, this is what I want, Galicia. More than I've ever wanted anything else in my entire life." He slowly kissed her eyelids, first one and then the other.

Galicia wondered if this would still be what Will wanted if he knew about Palestine's plight. Here she had been lecturing him about honor, yet it didn't speak well for her immortal soul that she needed to secure Will for herself before trying to help Palestine. But she was a woman in love who had just discovered the limits to her selflessness. Will didn't ever need to know the exact timing that had governed her decision to marry him as soon as possible.

4

Hijacked Happiness: March 1911

Galicia stood in Dr. Manning's doorway, unsure of herself. He rarely smiled and often looked as though he were nursing a severe case of heartburn. Had she had any choice, he was the last person she would seek out for assistance. Besides, as a practice teacher, she had real gall questioning a judgment that he himself, the director of the Virginia Colony for the Feebleminded, had probably made. But her only other option was silence. She had been struggling for several days against her own inclination to say nothing about the unjust fate of Palestine McClellan. She had finally realized that she was morally bound to help Palestine if she could, whatever the consequences with Will. Otherwise, she would never be able to live at peace with herself, so great would be her shame.

Dr. Manning looked up from the papers on his desk and gestured for her to enter. Standing up, he gave a courtly half-bow and said, "It's a pleasure to see you, Miss Hunter. You've been doing an excellent job here at the Colony this term."

"Thank you, sir. I'm enjoying my work here very much."

"I'm afraid not many could honestly say that." He gave a weary grimace. "For the most part, our patients are very troubled and disagreeable people." He gestured for her to sit in the chair facing his desk. Then he resumed his seat. "So what brings you here today, Miss Hunter?"

"I wanted to discuss a student of mine named Palestine McClellan, sir. She's been diagnosed as feebleminded. Yet from working with her, I feel certain she's not mentally impaired."

Dr. Manning frowned. "What makes you think not, Miss Hunter?"

"She writes well. She discusses what she's read with insight and enthusiasm. There's a marked difference between her and many of my other pupils."

Excusing himself, he left the room, then returned with the same manila file folder Galicia had already perused. After he had flipped through it, he observed, "Palestine McClellan roams the roads at night, searching for strangers with whom to conceive mulatto babies. How would you account for this anti-social behavior, Miss Hunter, if she is not feebleminded? Would you simply call her evil?"

Galicia lowered her head. She knew Palestine's first such baby had resulted from an excess of youthful ardor and from a paucity of information about human biology. She had no idea about the second. "Did anyone ever ask Palestine why she did this, sir?"

"There was no need to ask her. Her husband requested that she be committed here, and only he can request her release."

"For the rest of her life?"

"For the rest of her reproductive life. Her husband says he does not wish to pay for the upkeep of any more illegitimate imbeciles. Nor do the taxpayers of the state of Virginia."

"And who's to say that her children are imbeciles?" bristled Galicia, on Will's behalf.

"It's in the blood, Miss Hunter. The feebleminded pass their affliction to their offspring. And feeblemindedness breeds crime, alcoholism, and prostitution. Several states have already mandated sterilization for such people. And I'm happy to report that our legislators in Richmond are currently framing such a statute for Virginia as well."

"But Palestine McClellan is not feebleminded, sir." She felt frantic at Dr. Manning's circular logic.

Dr. Manning cleared his throat. "Forgive me for being so blunt, Miss Hunter, but I have thirty years of experience in the field of mental hygiene. Dare I suggest that I might be better equipped to identify feeblemindedness than an intern from the Leesville Teachers' College?"

"Please excuse my presumption, Dr. Manning." She hated herself for backing down, but this man was, after all, her employer.

Without his endorsement she wouldn't be able to graduate and move on with her life. "I'm just so concerned about Palestine, sir. She's my best student."

"I will take her situation under advisement, Miss Hunter. Thank you for drawing it to my attention." He got up and ushered her into the hall.

Galicia stood there, steadied by her hand against the cool tile wall. Having tried her best on Palestine's behalf, was she now justified in dropping her cause?

Dr. Hopewell, dressed in pale green scrubs, stood over Will, holding his right hand and poking and prodding at his extra digit, which grew from the joint between his thumb and index finger. The sunlight through the blinds laid stripes of bright and dark across them both. Will suppressed a smile at the thought that they must look like members of a chain gang. Yet Dr. Hopewell was one of the most respected men in Leesville.

During the Civil War, Dr. Hopewell had volunteered to run the Pest House. When the wounded of both sides rolled into Leesville in boxcars from the Virginia battlefields, those who were already dead were packed in salt and shipped home to their parents. Those with smallpox, measles, influenza, typhoid, or dysentery were sent to a clapboard farmhouse alongside the cemetery. Prior to Dr. Hopewell's arrival, half had died there and had been removed to graves in the field next door. But the doctor changed the menu to include fresh fruits and vegetables. He painted the walls black to rest his patients' inflamed eyes. He salved their weeping sores with his own concoctions of oils and herbs. He gave them shots of whiskey to ease their pain and fear. He put sand on the floor to absorb their bodily fluids and changed it often. Soon only five percent were dying at the Pest House. He was regarded as a genius by other doctors—and as a saint by soldiers and their families, both Confederate and Union. And despite his exposure to all this contagion, he himself was still alive. Dennis Freeman, Will's intern friend, was in awe of him.

"I assume you've thought this over carefully, Mr. Martin?" His white beard was closely clipped, and his white hair was tousled. His small, narrow nose and frameless round glasses made him resemble a snowy owl.

"Yes sir, I have," said Will.

"Well, I believe we can do a good job for you."

"Thank you, sir. I sure would appreciate it."

"Mr. Freeman said you wouldn't mind an audience of medical students at the operation?" He sat behind his desk and leaned back in his oak swivel chair, his elbows propped on its curved arms and his fingers knit together.

"No, sir."

"Then I'll schedule you for the first operation next Friday morning, if that suits you?"

"I'll be there." Will's crooked smile was the only outward evidence of his anxiety.

"Mr. Freeman also told me what a fine orderly you are, Mr. Martin. He said you can perform any task with either hand."

"Yes sir. Apart from my extra fingers, that's my only claim to fame."

Dr. Hopewell smiled. "He also said you had been inquiring about medical school."

Will nodded hesitantly.

"I might be able to find you a spot here at the medical college. The South is desperate for doctors and surgeons. That's why this school was set up during the devastation after the war. You have good hands, Mr. Martin—supple and compact, ideal for surgery. We've started a year-round program, so you could be out in under three years. What do you think?"

Will gaped at him.

"Are you interested?"

"Yes sir, but I ain't got...I don't have any money."

"That can all be worked out. Normally we require two years of college work as preparation."

Will hung his head. "Well, I guess that lets me out, sir. I had to drop out before high school to work in a lumber camp after my father was killed in an accident."

"Well, your year at the infirmary counts for a lot. But you'd have to take biology and chemistry in summer school to pass the entrance exam."

"I could do that," said Will with renewed hope. "But I was fixing to marry directly, sir."

"Well, congratulations! Ask my secretary for an application on your way out. Complete it and leave it with her, and I'll see what we can come up with."

After filling out the forms and returning them to the secretary, Will walked between the fluted columns fronting the granite building that housed the medical school. The street below was crawling with swarms of carriages, both steam-powered and horse-drawn, all competing for the same lanes with an incessant bleating of their horns.

Will Martin from Mulatto Bald a doctor? He held up his hands and studied them. Supple and compact? Apart from pitching a baseball, weaving cat's cradles, and chopping branches off trees, they had never been any use to him at all. A bully at the mission school named Sam Bradley used to suggest that he join the bearded lady and the three-legged calf in the freak show at the carnival.

But could he ever pass that entrance exam? Dennis was always spouting Latin phrases, but Will didn't know a lick of Latin. Dr. Hopewell would probably make allowances for his lack of academic preparation. But he doubted that Dr. Hopewell, who had grown up in Richmond, could even imagine the one-room mission schoolhouse on Mulatto Bald where the older children had taught the younger ones. Will could recite the books of the Bible at breakneck speed, but that was about it.

Dr. Hopewell didn't seem to think that his marrying would be a problem. If it turned out to be, he wondered if Galicia would mind waiting. But how could he himself stand to delay now that it looked possible to sleep beside her every night?

As her students filed out, Galicia asked Palestine to stay behind.

Palestine looked frightened, her green eyes squinting. "Did I do something wrong?" she whispered.

Galicia shook her head. "I just need to ask you a couple of questions."

Palestine sat back down and eyed Galicia warily. Galicia was not certain she ought to be doing this. She could probably be fired from the Colony and expelled from the teachers' college for exceeding her authority. She only knew that her upcoming marriage to Will would be forever blighted if she were unable somehow to resolve Palestine's dilemma.

Inhaling, she began, "You're my best student, Palestine."

"Thank you, ma'am." Palestine stared intently at the floor.

"Actually, I don't understand why you're here at the Colony. I read in your chart that you were placed here by your husband because you wandered away from home late at night. Is that correct?"

Palestine's chubby cheeks flushed a rosy hue. Galicia was forced to acknowledge that she was pretty—like a plump milkmaid. Galicia struggled not to picture Palestine and Will intertwined in the act of love, as she and Will had not yet been.

"Yes, ma'am."

"Do you mind if I ask why?"

Palestine looked around the room, as though searching for an exit.

"I'd like to help you, Palestine. I don't think you belong here at the Colony."

Palestine said nothing.

"Do you *want* to be here?"

"Kind of."

Galicia frowned. It hadn't occurred to her that Palestine might prefer the Colony inmates to her husband and children.

"Why did you go out wandering in the middle of the night, Palestine?"

Several times she opened her mouth and then closed it, like a fish gasping for air on a creek bank.

"His son," she finally murmured.

"Whose son?"

"My husband's son."

"What about him?"

"He came in there every night."

"Came in where?"

"Came into our bedroom."

"Where was your husband?"

"He drank so much whiskey that he just kept on snoring. Even when I begged him to help me."

"So you left the house at night to get away from your stepson?"

"Yes, ma'am."

"Was he the father of your babies?" asked Galicia, feigning ignorance of Will's role.

"The first baby had another daddy. But the second was from my stepson."

"Did you tell your husband this?"

"Yes, ma'am. But he asked his son, and his son said I was a...."

"It's all right. You can tell me, Palestine."

"He said I was a lying whore," she whispered.

"And your husband took his word over yours?"

She nodded numbly.

"What's happened to your own sons?"

"My husband kept them. I tried to reach the daddy of the first one to come get him. But everyone said he'd left the place where he used to live at."

Galicia concealed her flinch. Swallowing, she continued, "Is your husband nice to your sons?"

Palestine shrugged. She was shredding a scrap of paper with her fingertips, the nails having been chewed down to the quick.

"Would you like to go back home?" Galicia asked hopefully.

"Not if his son was to keep at me like that. But I do miss them babies."

"I'm very sad to hear this, Palestine. I'll do everything I can to help you."

"Thank you, ma'am," she said bleakly.

As Palestine walked out, Galicia tried to sort through her mess of motives, searching for a single one that was pure. But each was tinged by her augmenting fear of losing Will to this adorable, wronged young woman who was his first love and the mother of his only child.

Will lay on the draped table in the operating theater, students watching from behind the railing in the balcony. Dennis waved to him, and he smiled back bravely. Although he would have liked to see this operation performed on someone other than himself, he was glad they had decided to anesthetize him. A mask was placed over his mouth and nose. The lights glaring in his eyes and the murmurs from the students overhead quickly faded into darkness and silence.

When Will awoke, he was lying on a cot in a shadowy room. Raising his head, he looked down at his hands, which were tightly bandaged. He tried to move his fingers. He could have sworn the extra ones wiggled along with the others. Maybe Dr. Hopewell had decided not to remove them?

Swinging his feet to the floor, he sat up, his back bare in the flimsy hospital gown. His left thigh hurt like hell. Shifting aside the gown, he discovered that his thigh was also wrapped in gauze. Then he recalled Dr. Hopewell's warning that he would be taking skin from there to graft onto his hands.

He lay back down and thought happily about the plan Dr. Hopewell had outlined just before the operation that would allow him to attend the medical school. He couldn't wait to tell Galicia. She would be amazed.

A nurse walked into the room. "You feeling okay now, Mr. Martin?"

"Yes, ma'am. A little bit hungry."

"Well, that's a good sign." She stuck a thermometer in his mouth. Then she wrapped a blood pressure cuff around his arm, pumped it up, and read the dial. "Dr. Hopewell said you're free to leave once you're steady on your feet." She read the thermometer.

"Did he cut off my extra fingers?"

She looked at him quizzically. "Yes, sir. That's why your hands are all wrapped up like that."

"Well, I reckon I'll just go along, then."

"Are you sure you're feeling well enough?"

"Yes, ma'am. I'm fine."

Will rode the streetcar out to the teachers' college and walked over to Galicia's dorm, where he asked the receptionist to page Galicia. Then he went into the sitting room and plopped down on a sofa with a floral slipcover, feeling woozy.

"What's wrong, Will?" demanded Galicia, breathless from hurtling down the stairs. Seeing his face looking so gray, she was consumed with dread that he had somehow found out about Palestine.

He held up his bandaged hands. "Nothing's wrong. I've just brought you your wedding gift."

"What have you done?"

"I had my extra fingers removed this morning."

She stared at him. "Is that safe, Will?"

"The head of surgery done it. Did it. So I reckon it is. Now I'm just like everybody else."

"How amazing." She was surprised to feel a twinge of regret. There was something pathetic about the lengths to which they were both prepared to go to fit into this new place, which was so foreign to the world in which they had grown up. He had been her Heathcliff, wild and free, but she had helped tame him. Sometimes it felt like clipping the wings of an eagle.

"Something else," murmured Will, eyes closed.

"What?" She braced herself.

"I've been accepted at the medical college. If I can pass the entrance exam. But I have to go to summer school to pick up some of the subjects I lack."

Her mouth dropped open. "Will! That's incredible! But how can you afford it?"

"They've given me a scholarship. And I can keep my job at the Veterans' Home to earn living expenses."

Galicia gazed down at the Oriental carpet. "So I guess we won't be able to marry any time soon." Unmarried, Will would be even more vulnerable to Palestine's desperate plight. Galicia realized it was time for her to face a future without Will in it.

"I'm afraid not," he said with a hangdog expression intended to mimic her own. "Not any sooner than next weekend."

She looked up.

"They've given me an apartment in the administration building at the Veterans' Home," Will explained. "And Dr. Hopewell, my new advisor at the medical college, spoke to the president of the board here, who agreed to let you finish your degree while living off-campus with your new husband."

Galicia threw back her head and gazed up at the molded tin ceiling, trying to calm her careening emotions. She laughed incredulously. "Good lord, Will, what in the world did we ever do to deserve such luck?"

"Not a thing. That's why they call it luck."

A judge married them at the Leesville courthouse, which was guarded by a gigantic statue of a laconic Confederate soldier cradling a squirrel rifle. Dennis, a rose in his lapel buttonhole, was their witness. Afterwards, he treated them to a roast beef lunch at the Leesville Inn, served on a table with a white linen cloth, which was laid with heavy pewter plates and flatware.

Then they returned to their new apartment, two sparsely furnished rooms at the Veterans' Home, where they spent their first night together. By morning Galicia understood why Palestine had forfeited her future for Will. The only wonder was that Galicia herself had wasted so much time fending him off.

The next day she wrote a note to her parents, informing them of her marriage, of Will's acceptance at medical school, and of the fact that she no longer needed money from them. With dread she handed it to the postman when he arrived with the morning mail.

The following Monday morning Galicia sat once more before Dr. Manning in his office at the Colony. He sounded irritated when he asked, "What can I do for you *now*, Miss Hunter?" He rubbed his pocked jaw with one hand, as though it itched.

"I'm Mrs. Martin now, sir. I got married since I last saw you." She blushed just thinking about the fervent nights she and Will had passed, determined now to make it up to Palestine for having hijacked the happiness that probably should have been hers.

"Well, congratulations, Mrs. Martin." He tapped the tip of his pen on his leather blotter, signaling that he had no time for idle connubial chitchat.

"Sir, I took the liberty of speaking with Palestine McClellan the other day. And I learned that the reason she was wandering the roads at night was to escape from her stepson, who was raping her. With her drunken husband passed out at her side."

Clearing his throat, Dr. Manning asked, "Did she tell this to her husband at the time?"

"Yes, sir. But his son denied it. So her husband refused to believe her. But her second baby was fathered by this stepson."

Dr. Manning remained silent as he digested this unsavory scenario. Then he asked, "And you expect me to accept as reality the erotic fantasies of a confirmed moron, Mrs. Martin?"

Galicia felt a flash of anger. "Sir, I've already explained to you that Palestine is not feebleminded."

"And I suggested, did I not, Mrs. Martin, that you might lack the expertise to be a reliable judge?"

"Yes, sir, you did."

"Mrs. Martin, this is a good example of how one can sometimes fail to maintain sufficient detachment in a work setting. You must learn from this episode. Ask yourself why this particular woman's sad fate concerns you so profoundly as to cloud your professional judgment."

"Because it's not fair!" But if Palestine were not the mother of Will's child, would she still be flogging this dead horse? And was she flogging it from outrage at justice impaired—or from guilt?

"No one ever said that life is fair," replied Dr. Manning, in the soothing voice used by the orderlies prior to slipping a straightjacket onto a violent patient. "Some are born to wealth and some to poverty. Some are born with intelligence and others with psychiatric disorders. The justice of this is known only to our Lord. But to question it is to question the will of God. And that, my dear young lady, amounts to blasphemy."

5

Old Times There Are Not Forgotten: April 1911

Reaching the streetcar stop for the Veterans' Home, Will hopped down and jogged up the driveway, past the brick gateposts and through the grove of ancient oaks. Veterans in gray hats and gold-buttoned uniforms were standing around the garden of clipped boxwoods, which contained a riot of petunias, marigolds, zinnias, and snapdragons that had been force-bloomed in hothouses all over town just for today. The elderly soldiers swapped war stories, somber or hilarious. Some sat in wheelchairs. Many wore black eye patches or lacked limbs. Their wives stood beside them in their best dresses, wearing elaborate hats strewn with fake fruits and flowers. A banner draped across the facade of the administration building read "Welcome, 50 Year Vets!"

Will did a mental calculation: 275 residents at the Veterans' Home, a couple of hundred visiting vets and their wives, the staff of the home, town officials, ministers and politicians. Galicia was one of a half-dozen teachers in charge of pupils from the Leesville schools. This added up to several hundred participants. The cooks had been stockpiling food in the kitchen coolers for days. Buffet tables snaked through the grove beneath the stately old oaks, which had budded early, as though determined to contribute to the festivities.

Rounding the administration building, Will headed to the cemetery. Sloping bleachers had been erected at the base of Phantom's statue, facing the reviewing stand. The parallel rows of identical headstones stretched across the clipped lawn like incisors on parade. Will spotted Colonel Combes standing among them looking exhausted, having weeded and mowed all week long. Will waved, and the colonel nodded.

Then Will saw Galicia, surrounded by students from the Colony, each attired in a red, white, or blue robe, with a hat to match. Their faces had been painted the same color as their robes. The uniformed band members from Leesville High were clustered in the field alongside the cemetery, tuning up—the brasses slurring and bleating, the woodwinds tweeting and chirruping, the snare drums emitting nervous bursts like random gunfire.

Will pulled his watch from his vest pocket. It was nearly time to get started. Galicia and the other teachers began to arrange their students in a long processional line. The band director blew his whistle, and the members assembled behind the drum major in his tall hat and epauletted jacket.

The overseer of the Veterans' Home arrived with his staff. The mayor and his entourage escorted the dapper Senator Lackland, who had just arrived on the train from Washington. Half a dozen legislators from Richmond were already seated. The mayor and the senator climbed into the reviewing stand and started shaking hands and slapping the shoulders of their pinstriped confreres. The veterans and their wives drifted over from the oak grove and began filling the rows of wooden chairs on the flagstones between Phantom's statue and the VIP stand.

The drum major twirled his long baton and blew several blasts on his whistle. The drums rolled in unison, and the marchers stepped out in formation, weaving down the pathways among the headstones, their silver tubas and golden trumpets gleaming in the midday sun. In response to the drum major's whistle, they raised their instruments and launched into a march rendition of "Sewanee River."

The teachers sent their children up the steps into the bleachered box. As they took their places in their tri-colored robes and hats, the lineaments of the Confederate battle flag began to emerge. The veterans and their wives rose stiffly. The men removed their hats and placed them over their hearts, and their wives pulled lace handkerchiefs from their purses.

Soon the Stars and Bars stretched out below the larger-than-life brass Phantom. The children stood on their tiptoes and then bent their knees as instructed, so that the flag appeared to be waving and rippling in some invisible breeze. The band shifted from "Sewanee River" to "Dixie," and the veterans started cheering and whistling through their fingers. A few of the more spry scrambled up onto their chairs and emitted hoarse Rebel yells.

Once the last bass drummer had high-stepped from the cemetery to fall into formation behind Phantom, everyone sat down. The chaplain from the Veterans' Home took the podium, his bald head shining like an ivory cue ball. As though to compensate for the lack of hair on his head, he had grown bristly sideburns like scrub brushes down to his chin.

"Let us pray," he requested. Hundreds of heads bowed. "We are here today to honor those brave Southern heroes who first fired on Fort Sumter in that bay at Charleston fifty years ago today. We also want to honor the heroes of a hundred later battles, who sought to free our homeland from the heel of our northern oppressors. Many of these courageous soldiers have already gone to their celestial barracks in the sky. Some lie safely enfolded in the arms of the earth, beneath the rows of stately marble markers to my left. Seated here before me today are those surviving heroes who are so calmly and fearlessly awaiting the inevitable summons to pitch their tents on the campground of the Lord, where all wounds will be salved, where loyal comrades need part no more...."

Watching tears wet the furrowed faces as the veterans recalled their fallen friends, Will felt bewildered. Here he sat celebrating the fiftieth anniversary of the doomed Confederacy. Yet he was descended from Joshua Martin, the Pilot of the Blue Ridge. The Couchtowners had loathed the Martins because of Joshua's activities on behalf of the Union. No doubt the Leesvillers would have loathed Joshua, too. And Will had to confess that he, like Joshua, would probably have hidden in a hole in the ground rather than march to certain death in orderly ranks, as had the slaughtered comrades of these valiant veterans.

"...help us, Lord," the chaplain concluded, "never to forget the courage shown by the Southern people in our lost struggle to preserve our proud heritage from the ravages of the barbarian invaders from the north. Amen."

"Amen," echoed Will, meaning it. He admired the courage he himself would probably have lacked—even if he, like his distant uncle Joshua, did not particularly admire the cause that had elicited it.

Galicia watched for Will at the streetcar stop across from the mock Greek temple that housed the medical college. They were going to the stadium to watch the Leesville Rebels no doubt lose dismally to a semi-pro team from Richmond. While they ate their supper of hotdogs and peanuts in the stands, she would at last tell him about Palestine. She had been putting it off, not wanting to cloud their current happiness. Besides, Palestine seemed content enough at the Colony, participating in Galicia's classes with enthusiasm. The only burr in the ointment was the thought of Will's son, under the care of a drunken stepfather who was probably less than thrilled to have his wife's cuckoo in his nest. Or had he already farmed the little boy out to some other family?

Palestine had been scheduled to participate in the fiftieth anniversary of the Confederacy at the Veterans' Home a few days earlier. Galicia's sole hope had been that Palestine would prove unrecognizable to Will with her painted face, amid the hundreds of other students. As the inmates at the Colony had climbed onto the trolley, though, Dr. Manning's secretary had called Palestine aside and sent her to see Dr. Manning. Rescued from her own deceit, Galicia had pledged finally to confront Will with Palestine's unpleasant situation. Surely his running off with Palestine was no longer a threat now that he and she were married.

Will dashed out the door and down the steps of the medical school. Just as he reached her, a trolley arrived, its brakes screeching. They climbed on and got off two stops later at the ballpark.

A jostling crowd was slowly converging at the entrance to the field. Will kept his arm around Galicia, pressing her close, looking down at her from time to time with a besotted grin. It was still impossible for them not to touch one another whenever and wherever they were together. Once inside, they found seats overlooking the first baseline. Will waved down a vendor and bought hot dogs.

"When I was a boy chopping trees at the lumber camp," he said, unwrapping his hotdog, his thigh pressed firmly against hers, "I used to imagine that I would play pro ball when I grew up."

"It's not too late."

Will smiled. "Maybe I'll just do that. Hit the road with the Leesville Rebels."

"Don't you dare." Galicia knew that Will possessed a ruthless streak she had not yet witnessed. But Palestine had witnessed it just when she needed him most. He could have insisted that she elope with him and start a life in some distant place, but he had not. Was he capable of deserting Galicia if the going got tough? But he was all she had now. The reply to her letter to her parents announcing her marriage had been a polite note from her mother wishing her and Will well. Galicia could only imagine her father's unexpressed opinion.

"I was just kidding." He patted her hand, puzzled by her sudden ferocity.

As they ate, trying to avoid squirting mustard out the ends of their rolls, Galicia took the plunge: "I have some news, Will."

"What?" He dabbed with his paper napkin at a smear of ketchup in the corner of her mouth.

Trying to rally her courage, she studied the ballplayers in their baggy pants, dashing around the bright green field after the small white ball, like dogs playing fetch.

"What?" he prompted.

"One of my students at the Colony is Palestine Sanders from Couchtown."

Will choked on his mouthful of bun. "Palestine Sanders is at the Colony for the Feebleminded?"

Galicia nodded.

"But why? She's no more feebleminded than you or I."

"That's what I told Dr. Manning the other day. But he didn't believe me."

"Why is she there?"

"Her husband committed her." She told him the entire story, except for the fact that Palestine had been incarcerated at the Colony for a couple of months now.

He said nothing, his olive face darkening.

"Will, I do know that you had a child with her."

He looked at her with consternation. "How did you know that?"

Galicia smiled sourly. "Everyone all over Couchtown knew it. Nobody has any secrets in that place."

"Do you know what's happened to my son, then?"

"I think he stayed with Palestine's husband."

Will gazed bleakly at the green field. "Hell fire, the boy isn't even two years old yet. Is there any way to get Palestine out of there so she can take care of him?"

"Her husband is the only one who can get her released, but he doesn't believe her story that his son assaulted her."

Will studied her, his thoughts elsewhere. "I'll go talk to Dr. Hopewell tomorrow and ask if he'll speak to Dr. Manning. I think they're friends."

"Good idea. I never thought of that."

"How long have you known this?"

"A few weeks."

"Why didn't you tell me right away?"

"It took me a while to realize who she is. She's on my list as Palestine McClellan, not Sanders." Galicia vowed to carry this lie with her to the grave.

Will knocked on the frosted glass of Dr. Hopewell's office door. Dr. Hopewell called for him to enter.

Will removed his bowler, which Galicia had made him buy and which made him feel like Charlie Chaplin. "Good morning, Dr. Hopewell. How are you today?"

Dr. Hopewell's desk was piled with books and papers. "I'm in a hell of a mess, if you really want to know. But have a seat, Will. What can I do for you?"

Will sat in the chair opposite the desk. Struggling to sound detached, he said, "Dr. Hopewell, as you know, my wife is doing her practice teaching at the Colony."

Dr. Hopewell nodded.

"She brought to my attention the situation of one of her students from our hometown." He told Dr. Hopewell Palestine's story, omitting the identity of the father of her first child. "We can both attest to the fact that this young woman is not feebleminded. Is there any chance you could speak to Dr. Manning at the Colony on her behalf?"

Dr. Hopewell's face assumed a nauseated expression. Eventually, he replied, "My intercession won't be necessary, Will. Palestine McClellan has already been released into the custody of her husband."

"But that's wonderful! I guess my wife has more influence than she realizes."

Dr. Hopewell hesitated. "I'm afraid it's not that simple, Will. Dr. Manning told me that Palestine McClellan had already given birth to two feebleminded children. He asked me to clip her Fallopian tubes in order to calm her lustful tendencies. He said that was the only way she could return home to care for her existing children. Based upon the request of her husband, I performed this operation last week. Her husband took her back home yesterday. I shouldn't even be discussing her with you. But I'm very troubled by what you've just told me. If she's actually a normal, healthy young woman and not, in fact, feebleminded, I've done something reprehensible. The operation was performed against her will."

"But, sir, it wasn't *your* fault."

"I was the one wielding the scalpel, so I am responsible."

"But apparently Dr. Manning and her husband misled you."

"Dr. Manning may have been misled by her husband."

"And her husband by his sorry son," snapped Will.

"Well, did the stepson lie about not having raped her?" mused Dr. Hopewell, oblivious to Will's sudden seizure of fury. "Or was the young woman just trying to cover up her own moral frailties?"

Clenching his molars, Will said nothing. Palestine was incapable of lying, but he was too much of a coward to say so. Had her love for Will been a "moral frailty"? Was it a moral frailty to have been raped?

Dr. Hopewell murmured, "Sometimes life can turn very complicated."

But Will knew that Palestine's story was actually simple: the moral frailty had been his own. He had deserted her, and then he had pretended that she had deserted him and had moped around feeling sorry for himself. Had he insisted, she might have gone away with him. He could perhaps have rescued her from all the shame she had had to endure alone, and from the eventual assaults of her stepson. Will had claimed to love her, but he had failed her. If there were any way to make this up to her, he needed to do it. But they were both married now, and not to each other, so his options were few.

Since Will had to cram four years of high school and two years of college into the next four months, he had no time for self-recrimination. He worked all day at the infirmary, studying there during quiet periods. In the evenings he attended biology and chemistry classes at the local college, and he read textbooks half the night and on weekends.

Although Galicia had a teaching position at the Colony for the following fall, the school there was closed for the summer. So she took a job selling cosmetics at a department store downtown. The hours were long, but the work was easy compared to teaching the mentally disturbed. Besides, she and Will had a goal that inspired them both—preparing Will to pass the entrance exam for medical school and then getting him through the program that would make him a doctor. She brought his meals to his desk while he worked, and she coached him on grammar, vocabulary, and literature. She was determined to prove to her parents that she had made a good choice in picking Will as her husband, and he was determined to prove the same thing to all of Couchtown.

Will sat in his shirtsleeves and vest at Dr. Hopewell's sun-splattered desk. Looking at the exam spread out before him, he chomped anxiously on a wad of gum. Sweat dribbled down his forehead and stung his eyes as he scribbled with his pen, trying to solve a math problem. Thanks to Galicia's tutoring, he had already finished the grammar and vocabulary sections. But he would rather have plowed all day long with a stubborn mule than work with fractions.

Dr. Hopewell looked in from the hallway to give him a wink of encouragement.

Once he had disappeared, Will slipped the watch Galicia had given him as a wedding gift out of his vest pocket and consulted it. He got up and took the gum from his mouth. Fixing it on the end of the rod that opened the transom above the door into the hall, he stuck a page from the exam onto the gum. Then he raised the blind, opened the window, and lowered the pole through the opening.

When he pulled the pole back in, the paper was gone. Closing the window and the shade, he returned the gum to his mouth and the rod to the corner. He plopped back down in his chair and resumed his battle with fractions.

Glancing up, he saw Dr. Hopewell's stooped frame once again in the doorway. Blinking like a kindly owl, he smiled and raised a hand with crossed fingers.

As soon as he had vanished, Will felt the full extent of his guilt. Yes, he was cheating. He was deceiving Dr. Hopewell, who was probably the finest man and best doctor he had ever known. But otherwise, he had no prayer of passing this exam. He would be condemned to a lifetime of emptying the bedpans of dying soldiers, and Couchtown would be deprived of the doctor it needed so badly now that the dynasty of Moore doctors was drawing to a close. Four generations of Moores had served that area for over a hundred years, but none of the current Moore sons had gone into medicine, so old Dr. Moore was searching for his own replacement, and Will intended to volunteer.

Checking his watch, Will jumped up and grabbed the pole. Sticking his gum on the tip, he opened the blind and the window and thrust out the pole. When he drew it back in, the page of Latin translations, which Dennis had just completed out in the alley, was firmly attached.

6

Homecoming: December 1911

Although Will had always hitched free rides in empty boxcars late at night, he had bought Galicia and himself tickets between Leesville and Saltville in the passenger car. Now that he could actually see the view, he was startled by the speed at which the countryside flashed past, veiled in swirls of gritty smoke.

Silas was waiting for them at the small Saltville stationhouse, with its overhanging gables that formed a roof above the planked platform. Inspecting their clothing, he said, "My lord, y'all done gone citified on us!"

After welcoming Galicia into the Martin family, he pumped Will's hand. Pausing in mid-shake, he took Will's hand in both of his. Raising it, he inspected the scar. "Where's your extra finger at, Will?"

"I had them removed in Leesville."

"Well, I declare."

Silas tossed their bags into the wagon alongside barrels of salt and other goods for Galicia's father's store. The three climbed up on the seat. Silas shook the reins, and the horses plodded toward the pathway across the Blue Ridge.

"How's everybody back home?" asked Will.

"Fair to middling. Grandmaw's arthur-itis is so bad that she can't hardly walk no more. And she can't hear no more neither. Momma's all right, though."

"Do you have you a girlfriend now?" asked Will.

Silas shrugged bashfully. "Yeah, I reckon. She's a baby sister to that old girlfriend of yours."

"Palestine?"

"Yeah. Her parents don't like me no better than they did you."

They laughed uneasily.

"How is Palestine these days?" ventured Will.

"Hard to say. They don't never hear from her no more."

"And Uncle J.C.?"

"Still preaching up a storm."

"You'd think that man would run out of words."

"Lord, that man has got more words than a hound has fleas."

As they chatted about their endless parade of relatives, and Will's speech reverted to the dialect Galicia despised, she watched the valley fall away alongside them, the buildings of Saltville shrinking to the size of dollhouses. She was apprehensive about this visit, her first since her marriage to Will the previous spring. She and her mother had exchanged several letters full of the mundane details of daily life, but Galicia felt a chilly new distance between them. She prayed her family would treat Will kindly. If not, this might prove a short visit indeed. Should Galicia be forced to choose, she would choose her husband.

Once they reached Couchtown, Silas left them and their bags at the Hunters' house on the main street. Galicia's mother rushed out and exclaimed over their fashionable attire.

"Your father is at the store," she said anxiously. "You can run over there and surprise him, honey, while I feed Will a snack."

Galicia crossed the street and walked into the Five and Dime. She looked around for her father, dreading to hear whatever he might have to say. Matthew, who was cutting calico from a bolt for a customer, waved to her enthusiastically, scissors in hand, and pointed toward the back.

Galicia found her father in the storeroom in his shirtsleeves and bowtie, stacking crates.

"Hi, Daddy."

He turned toward her. To her relief, he smiled. Setting down a crate, he studied her. She walked over to him and they hugged awkwardly.

"Where's Will?"

"Back at the house."

After a long silence he said, "Well, look at you, Galicia. All grown up and married to boot."

"Yes, Will and I are very happy, Daddy."

"Well, I have to confess that I wasn't too pleased when we got your news, Galicia. But it sounds as though Will is determined to make something of himself, and I can only applaud that. He started off life with a big handicap, being a Martin from Mulatto Bald."

"Thank you, Daddy."

At dinner they were all on their best behavior. Will used flawless grammar and all the correct silverware.

"You playing any ball up there at Leesville, Will?" asked Matthew.

"No, I don't have time with medical school and all. But I've seen some pretty fine ballplayers pass through Leesville. They have a real stadium, and Galicia and I go to games every chance we get."

"What are your plans after medical school?" asked Mr. Hunter.

"We hope to come back here, sir. I'm going to ask Dr. Moore tomorrow if he'll keep me in mind as an associate once I graduate."

"It would be wonderful to have you back here," said Mrs. Hunter, unable to prevent her voice from conveying the doubt she was obviously feeling that Couchtown would welcome a Martin as their physician. They all knew it would probably take more than a new suit, a monogrammed shirt, and a fancy degree for townspeople to accept Will in such an intimate role.

The buggy Will and Galicia had borrowed from her father lurched up the new cart road that wound from Silver Valley to the summit of Mulatto Bald.

"I can't believe I've never been up here before," she confessed.

"No reason to have been, unless you wanted to buy you some good moonshine."

Will was nervous about bringing Galicia to meet his family. He wondered if she would be appalled by their cabins, which were crammed with children and devoid of comforts. He also wondered if they would be appalled by her, or rather, by his choice of her as his wife. In their eyes, the worst thing anybody could do was to "git above their raising," and he had certainly done that.

Will halted the horse before the cabin in which he had grown up. Seeing it through eyes now accustomed to city conveniences, he found it dismal. Molting chickens strutted around the dirt yard, pecking at chunks of fallen chinking. Rocks on the roof held down the lichened wooden shakes. He didn't dare look at Galicia to discover her reaction.

A half-dozen barefoot children in faded overalls and flour-sack dresses raced out the door and flung themselves at him. Laughing, he introduced them to Galicia one by one. They ushered Will and his fancy new wife in her skirted suit and flowered hat across the bare yard and into the house, where his mother greeted him with a fierce embrace.

"Momma, meet my wife Galicia."

His mother hugged Galicia. "I'm real pleased to meet you, Galicia honey. We've heard so many nice things about you."

"As I have about all of you."

"Grandmaw, this is my wife Galicia," Will yelled to the wizened little woman who huddled in her brown and yellow afghan by the fire. She didn't respond.

"She can't hear nothing no more," explained his mother.

They sat next to the old woman, who appeared to be in a coma. One of the boys sneaked over and slipped Will's watch from his vest pocket, huddling with the others in the rear of the room to inspect it.

As Galicia chewed homemade molasses candy and sipped herbal tea, she covertly inspected the dim interior—the bunches of herbs and strings of beans and apple slices hanging from the rafters, the rugs hooked from scraps of worn-out clothing, the quilts sewn from the same, the walls papered with bulging layers of newspaper. There were none of the knickknacks that proliferated around her mother's house—the needlepoint pillows and china figurines, the cut-glass vases and framed photographs. After the fleshpots of Leesville, it was like traveling several centuries back in time to pioneer days.

Will was regaling his siblings with an account of the flush toilet in Leesville.

"Why would you want that stuff floating around in a bowl of water where you had to look at it?" asked a younger brother with a dark face, Will's haunting blue eyes, and tight black coils of hair.

"Good question," agreed Will.

The children followed them outside, and Will distributed from a sack in the buggy an orange apiece, hard candy, and a bunch of wrapped presents for Christmas Day. Galicia watched them as they clamored around Will. They displayed several combinations of skin, hair, and eye color, as though each had had different parents. Maybe they had?

"So now you know," he murmured, as their carriage careened down the pathway toward Silver Valley.

"I had no idea."

"I have you to thank for getting me out of there. My only thought was to follow you wherever you went."

"Cream always rises. You would have done something wonderful with your life, Will, no matter what."

"No, I had to find a goal that would make me willing to leave behind everything familiar."

"Are you sorry you did?"

"You know that I'm not." He took her kid-gloved hand in his. But he did feel a fleeting stab of remorse. Life on the bald was hard, so pleasures were simple and valued. But no novelty could ever pique the jaded palates of Leesville, where many citizens appeared greedy, spoiled, and bored. He smiled, remembering the pleasure he and Palestine used to take in the headdresses they wove from oak leaves, honeysuckle vines, ferns, and cardinal flowers.

As they headed down Silver Valley, they passed a tumbled stone ruin grown up to sumac and wild blackberries.

"That's where my ancestors farmed before they moved up on the bald," said Will.

"Why did they move? This looks like much richer soil down here."

"My grandmother used to say that they were forced off this land."

"By whom?"

"I don't really know. It had something to do with the Cherokees getting rounded up and marched out west."

"Do you think some of your ancestors were Cherokees?"

"I don't know. My grandmother used to say they were Porterghee Indians."

"What's Porterghee? Portuguese?"

"Danged if I know."

"Wouldn't it be great if we could buy that land and build a house like that mansion in Leesville, the one with the flush commode?"

"Hold on here, girl! I'm not even out of medical school yet. Don't you go getting notions."

"But Dr. Moore told you this morning that he would keep you in mind as an associate, didn't he?"

"Yes, but a lot depends on what he means by 'keeping me in mind.' You know how people around here are. They'll never tell you no. They just string you along until you get fed up and go away."

"But he asked you to work with him when you can find the time, didn't he?"

Will nodded. "I'm sure he wants to see whether or not his patients would accept a Martin as their next doctor."

"Of course they would, silly." Galicia patted his hand, trying to sound more certain than she felt.

"I wouldn't be so sure, my love. You don't know what it's like to be a Martin from Mulatto Bald."

"I guess I'll be finding out. Because I'm Mrs. Will Martin now, remember?"

"You can't say people didn't try to warn you," muttered Will.

7

Mongrels: August 1913

At the head of the narrow cove sat a weathered plank house two stories high, with sagging porches upstairs and down. Will recalled having several fistfights as a boy with the man who now lived here. Sam Bradley, a couple of years older and twice as big around, had often suggested in the playground at school that Will join the freak show at the carnival because of his extra fingers. Sam had usually won their battles by sitting on him and squashing the breath out of him. Will wondered if he were still a bully.

Climbing the steps to the front porch, Will was greeted by Sam's wife, Laurel, a sweet woman with slumped shoulders and a defeated air. She and Will had also been at the mission school together. "Thank the Lord you've come, Will. I think Sam is near about dead."

"He got knifed?"

She nodded. "You know Sam. He got into a fight. I don't know what about. Nothing probably. Some of his lowlife friends carted him home."

Sam was lying on a bed in a darkened room, fully clothed, eyes closed. Will walked over to him. His flannel shirt was dark with blood. Will reached down to unbutton it.

"Take them weird fingers offen me, Will Martin," growled Sam without opening his eyes.

"Hello, Sam." This was not the time to point out to Sam that his remaining fingers were now the same as everyone else's.

"I want Doc Moore."

"I'm handling his house calls this summer."

"I don't want no Martin scum touching me."

"If I don't stitch you up right away, Sam, you'll probably die. Looks like your heart has been nicked and your chest is filling up with blood."

Dr. Moore was using this summer to find out how many of his patients would agree with Sam's opinion about Will's becoming their physician once he graduated next spring. Will was also getting credit toward graduation for this job, which forced him to apply everything he had learned at the medical college and plenty he hadn't.

"Well, I reckon I'll just go on over to the hillside, then, and get myself buried."

"I'm not kidding, Sam. That's where you'll end up if you won't let me stitch you up."

"I ain't kidding neither. I'd rather just go on to my Maker than to be doctored by one of them nigger Martins."

Will clenched his jaws to keep from punching a dying man.

"Sam honey, please let Will sew up that hole in your heart," pleaded Laurel.

"Shut up, woman. Go fetch Doc Moore like I done told you to in the first place."

"I'll go get him, Pa," said a small boy in the corner whom Will hadn't noticed.

"Well, go on then, son," gasped Sam.

The boy darted from the room. Will sat in a chair by the wall.

Opening one bloodshot eye, Sam demanded, "Why are you still here, Martin?"

"I'm going to wait in case you change your mind."

"I ain't gonna change my mind. You keep them damned deformed hands offen me. If Doc Moore don't come, then I'll just head on over to the graveyard."

Will watched the color start to drain from Sam's face. If Dr. Moore arrived in time, they would have to operate on the spot. He remembered Uncle J.C.'s sermons contrasting the eye-for-an-eye attitude of the Old Testament to the turn-the-other-cheek advice of the New. As a boy, he had returned insult for insult and fist for fist, often getting pulverized in the process. Now he usually turned the other cheek because he had realized that rage, unanswered, turned inward. Attackers performed revenge upon themselves without his having to lift a finger—as Sam was now doing, his breathing having turned shallow and raspy.

Thinking him unconscious, Will stood up and walked over to the bedside.

As he again reached down to unfasten the bloody shirt, Sam snarled, "I done told you to keep away from me, Martin. I know what you're a'doing: you're trying to kill me."

Before Will could deny this, Sam's head slumped to one side, and he was gone. Will bowed his head and wished his soul, if he had one, Godspeed. He had gotten used to death at the Veterans' Home. It no longer scared him. It was where everyone ended up. Knowing that made it easier for Will to love his enemies, or at least not to hate them.

Riding back to town, Will spotted Dr. Moore on a horse headed up the cart road. He was twisted in his saddle, and his face was ashen from the pain of his bulging disk. Behind him rode Sam's son on a saddleless work horse, his bare feet dangling.

"You're too late, Dr. Moore."

"What's happened?"

"A tamponade, I think. He refused to let me examine him. He insisted on you."

"Dead?"

Will glanced at the cowlicked little boy and nodded, recalling the awful moment when he learned that his own father had been killed by a flying log at the splash dam. He had had to drop out of school and work at the lumber camp so his family could eat. His childhood had ended from one day to the next. As would that of Sam's son. The boy's eyes opened wide, and his face blanched.

"I'm sorry, son," said Dr. Moore.

The boy kicked his horse savagely with his heels and jounced up the road toward home.

"Damn stubborn fool," muttered the doctor. "Well, while you were gone, Millie Harmon's husband came to fetch me. She's been in labor for over a day now. Sounds like a breech. Reckon you could run on over there?"

"Yes, sir. I'll go right now."

Gingerly, Dr. Moore turned his mare around and headed back to town at a slow walk, each step probably sending a wave of searing pain down his leg.

Several aproned women clustered around Millie, two holding back her knees so she could push harder, a third wiping her sweaty forehead, and a fourth helping her lean forward during the contractions. Finally, the baby's head popped out, a startled expression on the wizened little face. After a moment the mouth opened in a silent shriek of protest at the mistreatment Will had inflicted as he had repositioned the baby to descend the birth canal headfirst. The women began to laugh and chatter now that it appeared both baby and mother would survive.

As the miniature body, slick and perfect, slid into Will's waiting hands, Will said, "I'm sorry, little fellow, that I had to give you such a hard time."

Will tied off and cut the cord. As a grandmother carried the baby to the kitchen table to clean him up, he gasped and let out a loud wail. Everyone laughed.

While Will awaited the afterbirth, he remembered Millie as a dirty little girl in messy braids, a friend of one of his younger sisters. And here she was giving birth to her third child. All his life he had watched these women on the bald, often no older than fourteen when they began, bear a dozen or more children apiece. Most of the kids he had grown up with were conforming to this pattern as adults. He and Palestine would have been no different if her parents hadn't sent her away. But Palestine would never conceive again now, with her severed tubes, and it was his fault for having failed to help her when she was pregnant with his own child. He wondered if there would ever be a way to relieve the shame he felt, a shame he had never discussed with Galicia from fear of feeding the insecurities he was sure she must harbor concerning the situation. He tried to act with her as though he never thought about Palestine anymore, though he often did, especially here on the bald where he and she had spent their childhoods together. Life had seemed so sweet and innocent then. He and Palestine had wrestled and rolled in the fallen leaves like two puppies in a litter and had strung together necklaces of scarlet haws.

When the baby was reunited with his mother, Will sat at the kitchen table to fill out the birth certificate. "Do you have a name for him yet?" he asked Jerry, the harried father, who had been entertaining his two rambunctious toddlers during the endless labor. The small children now stood silently at their mother's bedside, awed by the tardy new arrival.

"Gibson Harmon, right, honey?" he called to his wife, who nodded weakly.

Will wrote that down, along with the time, date, and parents' names. "Race?" he asked.

"Millie and me is both Indian." Jerry's eyes shifted to a far corner.

Will wrote that down, not knowing if it were true or not. No one on the bald would ever admit to being Negro because then you lost any hope of voting or getting a fair trial at the courthouse. Besides, no one up here knew what the truth actually was, so they identified themselves as whatever would help them most. Those with dark skin, like Jerry, claimed to be Indian. The rest claimed to be white. The officials in town, several of whom had cousins on the bald, went along with this since it was impossible to prove one way or the other.

"I'll deliver this to the county clerk in Couchtown. You can get a stamped copy from him the next time you come to town."

Jerry nodded. He handed Will a burlap sack of green beans, saying, "This is all we got right now, Will. But I'll bring you some cash money once I sell my 'baccy in the fall."

"That's fine, Jerry. I know you'll pay Doc Moore when you can."

Exiting from the shack, which was roofed with rusted tin soft-drink signs, Will fastened his black leather medicine bag and the sack of beans behind the saddle and mounted Dr. Moore's gelding.

As he rode along the ridge down to Silver Valley, Will calculated that about half his new patients had been happy to see him, and half had not been. But only Sam had refused treatment. Dr. Moore was handling the office visits and the house calls in town. Will was assisting him in operations, tending the horses, and taking the house calls in the hills as well as the night calls in town. If both were still satisfied by the time Will and Galicia left for Leesville at the end of this summer, they would resume the arrangement after Will's graduation the following spring, and Will would gradually take over the practice so that Dr. Moore could retire. Those who doubted his abilities would have to get over their misgivings because he would soon be the only doctor for miles around.

Galicia sat atop a tall stepladder in her father's store, listing boxes of shoes on an inventory sheet. She recalled the morning Will had found her in this same spot after his pop foul hit her between the eyes. It seemed almost impossible now that she had not known him until that day. Now he was the center of her world. If she was not with him, she was thinking about him. She wondered what she used to think about before.

Motes drifted languidly in a shaft of golden sunlight slanting through the west-facing window. Soon she would return to their tiny apartment above the stables in Dr. Moore's barn. It was hard to know how to time their supper. As Will always said, Birth and Death didn't carry watches.

Climbing down the ladder, she called to Matthew behind the counter, "So long, Matt. I'm heading home now." He waved. She walked out the door and down the street, smiling at a circle of children playing jacks on a newly paved patch of sidewalk.

Hearing the horses snorting and neighing, she entered the stable and gave each his scoop of oats and a forkful of hay. Then she filled the crook of one arm with kindling and mounted the steps to the apartment. After starting a fire in the stove, she mixed batter and placed a tin of cornbread in the oven. Then she flopped down in one of the two armchairs in the cramped sitting area. Soon she was sound asleep.

She woke up, damp with sweat, to the odor of burning cornbread. Jumping up, she ran to the oven and removed the charred remains. Dumping them into the garbage, she started over again. As she slipped the pan into the stove, she heard the horses nickering, followed by the weary clomp of Will's boots up the steps.

"I fell asleep and burned the cornbread," she confessed, as he ducked through the low doorway into their dollhouse. The sun had set, and the room was shadowy. The frogs and night insects had begun their cantata by the creekside.

"It's late. You must be starved," he said.

"Not for supper." She smiled at him.

He walked over and took her in his arms. Pressed against his chest, she inhaled his familiar scent, mixed with the odor of horse lather and saddle leather.

"I should go down to the creek and wash off."

"Not a chance," she murmured, unbuttoning his suspenders.

"Lord, woman, what's happened to you? You used to be so prim that I didn't even dare pull out one of them ivory hair pins."

"You've made me a wanton woman, Will Martin." She sank to the carpet, dragging him down beside her. Even *Wuthering Heights* had not prepared her for the hungers he had unleashed in her. She had thought she was civilizing her wild mountain boy, while he had been turning her into a wild mountain girl instead.

8

A Roll of the Dice: November 1913

Will stood over the anesthetized patient, his hands deeply buried in her belly, suturing by feel with his left hand. Blood was seeping from her artery into "The Hole," as the other medical students called the abdominal cavity, as though it were a construction site. Dr. Hopewell stood beside him, with his gloved hands poised to intervene. The lights overhead were hot. Will felt sweat beading on his forehead between his cap and mask, soon to dribble into his eyes. Just in time, a nurse wiped it away with a towel.

A dozen students leaned on the railing above, concentrating as intently as spiritualists at a seance. After tying the last knot, Will withdrew the clamp. His friends in the balcony silently celebrated, as though he had roped a calf in record time. The nurse blotted up the blood in the cavity with gauze. As a second-year student sutured the incision, Will stepped back, rolled down his gloves, and lowered his mask, taking a gulp of fresh air.

"Well done," murmured Dr. Hopewell.

Walking from the operating room to the dressing room, Dr. Hopewell said, "You have no idea what an asset being able to work with both hands will prove, Will. I only wish I could!"

"I used to drive my teacher at school crazy, switching my pen from hand to hand. One time she tied my left hand behind my back, saying I'd have an easier life if I learned to be just right-handed."

Dr. Hopewell smiled. "Where are you thinking of practicing after graduation, Will?"

"My wife and I plan to head on back home to Couchtown. The only doctor there is over sixty and wants to retire. He's the one I worked for this past summer."

"So you're going to become a country doctor?"

"Yes, sir." But he didn't intend to confess to Dr. Hopewell his concerns about whether Couchtown would want a Martin from Mulatto Bald as their doctor. Dr. Hopewell didn't appear to find his heritage strange, so there was no reason to put that idea into his head.

"Well, that's an admirable ambition. But it will be a hard life, on call day and night all week long. If you should have second thoughts, I could probably find you a position here at the medical school. You have a rare talent for surgery—manual dexterity plus a risk-taking temperament."

"You're very kind, sir. But my wife trained on a scholarship at the teachers' college, and they expect her to go back home and help out there." He also didn't see the need to mention right now that his wife was pregnant and would probably not be teaching anywhere—a development that neither of them had intended, but that both had enthusiastically participated in.

"I would say you're both needed more there than here."

"Yes, sir, that's true enough." Will was resigned by now to the patronizing tone city folks adopted when discussing his highland home.

Pulling on his suit coat, he headed out the door and dashed to the streetcar stop just as one was pulling out. He jumped up on the back step and climbed into the car. Sitting down, he watched the storefronts parade past, with their elaborate facades that mimicked Renaissance palaces and Egyptian tombs. Although he loved surgery, his favorite part of the day was still ahead of him—bedtime, when he and Galicia snuggled up and told each other everything they had thought and done while apart. His only hope was that the presence of a new baby would not alter these precious times together too much.

The conductor, who had been working his way down the aisle with his pad of tickets, stopped beside Will. Will reached in his suit pocket for his fare and held it out to the conductor.

The conductor leaned over and said in his ear, "Let's not make a scene, boy. At the next stop just hop off and get into that car behind us."

Will looked up at him with consternation. "But I'm not colored, sir," he said in a low voice.

"You and I both know what you are," the conductor murmured.

The trolley screeched to a halt. The conductor took hold of Will's upper arm and assisted him to his feet. Will was too stunned to resist as the conductor escorted him to the exit. A couple of passengers looked up. The others didn't notice, or pretended not to.

"I'm sorry, boy. But if I let you ride up here, I could get fined. Too many fines and I get fired. Here's your ticket. Just climb on that car behind us."

Will stumbled down the steps. Rather than getting on the rear car, he stood there and watched the trolley move on down the tracks.

Galicia sat at her desk idly fingering the red-veined stone from her great-grandmother, Galicia Hunter, which hung on a gold chain around her neck. Her students were struggling over a passage in their readers. She always had them decorate the library in keeping with the seasons and holidays. At the moment, construction paper silhouettes of pilgrims, turkeys, and autumn leaves festooned the walls.

But any day now her pregnancy would start to show, and she would have to abandon this class that she loved so much. She had recently stopped wearing her corset and would soon have to let out the waistbands on her skirts. She hadn't yet notified Dr. Manning. He considered pregnant teachers a liability. He felt the students would be stimulated to lascivious thoughts and actions by the presence of someone who had so obviously indulged in the carnal pursuits denied to them.

Although Galicia was excited about this baby, she was apprehensive about giving up her job, which she enjoyed. She also enjoyed the salary, however modest. She and Will had always meant to have children, but they had not intended to have one so soon. Their brains had shut down that stifling summer evening when she had burned the cornbread. She had often wondered since about the awkward timing of this baby. She hated the thought that she might have gotten pregnant to put any idea of rescuing Palestine out of Will's head for good. But sometimes she thought that, just the same.

"Who can tell me about what she has just read?" asked Galicia.

Waiting for a volunteer, she thought about how Palestine used to participate in these discussions with such enthusiasm, sparking the rest of the class like the electric line overhead that propelled the streetcars. Galicia hoped she was okay back home with her rapist stepson. At least Will's son had his mother there to defend him now. She wondered if Will worried about them. They never discussed the topic. It lay between them like the corpse at a wake.

Will and Galicia sat at the small round dining table in their sitting room at the Veterans' Home, eating Will's favorite supper of soup beans, collard greens, and cornbread. Will was uncharacteristically silent.

"Is something wrong?" she asked. Her own stomach was churning mercilessly. She wondered who in the world named this condition "morning sickness." It afflicted her all day long.

Will looked up from shoveling beans into his mouth. His blue eyes squinted, as they always did when he was upset about something. He looked back down at his beans. They sat in silence, buttering and chewing their cornbread.

"What's going on, honey?"

He heaved a sigh. "I may as well tell you, Galicia. I got kicked off the streetcar today."

"You what?"

"Got asked to move to the colored car on the trolley."

Galicia stared at him. "But why?"

"The conductor apparently thought I look colored."

"Did you tell him you're not?"

"Yes, but he didn't believe me."

"So you just got off?"

"I was too shocked to make a fuss."

"Did anyone defend you?"

"No," he said bleakly.

Galicia studied his handsome face. It was dark, but no darker than that of many other whites. He had said his grandmother claimed to be part Porterghee Indian, whatever that was. All of a sudden,

Galicia realized that this action by a streetcar conductor concerned her for reasons other than just her love for Will. "One time you said my family and yours are related. Do you think that's really true?"

"I don't know. That's what my mother and grandmother always said."

"So if you're part Indian, or Negro, or Portuguese, or all of those, and if I am too, what's our baby going to look like?"

"After I got kicked off that streetcar, I went back to the medical library and spent a couple of hours reading up on genetics. I learned that when both parents are a racial mix, it's like rolling a handful of dice. Their baby could come out looking any which way—paler than the paler parent, darker than the darker one, or anything in between. Of course when it's something unexpected or unwelcome, people always accuse the mother of having messed around."

Galicia sighed. "Well, at least you know that I've never been with anyone but you." *Unlike you,* she added silently.

Will nodded.

"What should we do?" asked Galicia.

"Maybe we should move up north, if I could find work."

"I thought the Civil War was fought to end all this?"

"I guess it ended the slavery—but not the hatefulness."

Galicia sat at her desk watching her students work on a quiz. She couldn't tell if the churning in her stomach were morning sickness or anxiety from Will's streetcar experience the previous day. She had never paid much attention to skin color before. Most shades had been represented in Couchtown, and no one appeared to notice or care. They took people at their word about their ancestry. But Will's summary of genetics at supper last night had abruptly sensitized her to the topic. As she inspected the lowered faces of her students, she realized that the complexions of most were at least as dark as Will's— olive or ruddy, copper or deeply tanned. The hair of some was straight and silky, whereas others had springy curls—in many different shades of brown, black, and red. No blonds. But lots of blue eyes as well as various tones of green, brown, and black.

After class Galicia walked to the administration building and requested her students' records, which she had made a point of not reading before. Sitting down and working her way through the stack, she discovered that almost her entire class had come from rural areas and small towns in the Blue Ridge and the Cumberlands, along the southern and western borders of Virginia. The parents of several were labeled "vagrants." Many were referred to as "half breeds" or "mulattos." Their occupations were listed as farmers, basketmakers, weavers, harness makers, horse traders, and tinkers.

Leaning back in her chair, Galicia felt the coin drop: her "feeblemineded" students, although living in plain view, were not supposed to exist at all. They were descendants of Indians who had evaded the westward removal, of escaped slaves and free blacks who had fled the Tidewater and the cotton plantations of the Deep South, of all the dark-complexioned fugitives who had clustered together on remote mountaintops and in inaccessible swamps on poor land that the more fair-skinned settlers had shunned.

Her students were living proof that these despised groups and the encroaching white settlers had done more in past centuries than just hate and kill each other. Some had mingled and mated—and perhaps even loved one another. By locking their descendants up at the Colony until they were too old to reproduce, the state of Virginia was trying to exterminate them—and with them, all evidence that this miscegenation by their hallowed ancestors had ever occurred.

Will was one such descendant. She might be another. And the baby now sheltered in her womb was the innocent heir to all this illicit mixing. In a few months' time, their infant would emerge into a vicious world that would respond with contempt should his or her skin be the wrong shade. What could she and Will do to protect this helpless child that their passion had created?

9

The Perils of Pauline: March 1914

Will and Galicia were sitting in the new movie house in downtown Leesville, watching a locomotive hurtle along toward a young woman chained to the track. Driving the engine was the cad who had chained her there for refusing his advances. An automobile raced alongside the train, driven by her beau, who was intent on saving her. The piano player at the front of the movie house appeared to be having seizures as she pounded chords intended to convey the urgency of the situation.

Will reached over and took Galicia's hand. These movies were her only excitement these days—heroines climbing down knotted bedsheets to escape burning buildings, or trapped in boxcars on runaway trains. Since resigning from her job at the Colony, she mostly sat reading all day in their tiny apartment at the Veterans' Home. Sometimes she lumbered around the grounds chatting with the yardmen and the veterans out for strolls. She made perfect meals for Will and kept their home as spotless as an operating room. She also knitted and sewed little pieces of clothing. He only hoped she wasn't finding this routine as boring as he would. Presumably she had some inner dialogue going on with their baby that consoled her for having had to give up her career.

Once the beau had won the race, rescued his love from the tracks, and handed the cad over to the police, Will and Galicia followed the crowd from the theater over to the streetcar stop. Each time Will waited for the streetcar now, his scalp prickled with anxiety. He had been sent to the colored car a second time back in the winter. But otherwise no one seemed to notice or question his presence in the white car. He had not told Galicia about this second episode. She was alarmed enough over the first one. In the beginning they had discussed endlessly what they would do if their baby were born with dark skin. But for the last couple of months the topic had lain dormant between them, even though they had not found a solution.

The streetcar arrived, and Will and Galicia rode it home without incident. Back at their apartment they got ready for bed. As they lay under the covers, Galicia's belly began to distend.

"There he goes again!" she laughed. "Practicing his curve ball."

"Why are you so sure it's a boy?"

"I don't think a girl would punch and poke me so mercilessly."

Will lay his head on her belly and began to stroke the shuddering bulges and to sing softly: "Are you washed in the blood, in the soul-cleansing blood of the lamb...."

Gradually the baby's thrashing ceased, as though the infant were listening.

"If you turn our baby into a hard-shell Baptist, I'll kill you," said Galicia.

"Would you prefer a Presbyterian?" He started singing "Come, Thou Almighty King" in his rich baritone.

When Will had ended his serenade, Galicia said, "I feel like that girl chained to the tracks in the movie tonight."

He sat up and looked at her. "How do you mean?"

"This baby will be coming out soon. We don't know what he or she will look like, so we can't plan what to do. And there's no way I can escape this disaster that's rolling towards us like that locomotive engine."

"Except by having faith that, whatever happens, we three will be together and will make a happy life for ourselves somewhere on God's green earth. This isn't a disaster, Galicia. This is the most wonderful thing that's ever happened to either of us. This baby is the fruit of our love for one another."

Galicia took his face in both her hands and kissed his mouth. "Thank you, Will. You always know how to make me feel better."

Will turned off the table lamp and curved his body around hers, his arm across her side and his hand caressing her huge belly. As he lay there in the dark, he tried to heed his own words, but he was afraid. And he was mad that he had to be afraid. What kind of a world was this in which the arrival of an innocent baby might be a cause for alarm rather than rejoicing? They would love this baby no matter what, but how the poor child looked would determine the future for all three of them.

Will climbed on the streetcar at the stop near the medical college. As the car picked up speed, his scalp prickled as he watched an unfamiliar conductor move down the aisle collecting fares. When he reached Will, he looked up from his ticket book. Will studied his face. It remained composed. Will held out his fare. The man ripped off a ticket, handed it to Will, and moved on.

Will rode the car to the end of the line, the dock area on the banks of the James River where he had never been before. Hopping off, he followed a muddy path alongside the river to the shantytown where the Negroes lived, staining his dress shoes with orange clay as he dodged puddles filmed with mosquito larvae. The shacks, similar to those on Mulatto Bald, were the first to be inundated when the James overflowed. Most were flimsy old cabins with clutter in the front yards, and outhouses and livestock in the back.

The people Will passed smiled or spoke in greeting, none seeming surprised by the presence of a white man in their midst. Were they just being polite to a stranger, or did they see him as one of them? He came to a store housed in a rambling frame building. Going inside, he spotted people eating lunch at several wooden tables. He sat at an unoccupied table and read the menu written in chalk on a blackboard on the wall. A young woman in a red headscarf came over to take his order. He asked for soup beans, collard greens, and cornbread.

As Will ate, he reflected that the food and the housing in the shantytown were identical to what he had grown up with on Mulatto Bald. The soft accents and rhythms of the voices at the other tables as they joked and gossiped with one another were also familiar. When he had entered, the other diners had glanced at him as a newcomer, but no one had seemed startled by his arrival. He wondered if he and

Galicia and their baby could make a life for themselves down here. He probably could, and a baby could flourish wherever it was taken if it were loved and cared for. But Galicia's fitting in here was another matter. Her face was so pale that it turned bright red when she sat in the sun. She would stand out here like a nickel among pennies.

As he sopped up the liquid from his beans with a chunk of cornbread, he realized that although he had grown up in similar surroundings, he had not grown up knowing that he was the heir of slaves transported from Africa. Perhaps he was, but that possibility had gone unspoken on the bald. However horrible the history of these people in the shantytown, at least they *had* a history. And they had the self-assurance that came from knowing who they were and where their ancestors had come from, an assurance that he and most on Mulatto Bald lacked.

The bewilderment from all those years of uncertainty washed over him. Was he an Indian? A Negro? White? Portuguese? All of those? He didn't know. His mother and grandmother didn't know. No one on Mulatto Bald knew. And there was no way to find out. Even if someone had claimed to know, there was no way to prove it. Their ancestors had long ago simply clammed up, no doubt trying to protect their descendants from persecution, at the expense of robbing them of their identity. Soon he and Galicia would have a baby. Where could they take their infant so that he or she could feel some sense of safety and belonging? Probably it would be best just to go back home to Mulatto Bald, where no one asked you unanswerable questions or judged you by physical characteristics over which you had no control.

Riding the streetcar unchallenged back to town, Will climbed down and walked along the main street toward the medical college. For the first time he noticed the cement drinking fountains by the central square—two identical ones side by side. One had a metal sign hanging from it on a chain. It read "Colored." How could he not have noticed this before? He felt like Saul on the road to Damascus, with the scales falling from his previously blinded eyes.

Struggling to compose himself, Will went up the steps into the medical school and turned left into the library. From the rack of newspapers he took the pole on which hung that day's *Leesville Gazette*. He sat at a long oak table and spread out the paper. On the front page was a picture of a young man wearing only trousers, hanging by his neck from a tree branch. His bare chest glistened, and some of his ribs protruded through his charred flesh. The headline read "Angry Mob Burns 'Secret Negro.'" Will studied the grainy photograph. The man's face appeared pale, and his features looked European. The black hair hanging in his eyes was glossy and straight, like an Indian's.

Reading the article, Will learned that the man's chest was gleaming because he had been doused in coal oil. A group of white men had tortured him with red hot tongs for an hour before setting him on fire. Hundreds had watched. Some had brought picnics in baskets. The daughter of a prominent white merchant in the next county had been dragged from the site, screaming that she had not been raped, that the man was her husband, that she loved him, that he was not a Negro. The article said witnesses had been brought from Norfolk to testify in court that the man had been raised by black parents in the African community there. One of his executioners was quoted as calling him a "secret nigger." Authorities claimed they were unable to identify or apprehend the murderers, even though Will could plainly see the leering faces of two of them in the background of the photo.

Will's stomach clenched. Leaning back in his chair, he closed his eyes and tried to erase from his mind the image of the dangling man with the charred ribs. Unsuccessful, he pushed back his chair and stood up. Going into the bathroom, he went to the sink and filled his cupped hands with cool water. He splashed his face repeatedly.

With water still dripping from his jaws, he looked up to study himself in the mirror. A large, crooked nose. Absurdly long earlobes. Coarse black hair that kept falling into his eyes. Skin that turned as dark as a Bedouin's when he worked in the sun. The blue eyes of a sled dog. Weird looking, but surely not someone you would automatically pick out as colored? What had those conductors seen when they kicked him off the streetcar? Where was this mysterious line between black and white? But apparently appearances made no difference to men who believed that they could detect "secret niggers." Hearsay had maintained that the man was black, and that was enough evidence on which to murder him for loving a white woman.

Galicia's father wasn't thrilled about having Will as a son-in-law, but he would never turn him over to a lynch mob. Was there anyone else with a motive for such a thing? Palestine's father maybe. But Palestine's heritage was as confused as his own, and her father wouldn't want to draw attention to it.

Will drew a deep breath. He couldn't talk this over with Galicia. She had enough to worry about as she faced labor and childbirth. He could probably talk to Dr. Hopewell, who seemed without prejudice. During the war he had saved the lives of both Southerners and Yankees, blacks and whites, anyone unlucky enough to turn up at the Pest House. He appeared to live by the Hippocratic oath to do no harm, both in the office and out. In any case, he was as close as Will could come now to having a father.

Will leaned in the doorway, his arms folded across his chest, waiting for Dr. Hopewell to look up from his desk.

"Ah, Will. How long have you been standing there? What can I do for you?" He blinked his eyes behind his round rimless lenses, doing what Will had come to think of as his owl imitation.

"I'm sorry to interrupt you, sir."

"I've just finished what I was doing. Take a seat. I could use one of your amusing tales from the hills."

Will smiled weakly as he sat down. "Actually, I wanted to ask if you know anybody up north who might hire me after graduation."

Dr. Hopewell studied him. "I might. But frankly, they'd like you up there, with that accent of yours, just about as much as they like Yankees down here. Why would you want to go up there anyhow?"

"Well, my wife and I thought our baby might have more opportunities."

"Do you want my honest opinion?"

"Yes, sir, that's why I asked you."

"I doubt if you could find a job to match your skills up there right now. Things are still pretty raw between the North and the South."

"But my people fought for the Union."

Dr. Hopewell blinked. "Did they really?"

"Well, they mostly hid out in the hills. A few enlisted in the Union army. A few in the Confederate. Others burned railroad bridges for the Yankees. One led escaped prisoners across the Federal lines into Kentucky. Half a dozen got shot dead for it."

Dr. Hopewell shook his head. "I never knew that."

"I don't spread it around freely. I reckon I could get run out of Leesville."

Dr. Hopewell nodded. "Those were awful times, Will. The killing just went on and on. It was so pointless." He shook his head vigorously, as though trying to rid himself of his memories of the boxcars stacked with the corpses of handsome young men packed in salt. "Will, you were accepted here with the expectation that you would stay in the South. There are plenty of doctors up north, but not so many down here. You are badly needed here."

"Yes, sir. Well, I guess I might as well tell you my reason: I get sent to the colored streetcar from time to time. So I'm worried about what that means for my wife and our baby."

Dr. Hopewell frowned. "Are your people mixed?" He asked this as calmly as if discussing the weather.

"I think so. But we don't know what the mixture consists of. My grandmother always used to say we were Porterghee Indians."

"Portuguese?"

"I guess so."

"It's possible. This whole region used to be owned by Spain. I'm sure there were some Portuguese around in the old days—sailors, soldiers, explorers, settlers. Some slaves came from the Portuguese colonies in Africa."

"Well, I don't see how my ancestors could have known the word Porterghee if there weren't some basis in truth. They weren't educated people. I doubt if they would ever have even heard of a country named Portugal. But it doesn't seem to matter nowadays whether you're Indian or Negro or Portuguese or gypsy or whatever. If you look dark, you're colored and you can't ride the white streetcar or drink at the white water fountain."

Dr. Hopewell nodded with his eyes closed, as though in pain. "You're right, Will. Something horrible is happening in Virginia right now. There are people behind the scenes, some of them men I've considered my friends, like Dr. Manning at the Colony, working to pass laws that will categorize everyone as either Negro or white. Nothing else, and nothing in between."

"What about Indians?"

"They claim the Indian tribes have all intermarried with blacks and are therefore black themselves. If these men succeed, there will no longer be any Indians in the state of Virginia. If it weren't so horrifying, it would be amusing because the fanciest families in Virginia claim descent from Pocahontas. So if these new laws pass, many of our honored gentry will be designated Negro."

"But why now?"

"I think it's a reaction to the tiny bit of power blacks gained after the war. Some whites want Negroes back in their place—and certainly not mating with whites and 'polluting' our pure Anglo-Saxon bloodlines. You should hear Dr. Manning. He regards racially mixed people as the scum of the earth, far inferior to blacks. He plans to eradicate them by sterilizing them all."

Will hid his flinch as he thought about Palestine. "But racial mixing must have gone on since time began, sir."

"Haven't you learned yet that that's one of the things we don't talk about in Virginia, son?" Dr Hopewell smiled bitterly.

"And the people who can't hide it just vanish into the swamps or onto the ridgetops where the Anglo-Saxons won't have to look at them?"

Dr. Hopewell nodded. "I think our legislators in Richmond have lost what little sense they ever had. They've just passed a new statute mandating segregated housing. Have you seen that memo?"

Will nodded no.

Dr. Hopewell rifled through a stack of papers on his desk and passed a sheet to Will.

Will read, "The preservation of the public morals, public health, and public order in the cities and towns of this commonwealth is endangered by the residence of white and colored people in close proximity to one another." Skimming the rest of the memo, he discovered that all municipalities in the state were now required to set up segregation districts in which the other race would not be allowed to live.

"I don't know where this is all leading, Will. But I'll be frank with you: if you were to get classified as colored and your wife as white, your marriage would be illegal and your child illegitimate. And she could go to prison for two to five years."

"And I could get lynched. Did you see today's paper?"

Dr. Hopewell nodded. "I wasn't going to mention that."

"What in hell can we do?"

"Dr. Manning and his colleagues are constructing a hell right here on earth. And I'm just waiting for them to turn on me for not joining their witch hunt. They'll probably label me a 'secret nigger' before this is over. For all I know, I may be one. And Dr. Manning may be, too. Why else would he need to be so rabid about denying it?"

They sat in silence for a while.

Then Dr. Hopewell said, "I just heard that a new town is being built as a base for northern industries. It's just across the state line in Tennessee. They need some good doctors. You could get a fresh start in a new place."

"Would it be any different down there?"

"The town will be full of folks from the north and from southern cities, professional people with education and degrees. I doubt if you and your wife would stir any notice in a place where everyone will be too busy building a new town to go looking for trouble."

They studied one another. Will felt a flicker of hope. "Thank you, sir. That sounds interesting. Could you put me in touch with whomever is in charge?"

As he walked down the hallway toward the exit door, Will reflected that fleeing Virginia to protect Galicia and their baby would leave his firstborn more unprotected than ever. He had done nothing so far to help his and Palestine's son. He had thought about sending Palestine some money, but her husband might punish her for such proof of her involvement with another man. Sometimes he imagined going out to the old man's farm and hiding in the hayloft and watching to make sure Palestine and his son were being well-treated. And if they weren't....

This was where his heroic fantasy always bogged down. If they were being mistreated, what on earth could he do about it? If only he were one of those Old Testament patriarchs Uncle J.C. used to carry on about, with a passel of wives and children, goats and sheep, camels and tents and carpets. He and Galicia and Palestine and their children could become nomads, folding up their tents and moving on whenever they had outstayed their welcome.

By loving Palestine, he had done her damage. And there appeared no way to make it up to her now that he was married to Galicia with a new baby on the way. He vowed to do a better job of protecting and providing for Galicia and this new baby. It was the only form of penance he could think of. He felt like a carrier of the plague, running around ruining the life of every woman he ever loved. Galicia's father was right not to want her mixed up with a man from Mulatto Bald.

Galicia tossed the *Leesville Gazette* on to the carpet beside the couch on which she was lying. She placed her forearm over her eyes and tried, without success, to erase the image of the young man hanged and burned in front of a cheering crowd for loving a white woman. What in the world was wrong with these people? They applauded those who hated and murdered those who loved.

She could feel her baby cavorting in her womb. It was nice the poor creature was having so much fun in there because when he or she emerged, the fun might cease for all three of them. She and Will had married three years ago today. Life had seemed so simple then, and the future so rosy.

The door opened. Galicia sat up and watched Will walk through it in the three-piece suit he always wore to classes. He came over to the couch and looked down at the newspaper.

"So you saw it?"

Galicia nodded.

"I wish you hadn't."

"Believe me, so do I."

"Well, we're not going to sit around here moping all evening. I'm taking you out, just as I promised, to celebrate our anniversary. There's a new *Perils of Pauline* on at the theater. And I've made reservations at the Leesburg Inn for dinner afterwards."

"Good idea." Galicia struggled to her feet and went into the bedroom to change into her best maternity dress, a tent-like garment with a layered skirt that came to her ankles. She put on some of the make-up she had bought on sale from the cosmetics counter at which she had worked a couple of summers ago, and she hung the reddish black stone handed down by her distant aunt Galicia around her neck on its gold chain.

They sat in the theater holding hands while Pauline ran a gauntlet of Indians wielding clubs. They had kidnapped her from her family's wilderness cabin. When she reached the end of the row of tormentors, she dodged their grasp and kept running. As she careened down a hillside and appeared on the verge of escaping, her pursuers rolled a boulder to the top of the hill and then pushed it down the slope. Pauline glanced behind her to discover a huge rolling rock about to overtake her. She stepped aside just in time to avoid being flattened like a pancake. A posse of cowboys greeted her at the bottom of the hill and shot down the approaching Indians.

"No wonder everyone hates Indians," muttered Will as they stood up and moved toward the exit.

"Who hates Indians?"

"Dr. Hopewell told me today that the state of Virginia is trying to legislate them out of existence. Your old boss at the Colony, Dr. Manning, is one of the ringleaders."

"That doesn't surprise me a bit. He used to insist that feeblemindedness was hereditary and caused crime, alcoholism, and prostitution. Most of my students were racially ambiguous, and he had total contempt for them."

As they reached the sidewalk, Galicia glanced over at the iron staircase on the outside of the theater, which descended from the balcony. It was lined with exiting black people in their Sunday best, chatting among themselves about Pauline's latest escapade. She nudged Will and nodded toward the staircase. "I never noticed that until tonight. Did you?"

Will nodded. "I seem to be noticing all the outrages I've managed to ignore until now—now that they may apply to me and my family. I'm embarrassed that I didn't notice them before, on behalf of humanity in general."

Will had arranged for them to be seated at the very table in the Leesburg Inn at which Dennis had treated them to their wedding lunch. It was covered with a starched white linen cloth and laid with heavy pewter plates and cutlery.

"Strange to think that lunch with Dennis was only three years ago," mused Galicia. "It feels like another lifetime. A much more innocent lifetime."

"Are you sorry we married?" Will straightened the knot of his tie and checked the folds on his shirt collar.

"You know I'm not." She removed her slipper and stroked Will's calf with her foot.

"I have a plan to propose." He told her about the new industrial center being built across the state line in Tennessee.

"Couldn't we just go back to Couchtown as we had planned?"

"I don't think so, my love. Dr. Hopewell says Dr. Manning and his gang are working to segregate the entire state. That will eventually include Couchtown. They've already passed a segregated housing statute for the cities. By the time they get through, you and I might find ourselves on opposite sides of their color line. You could go to prison and I could get lynched. Then what would become of our child?"

"Couldn't we just live in Couchtown and wait to see if it gets that bad? Maybe Dr. Hopewell is wrong."

"It takes a long time for a doctor to build a practice. It's not that easy to start over. Besides, do we really want to be looking over our shoulders all the time, waiting for the ax to fall?"

"But wouldn't we be doing that in this new town, too? Is Tennessee any more tolerant than Virginia?"

"Not more tolerant, just less organized. Tennessee has passed some horrendous laws, too, but Dr. Hopewell thinks everyone will be too busy building this new town to notice or care about the color of people's skin. In any case, no one in Tennessee is likely to have heard of the infamous Martins from Mulatto Bald."

"Let me think about it. It's not a bad idea."

10

Holston: May 1914

Will and Galicia once again rode the train to Saltville, but this time they remained in their seats at the rail yard as boxcars carrying parts for the salt works were uncoupled onto a siding with much banging, clanking, and jerking. Then the train continued southward, chugging through the craggy foothills that separated the Shenandoah Valley of Virginia from the Holston Valley of Tennessee.

Will pointed to a deeply rutted dirt trace that ran alongside the tracks for a certain distance. "That's the Great Wagon Road. Settlers from Pennsylvania followed it into Cherokee country a hundred and fifty years ago. And before that it was a branch of the Great Warriors' Path that connected the northern and southern tribes."

"You're turning into a regular fount of knowledge."

"I probably should have been a teacher like you. I love history. It's like peeling the layers of newspaper off a wall in an old house." He paused. "But you people in Couchtown probably ordered your wallpaper new from Richmond, didn't you?"

"Newspaper would have been more interesting than those floral patterns my mother used to pick."

"That's how we learned the alphabet up on the bald. From the headlines on the newspapers pasted on our walls to keep out the drafts."

Galicia smiled. "Tell me some more tragic tales from Miserable Mountain, my darling."

"But it's true," he insisted indignantly.

Galicia realized that he had many sensitivities about his childhood that she would never understand, and that it was probably better not to tease in unfamiliar territory. Chastened, she took his hand in hers and squeezed it. He squeezed back in forgiveness. Glancing around to make sure no one was watching, he patted her swollen belly affectionately.

The train descended into the Holston Valley. The tracks paralleled the Holston River, which was lined by verdant trees with branches that hung out over the water, swaying and dipping like oars as the rail cars roared past. Across the river ran a long, low mountain, fluted like a pastry crust with deep coves.

"That's called Hunger Mountain," said Will. "Some early settlers starved to death up there during one harsh winter."

Galicia shivered, even though her armpits were sweaty.

On the outskirts of the town of Holston, the train passed a boatyard with decaying wooden wharves that were collapsing into the river.

"That's where Donelson's flotilla of flatboats embarked for Nashville in 1790. A boatload of smallpox patients at the rear was massacred by Cherokees. Much to the later regret of the warriors, who also came down with smallpox and spread it throughout their villages."

"How do you know all this?" asked Galicia. Although Will had not had much formal education, his love of knowledge was so great that he soaked it up like thirsty soil wherever he went.

"The Cherokees called that big island in the middle of the river Peace Island. No violence was allowed on it. They negotiated treaties there."

"What's that ugly building on Peace Island?"

"It's a sawmill for the new chemical plant. They use chemicals extracted from wood to produce camera film."

The two disembarked before a boxcar that served as a station-house. Across the tracks loomed a hill veiled in dust, where several roaring steam shovels were unearthing huge slabs of rock.

Grabbing their bags, Will led Galicia around the boxcar to the main street. It stretched past many littered vacant lots to a red brick church with a white steeple. An emaciated Holstein meandered along the deserted thoroughfare of packed clay.

"Well, here it is: our new hometown," announced Will, with an enthusiasm that eluded Galicia.

"Very nice." Lacking the conveniences of Leesville and the familiarity of Couchtown, Holston appeared the worst of both worlds. But she was determined to hold her tongue. It wasn't as though they had the option of returning to Virginia.

Will hired a horse-drawn wagon out front to convey them and their trunks to the house he had rented. The sway-backed horses, driven by an old man in a black felt hat, plodded down the main street past the cow with its concave belly and xylophone ribs.

"This area used to be called Peace Island Flats," Will cheerily informed her. "The Cherokees and the white settlers fought a battle on this very spot. The settlers won and forced the Cherokees to hand over Peace Island."

"That's terrible," murmured Galicia, more despondent by the minute.

"Not for the whites. They needed this level valley land for farming."

Will pointed out the office he had rented on the second floor above a pharmacy. "That drugstore has a soda fountain that makes great ice cream sodas."

Galicia nodded unhappily. The few existing stores had facades of maroon brick higher than the roofs behind them, making the street resemble a stage set for a Wild West show.

"This area, like Couchtown, was part of that border region called the Squabble State. First it was in Virginia, then North Carolina, then the short-lived state of Franklin, now Tennessee."

"How interesting." Galicia struggled to dredge up enthusiasm for this forlorn place. "And where is Couchtown from here?"

He pointed east toward high mountains that receded layer upon layer into the distance. "It's only about fifty miles as the crow flies. But the mountains are so rugged that you'd have to go back to Saltville and head southeast by wagon to get there. The men from Couchtown who joined the Union army traveled those mountains on foot. They would have crossed Peace Island on their way to enlist in Kentucky."

"Why would Virginians have joined the Union army?"

He looked at her with surprise. "They's a'plenty that did."

Galicia raised her eyebrows, their signal that he had just lapsed into his native tongue.

"My ancestor Joshua Martin used to lead them to Kentucky," continued Will, as though his slip had never occurred. "Until his brother Abner killed him."

"But my family is related to Abner Martin. He rode with Jeb Stuart."

"Then you're also related to Joshua Martin. And to me. We've discussed this before. I thought we had it settled."

"But my father always said that there are two different Martin families in Couchtown."

"Far be it from me to contradict your honored father. All I'm saying is that my ancestors Joshua and Abner Martin were brothers. And that Abner led a group of Confederate soldiers that killed Joshua."

"I never heard that before."

"They say the winners write history. I guess the South won in downtown Couchtown."

They passed a field crammed with canvas tents that had probably been white at one time, but were now stained orange from the clay soil.

"What in the world are those?" asked Galicia.

"The workers building the town and the factories live there. That fellow named Walter Merilee—the one who works for the group that has guaranteed me a salary until I get my practice going—found us a house across the street from his. He says we're very lucky to have gotten it."

"I wouldn't have done well in a tent." Galicia strove for an amused tone that came out pathetic instead.

Their new house was a small stuccoed hacienda on an unpaved road named Chickasaw, which was lined with other haciendas. Inside it sported mustard yellow walls.

"All I bought was a bed and a sofa," Will explained. "You have such good taste that I assumed you'd rather furnish it yourself."

Galicia cast him a weary smile. She felt almost as excited about furnishing this fake pueblo as she did about living in a town with clay streets stained red by the blood of slaughtered Cherokees.

"Look!" He flipped a wall switch, and a bare bulb dangling from the ceiling on a frayed cord illuminated. "Electric lights!"

All Galicia wanted was to run into the bedroom, slam the door, throw herself onto the new bed, and weep. Instead, modeling herself on the brave settler wives who had silently starved to death on Hunger Mountain, she forced a smile and said, "This is wonderful, Will."

Will went out back and drew water with a hand pump. Then he built a coal fire in the kitchen stove and set the water on to heat. He insisted that Galicia disrobe and sit cross-legged in a nickel tub in the middle of the kitchen floor. Carefully mixing the hot water with cool, he trickled it over her shoulders and down her veined belly. After soaping her, he rinsed her with another pan of tepid water.

As they lay in bed, Will asked, "So what do you think of our new home, darling?"

"Ask me tomorrow." She was determined not to whine, however tempting the invitation he had just handed her. "I'm too tired right now to think much of anything."

Will reined in Fleet, a chocolate gelding, his favorite of the three horses he had bought at a livestock auction. Climbing down from his new buggy, he waved to Mr. Marshall, who had tied his horse to a fencepost and was waiting by the gate. The twilight was a soft brown velvet, like the fur of a bat.

Will unharnessed Fleet. Then he grabbed a saddle from the buggy and strapped it on Fleet's back. Fastening his medicine bag behind the saddle, he mounted and nudged Fleet with his heels. They headed through the gate.

"Thanks for coming so fast, Doc," said Mr. Marshall.

"How's he doing?"

"Not so good. His face is done gone gray. I reckon he's a'dying."

"Maybe not. Let's get on up there and see."

Will clicked to Fleet, who shifted into an easy canter, throwing up clods of the rich topsoil left by the spring floods. Fleet was proving himself as adaptable as his new owner, transforming from a carriage horse to a saddle horse as required. Similarly, Will himself often consulted his surgery text on his office desk as he performed operations that he had never even witnessed in medical school. Filling his new roles was frightening, but not nearly so frightening as riding the Leesville trolley.

A redbone hound chained to an old oak bayed a mournful greeting as the two riders approached the cabin, a chinked log structure identical to those on Mulatto Bald. A flock of chickens roosting in the rafters rustled and clucked, sending down a shower of fluffy white down as Will crossed the porch.

The dark, smoky room was packed with silent people. Sniffing, Will picked up the sour stench of infection mixed with that of sweat, spoiled food, and pipe smoke. The old man lay on a bench by the fireplace, panting like an overheated hound. Will asked Mr. Marshall to hold up a lantern so he could examine him.

Noting the old man's grunts and winces in response to his probing fingers, Will decided his appendix was about to rupture. He had to operate right away.

Hastily, Will spread a clean sheet from his bag on the kitchen table. Mr. Marshall and two of his sons removed the man's filthy overalls and underclothes and then lifted him like a bundle of kindling onto the sheet. Will draped him with a second sheet.

Taking out some instruments, Will laid them in a pot of water boiling on the stove. He placed a gauze mask over the man's mouth and nose and showed Mr. Marshall how to drip the ether onto it. Then he scrubbed his hands carefully in a pan of sterilized water before pulling on his boiled gloves.

After taking the man's pulse and lifting his eyelid to make sure he was out, Will picked up the scalpel. Behind him he heard a male voice leading the others in prayer. He bowed his head, closed his eyes, and mouthed a quick amen. Then he began his incision.

Positioning two sons to hold the cut open with sterilized spoons, he thrust his hands into the man's abdomen, identifying organs and muscles, blood vessels and cushions of fat by feel.

His audience was softly singing,
"When my feeble life is o'er,
Time won't be for me no more.
Gently guide me safely home
To Thy kingdom shore, to the shore...."

Will forced himself not to join the baritone, who was struggling to stay on key. He suspected the family might find a singing surgeon unnerving. At last reaching the appendix, which was badly swollen, he tied it off and clipped it out.

As he took the final stitch closing the incision, he heaved a sigh of relief and wiped the sweat off his forehead with his shirtsleeve.

Following Mr. Marshall back to the road, Will recalled hearing at medical school about doctors murdered by distraught family members when patients died. If that appendix had burst, he might have met his Maker in that remote cabin, serenaded by the family choir. Luckily, this scenario had not occurred to him at the time or else his hands would have trembled so badly that he might have botched the operation. It was a relief to have his patients so pleased to see him. Knowing nothing about the unsavoriness of Martins from Mulatto Bald, they sometimes mistook him for Jesus at the Second Coming.

As the buggy bounced from rut to rut like a cork in a creek, Will slumped in the driver's seat. If he fell asleep, Fleet would haul him back to the stable in the alley behind his office, where a nosebag of oats and all Fleet's horse buddies awaited him. But trying to sleep in a lurching carriage was almost as difficult as napping on a camel. It might prove dangerous as well. He had heard of doctors on house calls being robbed for the drugs in their satchels. He carried a pistol in his bag, but he would never be able to find it in time to fend off a desperado.

The major worry preventing his slumber, though, concerned the baby soon to emerge from Galicia's womb. Would he be there when Galicia went into labor, or would he be stuck at some distant farmhouse? If their baby were born with extra fingers, he had decided to remove them right away to spare the infant the insults he had endured as a child. If you got them quickly enough, you could just tie them off with a catgut thread and strangle them.

If the baby had dark skin, he wondered if they should move to Richmond or Nashville and try to live as Negroes. Would anyone ever believe that Galicia, with her pale skin and wavy auburn hair, was a Negro? Or should they just move up north and hope that racially complex families were more tolerated up there?

If only he had insisted on marrying Palestine, they would have remained on Mulatto Bald and none of these problems would now exist. Maybe there was more wisdom than he had realized to his neighbors' warnings not to get above your raising.

Galicia was stitching a living room curtain on a foot-pedaled sewing machine. The material, which she had bought at the dry goods store on the main street, featured a swirl of golden roses and greenery that coordinated well with the mustard walls. Working with the fabric had cheered her to the point of actually believing that she and Will could establish a happy life here in their adobe hut on Chickasaw Road. She was trying to maintain the mindset of a sturdy pioneer wife.

She heard a knock at the front door. Untangling herself from the material, she got up and lumbered over to answer it. Standing on the step was a tiny woman with lips that formed a bright red bow.

"Welcome," said the woman. She extended a pie.

Taking it, Galicia said, "How marvelous! Thank you so much."

"I'm Marianne Merilee. I believe our husbands have already met."

"Oh yes, your husband is the lawyer who helped mine find this house. I'm so happy to meet you. I'm Galicia Martin. Won't you come in?"

They stepped over and around the scraps of cloth strewn across the living room floor.

"Forgive my mess," said Galicia. "As you can see, I'm sewing curtains."

"What a lovely fabric!"

"Thank you. I like it too."

They sat on the sofa, and Marianne recounted her entire life history, involving a childhood of privilege in Roanoke, followed by marriage to Walter Merilee, a graduate of the University of Virginia. Walter was a lawyer for the consortium of industries developing Holston. "And now we live just across the street from you," she concluded breathlessly.

"In that half-timbered house?"

"Yes. We're just renting there until our house up on Tuscarora Heights is finished."

"How long have you been here?"

"About a year now."

"Are you enjoying it?"

"Very much. It's so exciting to be in on the ground floor of a brand new city. Walter says Holston will become an industrial center for the entire South, like Pittsburgh up north."

Galicia nodded.

"I must confess that I miss Virginia, though. Don't you prefer Virginia to Tennessee?"

"I don't know. I just got here."

"George Washington, Thomas Jefferson, James Madison, Patrick Henry, Robert E. Lee." She sighed. "Who all famous ever came from Tennessee?"

"No one that I know of," admitted Galicia.

"The wives of the plant managers from New York and Boston swan around Holston as though they're God's gift to the South. But they dress as badly as their maids. And they have no personal charm whatsoever."

"I haven't met any yet."

"Well, I promise you will soon see what I mean."

As Galicia returned to her curtain following Mrs. Merilee's departure, she tried to sort out the politics of the Holston wives. Apparently, those from the North felt superior to those from the South. But those from Virginia felt superior to everyone.

Will walked through the door, his boots and trouser legs splattered with orange mud.

"How's my beautiful bride tonight?" he demanded.

"A bride no more, that's for sure." She struggled to her feet and waddled over to kiss him, both leaning over her belly to accomplish this.

"Have you eaten?" she asked.

"A patient's family fed me."

"How about some apple pie? Mrs. Merilee across the street brought us one."

"I'd love a piece."

They sat on the couch while he ate. "Delicious," he said. "Tell me about Mrs. Merilee."

She related what she had learned. "She's homesick for Virginia. The more she talked about it, the more homesick I got myself."

"Never forget that 'secret Negro' who got lynched for loving a white woman."

"No, of course you're right."

"Besides, Virginia is only a few miles from here. You can cross the border any time you want to."

"You know that's not what I mean. Being a Virginian is a state of mind."

Will laughed. "So you don't need to actually go there then, do you?"

She smiled.

"Did you eat supper?" he asked.

"Hours ago."

"I'm sorry you have to eat alone so often."

She shrugged. "I signed on as the wife of a country doctor."

"Would you do it again, knowing all that you know now?"

"I like having my own personal physician. It makes me feel like royalty."

"Not that I'm ever here to attend to you."

"Just as long as you're here when this baby decides to emerge."

Later that night Galicia awoke with a start and sat straight up. She
was clammy with sweat, and her heart pounded like a bass drum.
Fighting through the fog in her brain, she realized that she had been
dreaming about carrying a dark-skinned baby through a warren of
trash-strewn alleys, trying to hide it and nurse it at the same time.
Menacing people kept looming up out of the shadows. The baby
whimpered and gave them away. The pursuers surrounded her and
the baby and started sneezing, spewing them with mucous, like
snakes spitting venom.

Galicia strolled down the main street of packed clay from the dry
goods store to meet Will for lunch at the drugstore below his office.
She had to amble with her legs well apart, lurching from one to the
other like a drunken sailor on shore leave. Despite her best efforts to
think about other topics, she kept returning to her nightmare. Were
such vivid dreams omens, she wondered, or were they just a product
of her anxiety over the impending birth? What if the baby sheltered in
her womb were in fact dark-skinned? Where could the three of them
go next in search of acceptance?

Having spotted her out the window, Will came dashing
downstairs in his white coat, his stethoscope dangling from his neck.
They sat in a back booth and ordered grilled cheese sandwiches and
chocolate sodas from a gum-chewing waitress with a yellow pencil
stuck behind her ear.

"Do you remember the sodas I made for us that day you first
came to see me at my father's store?" She pictured him in his faded
overalls and undershirt, with his slate blue eyes, crooked nose, and
long earlobes.

"Best soda I ever drank!"

"Did you ever imagine that day that we'd end up like this?" She
patted her huge belly.

"It was definitely my goal."

"I'm shocked that you'd have thought that way about a
respectable girl like me!" She smiled, remembering that she had been
thinking of him in exactly the same way—except that *he* had not been
respectable. A startled grimace contorted her face.

"What's wrong?" he asked.

"I think my water just broke."

He looked both awed and terrified.

"Don't just sit there. You're the doctor. Tell me what to do."

"Let's go up to my office." He rushed over to the waitress and explained what had happened in a hushed voice. She gave him her apron. He tied it around Galicia so as to conceal her damp skirt. As they exited, the other customers began to discuss why Doc Martin's wife had just raced out wearing an apron tied on backwards.

Will helped Galicia up the steps, through his reception room past some waiting patients, and into his examining room. Sitting her on the table, he fluttered ineffectually around the room.

"Will, I do not want to have our baby here in this office."

He stopped pacing to look at her. "But all my instruments and drugs are here. And my nurse can help with the delivery."

"We need to do this ourselves. You deliver babies alone all the time out on those farms. So go down to the stable and hitch the horse to the buggy and drive me home."

He knew it was as pointless to argue with a woman in labor as with a man in love. Clomping down the steps, he grasped her rationale: she wanted them to be the first to see the color of their baby's skin and make whatever decisions were required.

He tripped over a water bucket in the stable. Then he buckled Fleet's harness on upside down, while Fleet gazed at him quizzically. But finally he managed to drive the buggy down the alley and around the corner to his office door. He and his nurse helped Galicia down the steps and into the buggy, while townspeople watched from the sidewalks and through the windows of the soda shop.

Helping Galicia into their house, he made her as comfortable as possible in their bed.

"Thank you, darling," she said, just before being hit by her first contraction.

Their daughter was born toward midnight. She had five tiny fingers on each hand and five toes on each foot. Her face was ruddy, unlike either parent, and she had a full head of glossy black hair like her father's. Her navy blue eyes studied her parents with bewilderment. She pursed and unpursed her lips, as though uncertain what to do with them. But once Galicia gave her her nipple, she sucked contentedly until her eyelids began to flutter slowly shut, like the wings of an exhausted butterfly.

11

Half-Breeds: 1920

Galicia surveyed the five linen-clothed bridge tables arranged around her living room. They were set with the china and silver she had bought once her house on Tuscarora Heights was finished. The ladies about to arrive all lived on Tuscarora Heights—or wished they did. A few still rented down on Chickasaw Road while their new houses up here were being completed. Those who actually owned houses on Chickasaw Road were tradesmen and storeowners. Their wives belonged to the Daughters of the Confederacy. Galicia had toyed with joining the DOC. Fortunately, Marianne had warned her in time that the Daughters were common.

Galicia strode into the kitchen, where Iona, her cook, was mixing the chicken salad with which to fill the pastry shells still baking in the oven. "Did you chill the tea, Iona?"

"Yes, ma'am."

Iona's white uniform dress hung lankly on her bony frame. She looked like a scarecrow disguised as a registered nurse. To Galicia's annoyance, she insisted on wearing her stockings rolled down to her ankles with thin white socks over them, and she sometimes dipped snuff when she thought Galicia wasn't looking. "Not too much mayonnaise, please. You know how those ladies are always watching their figures. Is Linda minding Hunter?"

"Yes, ma'am. They're out back."

Galicia looked out the window. Hunter stood by the fishpond in her fringed cowgirl skirt, vest, and boots, her pistol leveled at Linda, Iona's granddaughter, who wore a headdress of feathers atop her curly black hair. Linda had an arrow tipped with a suction cup drawn back in her bow and aimed waveringly in Hunter's direction. The honey-toned puppy leapt back and forth between the two, trying to force them to play with him instead.

The girls threw down their weapons, picked up the puppy between them, and dropped him into the fishpond. Both shrieked delightedly as the yapping creature struggled to scale the concrete bank, which was slippery with algae. The alarmed goldfish huddled beneath lily pads in a far corner.

Galicia walked into the dining room, where her mahogany table was laid with gleaming silver platters and serving pieces. An ivory magnolia blossom floated in a cut-glass bowl, filling the room with its intoxicating scent.

Iona carried in a silver tray of miniature country ham biscuits. She glanced with a blank expression at the wallpapered mural above the table. It featured a wharf onto which cheerful slaves were hoisting cotton bales. In the background, a hoop-skirted belle was ascending into a carriage beneath the portico of a white-columned house similar to the one in which Galicia was now living, which had been modeled on her favorite house in Leesville, with its two-story white columns and leaded glass fanlight.

The doorbell rang. Galicia went to the door and opened it. There stood Marianne Merilee in a robin's egg blue tunic with a mid-calf length skirt that revealed her shapely ankles, a narrow-brimmed hat with a protruding partridge feather, a fox fur stole and matching muff, and heels so high that she looked like a ballerina en pointe. Galicia took notes for her next shopping trip to Knoxville. Marianne kept up with all the latest fashions. Now that the war in Europe was over, women were replacing the colors of mourning with cheery pastels. Marianne had even confessed to having given up her corset for the latest undergarment from France called a brassiere. It supported your breasts but let your belly bulge freely.

"Come in, Marianne. Lovely to see you. You've bobbed your hair!"

"I thought I needed a fresh look. Do you like it?"

"I love it! What does Walter think?"

"He hates it. He thinks I look like a boy."

They entered the living room, sat on the velvet-upholstered Empire sofa, and turned to face one another.

"So, I suppose you're serving your wonderful lime ambrosia salad today?" asked Marianne, her bright red lips turning up at the corners in abrupt right angles.

"Yes, I am."

Marianne lowered her blue-shadowed eyelids.

"Is something wrong?" asked Galicia.

"I promised I wouldn't tell you."

"Tell me what?"

"I'm afraid I can't say."

"If you can't say, Marianne, why did you bring it up?"

"I simply asked if you were serving Evelyn's salad today."

"*Evelyn's* salad?"

Marianne's rouged cheeks turned even redder.

"Does Evelyn think she owns that salad? I found the recipe in the *Ladies' Home Journal*, May issue."

"Yes, after eating it first at Evelyn's."

"But I've eaten that salad all over town!"

"I'm not the one you should be explaining this to."

"I have nothing to explain," insisted Galicia. The rules that governed recipe patents in Holston still eluded her. In Couchtown women had been flattered when others requested their recipes. Here, imitating a recipe could get your name removed from important guest lists.

"Don't get mad at the messenger, Galicia. I'm just telling you this because I'm your friend."

The doorbell rang again. On the porch stood Betty Moody in a maroon silk tunic and calf-length skirt. She too had bobbed her hair. Suddenly Galicia felt like a pioneer wife in her ankle-length skirt and long hair.

The three women perched along the sofa like doves on a power line.

"Did you hear what Pegasus has been reading for today's meeting?" asked Betty.

Pegasus was the book club formed by the wives of the plant managers from the North, most of whom had attended elite women's colleges up there. Their first project had been to establish a public library downtown and persuade their husbands' companies to finance it. Word had gotten out that they felt the wives from the South didn't possess the education or literary sophistication necessary to join Pegasus.

In response, Galicia and Marianne had formed the Old Dominion Club. To qualify for membership, your ancestors had to have come from the Virginia Tidewater. Although Pegasus could dismiss the Daughters of the Confederacy as nothing more than the spawn of rebel riffraff, they had more difficulty snubbing Tidewater Virginians, whose forebears had, after all, settled at Jamestown some thirteen years prior to the *Mayflower*'s arrival at Plymouth Rock.

The meetings of the Old Dominion Club featured papers by the members on famous Virginians. Betty was speaking that day on Captain John Smith and his rescue by Pocahontas from death at the hands of the Powhatan Indians.

"Does anyone really care what Pegasus is reading?" asked Marianne.

"What *are* they reading?" asked Galicia.

"Something called *Moll Flanders*," said Betty. "I'm told the main character is"—she paused to gaze at them with alarm before whispering—"a prostitute!"

Galicia made a mental note of the title. She was reading their list in secret. She agreed that she was not up to their level yet, but one day she would be. After all, she was a graduate of the Leesville Teachers' College, and she intended to be the first Southerner invited to join Pegasus.

Will used his three-wood to drive his ball from the eighth tee. Then he teed up a second ball and took out his left-handed three-wood. When nobody at the clubhouse was looking for a game, he often played himself. That particular afternoon his left hand was ahead by two. He had picked up golf easily because the swing was so similar to a baseball swing. Now he won most of the tournaments, which didn't endear him to the other men, especially those from New York and Boston, who ranked others by their golf handicaps.

Replacing the club, he hitched his leather bag over his shoulder and set out after his balls. He often played until dusk, delaying his return home as long as possible. Golf was probably a safer distraction than a mistress. Apparently Galicia agreed because she had bought him a complete golfing outfit the last time she went shopping in Knoxville—tweed cap, tattersall shirt, knit tie, pullover sweater, tweed plus fours, and argyle socks. He felt like the Jack in a deck of cards.

Ever since Hunter's birth, he and Galicia had been distant from one another. He blamed himself. From time to time he still pictured that pale young man glistening with coal oil, his charred corpse hanging from an oak limb, because of his misplaced love for a white woman. This seemingly indelible image, plus his anxiety about extra digits and his guilt over Palestine's fate, had probably traumatized him into avoiding the act that might result in another pregnancy. At first Galicia had tried every strategy she could devise to help him overcome his "difficulty." But she had finally accepted defeat. Now she was so absorbed in her political struggles with the other wives in Holston that she seemed oblivious to him—so long as he kept their ever-mounting bills paid.

He sometimes thought wistfully about their nights together in the little apartment in Leesville, sharing the events of their days and then making love half the night. He missed that closeness, but not enough to risk having another baby.

Occasional letters from Dr. Hopewell in Leesville confirmed that Will had been smart to leave. Dr. Manning and his crew were on the march, lobbying the legislature to pass a bill that would define anyone with a single drop of Negro blood as colored, including all Indians. Dr. Hopewell told him about a white man about to be arrested for having a black wife. When the sheriff arrived in his doorway, her husband had pricked her finger with a needle and licked the blood off to prove that he had Negro blood in him and was therefore Negro himself.

Will chipped his left-handed ball on to the green within a foot of the hole. But the right-handed one lay in the sand trap alongside the green. Blasting his way out with his wedge, he dropped it two yards from the flag.

As he putted, Will thought about how hard Galicia and he had worked to educate themselves for their careers. They had built a handsome house and filled it with antiques and Oriental carpets. They had produced an adorable daughter. No one in Holston had ever questioned their membership in the white race. They had fought the whole world in order to be together, and they had achieved more than they had ever dreamed possible. Why, then, did he feel so empty inside?

Galicia had insisted he give up his horses and house calls to open a clinic. Of course, she was right: he could treat a dozen patients there in the time it took him to make one house call. So he no longer cantered through forests to perform operations on kitchen tables. He had felt like a hero back then, helping those with no one else to look to. Now he was nothing but a corporate gigolo, repairing the prolapsed organs of the wives of Holston plant managers. So far he had done bladder repairs to solve the incontinence of three members of the Pegasus Book Club. Galicia would have loved to have this information as ammunition in her power struggles, but his sense of professional ethics made it impossible for him to give it to her. He felt useless—as a gossip, a husband, and a doctor.

Pocketing his balls, Will headed toward the ninth tee, his favorite hole. The fairway ran between a wooded foothill and the river. A slice landed you in the water, and a hook in the trees. You had to drive right down the middle, high enough to avoid a sand trap but short enough not to miss the green and roll down the hill behind it.

Walter Merilee and Hal DeWitt, the president of the pulp mill, were standing alongside the ninth tee, watching a third man loft his drive into the river, where fish killed by a spill at the chemical plant bobbed by the shore. Last month in the clubhouse, Hal had drawn him aside. With a sheepish grin, he had asked Will to "tighten up" his wife Barbara, who had recently given birth to their fifth child. Will had done so with a few well-placed stitches. No doubt Hal was now a happy man.

"Why, it's Dr. Martin!" exclaimed Walter.

The other two turned toward him. Will shook hands with Walter and Hal.

"Mr. Frye, this is Dr. Martin, head of the Holston Clinic," said Hal.

Mr. Frye's belly formed a green mound like a grassy grave beneath his golfing sweater. He shook Will's hand, saying, "Quite a nice little town you have here, sir."

"Thank you, Mr. Frye. We like it."

"We're trying to persuade Mr. Frye to build a printing plant here in Holston," explained Walter, giving Will a look fraught with urgency.

"No persuasion needed," said Mr. Frye. "I was convinced as soon as I saw this marvelous golf course!"

The other three laughed politely.

"You have to admit that it makes sense, Mr. Frye," said Hal. "My mill supplies your paper. The cotton mill supplies the cloth for your book covers. We all save charges for shipping crates and fees."

"Plus, you have an endless supply of pure Anglo-Saxon labor," added Walter. "Men starving on their farms in the hills. Men eager for work at wages half of what you're paying in Massachusetts. Men so grateful for steady employment that they would never dream of unionizing. God-fearing men with a strong Protestant work ethic. Men whose ancestors cleared this region of Indians and defeated the British at King's Mountain. Help me out here, Dr. Martin," said Walter with a laugh. "You're from these parts, and you know your history better than I do."

"Men who fought for the Union and were persecuted for it?" suggested Will.

Walter and Hal shot him bewildered glances.

"Is that so?" said Mr. Frye. "I didn't know that Tennesseans supported the Union."

"Thirty thousand joined the Union army," said Will. "Most endured harassment by their Confederate neighbors, and thousands died in battle."

"Pure Anglo-Saxon patriots who fought first to establish the Union at King's Mountain, and then to save it from dissolution during the Civil War," mused Mr. Frye, gazing off into the distance. "Men loyal to Abraham Lincoln, even when those around them were branding him a tyrant." He gave the others a steely stare. "Fine, brave mountaineers, mired down in poverty, ridiculed as hillbillies by the North and the South alike. It's not just. I believe you have just convinced me, sir."

Walter and Hal looked at Will with astonished gratitude.

Will shrugged modestly.

"Won't you join us and make it a foursome on the back nine?" asked Hal, a former captain of the Princeton golf team who had been known to hide in the bushes outside the clubhouse to avoid playing with Will.

Hal turned to Mr. Frye to add, "Dr. Martin is the best golfer in town. He beats the pants off us all, with both his right-handed swing and his left."

Mr. Frye studied him. "How intriguing. Where are you from, Dr. Martin?"

Will pointed toward the mountains across the river, which were turning purple in the sinking sun. "Fifty miles that way, as the crow flies. I'm one of those Anglo-Saxon patriots down from the hills."

Will smiled wryly. His whole life had consisted of playing roles, so he might as well play the Anglo-Saxon patriot one, too. Galicia was pretending to be a Tidewater Virginian now. And if he and she had tried to live as blacks, they would still have been playing roles. They were not "passing" as white, because passing implied that you knew you were black and were masquerading as white. But he and Galicia had no idea who they really were. The last time they had visited Couchtown to show the baby to their parents, everyone had treated them like rich city snobs. They had become two people who fit in nowhere. All they had now was each other, but even that apparently wasn't enough to heal their unspoken rift and bring them together again.

In the clubhouse as they sat on a bench changing their shoes, Walter said quietly, "That was a clever ploy, Will, about the people in these mountains having fought for the Union."

"Six of my ancestors were shot dead for it."

"But Marianne says that Galicia's people were from the Tidewater. She says they rode with Jeb Stuart during the War."

"Her people may have ridden with Jeb Stuart," said Will, "but mine blew up railroad bridges for General Grant." He barely managed to restrain himself from ruining Galicia's social standing in Holston for good by admitting that he and she were cousins.

"Ah, a mixed marriage, huh?"

Will grimaced. "I guess you could call it that."

As Walter led Mr. Frye to his car, Hal said, "May I have a word with you, Will?"

Resting his foot on the running board of his Packard, Will turned to face him.

"I'd like to offer you a job."

Will looked at him questioningly.

"It's important to us that our workers stay healthy. I'd like you to consider coming aboard as our medical officer. I've heard my men talk about you. They like and respect you. I know you're not really one of them, but you do have the common touch."

Will raised his eyebrows. He had assumed that his accent still gave him away as "common," despite Galicia's coaching. "Well, thank you, Hal. But I'm doing pretty well right now with my clinic."

"I'll buy you out and bring in a new doctor to run it. Plus, I'll match what you're clearing right now as a salary, and increase it by ten percent."

Will said nothing, recognizing a poker game. It was bluffing time.

After a long silence Hal said, "All right, Will: twenty-five percent."

"What would my duties be?"

"You'd establish an infirmary at the mill. We'd hire a nurse to help you staff it. You'd also make house calls to the workers' families in the mill village. And I'd like you to recommend improvements at the mill and in the village to prevent diseases and accidents."

Will felt a surge of excitement for the first time since he had hit a hole-in-one the previous spring. "I can't say I'm not interested, Hal. But I need to talk to Galicia first."

"Of course. Take all the time you need, Will."

"Thank you for the offer, in any case. I'm really honored."

"The honor would be entirely ours."

Will smiled. "I see you've mastered the Southern formulas for courtesy, Hal."

"I'm trying to," he confessed with a grin. "Oh, and by the way, thanks for fixing up the wife." He gave Will a rakish wink.

Galicia lay in the lamplight, intently reading *Moll Flanders*.

"Is that book any good?" Will was stretched out beneath the sheets in the royal blue silk pajamas she had given him for his birthday. He felt like the harem eunuch.

She nodded.

"Honey, I hate to interrupt you, but I need to discuss something with you." She turned her head to look at him, appalled to have just read that Moll, the main character, had been released from an English jail and transported to a Tidewater plantation as an indentured servant. But this author Daniel Defoe had lived in England, not Virginia, so he probably didn't realize that the English in the Tidewater *owned* the plantations; they did not work on them.

Will told Galicia about Hal DeWitt's offer. "So what do you think?"

She studied him thoughtfully. Will enjoyed a lot of prestige as the head of his own clinic, treating the families of the factory managers. But apparently he would earn more money treating the workers. Hal DeWitt was one of the most important men in town. Barbara DeWitt was a graduate of Mount Holyoke College and a founder of Pegasus. This new job would mean dinner parties with the

DeWitts and their friends from the North. Eventually it might lead to an invitation to join Pegasus.

"Which would *you* prefer?" she asked, so that, if he made the right choice, he could feel that it was his own.

"I'm tempted to accept the job. I like the idea of treating the mill workers. It seems more real than what I've been doing."

"Why are factory workers' illnesses more real than those of management?"

"I just meant that the workers need my services more. The managers will always find good care. They can afford to go to Roanoke or Knoxville."

Galicia sighed. Will was such a bleeding heart that he didn't charge anyone who couldn't afford his fees. The garage was full of moldy country hams he had accepted in lieu of payment. And he gave money to anyone who asked, ignoring the fact that decent people never asked. Without her guarding their checkbook, they would have been forced to move up on Hunger Mountain amid the colony of drones created by his misdirected generosity.

"Do whatever you think best, darling."

"I guess I'll accept Hal's offer, then."

She reflected that he was still so handsome, despite his thinning hair. "Will, do you really not want any more children?" she asked, even though she knew better than to pick scabs off old wounds.

"Oh Lord, Galicia, let's not get into that again."

"I've finally figured it out: since Palestine McClellan can't bear any more children, you think you shouldn't either. But why must I be punished for your sins?" She felt a stab from her conscience. She had performed terrible sins of omission against both Palestine and Will. But at least Will didn't know this.

His face contorted. Clenching his molars, he rolled over and turned his back on her.

Closing her book and laying it on the bedside table, she turned off the lamp. Wrapping her arms around her spurned body, she turned her back to Will's. She wondered if this loveless marriage were her punishment for having kept Will and Palestine apart.

Would he have deserted her for Palestine if she had given him the choice?

Still, Galicia had to acknowledge that if Will hadn't rejected her, she might have rejected him. It was impossible for her to erase the memory of the anxiety that had gripped them both in Leesville during her pregnancy. Nor was it possible for her to erase the image of that young man hanging by his neck, doused in coal oil, for the sin of loving a white woman. If they hadn't left Virginia, that could have been Will. She shuddered.

She couldn't seem to get the photo out of her head, but she could choose not to dwell on it. So she forced herself to concentrate instead on the topic of pickpockets and whores from English prisons infesting the Tidewater during colonial days. Could this be true? If so, what would it mean for the Old Dominion Club that Pegasus now knew that not everyone in the Tidewater had been an aristocrat? Had they discussed this at their last meeting? What if word got out?

Will sat beside Hunter on the wooden bench, waiting for the movie to begin. The Rodeo Roundup was one benefit to working at the mill that Hal had neglected to mention. The children of the employees got to watch a free cowboy movie every Saturday morning in the cafeteria. Most men in Tuscarora Heights played golf on Saturdays, but he preferred to spend them with Hunter, whom he rarely saw otherwise, since he left for work before she woke up and often came home after she was asleep. Besides, although he didn't admit it to other adults, he adored Tom Mix and Tony the Wonder Horse.

Various people from the mill village whom he had treated waved to him, and he waved back. Toward the front he spotted his nurse, Nora Porter, seated beside a small boy he supposed was her son Sidney. It was startling to see her dressed in something other than her crisp white uniform. She wore a coral silk tunic that molded her large breasts too closely for his own comfort. The way they bounced and swayed when she strode down the hallway at work suggested that, like most other women in Holston, she too had abandoned her corset. The brassiere was a godsend to men and women alike.

Fortunately, the lights dimmed, and Miss Penrose, the organist from the Baptist church, launched into a frenzied allegro on the piano, like bees swarming. Silently howling Indians on horses, their faces painted in alarming patterns, filled the screen. They were circling a flaming farmhouse, shooting arrows and hurling tomahawks.

No wonder they needed to be exterminated, thought Will. He leaned forward, resting his elbows on his knees and his chin on his fists, and awaited the arrival of Tom and Tony the Wonder Horse. It soon became clear that the problem wasn't the Indians, who possessed a certain savage dignity. Nor was the problem the white settlers, who were bringing civilization and its glories to the frontier.

The real problem was a surly Indian named Two Hearts. Tom Mix, in the subtitles that Will quietly read to Hunter, referred to Two Hearts as "a low-down, lying, thieving, and deceiving half breed." It seemed that he had incited his otherwise docile tribe to murder and arson because he hated his white trapper father, who had rejected him and his Indian mother. Once Two Hearts had been slain by the disgruntled Indians, as studded with arrows as a hound's nose with porcupine quills, racial harmony once again reigned in Buffalo Flats.

As the lights came back on, Will said to Hunter, "What would you say if I told you that your father is a low-down lying, thieving, and deceiving half breed, just like Two Hearts?"

Hunter giggled. "No, you're my own sweet daddy." She hesitated. "Is that really true?"

"Yes."

"Does Mommy know?"

"Yes."

"Is she a half breed, too?"

"She certainly is," he said, cheerfully anticipating Galicia's outrage when Hunter questioned her.

"But that's horrible, Daddy. Indians are mean, bad people."

Will sighed. "But the white settlers were stealing their land, honey, where they had lived for many, many years."

"They all could have shared it."

"The Indians tried to share it, but the settlers wanted it all for themselves."

Hunter frowned. "I don't believe you, Daddy."

He laughed and shrugged. "I warned you that I'm a lying half breed, didn't I? Let's go downtown and drink chocolate ice cream sodas for lunch."

He nosed the Packard left off Shawnee Avenue on to Chickasaw Road so that he could drive past the little stucco house in which he had learned that the buxom Nora Porter lived. He loved the cheap Midnight in Paris perfume she wore at work. Galicia used to wear it when she worked at the cosmetics counter in Leesville. He found it much more alluring than the Narcisse Noire Galicia now wore, along with every other matron on Tuscarora Heights.

Hunter said, "I love you anyway, Daddy."

"I love you, too, honey. Don't pay any attention to me."

"I won't," she promised him.

Will was certain the old woman lying in the iron bedstead, bathed in her own sweat with fleas hopping around her like popcorn popping, had typhoid. This was the third case in the mill village.

As he explained to the teenaged daughter how to care for her grandmother while her parents worked, he watched several small children eating their lunch of packaged cupcakes and soda pops, clawing at their no doubt lice-laden heads. While he considered whether to quarantine the whole family, a giant rat lumbered like a pet groundhog across the linoleum floor.

Exiting into the road of identical frame houses, he turned to inspect their exteriors. Although only a decade old, they had been so poorly built that they looked much older. Inside you often saw daylight through the cracks. In cold weather the occupants had to load their coal stoves so full that gritty smoke seeped out the lids and filled the rooms. Tuberculosis, pneumonia, and influenza were rampant.

Between two houses he saw hogs rooting in the sinkhole where residents tossed their garbage. Beyond that stretched a row of outhouses. The bank on which they perched sloped down to the stream from which residents hauled their water. The water itself ran milky with waste from a dairy upstream, which was probably the source of the typhoid.

Shaking his head hopelessly, Will tiptoed through the mud to his Packard, trying to figure out how to tell Hal DeWitt that the only way to assure a healthy work force was to tear down this disgusting village and start over. At last reaching his car, a black island in the sea of orange mud, he climbed in, smearing the clay caked on his shoes onto the floor mat.

As he drove back to the mill, he itemized the jobs ahead: The so-called houses needed new siding and indoor bathrooms. The water, electric, and sewage lines needed to be extended out from town. As did the garbage pick-up. The roads should be paved to get rid of the pools of stagnant water in which mosquitoes bred. The livestock had to be eliminated, or at least fenced. An extermination program would be necessary to get rid of the fleas, rats, and lice. And that was just the beginning. He would write Hal a memo back at the infirmary. It would be interesting to see if Hal would put his money where his mouth was.

As he turned off Chickasaw Road into the mill yard, a man operating a big yellow crane waved to him. Recognizing Ray Wilson, the father of the family he had just visited, he waved back. When Ray had arrived at the infirmary to report his mother's illness, he had talked about that dismal village as though it were Jerusalem, its orange clay streets paved with gold.

No one knew better than Will what it was like to scratch a living from a dirt farm in the hills. But had life improved for those who had deserted such farms to work in the factories of Holston? Survival had been a challenge on Mulatto Bald, but you could grow vegetables and keep a cow and a few chickens. You could hunt game in the forest. The creeks you drank from ran out of springs in the hillsides, and your wastes went into deep holes in the ground. Even though their lives had been short, people's ancestors had built their cabins to last. If you kept the walls chinked and well padded with newspapers, they held in the heat from the stone fireplaces.

The so-called progress in Holston was starting to look to Will like more of the same, only worse—the rich getting richer off the back-breaking labor of the poor. The workers needed a union such as some of the miners in the nearby mountains had formed. He wondered if he were turning into a Communist. He could only imagine how that would affect Galicia's social standing in Holston.

Parking the car, Will walked into the administration building and along the corridors to the infirmary. He entered to discover Nora Porter sitting at the intake desk in her white uniform, powdering her eye in the mirror of her compact. The eye looked swollen and bruised.

"What's happened, Mrs. Porter?" Although he would do anything to avoid a frank discussion with Galicia, he never beat around the bush professionally.

"I ran into a door."

"What was his name?"

She looked up with a startled smile that revealed a smear of lipstick on an upper bicuspid.

"Did someone hit you?"

"Yes, sir," she confessed shamefacedly.

"Well, don't put up with it."

"What else can I do, Dr. Martin? I can't leave him. We've got a young child."

"So it's your husband?"

She nodded.

"You can threaten to leave if it happens again, Mrs. Porter. And if it does, then please leave. You have a good job here. You'll manage. It beats being dead. I've seen a lot of these cases. They almost always go from bad to worse."

She nodded doubtfully.

"Do you want me to go talk to him?"

She gave a startled laugh. "It would make him even madder if he knew I had spoken to you about it, Dr. Martin."

"When I was a boy up in the mountains, if a woman was beaten by her husband, all the men got together and went over and pounded him to pulp. That usually ended it. Just say the word, Mrs. Porter, and I'll gather up a gang and head on over to your house."

"Thank you, Dr. Martin. You're sweet. I'll remember that." She smiled at him gratefully as his nose picked up the scent of her Midnight in Paris perfume and his guilty blue gaze skittered across the two fetching white mounds atop her chest.

"Now, I want everbody in this church who agrees that it's a sin in the eyes of the Lord to play cards...to stand up right now!" shouted Mr. Gibbs, the preacher at the First Baptist Church.

His face was so red that it looked to Will as though his necktie, which was dotted with tiny golden crosses, must be about to strangle him.

The church rose as one.

"Now everbody say a-man!"

"A-man," echoed the congregation.

Will had remained seated. When Hunter saw him, she sat back down. Galicia looked over to discover them both sitting. She gestured for them to get up. Will grinned at her.

"Say a-man!" repeated Mr. Gibbs.

"A-man!" the audience chorused.

"One more time: a-man!"

"A-man!"

"I can't hear you! Say it louder!"

"A-man!"

"Say what?"

"A-MAN!" they shrieked, as though cheering a touchdown.

Mr. Gibbs motioned for the congregation to sit, eying Will. The rows of ushers sitting in the amen corner behind Mr. Gibbs also eyed him. Walter Merilee frowned questioningly. Galicia was furious that Will had refused to be an usher, since several factory managers were.

The members of Pegasus attended the Episcopal chapel, a quaint, ivy-infested stone manse that belonged on some windswept moor rather than on a gullied hillside overlooking Shawnee Avenue. Galicia had insisted that they attend services there a couple of Sundays. But Will had refused to continue, maintaining that preachers who spoke in verbs that ended in "eth" made his skin crawl.

"All right now!" continued Mr. Gibbs. "I want everbody who agrees that it's a sin straight from Satan to play golf on Sunday...to stand up right now."

Will watched his golfing buddies in the amen corner stir, hesitate, and then rise to their feet in their pinstriped suits.

Again Will remained seated, flanked by his loyal daughter.

"Get up!" hissed Galicia.

"Now I want everbody to shout a-man like good Christians storming the gates of Heaven!"

"A-MAN!" they howled.

Galcia glared at him. He winked at her.

"I've never been so humiliated," muttered Galicia as they headed in the Packard to the Holston Inn for the lunch buffet.

"How could I stand up when I don't agree that golf on Sunday is a sin? I've known some nutty preachers before, but Gibbs takes the cake. He makes Uncle J.C. look almost sane."

"You make me so mad that I could just scream!"

"Everybody scream 'a-man!'" called Will.

"A-man!" shrieked Hunter from the back seat.

"See?" said Galicia in a low voice. "You're teaching our daughter to mock things she doesn't even understand."

"There was your entire bridge club standing up and agreeing that playing cards is a sin. How can you all play bridge together twice a week if you think it's a sin?"

She turned her head and gazed out the window.

"Mommy, is it true that we're Indians?" asked Hunter.

"Of course not! Where did you get that idea?" She shot Will a venomous look.

"That's what Daddy says."

"That's because Daddy likes to cause trouble. Daddy got so used to being an outcast as a boy that he can't get over it now. He thinks it makes him special. He doesn't realize that it just makes him ridiculous."

"What's an outcast?" asked Hunter.

"It means someone who is less of a hypocrite than the people around him," said Will.

"Daddy says he's a half breed and so are you."

Rolling her eyes at Will, Galicia said, "It's possible that we may be a tiny bit Indian, Hunter. But if we are, it's because we're descended from Pocahontas, who lived in the Virginia Tidewater."

Will burst out laughing.

"Who's that?" asked Hunter.

"Pocahontas is the Indian princess who saved the life of Captain John Smith." Galicia determinedly ignored her husband.

"Who's Captain John Smith?"

"He's the brave soldier who started Jamestown, the first town in the United States, which was also located in the Tidewater."

"Was he an Indian, too?"

"No, he was from England, just like many of our best ancestors. The ancestors we prefer to speak about."

"Where's England?"

"It's across the ocean in Europe."

"What's Europe?"

"Oh, do stop it, Hunter!"

Will was grinning merrily.

"You enjoy embarrassing me, don't you?"

"I can't deny that I do, Galicia. You're so danged embarrassable that I just can't help myself!"

"You don't care two hoots about any of this, do you?" She gestured wildly around the car. "As far as you're concerned, we could be living in squalor on Mulatto Bald with the rest of your retarded relatives!" She started crying, rummaging through her handbag for a handkerchief.

"What's wrong, Mommy?" Hunter leaned over from the back seat.

"Nothing, honey. Your daddy is just driving me crazy. Don't pay any attention to us."

"That's what Daddy says." Bewildered, she looked back and forth between her weeping mother and her grinning father.

12

Home to Roost: 1927

Hunter sat at the mahogany table, eating the chocolate cake Iona had baked, listening to her parents argue. They had argued her entire life. She wished they would stop. Her friends' parents were nice to each other, or at least polite.

Her mother had just announced that she had been elected the first president of something called the Colonial Dames. She explained that this new club had been formed by merging the Pegasus Book Club with the Old Dominion Club. To join you had to have ancestors from either the *Mayflower* in Massachusetts or Jamestown in Virginia. Her mother had been the unanimous choice for president because she had both.

Her mother loved her clubs, and her father could have just congratulated her. Instead, he asked in his most smart-alecky voice, "Since when did you have ancestors on the *Mayflower*, Galicia?"

Hunter wondered why someone so handsome had to be so mean. He was wearing his three-piece suit and tie from the office, and his black hair was tinged with silver, like the lawn after a heavy frost. If he weren't such a jerk, she could see how her mother might love him.

"The Hunters were Quakers from Philadelphia," her mother replied in her my-people-are-better-than-yours voice.

"I didn't realize that Quakers were also Pilgrims."

"The immigrant Hunters arrived on the *Mayflower*," she explained patiently. "Then their descendants moved south to Philadelphia, where they converted to Quakerism."

"Prior to moving south to Couchtown and becoming Baptists? My, my, what a fickle bunch!"

Hunter hated how her father always made fun of her mother's familial fantasies, which apparently gave her pleasure. As did her pathetic attempts to look like a flapper, with her dropped-waist dresses and her short hairdo with a curl beneath each earlobe. After her father mocked her, her mother would turn mean, sometimes to him, sometimes to Hunter, sometimes to Iona.

"That's certainly preferable to perching on the same mountaintop for centuries, like petrified buzzards," retorted her mother, sniffing.

Hunter tried to distract them from their dislike of one another by asking, "Mother, I don't see why I can't switch to tap."

Hunter didn't want to admit that she was having trouble getting up on her toes in ballet class. She had recently put on a lot of weight, mostly in her chest and hips. Her breasts had gotten so big that she had to bind them with an elastic bandage in order not to look ridiculous in her tutu. Apparently becoming a woman mostly involved bleeding and bloating. She would rather stay a child, but she didn't seem to have a choice.

"You may not switch to tap, and that's that!"

"But why not, Mother?"

"Tap is common, Hunter. Tap dancers perform in vaudeville shows."

Her father raised his eyebrows. "You used to love vaudeville shows in Leesville, as I recall, Galicia."

Hunter tried to picture her parents as fun-loving youths who enjoyed one another's company. But it was impossible.

"You let Daddy drive that horrible old broken-down Packard. That's pretty common, if you ask me."

"In the first place, I don't 'let' your father do anything. He always does exactly as he pleases, no matter how much it upsets me. And in the second place, we *didn't* ask you."

The doorbell rang. All three looked at one another. No one in Holston ever came calling unannounced during the dinner hour.

"Would you answer that please, Iona?" called her mother.

Iona loped in from the kitchen and over to the door, her white uniform flapping on her bony body like a flag of surrender.

Hunter heard her say, "Deliveries go to the kitchen, boy. What you be bringing here this hour of the night anyhow?"

After an inaudible reply, she said, "They be eating supper right now."

"Who is it, Iona?" asked her mother.

Iona peered around the corner of the door. "Boy name of Billy McClellan. Says he needs to see you, Doctor. I done told him to go around to the kitchen, but he won't do it."

Hunter watched her parents exchange shocked glances.

"Thank you, Iona." Her father pushed back his chair and got up. "I'll handle it."

He hurried to the door and ushered the caller into the hall. The boy looked about sixteen. Tall and slender, he wore a suit with sleeves and trouser legs that showed his wrists and ankles. His face was the color of wildflower honey. He was handsome, but he needed a haircut. His dark hair was hanging in his eyes, and he tossed it back with a jerk of his head.

"How do you do, sir?" he said carefully, as though reciting a poem he had memorized for English class. "My name is Billy McClellan. My mother, Palestine McClellan, told me to look you up once I got to Holston."

Her father stared at the boy without saying a word—for once in his life.

Billy continued, "She said you was her best friend growing up back in Couchtown, and maybe you would remember her and help me to find a job here in Holston."

Her father stammered, "Uh, uh, where are you coming from, Billy?"

"I hopped a boxcar down the valley from Saltville." He shrugged sheepishly.

"Well, come right in." Her father stepped aside. Billy walked into the dining room, carrying a bulging canvas bag in one hand and a brimmed wool cap in the other.

"This is my wife, Mrs. Martin, and my daughter, Hunter."

"Pleased to meet you, ma'am. And miss."

"Have you eaten?" asked her mother in a tense voice.

"No, ma'am. Not all day long."

"Please have a seat."

Billy sat down. Hunter watched her parents stare at this boy with wide eyes. Hunter stared at him, too. She had never before seen a Negro sitting at their dinner table. But was he a Negro or not? Probably not since he was sitting at their dinner table. He looked halfway between a Negro and a white boy—with caramel skin and black hair, but blue eyes.

Her father called into the kitchen, "Iona, could you please bring this young man a plate of food?"

Iona carried in a plate and laid it before Billy with an appalled glance at Hunter's mother.

While Billy ate, Hunter's father asked hesitantly, "Where did you come from before Saltville, Billy?"

He replied between bites, "My momma and me lived on a farm near Independence, Virginia, with my stepdaddy. Him and his sons didn't much like me because"—he paused to chew and swallow—"because I had a different daddy. They used to beat me with tobacco poles. My daddy died in a logging accident before I was borned, but my momma says I look like I do because he was a big, tall Indian man, the onliest man she ever loved. When I got bigger, I started fighting back. The other day I got so mad that I burned down the barn. So my stepdaddy was fixing to ship me off to the Colony for the Feebleminded in Leesville. But Momma said that they operate on you there so you can't have no kids and that I might like to have some one day. That's when she thought of you. So she asked her momma to find out where you was at now."

"You can sleep here tonight, Billy," said her father in a choked voice Hunter didn't recognize. "We'll think of a job for you in the morning."

"Thank you, sir. I sure do appreciate you. And you, too, ma'am. And miss."

Hunter rode in the back seat of the Packard while her father drove Iona back to her apartment in the Negro section of Holston, beyond the railroad underpass down by the river. Iona always refused to ride anywhere but in the front seat. Clutching a jar of bacon grease from the Martins' kitchen, she muttered to herself the whole way about white people who displayed their trashy upbringings by letting Negroes off the street eat at their dinner table.

"Daddy, who is that boy?" asked Hunter on the trip home.

He hesitated a long time before replying, "His mother and I were great friends when we were children." In the light from the dashboard, he looked as though he were about to cry.

"What's wrong, Daddy?"

"Nothing, darling. Everything is fine."

Hunter could tell he was lying.

When they got back to the house, her mother had already settled Billy into the maid's room off the kitchen. Hunter followed her father upstairs. She went into her parents' bedroom to kiss her mother good night and found her huddled under their covers with an ice pack on her forehead.

As Hunter left the room, she heard her mother moan to her father, "What are we going to do?"

Hunter lingered in the shadowy hall next to the cracked door.

"Palestine did her best for sixteen years, and now it's my turn," her father replied.

Before tonight, Hunter had never heard the name Palestine outside of church. Who in the world was she?

"You're not going to let him *stay* here?"

"I'm certainly not going to turn him out into the street like some stray cur."

"What will people think?"

"Who knows? Who cares?"

"Couldn't you give him train fare to New York and mail him a check every month?"

"He's just a boy, Galicia. Other people helped me when I was in his situation."

"All he's asked from you is a job."

The door swung shut, turning the hallway dark. Hunter tiptoed back to her room.

Hunter and Billy sat cross-legged by the fishpond, tossing cracker crumbs to the goldfish and laughing at their greedy antics. Hunter had just gotten home from school, and Billy from the golf course, where he worked afternoons on the maintenance crew and caddied for the golfers. In the mornings a retired teacher tutored him in her father's den.

"Didn't you ever go to school?" asked Hunter.

"The white school wouldn't take me, and my mother wouldn't let me go to the black one. She said it wasn't right how Negroes got treated, but since I was an Indian, I shouldn't be treated like a Negro. Besides, my stepdaddy wanted me to work on the farm. But my momma learned me my letters and numbers. I know how to read and write. I just don't know much else!"

"I wish I didn't have to go to school."

"You shouldn't say that. It's really important to get an education. Otherwise, you end up like me, toting other people's golf bags."

"I think it would be fun to work outdoors."

"Well, since I've done that my whole life long, I think it would be fun to sit at a desk and read some interesting books."

"Let's ask my father if we can swap."

"You're just a tiny little thing. You wouldn't be able to carry a big old golf bag."

"But I'm strong." She flexed her arm.

He poked her muscle and laughed. "You're about as strong as a gnat, Hunter."

"Do you like it here with us, Billy?"

"Yeah, I like it real good. I miss my momma, but nobody else. Your parents are really nice. And Iona, too."

"Iona is pretty grumpy sometimes."

"She's okay now that she's gotten used to having me in the basement."

Her parents had turned the basement into an apartment for Billy. They had set up some of their old furniture down there. He had his own entrance and could go up the steps to the kitchen and ask Iona for food whenever he wanted.

"I bet I'm stronger than you think," said Hunter. "Do you want to arm wrestle?"

Billy laughed. "No, let's go down to the woods. There's something I want to show you."

They got to their feet and walked across the back yard, past the shed where Hunter's pony had lived when she was a child. Just across the wooden fence was a forest that stretched down to a narrow valley. Through this valley ran a creek strewn with boulders. After climbing the fence, they followed a faint path through a grove of ancient oaks to the creek. They walked along the bank until they came to a marsh overrun with ferns and with tall stalks that bore spiky green leaves and scarlet flowers. Feeding on the bright blossoms were dozens of darting hummingbirds.

"Oh my goodness," exclaimed Hunter.

"Amazing, huh?"

"Amazing." But what was most amazing was that Billy should find it amazing and should want to share his amazement with her. The boys she knew at school were only interested in ball games and fistfights. But Billy was older than they were. Maybe boys improved with age?

He led her over to a flat ledge by the stream and made her sit down. "You wait here. I want to give you something."

She sat there watching the whirring green and red humming-birds while Billy rambled through the woods nearby, cutting ferns and flowers with a knife he had pulled from his pocket. He returned with an armload of purple oak leaves, cardinal flowers, and greenery, which he dumped beside her on the rock. Then he sat down and began selecting things from the pile, braiding them together with honeysuckle vines that still sported some of their fragrant white flowers.

By the time he had finished, he had woven an elaborate headdress, which he placed carefully on her head.

"There! Hunter Martin, I crown you the princess of this forest!" He bowed low with one arm outstretched, like a prince in a fairy tale.

She giggled nervously. She had never before known a boy who liked to play with flowers. He carefully pulled out the yellow stamen of a honeysuckle blossom so that a tiny drop of nectar quivered at its tip. He held it to her mouth and placed the droplet on her tongue.

"And I am your obedient servant," he announced. "Your wish is my command!"

Noticing that the sun was about to sink behind the trees, she said, "Well, my first command is that you lead me back home. Because it's almost time for supper."

They ran along the twisting paths up to the wooden fence. Climbing the fence, they dashed across the green lawn, Hunter holding her crown of flowers steady on her head.

Her father was standing by the fishpond looking worried. "There you two are!" Then, as he noticed Hunter's headdress, he seemed to freeze. "Where did you get that beautiful bonnet?"

"Billy made it for me."

"You made it, Billy?"

"Yes, sir. My momma learned me how."

"Your mother and I used to make hats like that when we were kids." It looked to Hunter as though he were about to throw up.

13

Mountain Meadows: 1930

Hunter stood in the driveway beside her father's new Cadillac. It was dark blue with a white hood and whitewall tires. Billy walked out of the house, a suitcase in each hand. As he opened the trunk, she looked out over her hometown, which stretched from the foot of Tuscarora Heights. Holston was completely built up since her childhood, with street after street of houses and shops. Through the center of town ran the murky Holston River. Downriver lay Peace Island, crammed with multi-windowed factories, holding tanks, and smokestacks. Ringing the island were train tracks lined with open cars mounded high with shiny black coal.

This scene always struck Hunter as odd because right beyond the fence at the foot of her parents' back lawn lay an untouched forest where she and Billy spent most of their spare time now, wading in the creek and sunning and picnicking on the flat rocks. He had taught her the calls of the birds that lived there, the names of the plants, and the habits of the insects and animals. Sometimes they rode their bicycles along the logging trails that wound deep into the heart of the forest. It was as though these two worlds—the forest and the factories—existed side by side with no connection between them.

The mountains beyond Holston were scarcely visible in the haze from the factory smokestacks, which gave off a sickly sweet, acrid odor that you could smell all over town. A new road cut right through those mountains to Couchtown, where Hunter and her parents hadn't visited since Hunter was a baby. Her parents kept in touch with their parents via letters, photographs, and phone calls, but getting to Couchtown from Holston had been a challenge until now. First, a train trip to Saltville. Then a wagon ride for many hours across the Blue Ridge. As the years passed, her parents found more and more excuses not to make the grueling journey. Hunter had the impression they didn't really like Virginia. Her mother always talked about how superior Virginia was to Tennessee, but she never went there, even though the state line was only five miles north. But with the new Cadillac and the new road, her father had decided they needed to go to Couchtown to check on their elderly parents. He thought they could now get there in about ten hours, depending on how many flat tires they had.

Hunter was pleased that her parents were willing to spend ten hours together. Ever since Billy's arrival three years earlier, they had seemed much happier together. She often heard them through her bedroom wall late at night talking in low, urgent voices, like Bolsheviks plotting a bombing. But during daylight hours they seemed relaxed and cheerful for a change. Several times she had seen them kiss in a way that embarrassed her. Her father became especially cheerful whenever Billy stopped by from his apartment over the equipment shed at the golf course. One thing was certain: Hunter was happier since Billy's arrival.

Billy carried out a couple more suitcases, loaded them in the trunk, and slammed it shut. He slid behind the wheel, and Hunter got into the front passenger's seat. Her parents had insisted on squeezing into the narrow back seat together.

"This feels like a double date," quipped her father.

"Father, please promise you won't be corny all the way to Couchtown," Hunter requested.

"You've got to admit that this car beats your old Packard, don't you, dear?" said her mother.

"I loved that car," her father moaned.

Hunter turned around to look over the back seat. Her mother wore a new forest green velvet cloche with a dotted net veil.

"Nice hat, Mother." Hunter had recently decided to stop calling her parents Momma and Daddy. It sounded so childish now that Billy had made a woman of her.

"These dots on the veil make me feel as though I'm being circled by flies," her mother said merrily.

Hunter watched her father reach over to take her mother's hand in his. She didn't know whether to be disgusted or pleased that they were apparently going to "spoon," as they called it, throughout this tedious trip. She wished she and Billy could be spooning in the back instead. But her parents would have had heart attacks. They referred to Billy and her as "the kids" and treated them like toddlers.

Hunter studied Billy's handsome caramel face and his slicked-back black hair. He shaved every day now, and she was fascinated by the scraggly moustache he was trying to grow. He had been disappointed to discover that his facial hair was not as thick as that of other boys his age. But he explained that Indians didn't have heavy beards.

Billy had been appointed head of the maintenance crew at the golf course and lived above the shed where the grooming equipment was stored. The clubhouse had expanded to include a ballroom and a grill with a bar. On weekends Billy worked there as a bartender. But Hunter's father wanted to send him north to college and medical school now that his tutoring with the retired schoolteacher had prepared him to pass the entrance exams. Hunter hoped Billy would stay in Holston until she graduated from high school the following year and went to Bryn Mawr. If they were both up north at school, they could still see each other often.

The new "road" was a glorified cart path. It switchbacked up and down the forested mountainsides and meandered along the streams and across the fords. Each time a stone punctured a tire, they all got out while Billy jacked up the car, removed the tire, patched the inner tube, pumped it back up, and then reattached the wheel.

When the sun was overhead, Hunter's mother made Billy stop the car and get the picnic basket from the trunk. She spread a red checkered tablecloth on a grassy green bank alongside the road and laid out fried chicken, deviled eggs, potato salad, baked beans, and coleslaw. As her parents filled their plates, Hunter announced that she and Billy were going to follow a stream by the road to its source so they could fill the canteens with fresh water.

"Good thinking," said Billy in a soft voice as they left her parents by the roadside.

Well into the forest, they stopped in a patch of ferns. Billy set the
canteens on the ground and took Hunter in his arms. They kissed so
intently that the stubble on his jaws scratched her face raw. Then they
sank to the ground on a mattress of leaves and pressed the length of
their bodies together.

After their return from the forest with the dripping water bottles,
Hunter and Billy lounged in the shade by the roadside where cars
never passed and ate enough food for a small village.

"I can't wait for you kids to see where Mrs. Martin and I grew
up," said her father. "You probably don't remember it, Hunter."

"I'm looking forward to it, sir," said Billy as he twisted apart the
bones of a chicken wing. "My mother never took me to Mulatto Bald,
but she used to talk about it all the time."

"I'm afraid your mother's parents aren't there anymore," said
Will. "My mother said they sold their farm and moved to Florida."

Billy shrugged. "I never knew them anyhow."

"Apparently, that area has changed a lot," cautioned Hunter's
mother. "Couchtown is a tourist mecca now. That rail line the timber
company laid has been extended north to Richmond and south to
Charleston."

"I'm sure it's changed some," said her father. "But you can't
move mountains."

"No, but you can flood valleys. My father says Silver Valley is a
lake now. And there's a new hotel up on the bald."

"Yes," said her father impatiently, "but the bald itself is still
there. That's my point."

"Honey, I just don't want you to be disappointed if it's different
from what you remember."

Her father shrugged. "How different can it be?"

Back in the car, Hunter's father and Billy started harmonizing on
a hymn. Hunter already knew that Billy had a beautiful voice. Before
they had made love for the first time, she had been lying on a
limestone ledge along the creek below her house. She was wearing a
necklace he had strung from scarlet haws and crabapples. He started
singing a lullaby his mother had taught him:

"Blacks and bays, dapples and greys,
Running in the night.
When you wake, you shall have
All the pretty little ponies."

She fell asleep. When she woke up, she knew what needed to happen next. She rolled over and drew Billy to her.

He whispered, "I don't ever want you to do anything you don't want to do, Hunter."

She whispered back, "But this is what I want, Billy."

The hummingbirds whirring in the cardinal flowers, the frogs hiding in the watercress, and the locusts clutching the tree bark serenaded them as she and Billy became one.

But Hunter had never before heard Billy sing with her father, although Billy said they always sang together when he drove her father to conferences and consultations. They were good. Their voices wove in and out and around each other like two stray dogs meeting for the first time. As the Cadillac careened from rut to rut, alarming flocks of birds into flight, they sang, "Are your garments spotless? Are they white as snow? Are you washed in the blood of the Lord?"

It was dark when they reached Couchtown. Hunter's grandparents, alarmingly gray and wrinkled in person, in contrast to their photos, welcomed them at their house on the main street.

"So this is Billy?" exclaimed her grandmother. "We've heard so many nice things about you, Billy. I know that you're a big help to Dr. and Mrs. Martin—doing their yard work, and driving and caddying for Dr. Martin."

"They're a big help to me, ma'am." He smiled at Hunter as her grandmother led him down the steps to the maid's room in the basement.

The next morning, Hunter's grandparents—her mother's parents—joined the four in the blue and white Cadillac as they headed to Silver Valley.

"Now I don't want you all to be too shocked, Will and Galicia," said Hunter's grandfather, who wore a little red and white polka dotted bow tie that no man in Holston would be caught dead in. "So I need to warn you that the federal government has built a dam across the Sturgeon River to generate power for the factories down in Holston. It's turned Silver Valley into one big lake."

"Stop here," Hunter's father told Billy when they reached a pull-off that overlooked the new lake. They all climbed out and surveyed the vast silver sheet of water that lapped against the surrounding hillsides. Tree branches and fence posts still poked up out of the water near the red clay shore.

"Somewhere under there is where your ancestors used to farm," he informed Hunter in a dazed voice.

"We lost lots of good farm land in order to electrify Holston," said her grandfather. "I hope it was worth it?"

Hunter watched her father shrug. "I don't honestly know, Mr. Hunter. Holston is certainly different from Silver Valley. But an improvement? I'm not so sure."

They clambered back into the Cadillac, and Billy drove them along a road that circled the lake. At the foot of what had once been Silver Valley, they arrived at a turnoff marked by a huge billboard featuring an Indian chief in a feathered war bonnet. It read, "See Indian Rock Cave." They followed the arrow on the billboard up the winding access road. Will parked the Cadillac beside a souvenir stand overflowing with moccasins and tomahawks imported from Japan.

Outside the cave mouth loomed a giant wooden cigar store Indian some thirty feet tall. An arrow-shaped sign pointed into the cave. It read, "Authentic Red Indian Rock Paintings."

As Hunter, Billy, and her family joined a busload of Baptists from Birmingham by the cave mouth, her father said, "My ancestor, Joshua Martin, was shot to death right here in this very spot."

"What for?" asked Hunter.

"During the Civil War he led escaped Union prisoners through this cave and over into Kentucky."

"I thought we were supposed to be Southerners?" said Hunter. "If not, how come I have to be in this Plantation Ball thing that the Colonial Dames are putting on?"

"There were two different Martin families in these parts," Hunter's grandfather explained to her. "Your father's Martin family on the bald fought for the Union. My Martins down in Couchtown were Confederates who rode with Jeb Stuart."

Hunter nodded politely. She watched her father roll his eyes, grateful that he had apparently decided to keep to himself whatever sarcastic comments were going through his head.

The group followed their guide, who was dressed in a doeskin squaw outfit, along the hand-railed path into the cave, which was illuminated by flickering electric wall sconces. They passed a milky quartz formation that looked like a frozen waterfall. Then they entered an open area filled with a forest of bizarre pointed rock formations rising up from the floor and hanging down from the ceiling. The guide pointed out one that she claimed resembled the profile of an Indian chief. One of the Baptists pointed out another that he insisted looked like Jesus. Hunter couldn't see it herself, but the other Baptists agreed.

As they approached the heart of the cave, they heard a roaring sound that the guide said came from an underground river. Then they saw a high wall directly in front of them, lit by spotlights shining up from the floor. It was covered with herds of charging animals painted in red, tan, and black. Tiny black stick-figure hunters bearing spears and bows were about to be trampled by rampaging deer, buffalo, bears, and panthers.

"This is the best example of Indian rock art east of the Mississippi," recited their guide, clandestinely consulting her notes in the dim light. "It is believed to have been painted by the ancient Indians who inhabited these mountains long before the first white settlers arrived from the Virginia Tidewater."

Hunter wrapped her arms around herself and shivered in the damp gloom. Billy moved slightly to his left so that his hip and leg pressed against hers. Then he moved his arm over so that his hand could caress her buttock in the shadows. Sometimes she thought she would die from happiness at being loved by him.

Piling back into the Cadillac, they descended the access road until they entered the main road, which continued along the ridge that rose up to Mulatto Bald. Reaching the summit, they were greeted by another billboard, this one reading, "Welcome to Mountain Meadows: Luxury Living at the Top of the World!"

All but a handful of the cabins Hunter's father used to talk about were gone now, leaving many vacant lots that were marked off with stakes and string, onto which were tied scraps of cloth.

Along one side of the main road rambled a vast stone fortress with hundreds of windows that overlooked Silver Lake and the mountains that receded ridge after ridge into North Carolina. This lodge was landscaped with thickets of blooming rhododendron and mountain laurel. A sign out front consisting of letters burnt into a large wooden slab read "Mountain Meadows Inn." A golf course stretched behind the inn, on which men in tweed plus fours and Scottish caps crowned with pompoms were chipping and putting.

"I thought you said you grew up really poor, Father," said Hunter. "But this is beautiful."

"It's changed," he said in a stricken voice. "Everything I used to know is gone now. It's like waking up from a dream."

"I thought you'd be impressed, Will," said Hunter's grandfather. "People ride the train up from Florida and South Carolina to keep cool in the summer. And they come down from New York and Boston to recuperate from TB. The depression has slowed things down a bit, but it'll recover. People will always need vacations."

Hunter studied her father. He didn't look impressed. In fact, he looked upset. But he said nothing to contradict Hunter's grandfather.

Next they arrived at a half-timbered Tudor house.

"This looks like Snow White's cottage," observed Hunter as they pulled into her grandmother Martin's driveway. "Is this where you grew up, Father?"

"No. That cabin was pulled down. I had this one built for my mother a few years ago."

Grandmother Martin was stooped and wrinkled. Her crooked cane and large curved nose made her resemble the witch in Hansel and Gretel. After welcoming them, she gave everyone a tour of her house. Hunter was baffled when she demonstrated how the electric lights and flush toilet worked, as though everyone didn't already know that. Then they sat around her fireplace, which she explained had been built with stones salvaged from the fireplace in her old cabin, the one in which her son Will had grown up.

"Where has everyone gone, Momma?" asked her father in a bewildered voice.

His mother shrugged. "They've all gone away now but me, son."

"Where to?"

"Off to the cities, I reckon. Lots to Holston to work in the mills. Some up to Detroit to work in the auto plants. A few to Illinois to work in the canning factories. Some to Birmingham to work in the steel mills. Lord, I don't know where all they've gone to, son. But we don't have nothing to offer young people no more."

"They just can't stop taking our land, can they?" her father muttered. "First, they drove us out of the Smokies. Then out of Silver Valley onto this bald. Now they've flooded Silver Valley and taken over the bald."

"You sound just like your grandmother, Will-Usdi," murmured his mother.

Hunter's mother sighed. "There he goes again," she said to the others. "Will, if you miss your lost tribal days so much, why don't you just go live in that cave and chip arrowheads for the tourists?"

Everyone laughed except her father.

As they drove back to Holston, Hunter turned around and said to her parents in the back seat, "Grandmother Hunter told Billy and me all about you two."

"What did she tell you?" asked her mother, sounding nervous.

"She told about how she and Grandfather didn't want you to marry Father because he was so wild. But how you two were so much in love that you just ran off to Leesville and got married, and never cared what anybody else in the whole world thought about it."

Her father nodded. "I guess that's just about the truth, isn't it, Galicia?"

Her mother smiled. "Yes, I guess it is."

"I think that's great, sir!" called Billy from behind the wheel.

"Well, I'd say it's worked out fine." Her father took her mother's hand in his with a tired smile.

Hunter studied them and tried to imagine them as much in love as Billy and herself. But she just couldn't picture it. They were so proper and boring. It was impossible that her father had ever made her mother gasp and moan the way that Billy did her. It was too silly even to think about. She giggled.

"What's so funny?" asked her father.

"You two. You're hilarious!"

"We are?" asked her father, looking pleased.

14

The Plantation Ball: 1930

"But I don't *want* Timmy DeWitt as my escort for the Plantation Ball," groaned Hunter, standing in the fitting room at Iverson's Department Store as the seamstress pinned up the hem on her new dropped-waist sea foam chiffon ball gown.

"It's already arranged." Her mother was sitting in a bentwood chair instructing the seamstress. "Timmy has been accepted at Princeton. He'll be able to arrange dates for you with his friends when you're at Bryn Mawr."

"I hate Timmy DeWitt!"

"Well, he told his mother he doesn't like you either, dear, so it should work out just fine. After all, it's only for four hours."

"But we'll have to go to those stupid waltz lessons together beforehand. Why can't Billy be my date?"

"Billy? Billy's going to be bartending that night."

"It's because he's not the right color, isn't it? Why don't you people ever tell the truth?"

"Hunter, it isn't appropriate for you to think of Billy as someone to date. He's our yard boy. He's your father's caddy and chauffeur. You're going to the ball with Timmy, darling, and that's that."

"I may *go* to the ball with him. But I won't *leave* with him."

"Fine. It's all settled." Hunter's mother took a small package from her handbag and handed it to Hunter.

"What's this?" Hunter ripped off the paper and opened the box, removing a dark red stone on a gold chain.

"My parents gave it to me when I was sixteen. So now that you're sixteen, I'd like you to have it. It belonged to my great-grandmother, who was named Galicia Hunter. It's been passed down to each Galicia in our family for many generations now. But since we named you Hunter and there's no other Galicia in the family right now, my parents agreed that you should have it.

"I always thought it was just a stone someone had picked up in a creek. But I had it cleaned and reset, and it turns out to be a ruby. I have no idea where my cavalier forebears in the Tidewater might have acquired such a beautiful ruby. They probably brought it with them from England. They had to leave their estates in a hurry after the beheading of Charles the First by Oliver Cromwell, so their jewelry may have been their only portable wealth."

"Thank you, Mother. It's really gorgeous." Hunter unclasped the chain and put it around her neck, politely ignoring her mother's latest ancestral litany. Looking into the mirror, she saw the ruby lying in the hollow of her throat, scintillating in the florescent light. "I'm going to wear it to the ball with my gown."

"It looks even better on you than I had imagined, with your black hair and amber eyes and ruddy skin." Her mother took a handkerchief from her pocket book and dabbed with it at the corner of her eye.

After arriving home from her waltz lesson with Timmy DeWitt, Hunter went up to her bedroom and changed into her riding clothes and boots. Taking her bicycle from the garage, she rode it down the driveway and along her street until she reached the turnoff to the country club. She pedaled toward the club under a clear blue sky. She and Billy were going to bike out to a farm where the farmer let them ride his horses. Arriving at the entrance to the golf course, she dismounted and waited for Billy.

Billy was late. The sun was sinking slowly toward the horizon. It was unlikely they would have time to get to the farm, ride, and return home before supper. Hunter started to worry. Billy was never late, at least not when he was meeting her.

Finally she spotted him on his bike, pedaling slowly down the lane from the course. Relieved, she felt a stab of annoyance that he wasn't hurrying. She wondered if he were losing interest in her now that she had given herself to him completely. She had resisted him for a long time, even though he had wanted her so badly. And then that day on the limestone ledge by the creek she had finally wanted him just as badly. And now they couldn't seem to stop, even though they knew it would be a disaster if they should make a baby. But all either of them lived for anymore were those stolen moments when they could touch each other's bodies in the forbidden places. Or at least that was all she lived for. Billy apparently had other more compelling interests now.

When Billy reached her, Hunter saw that his face was bruised and crusted with blood. She gasped. He looked up, his blue eyes lifeless.

"Billy, what's happened?"

"I don't want to talk about it."

"Let me look at you."

"No, we need to get out of here fast."

"Why?"

"I'll tell you later."

He pedaled down the road and Hunter followed. After several minutes he braked and climbed off his bike, so Hunter did too. They rolled their bikes into the woods and stashed them behind some bushes. Then they stumbled down a rocky path that led by a back way to the stream below Hunter's house. Billy was limping badly.

When they reached the creek, he lay down on the limestone ledge where they had first made love. Hunter sat beside him and examined his wounds. She removed her jacket and her shirt. Wearing only her brassiere, riding pants, and boots, she wet the shirttail and used it to gently wash the caked blood off his face. A cut along one side of his nose looked deep and ugly. It had just barely missed his eye, which was ringed with black, like a raccoon's. The cut was still oozing globs of clotting blood.

Once he looked more human, she asked, "Are you going to tell me what happened?"

Suddenly Billy started shaking with sobs. Stunned, Hunter leaned over and held him in her arms as he cried.

When he finally stopped, she said, "Billy, who did this to you?"

He sat up. His eyes had gone steely, like those of the sheriffs in the cowboy movies of her childhood when the bad guys arrived in town. "The other caddies don't want me to work at the golf course anymore."

"Why not? You run the place, don't you?"

He looked at her sullenly. "They said to stay away because I'm a Negro. I said I'm an Indian. They said the Indians all got sent out west, and that Indians are just 'red niggers' anyhow."

"My father will be furious. He'll run them all out of town."

"No, I don't want him to know, Hunter. This is my fight."

"Of course he's going to know, Billy. You look like you've been run over by a truck."

"If I tell on them, they may kill me next time."

"They could never get away with that."

"Whether or not they got away with it wouldn't matter to me because I'd be dead." Billy smiled for the first time. Then he winced because the smile opened the cut down the side of his nose. "There's another reason I can't turn them in."

"What's that?"

"They said they'll tell your father what you and I do in the woods together. One said his uncle was a Ku Kluxer who would love to lynch me for messing around with a white girl."

Hunter glanced frantically at the rhododendrons all around them. "They've been watching us?"

"I don't know how they know, but they know."

They sat there for a long time, watching the shadows lengthen across the rocks and listening to the rushing of the water.

"Billy, we need to go back to my house and let my father stitch that cut. It looks horrible. It could get infected. You could look like Frankenstein for the rest of your life."

"I'll go. But I'm going to make up some story. I'm not going to rat out the other caddies. Promise you'll back me up."

"Okay."

They walked slowly up the hill to Hunter's back yard and climbed the fence. As they crossed the lawn to the house, Hunter's father came out the door. "Thank God you're okay, Billy. Hal DeWitt phoned to tell me that some of the other caddies attacked you with a three iron behind the clubhouse. He saw it happening from the bar. But by the time he got over there, everyone had taken off. Are you all right?"

He studied Billy's limp and his lacerated face as they approached him. "No, you aren't all right at all. Come into my den."

Billy dragged his leg down the hall and into the den. Hunter followed with her bloodstained shirttail hanging out.

Billy sat in a desk chair, and Hunter's father gingerly touched the cuts and bruises with his fingertips. "I need to take some stitches. We'll go to the clinic in a minute. But first tell me what happened. I guess we never should have made you head of the maintenance crew over boys who had been there longer."

Billy sat silently. Hunter could tell he was trying to compose a plausible lie. But what was the point, since her father already knew who his assailants were?

Hunter said, "They told him he couldn't work there anymore because he's a Negro."

Her father flinched. "What did you say, Billy?"

"I said my father was an Indian and that's why I look like I do. They said Indians are red niggers, and that I wasn't nothing but Doc Martin's house nigger."

Hunter's father looked as though someone had kicked him in the stomach.

"Whichever boys did that will never work at that golf course again. I'll have them arrested for assault and sent to reform school."

"Please don't do that, sir. They would kill me first. You know what those guys are like."

The three were silent for a long time. Finally Will said, "Billy, I think it's time for you to head up north to school. We need to get some applications and start that process."

Billy looked up at him, squinting with pain. "All right, sir."

Hunter's heart sank. She would have to stay in Holston for another year before she could go to Bryn Mawr. How could she bear it here without Billy, especially now that the caddies would brand her a slut and spread it all over town?

"But I wouldn't want to go up there without Hunter, sir."

Her father blinked. "Excuse me?"

"I guess you realize that Hunter and I are in love, Dr. Martin?"

Her father opened his mouth, but no words came out.

"I know she's too young to marry me now. But I wanted to tell you that's our plan, so that you and Mrs. Martin won't think we've been sneaking around behind your backs.'"

Her father stared at him with wide eyes.

"Once Hunter has graduated, we'd like to get engaged, sir. With your permission, of course. I reckon maybe you think we're too young, sir. But Hunter told me that you weren't much older than me when you married Mrs. Martin."

Will nodded numbly.

Hunter felt proud of Billy for daring to proclaim their love to her father. She waited nervously for a blessing that didn't come.

"I guess maybe you think I can't support Hunter, sir," Billy continued anxiously. "But I've saved a lot of money from my jobs, and you know that I'm a hard worker. Besides, Hunter and I don't need a fancy house or a big car. All we want is each other."

Will remained as motionless as the wooden Indian outside the cave in Silver Valley.

"Well, I guess you mind my color, too, then, Dr. Martin." He hung his head. "But Hunter says you and Mrs. Martin might be part Indian yourselves."

"Yes."

"So Hunter is, too. So you must not mind if I am, sir?"

"No," said Will, shaking his head.

"So may I ask, sir, what the problem is with Hunter and me loving each other?"

"I thought you understood," murmured Will.

"Understood what, sir?"

Will drew a deep breath. "Billy, you can't ever date Hunter because she's your half-sister."

Hunter gasped. Billy's face convulsed. No one uttered a sound. Hunter could hear her mother's antique clock ticking in the living room, as loud as a forest full of locusts.

Finally Billy said, "I'm disappointed in you, sir. I've never known you to lie. Why don't you just come right out and say that you don't want your daughter to marry a colored man? Whether my daddy was an Indian or not doesn't matter to you because my face is dark. So in the eyes of the world, I'm a colored man."

"Billy, listen to me: you're my son."

Billy stared at him. "That's not true, Dr. Martin, and you know it. If you were really my father, you wouldn't have let my momma get raped by my stepbrother, or me get beaten with tobacco poles by that sorry old man and his rotten sons. And when I got to Holston, you'd have claimed me as your son, no matter what, instead of sticking me down in your basement. If you ask me, sir, the worst kind of bigot is the man who pretends that he isn't one."

Will closed his eyes. Billy stood up and grabbed Hunter's hand. The two of them walked out.

Hunter and Timmy DeWitt waltzed to "The Blue Danube," veering in and out among the nineteen other couples like stock cars circling a racetrack. She could see her parents sitting at a satin-draped table, watching her with tentative smiles. Her mother wore a gold-sequined dress with a dropped waist and a short skirt. It was a definite fashion error. Her father wore a tuxedo with satin lapels and looked as handsome as a movie star. She would miss them. Her father took her mother's hand, encased in an elbow-length kid glove, and patted it. At least they would still have each other.

The previous night, the three of them and Billy had had a family conference around the mahogany table in the dining room after Iona went home. Her parents had apologized for not telling Hunter and Billy that they were half-siblings right from the start. They explained their convoluted motives and asked for forgiveness. Their intentions had been good, they insisted, even if the results were now painful for Billy and Hunter. But luckily, no harm had been done. It was clear to Hunter that they didn't realize that she and Billy had been lovers for several months now, and that their giving each other up was out of the question. They spelled out a plan for Billy to go north to college and medical school, figuring that the time apart would allow both

Hunter and Billy to shift their love into emotions more appropriate for siblings. Each could find a new romantic interest to salve the pain of this loss. Her father said he hoped that Billy's having found his father would provide consolation to Billy for having to renounce his first love.

As Hunter walked Billy to his bicycle in the driveway afterwards, he said bitterly, "They're lying, Hunter. They just don't want me in your family. They want you to be with a boy like Timmy DeWitt, whose parents come from up north and have lots of money. But do you still want me?"

"You're the only boy I've ever wanted, or will ever want, Billy."

As the calls of the night insects pulsed in the forest at the foot of the lawn, Billy outlined his plan that would allow them to be together for the rest of their lives.

Now, at the dance, Hunter glanced over to the buffet table. Billy stood behind the punch bowl in his white jacket, his hands clasped before him and his face somber as he watched her dance with Timmy. He still wore a bandage over the cut down his nose. The bruise around his eye had faded to yellows and greens. Their gazes locked, and he winked at her with his good eye. She felt his wink in the pit of her stomach. Smiling, she winked back. By midnight, their life together would have begun. She would miss her parents, but not as much as she would miss Billy if he went north without her.

After the waltz, Hunter went over and asked her mother, "May I borrow your husband for a dance?"

Timmy DeWitt, standing behind her, invited her mother to dance.

Hunter laid her corsaged wrist on her father's shoulder, and they moved out onto the floor. Hunter leaned back to gaze up at him. He looked down, smiling uncertainly.

She smiled, her red lips trembling, a tear rolling down one cheek. "I love you, Father. No matter what. Don't ever forget that."

"I love you, too, honey. You look beautiful tonight. We're so proud of you. And I'm sorry about Billy. I know how hard it is to have to give up your first love. I had to do that, too. She was Billy's mother, as a matter of fact."

"Everything will be fine." Hunter smiled up at him, amazed that he insisted on continuing to embroider this lie about being Billy's father.

At the end of the song, Hunter and Timmy escorted her parents back to their chairs. Hunter leaned over and kissed her mother on the cheek. Gazing at her for the last time, she said, "I love this ruby, Mother. Thank you for it. I will wear it always and think of you."

"You're quite welcome, dear."

Her mother frowned, seeming taken aback by her intensity. Hunter realized that she needed to act more like her usual moody self so as not to incite her parents' suspicions. Besides, she might have to sell this ruby to help finance her new life with Billy.

Next, Timmy and Hunter invited Barbara and Hal DeWitt to dance. Hunter smiled to herself. Whatever momentous dramas might be going on underneath the surface, all the children of Holston had been trained to maintain proper appearances.

After the required parental dances, bedlam broke loose as the debutantes and their escorts abandoned each other to dance the Charleston with their secret crushes. Their parents did the same. It was frightening watching the Colonial Dames trying to imitate Josephine Baker at the Folies Bergere. But Hunter noticed that her parents were slow dancing cheek to cheek with each other to the fast music. It pleased Hunter that this was the final image of them that she would carry with her for the rest of her life—together and smiling. She blew them an imaginary kiss and then went over to the buffet table to find Billy.

She and Billy raced out to the parking lot and climbed into her parents' Cadillac. Using his set of keys, he started it up and drove to her house. She rushed inside and changed her clothes, leaving her gown spread out on her bed. They had to hurry. The coal train to Leesburg would pass through Holston in half an hour. They would leave the Cadillac at the bus station so her parents would be kept busy trying to track them along the bus routes while they rode boxcars north to New York City.

From her desk drawer, she took the note she had struggled over for a long time and carried it down to the kitchen. Removing it from its envelope, she reread her words:

"Dear Mother and Father: Billy and I are going to some big city out west where people whose skins are different colors can love each other without upsetting everyone. We will leave your car in the parking lot at the bus station. Please don't worry about me. Billy loves me and will always take good care of me. Thank you for everything you have done for us both. I know you will eventually understand and forgive our decision, since you two did the same thing—so much in love that you eloped to Leesville all those years ago. I will love you always. Hunter."

She propped the note against the sugar bowl on the counter and ran out the back door to the Cadillac idling in the driveway.

Acknowledgments

Special thanks to Ina Danko, Deborah Deutschman, Niota Hensley, and Carol Edwards for careful readings and good suggestions.

Thanks also to Wayne Winkler for introducing my manuscript to the wonderful people at Mercer University Press, especially Marc Jolley and Marsha Luttrell